The Rain

Evil Returns to Cades Cove

Cades Cove Series
Book Two
by
Aiden James

BOOKS BY AIDEN JAMES

CADES COVE SERIES
Cades Cove
The Raven Mocker
Devil Mountain

DYING OF THE DARK VAMPIRES
With Patrick Burdine
The Vampires' Last Lover
The Vampires' Birthright
Blood Princesses

THE JUDAS CHRONICLES
Immortal Plague
Immortal Reign
Immortal Destiny
Immortal Dragon
Immortal Tyranny
Immortal Pyramid
Immortal Victory
Immortal Supremacy
Immortal Storm

NICK CAINE ADVENTURES
With J.R. Rain
Temple of the Jaguar
Treasure of the Deep
Pyramid of the Gods
Aiden James only
Curse of the Druids
Secret of the Loch
River of the Damned

Published 2019 by
Manor House Books

Copyright © 2010 by Aiden James

Cover Art: Michele Lee, Blue Sky Design ~
Boston

Printed in the United States of America.

Third Edition

THE RAVEN MOCKER

THE CADES COVE SERIES - BOOK TWO

AIDEN JAMES

To those who wonder about the occasional tingle up the spine… and casting a look over a shoulder to find no one's there.

"There are no haunted places, only haunted people."
—Robert Baker & Joe Nickell

"It's best to leave the 'dead and buried' undisturbed. Pray they stay at peace, sleeping in the bosom of The Great Spirit."
     —Evelyn "Two Doves Rising" Sherman

Chapter One

A sudden gust carried snow flurries into the anthropology department's long corridor before the main entrance closed, the security latch locking. The entire building sat deserted, as did much of the University of Tennessee's Knoxville campus. Most everyone, the faculty included, had left earlier that afternoon for winter break. Everyone, that is, except Eddie Krantz and his fiancée Cynthia Towner.

"We'll be in here fifteen to twenty minutes, tops," said Eddie, removing his scarf and brushing a thin layer of snowflakes from his coat.

Blonde and handsome with serene blue eyes, he cracked a tense smile in hopes she would remain patient. Anxious to begin their trip to Miami Beach, it was imperative he completed the last-minute task given by Dr. Walter Pollack. As a first-year archaeology intern, he could ill afford displeasing the professor. Let the boss down just once, and kiss any chance of better projects goodbye.

"What does he want you to do again?" she asked, impatiently.

Cynthia removed her knitted cap and earmuffs. Her long dark brown hair no longer confined, it smartly framed her delicate features and emerald eyes within a soft oval face.

She followed him to the second floor, to a small lab at the end of the dimly lit hall. The echoed clicks from their shoes accentuated the building's emptiness.

"He needs me to double-check the tag numbers against the journal entries on some bones we removed from Cades Cove last month."

He unlocked the lab's door with a security card, and pushed the door open. Once he flicked on the overhead fluorescent light, Eddie motioned for her to enter first and then closed the door. Spartanly furnished, the small room contained two tables and a stool, along with a small wooden cabinet and stainless-steel sink.

A complete human skeleton was laid out on the table nearest to the sink. The aged bones, darker than what one might normally expect to find, were covered with unusual grooves, and the hands and feet were grotesquely elongated in comparison to the rest of the skeleton. The overall massive size was unusual. The lower legs and feet lined up in neat rows next to the core of the frame, indicating whoever the bones belonged to had stood much taller than the six-and-a-half-foot table.

"Wow... so this is what you were talking about last month, after your team finished that dig. Right?"

Unlike some females he'd dated, Cynthia seemed intrigued by the remains, especially the apparent deformities. It was one of the things that endeared her to him. She had nearly finished her undergraduate studies in microbiology, and currently planned to attend med school within the next three years. It depended on when he finished his graduate work.

He nodded, watching her fascination and pleased the ticking-timer for him to hurry had been paused. He needed to take care of Dr. Pollack's directive quickly. He moved to the cabinet and opened it. The professor's journal sat on the top shelf. Eddie grabbed the journal and returned to the table, opening to the ledger pages for this particular specimen.

The only skeleton left to confirm, two-dozen others had already been verified and taken elsewhere for safekeeping. Like them, this one would be moved to a cold storage unit set up in the basement of an abandoned dormitory near the McClung Museum. Eddie had been charged with verifying the bones, carefully wrapping the remains, and then placing them inside a steel travel case waiting beneath the table. Another of the professor's assistants would pick up the case later and take it to the storage unit.

He set out to complete the assignment in earnest, while Cynthia continued to study the remains. She frowned.

"What do these belong to?"

She pointed to a pile of sharp jagged teeth located near the bottom edge of the table. More than a dozen in total, each tooth curved slightly along its two to three-inch length.

"Some animal, Cyn," Eddie replied, tersely. He barely looked up from the ledger. When he felt the heat from her glare, he looked up again, offering an apologetic smile.

"Our preliminary findings were the teeth belonged to some kind of big cat that's no longer around here."

"You mean extinct? That would make it prehistoric, right?" she persisted. Her gaze followed the skeleton's length, settling on the skull. "It's got a head bigger than Shaq's." She shot him a wry smile. He responded with another pithy glance.

"Do you remember anything else I told you, before the Indian activists closed the site?" he asked, not immediately catching her allusion to the former star basketball player.

He regretted the smugness slipped through unchecked. Yet, hoping she'd let him finish the task uninterrupted, he tried to ignore the sting on her face from his latest barb. Her lower lip quivered, likely in sullen anger.

Well here's something not so endearing. Jesus, she'd better learn to not be so damned sensitive. Otherwise, she's never going to amount to anything in the medical field....

"This is the most unusual specimen recovered from the dig," Eddie continued. "Dr. Pollack's really excited about the skull, since the cranial capacity is bigger than modern man, even rivaling that of *Cro-Magnon*. Remember now?"

Cynthia nodded weakly, and looked at the bones. The skull's lower jaw curved to a point, a very unusual feature for any human. The entire skull lacked teeth, except for several worn molars. The sockets where the incisors and canines should have been were empty.

"Where are *its* teeth?"

Her sarcastic tone needled him. He looked up sharply from the ledger.

Did she really need to go there?

"Well," he began, frowning as he watched her gaze shift from the animal teeth to the skull and jawbone. "We might've lost them when we separated the skeleton from the girl's remains I also told you about."

The look on his face wasn't so apologetic, imploring her silently to please let him finish the rest of his verification undisturbed. He lacked half a page and then it was on to packing up the bones and getting the hell out of this place.

"Are you talking about the murdered girl from the early nineteen-hundreds, whose remains were reburied right after Thanksgiving?"

He confirmed with a nod.

"Did you ever read the story about that?" She waited for his response, which was simply a negative headshake.

"It was in both the Knoxville and school papers, as well as the news on TV," she said. "The girl's remains were reburied in one of the churchyards in Cades Cove, and the service was a Scottish-Native American ceremony."

She didn't go on when his only response was a tepid grunt. Perhaps to get his attention, she picked up a handful of the animal teeth. When he still ignored her, she moved to the skull and placed the teeth inside several of the empty sockets. A slight gasp escaped her mouth when all but one fit perfectly, and the other was just slightly loose. She was adding one of the longer teeth to a matching socket when he noticed what she was doing.

"*Stop* that!"

She withdrew her hand, seemingly wounded by his rebuke.

He glared at her, poised to offer a stronger rebuke. But first he turned his attention to the skull. Prepared to carefully remove the sharp canines from the skull's mouth, he hesitated, pulling his hand back.

My God, that's creepy!

"This is really going to be bad if you jammed them in there." Eddie was determined to find a distraction from thinking about how the teeth looked so...so *natural* in the skull. For some crazy reason, the teeth made the thing look alive, as if his hand ventured too close, he might lose a finger or two. "Dr. Pollack told us last week that advanced carbon dating has proved this particular skeleton comprises the oldest human remains ever found in North America. He'll have my ass in a sling if I can't get the teeth out."

"I'm sorry—I didn't mean to mess anything up."

This time, she did look like she'd cry. He wondered if the skull creeped her out as much as it did him.

"It's okay, Cyn," he assured her, forcing himself to sound compassionate while he gently removed the first tooth. The thing looked less sinister, and he moved on to removing the rest of the teeth. "Just give me a few more minutes. I promise to hurry to wrap this up."

Cynthia moved to the lone stool in the room, pulling it to the door while she waited. She tapped her feet lightly to let him know the 'timer' was back, full on. Aside from her usual impatience, he wondered if she shared his mental picture of what the skull might look like if all of the curved, sharp teeth were in place. Given its gangly height and other apparent deformities, the teeth made it look alien despite its human characteristics. Definitely predatory. *Thank God it's dead!*

"Okay, that should do it!" he announced a few minutes later, feeling immensely relieved.

Eddie removed the protective case from beneath the table and carefully placed the bones inside. He closed the case, sliding the journal into a sealed sleeve along the steel container's side. Only the teeth remained, to be cataloged and removed for storage the following day by another assistant.

The fact Cynthia didn't reciprocate his radiant smile after he had locked the case and slid it back under the table wasn't an immediate cause for concern, since he had a fifteen-hour car ride to work on fixing that. Ready to enjoy their shared holiday break, Eddie nearly skipped down the stairs to the main floor with his gal following close behind.

On the way downstairs, a loud thud startled them, accompanied by the sound of a door handle jiggling. The latter noise echoed eerily from upstairs. He crept warily up the stairs to take a look. The noises stopped when he stepped into the deserted hall. Nothing seemed obviously out of place, but the air had become much colder, revealing his chilled breaths. As he approached the lab they had just left, Eddie became aware of a peculiar sensation that grew stronger, until the tender hairs along the back of his neck sprang to life.

It sure as hell feels like someone's watching me... but there's nobody here!

The door was now slightly ajar, and he assumed he must've left it that way. He pushed the door open and stepped inside, quickly flipping up the light switch. Everything was as he left it, including the case. It sat upon the floor, closed and locked. However, the air felt charged, and much colder.

This place is starting to really freak me out... time to leave!

"Ed?" Cynthia's worried voice echoed weirdly from the edge of the hallway, near the stairs.

"I'll be right there!"

His nervousness embarrassed him. Normally, he wasn't one to let weaker emotions govern his behavior. But it was hard to remain stoically rationale when his eyes were playing tricks. As he turned off the lab's overhead lights and prepared to close the door, he could've sworn something moved toward him in the dimness… something darker than the deep shadows of the windowless room. The ink-like form reached him just as he pulled the door shut. For a moment, he simply stared at the closed door, expecting some other crazy shit to happen.

Not about to venture inside the room a third time, he hurried to rejoin his fiancé at the end of the hall, casting several uneasy glances over his shoulder along the way. He led her out of the building in haste. Despite December's wintry chill outside, the air seemed warmer than it did on the second floor. Together, they hurried to his Mazda, jumped inside, and the car swerved out of the parking lot before either one had their seatbelts fastened.

Eddie couldn't vouch for Cynthia, but that strange feeling of being watched by someone or *something* unseen stayed with him until the University's campus was no longer visible in the rearview mirror.

There had to be a logical reason for what happened—just had to be. It's what he kept telling himself all the way to Miami Beach.

Chapter Two

The Delta 747 jerked and dipped, as flight 1409 approached the eastern edge of Denver's metro sprawl. Ruth Guarnier tightened her grip on the left arm of the seat. Gazing anxiously out her window, she was thankful no one seemed to notice her surprised gasp. Nearly a decade since her last trip to Denver, she had forgotten the turbulent winds for which the region is well known.

She sighed. Much of her nervousness was hidden behind gentle brown eyes. Only the fine lines around her mouth, as she pursed her lips, gave evidence her teeth were tightly clinched. A handsome woman in her early sixties, she rarely looked her age. Dressed in a sharp burgundy pantsuit, her hair had been freshly accented the day before with enough brunette shade to lessen the light gray.

Her seatbelt secured in accordance with the advisory light above her seat, she quietly opened her carry-on bag. Call it superstition, or perhaps a compulsory need to ensure the jewels were still there. Either way, she couldn't stop herself. They remained safely wrapped in protective tissue inside the rectangular box that had been their home for much of the past forty years.

"It's time, David," she whispered, relaxing her jaw as she unwrapped the largest gem.

Being the only passenger sitting in her row allowed ample opportunity to feed her obsession, to look one last time before the plane's descent into Denver International Airport. She raised her head above the seats to check on the stewardesses' location. For the moment, they were busy collecting empty glasses and trash in the plane's coach section. She could count on another minute in relative privacy, so she uncovered the clear oblong diamond resting inside the box.

A flawless gem nearly two inches in length, and half that size in width, Ruth couldn't remember the exact carat weight from its last valuation, shortly after her husband, Peter, passed away twenty years ago. It was enough to push the stone's value to well over two hundred thousand dollars—a conservative estimate, since the Atlanta-based appraiser told her at the time how the smooth surface and near pristine condition of the jewel added an undetermined amount to its worth. Not to mention, the non-faceted stone had been polished without obvious tool marks. She crinkled her nose studying it; amazed, as she often was, that something so wondrous found its way into her family's otherwise sordid legacy.

The remaining three jewels in the box were similarly shaped and non-faceted, although not as large. These consisted of a smaller yellow diamond and two sapphires, one a brilliant blue, the other a deeper purple hue.

Ruth smiled sadly as she considered their inestimable value and cost to her family, since the jewels once belonged to a larger collection of her grandfather's. The immense wealth had come with a far greater price than the gemstones could ever repay. Anyone unfortunate enough to live under the unmerciful control of William Hobbs Sr., the lecherous old codger who survived far longer than a judicious God should ever allow, could never be compensated for the endless tyranny that reigned for decades through his male descendents.

But this was a time to rejoice, and not fret about past injuries. The man had been long removed from this life, and not all of his descendents took after him. Her beloved nephew, David Hobbs, was nothing like his great grandfather. Nor were his sons, Tyler and Christopher, who took after their father, thank the Lord. And, to think she'd be spending the Christmas holidays with them all! She pinched herself earlier, while waiting in Chattanooga's airport for her flight, just to make sure it wasn't a dream.

She especially looked forward to visiting with Miriam, David's lovely wife, and her grand niece, Jillian. It would be so much fun to take everyone shopping for something instead of mailing gifts, as had always been the case. A great surprise awaited David and Miriam, in addition to the four precious jewels. She carried trust papers, entitling David and his heirs to a large inheritance mentioned briefly to him in October, when he came to Tennessee on a business trip. Her only regret was the gems were an incomplete set, as she had misplaced a quarter-sized ruby. Unlike the other stones, the ruby was circular in shape, and thinner in width. She hoped to look for it again when she returned home in early January.

Satisfied for the time being, she wrapped up everything and placed the box back inside her carry-on bag, and locked it. She returned her attention to the view through the window. The plane veered further to the west, following a predestined approach to DIA. The landscape below was white, as the city and surrounding areas had been blanketed by several snowstorms during the past week.

Landing soon, she started to smile, until an uneasy feeling washed over her. It wasn't the first time this had happened lately, and the feeling always came with the same thought. Something was strangely mysterious about David when she last saw him in October. She recalled his abhorred reaction to what they discussed briefly from her past… about a family ghost.

Ruth chuckled lightly and shrugged, pushing the worrisome thought from her mind. She focused instead on the snow-covered roads and houses becoming clearly defined, as the plane began its final descent.

Chapter Three

"Get a move on it, kids!"

David Hobbs stood waiting at the foot of the stairs near the foyer of his family's spacious home in Littleton, Colorado. Dressed in a blue turtleneck sweater and his favorite pair of Wranglers, he absently stroked his closely cropped blonde beard. Strong and handsome, with warm eyes that morphed between hazel and bright green depending on his mood, he cleared his throat in preparation for a more urgent command to get the children's attention. Excited their great aunt was coming to Denver to spend the Christmas holidays, they chased after one another across the upstairs landing.

"Kids!"

"We're coming, Daddy!"

Jillian Hobbs, David's twelve-year-old daughter limped around the corner of the landing, nearly tripping on her way downstairs. Dressed in jeans and a Denver Broncos sweatshirt, she was already a tall, slender beauty with the same hair and eyes as her father. She smiled warmly at her dad while heading down the stairs, despite her hips' stiffness due to the painful flare-ups she often dealt with.

He felt a momentary tug on his heart beyond empathy for her present discomfort, realizing in a couple of years she'd likely start dating. Luckily, her older brother, Tyler, was even more protective than David. He and the youngest

Hobbs, Christopher, were dressed in similar winter attire and followed close behind her. Tyler, fourteen, favored his mother, with the same dark hair and piercing blue eyes. Still, he carried David's strong physical stature and cynical humor.

"Ty's letting me play with his 3DS, Daddy!" Christopher announced excitedly.

Closely resembling his older sister at nine years, including the same impish smile, Christopher raised the device in the air while pointing at it, nearly running over his sister on the way downstairs. He heeded his dad's warnings to slow down and not pull on the evergreen garland hung a few days earlier.

"Well, let's get this show on the road." David's expression softened now that he had their collective attention. "Where's your mom?"

"Right here." Miriam's snow boots clicked against the dining room's oak floor as she approached the foyer where everyone else was gathered. Her smile and radiant complexion seemed to set the air around her aglow—or maybe it was the luminance in her sky-blue eyes that sparkled with the same excitement as the kids.

David thought she looked delicious in the knit sweater and leggings she chose to wear that afternoon, wishing he could whisk her upstairs to ravish right then. But beyond impractical with the kids present, they were already running late to pick up his aunt. He ushered everyone outside, pausing to make sure Sadie, the family's Yorkshire terrier, had enough food and water to last until their return home later that afternoon. Then he joined his family already piling into the minivan idling in the driveway.

* * * * *

"Sadie's acting strange again," Miriam whispered, once on the highway heading north to Denver. Determined to keep her voice low, she glanced behind her at the kids, who were preoccupied with their tablets and MP3s. "Did you notice how she went right under the couch once she realized we were leaving?"

"Yeah, I did," he said, glancing her way before making a move to get in the fast lane. "She's been skittish for the past few days, and won't go outside without someone right beside her. I see she's sleeping in Jill's bed again."

"She's been like that since last Saturday, when we returned home after picking up the Christmas tree."

"It's been that long?"

Surprised, he pulled his eyes from the road to regard her. Miriam kept her attention straight ahead, as if not wanting to debate when the feeling inside their home had changed. In truth, he noticed something had been amiss since the previous Saturday, as she stated. But to him, the change was subtle, like a low hum in an older appliance, as what happened when the refrigerator started to die last summer. It took months before the unit finally died, but the warning at first had been almost unrecognizable.

The sensation of something being 'off' became more noticeable as the night wore on, and David initially chalked it up to the presence of the ten-foot Douglas Fir standing in the living room. It wasn't until the next morning that the feeling seemed more like an invisible intruder had invaded their residence during their brief absence. Still, he assumed the dog's nervousness had more to do with the tree's presence, since Sadie often barked when a new piece of furniture was brought home, or how she reacted when the new fridge was delivered last September. He reasoned the tree could've looked like a bristly monster to a color-blind animal with limited depth perception.

"Maybe we should take her to the vet again."

He made sure his response was nonchalant, hoping to draw any other observations Miriam might be pondering at that moment.

"Perhaps we should," she replied evenly, as if aware of his tactic. "But the dining room has felt like an icebox since then, too."

She looked at him when he didn't immediately respond. He offered a warm smile, and hoped she'd take it as the compassion he intended and not condescendence.

"Don't act like you haven't noticed it too, hon. I've seen you look over your shoulder the past few days and shake your head when you didn't see anything." She sent another cautious glance toward the back seats. The kids remained lost in their cyber-worlds.

"Yeah, okay… so maybe I've sensed a few odd things this past week," he admitted, keeping his focus on the road. "The chill in the dining room is a little creepy. But, if not for what happened in October, I wouldn't think much about it. Lots of homes have rooms that can't seem to stay warm, and the weather has been cold as hell the past couple of weeks."

It could make sense, since most of Colorado and the Midwest had been blanketed with heavy snows and near-arctic temperatures during much of December so far. But, the space heater he recently added to the dining room did little to warm it. It made it damned near impossible to deny the reality that something else kept the room so cold.

But what creeped him out most was the fact the icy feeling periodically moved elsewhere on the main floor, as if some large unfriendly presence would take a tour of the house. He witnessed it while getting something to eat from the kitchen, and again while adding additional logs to the fireplace in the living room. The small hairs on his neck and arm perked up when he felt the coldness invade the warmth.

If not for the terrifying experience in October, when his family survived a violent haunting that claimed the life of his best friend, David would've thought most, if not all, of what happened during the past week was rationally explainable. The earlier experience changed the way he viewed the world forever.

When the haunting ended, after David returned to the Smoky Mountains of Tennessee to resolve his ancestors' sins and bring peace to the tormented spirit of Allie Mae McCormick, a feeling of serenity followed him home. One that lasted until it ebbed away the past week.

"Don't worry darlin'. I seriously doubt it's her." He smiled confidently. Miriam shot him an imploring look begging him to be right.

"I just want things to be peaceful... at least through Christmas." She sighed and turned the radio up, signaling she was done talking about it.

Late afternoon snow flurries intensified their assault on the minivan. Watching the swirling stream of snowflakes while listening to holiday melodies served as a soothing distraction—until they reached the exit ramps for Denver International Airport, beyond the eastern side of Denver's metro sprawl. Miriam picked up the conversation again.

"Did you happen to mention anything about Allie Mae's ghost to Ruth when you visited her in Chattanooga?" Miriam sounded a lot more worried, and it revealed what she had thought about for much of the past half hour.

"No, I didn't," he replied, reflecting on the parting conversation with his aunt in October. They had met for lunch at a steakhouse just outside Chattanooga's airport.

At the time, Aunt Ruth was the one to mention a ghostly encounter, and not him. It was a ghost from her childhood that involved her great uncle—David's great, great uncle—Zachariah Hobbs. He realized from what the mysterious entity foretold to his aunt as a child, about Zachariah's impending death, the very same entity came back sixty years later to wage war with David and his family. He only hoped she hadn't noticed how the encounter she described had chilled him—other than spraying his iced tea through his nose when she related the entity's promise of revenge upon Uncle Zach for his part in her murder.

"I just want Ruth to have a great time while she's here," said Miriam, letting out a slow, deep breath before looking out her window at the swirling snow. "I want it to be really *special*."

"Everything will be fine, babe." He reached over to gently pat her thigh above the knee. "Auntie's going to have a great time. A truly *fantastic* time—I promise!"

If they started his aunt's visit on the right foot, David reasoned it could buy him some time to figure out what to do about the troublesome situation in their house. Miriam nodded and began to relax, until Christopher spoke up.

"Where's Auntie Ruth going to sleep?"

They both whirled their heads in his direction, fearful of what he might've overheard. He had his headphones pulled down and a dormant game resting in his lap.

"Is she going to sleep on the sofa in the living room, or in one of the guestrooms upstairs?"

"Honey, she'll be staying in the guestroom next to your bedroom and Jill's," said Miriam. "I've already prepared the room for her, since she told me at Thanksgiving that she wanted the one closest to you kids."

Christopher nodded, thoughtfully, shooting a worried look toward Jillian, who sat in the seat to his left. She, like Tyler sprawled out in the bench seat behind her, jammed to the music in her iPod. Christopher leaned closer to his mom.

"I'm glad Auntie Ruth won't be sleeping on the sofa, Mommy." The look on his face confirmed his relief. "I don't think the old tree man would like it if someone slept in the living room." He lowered his tone to emphasize his seriousness.

"Old tree man? What are you talking about, Chris?"

Hoping his tone sounded playful, the solemn look on Christopher's face worried David.

"The man in our house," he replied.

As if realizing he might be in trouble for not sharing the information sooner, Christopher began to fidget. He lowered his eyes to avoid his mother's stunned look and his father's probing gaze in the rearview mirror.

"*What* man in our house?"

Miriam's alarm drew a curious look from Jillian, who might've removed her headphones if not for her dad's mouthed assurance everything was okay. She looked at Christopher and searched her mom's face for confirmation of what her dad said. Miriam forced a warm smile and repeated David's assurance, until Jillian again grooved to her private musical bliss.

"Can you describe the man you're talking about, son?" David posed the question tenderly, keeping his eyes on the road while studying his son through the mirror.

"Yes," said Christopher, hesitating until he received another assuring look from his mom. "He's really thin and very, very old. He's a lot taller than you, Daddy, and has lots of deep wrinkles in his face and body that look like the bark on scary trees. You know, the ones in Halloween pictures? …And, he's got no clothes! His hair is gray and really long, with black feathers stuck in it. He likes to touch the feathers with his fingernails that are really, really long—just like his toenails, too, with the tips curled in.

Oh, and his eyes are yellow, like the Patterson's tiger cat Sonya. I've only seen him a few times."

"Where did you see him, honey?" asked Miriam, her voice soothing, although David could tell she barely restrained her fear.

"In the living room," said Christopher. "Most of the time he just sits on the sofa staring straight ahead, like he's daydreaming. But the other night I watched him follow Daddy from the kitchen to the fireplace. The night you made me sit at the table until I finished my peas and cauliflower, Mommy."

The minivan reached the entrance to the short-term parking area nearest the baggage claim where Ruth's flight was scheduled to arrive. Anxious to ask more questions, David focused instead on finding a parking space.

"Why didn't you tell us about this earlier, honey?" Miriam kneaded her knuckles, but her tone remained calm.

"I was going to tell you and Daddy," he said, after another moment's hesitation. "The man looked like he might hurt Daddy."

David shot a concerned look at Miriam, who gasped, but muted her reaction when Christopher dropped his gaze to his lap again.

"Then he looked at me and smiled a little, and acted like he wanted to tell Daddy he was sorry, right before he disappeared. Didn't you see him? You looked right at him, Daddy. More than once that night...."

His voice trailed off and his eyes turned misty. Miriam reached back to give him a hug. When he started bawling in her arms, Jillian and Tyler took off their headsets.

David immediately assured them that everything would be all right.

If only he believed it. Instead, he pictured the chilled presence in the living room, leering at him as some grotesque ancient man.

How in the hell is this even possible? Not another haunting just two months after the first one!

The unenviable task of trying to keep this shit away from Auntie's awareness was all he could think about as he pulled into a vacant parking spot.

Chapter Four

John Running Deer gazed through the large picture window in his upstairs loft, studying the shadowed, snow-covered treetops on either side of his secluded Smoky Mountain cabin. Twilight drew near, chasing the setting sun that had broken through the cloud cover, only to rapidly disappear behind the hills to the west of his home. Light snow flurries continued to twist and fall through the air, like tiny diamonds floating within the security lights' glare beneath the cabin's eaves.

For the moment John frowned, his deep brown eyes squinted in an effort to discern some unseen menace camouflaged within the approaching darkness. The wind, which had shrieked and howled for much of the day while pushing drifts of powdered snow up to the cabin's front door, was now silent—as if listening, waiting for what would come next.

Before he turned away from the window, a soft whistling sound drew his attention in the distance. It grew louder as it approached the cabin from the north.

The anisgina comes again!

He closed the window's heavy curtains, and hurried down the narrow staircase to the main level, where Shawn, his prized Siberian husky, waited. The dog whined as he followed John, watching him close the remaining open curtains and make sure both the front and back entrances to the cabin were securely locked with the deadbolts set. By the time John finished, the sound had become a near-deafening roar, announcing the arrival of a restless spirit whose anger had been repeatedly directed toward him. The entity's physical remains were recently unearthed from its ancient resting place in a sacred Cades Cove ravine.

The terrible attacks he endured the past few weeks always started with the same distant whistle; one he first mistook as the wind rustling through tall white pines, oaks, and maples in the surrounding forest. But whenever it reached his property, the sound always became deeper and much more intense, resembling an enormous swarm of angry hornets.

Each time, it sent debilitating chills through his entire being, and rendered useless his knowledge of ancient Cherokee spells. Even the privileged training received in his youth, when he was next in line to become a revered shaman didn't help. The colorful dream catchers and spirit chasers covering every wall of the cabin swayed as if in symphony with one another, lifted by some unseen hand moving along the inside perimeter of his home.

Especially unsettling, the swarm would move up the windows and doors, and across the cabin's roof as the entity sought entrance to his home. Fearing tonight might be the occasion when it finally found a way inside the cabin, John hurried to add another log to the fire burning within the large stone fireplace in the living room. He offered a fervent prayer that the existing blaze would prove strong enough to keep the spirit at bay.

"It's all right, boy," he sought to assure Shawn, who continued to whine and pace nervously, despite the log's immediate impact on the fire's brightness.

After scanning the living room to verify he and the dog were truly alone, he sat in his recliner. He pulled a colorful afghan over his shoulders, since lately he struggled to stay warm despite being attired for cold weather, wearing a thick flannel shirt and thermal snow pants.

Shawn nudged him with an imploring look in his pale blue eyes, his snow-white fur muted in the dimness. Perhaps he noticed his master had aged several years over the past two months, as John's dark braided hair was grayer than it had been when he first met David Hobbs in October. The lines on his face had become more pronounced. Still virile and handsome for a man well into his sixties, the entity's aggression steadily drained away the strength and peaceful disposition that were his hallmarks.

It made him reconsider his determination to keep working as a ranger for the national park service until the age of seventy-two, just five years away. After spending the last forty-three years as one of the more knowledgeable and popular tour guides on the Tennessee side of The Great Smoky Mountain National Park, he honestly didn't know what else he would do. However, if the current siege on his home and state of mind continued, he might have to find something else. Perhaps it would also mean leaving the land that had once been the cherished domain of his Cherokee ancestors.

Aware of his beloved pet's need for protective assurance, he reached down to massage the area beneath Shawn's chin. He continued until the unsettling noise diminished, signaling the assault's end. The angry spirit had moved on to some other destination.

John picked up a Christmas card from the coffee table next to his chair. The card was still inside its open envelope, and it came from David and his wife, Miriam. He had read David's note contained within it several times. Soon, the card would join the others he received from his daughter, Joanna, and his granddaughters, Evelyn and Hanna on his mantle.

The Hobbs' card included a small family portrait, framed in an embossed holly print on gold foil. He removed the photograph and held it in his lap, once Shawn curled around his feet. He reflected on David's visit to the cabin just before Halloween, the first time the sound of swarming hornets plagued his home. At the time, he and David were under continuous assault from the angry ghost of a Cades Cove teenager who blamed David for her terrible murder.

Allie Mae…may you remain at peace within the bosom of the Great Spirit.

If not for his granddaughter Evelyn, whose talent and skills in the shaman ways exceeded his, the spirit would've prevailed in taking his friend's life. After David confronted his ancestors' role in the crime committed against her in the ravine, John hoped to provide lasting peace for her spirit by locating her remains and arranging a proper burial elsewhere. That part of the plan went well enough, with Evelyn invoking a Cherokee blessing when the bones were reburied in the McCormick section of the old Methodist Church's cemetery in Cades Cove.

But other ominous events ensued once Allie Mae's bones were unearthed from beneath a heavy stone slab that had rested on top of them for more than ninety years. The slab turned out to be part of an ancient temple, and actually was part of the structure's ceiling, according to Dr. Walter Pollack from the University of Tennessee's archaeology department. But, there was more. Other bones lay buried underneath Allie's crushed skeleton. These remains hadn't seen the light of day in more than a thousand years. Discovered alongside the much older skeleton was a jeweled scepter made of solid gold with an ornate handle and ivory blade.

They found other skeletons in the ravine as well. Most of these showed signs of violence, along with Anglo-American armor and jewelry from the early 1600s. When all of the skeletons and the splendid scepter had been removed from the ravine, and brought to the Frank H. McClung Museum for further examination, the hostile visitations to the cabin soon followed.

John and Evelyn sought legal injunctions to stop the excavation, and restore the older skeletons and other artifacts back to the original gravesite in the ravine. Meanwhile, the swarming menace grew stronger by the week. Evelyn was convinced the entity behind the current mischief was the very same one that fueled Allie Mae's thirst for vengeance and exaggerated strength in October.

John intended to take up the legal battle again in January. He felt confident the NCAI would be successful in getting the remains returned to the ravine, since some of the skeletons had been confirmed as Native American. Getting the scepter returned remained the bigger worry. Inconclusive as to which ancient race of people it belonged, the University dug their heels in for a potential protracted court war for its ownership. Using the unusual appearance of the largest skeleton to support their stance, the archaeology department recently issued a statement claiming the scepter and skeleton belonged to an undetermined "non-Indian race".

John lingered over the Hobbs' portrait for another moment, listening to the low gusts of wind outside and pops from the hickory logs burning in the fireplace. He hoped the holidays would be a blessed time for David and his family. He started to smile, but stopped.

I've got to warn everyone...right now!

He hastily stood and moved to the small cove where his phone sat, next to the refrigerator. He pulled out a number from his wallet and dialed it. After five rings the call went to voicemail, and John let out a low hiss of frustration.

"Peter, this is John Running Deer again," he said, his tone worried. "I need for you to call me back once you get this, and you have my number at the cabin. It doesn't matter what time—just call me. Thanks."

Dr. Peter Kirkland, a prominent member of the University of Tennessee's forensic staff in Knoxville, had known John for almost twenty years. Their recent disagreement over who held the true rights to the ravine's remains and artifacts threatened to end their longtime friendship.

After he hung up, John remained in the kitchen. The powerful premonition from a moment ago grew stronger.... *Something very bad will happen soon!*

Peter's role left him in terrible danger, although the professor, a pragmatist to a fault, would never believe in an ancient entity or curse unless either one bit him on the ass. As for David Hobbs... John fervently prayed that the other half of his premonition wasn't true.

5:35 p.m. Two hours ahead of Littleton, Colorado. In all likelihood, the Hobbs' family would be out doing last minute Christmas shopping. David mentioned a relative coming from out of town this weekend when they last talked, a little over a week ago. Regardless, John felt he had to warn him.

Ignoring Evelyn's admonition not to say anything until after the holidays, he grabbed the phone and dialed David's number. Pressing the receiver tightly against his ear, he waited impatiently for the crackling line to Littleton, Colorado to connect.

Chapter Five

"Auntie! Over here!"

David waved his arms to alert the smartly dressed older woman in the long beige overcoat that he and the rest of the family waited by the assigned luggage carousel for flight 1409. At first, Ruth Guarnier didn't see him or his antics, lost in the confusion of the holiday bustle pervading Denver International Airport. Once he took a few steps toward her, weaving through the crowd of travelers anxious to grab their bags and skis, she saw him and smiled. She moved as quickly as her arthritic knees would allow.

"Well, David, I made it here in one piece, don't you know!"

She set her carry-on bag and purse at her feet to give him a hug. He responded in kind, nearly lifting her off the ground. She uttered a slight yelp.

"It's so good to see you, Auntie!"

Miriam and the kids navigated the stream of travelers to join them.

"Mir... it seems you haven't aged a bit since I last saw you. Why, you're lovelier than a winter songbird!" Ruth broke her embrace with David and reached for Miriam. "It's so *good* to see you, dear!"

"I've missed you so much, Ruth!" Miriam's shoulders trembled as she fought to keep from crying. "It's wonderful to have you here with us—*so* wonderful!"

"There, there, dear," said Ruth, soothingly, as the two hugged tightly. "I've missed you, too, you know."

Despite frequent phone conversations between the two, until October, the anger and deep-seated resentment her nephew previously harbored against her made it difficult to arrange a meaningful visit. Since she understood the painful history behind his animosity, she had always been very willing to forgive.

David guided everyone closer to the carousel and out of the stream of traffic, which included less and less smiling faces for having to go around the group huddled in the middle of the aisle.

"Well, now…. Jill, I see you're growing up to be such a beautiful young lady!"

Ruth stopped to admire her grandniece once they reached the carousel area, after Tyler had taken her claim tickets to retrieve the luggage. Jillian blushed, but managed a smile showing dimples she inherited from her aunt's side of the family. Ruth sighed softly, reminiscing about a younger version of David, who passed his good looks on to his daughter.

"And Chris, my gosh, you've grown up too!" She stepped back to admire David and Miriam's youngest child. "You probably don't even remember your Aunt Ruth, do you, darlin'?"

"I was just a baby back then. Mommy told me that."

Christopher blushed, looking at his shoes. He raised his eyes slowly, smiling at her.

"Well, then, we need to get reacquainted."

She reached out a hand, and he eagerly placed his hand inside hers. Tyler returned with her bags from the carousel, and once she saw him, she gasped in surprise.

"Boy, you're the spittin' image of your great, great, *great* Uncle Zachariah Hobbs!" she marveled, unaware of the uneasy looks on the faces of Miriam and Jillian. "Has anyone ever told you that before? I know there's a picture of Uncle Zach in the photo album I gave to your father back in October."

"Yeah, Dad showed me." Tyler blushed.

"Um-hmmm." She shook her head as she continued to study him. "David told me during our visit that you're quite a hit with the young ladies in your school, Ty. And, I understand that the other young men admire you, as well. No doubt you'll do us all proud, son."

Tyler returned her warm smile with a shy grin, and by the time she looked at everyone else again, the troubled looks on Miriam and Jillian's faces had faded. Busy watching everyone else's reactions, Christopher tightened his grip on his great aunt's hand. Not to be outdone, Jillian moved to Ruth's other side and cupped her arm inside hers, drawing a look of surprised joy.

"So, how was your flight from Chattanooga, Auntie Ruth?" Jillian asked, letting her hand slide down to clasp Ruth's.

"Oh, it was fine, dear… maybe a little bumpy once we got close to Denver," she said, beaming from the reception she received. "But I made it in one piece!"

Her eyes twinkled, drawing another blush from Jillian.

* * * * *

They left the baggage area and returned to the minivan. Tyler led the way, still carrying his great aunt's coat bag and one of her suitcases. Ruth and his younger siblings followed close behind him. David carried her other suitcase, and walked a short distance behind with Miriam to talk.

"She's such a sweet woman," said Miriam, quietly. "I've really missed her."

"Believe it or not, I have too," said David. "Hopefully things will be a lot better between she and I."

He smiled, but Miriam was frowning.

"What's up?"

"Are you sure you didn't tell her anything about what happened to us back in October?"

"I'm sure."

October… the most regrettable month of my entire life!

He had denied the fact an angry ghost followed him and Miriam home from Gatlinburg, Tennessee in mid-October, where they celebrated their fifteenth anniversary. By the time he fully accepted the reality of Allie Mae McCormick's spirit and her violent tendencies, she had murdered his best friend, Norm Sowell, and also attempted to kill Tyler. It's what took him back to Tennessee. He visited with his aunt before returning to Gatlinburg.

"What's up, hon?" she asked, obviously in response to his slight grimace.

"Nothing." He sought to hide his gloomy thoughts behind an exaggerated smile. "Just thinking about how much fun it'll be if the old tree man decides to become a little more active while Auntie's here with us."

Not his original thought, but a quick and logical leap once he left the mental imagery of the previous haunting. After all, the month and a half of peace following Allie Mae's expulsion from their world could only mean something if the latest situation hadn't occurred. All bets were off now. They had moved into uncharted territory with an entity that seemed quite irritated with him again.

"I've decided to call Sara tonight, once we get settled in for the evening," she advised. "Please don't try to talk me out of it, okay?"

Sara Palmer, a gifted parapsychologist, was a good friend of Janice Andrews, Miriam's best friend. David had thought of her as a New Age crackpot until her insights proved helpful in banishing Allie Mae's spirit. Since then, Miriam remained in contact with Sara, as much for friendship as additional guidance.

"Okay, but aren't you a little concerned having a witch lady show up with feather dusters and incense will make Auntie a little suspicious?" he asked, attempting to do just what she warned him against—to talk her out of it. "It's not like Sara will show up with a white-bearded fat man in a sleigh drawn by a dozen reindeer."

"Don't be silly!" she countered. "You know fully well she'll know how to handle this discreetly. If I'd followed my gut instinct last time and called her right away, instead of waiting on you to get us into deeper trouble, maybe things wouldn't have gotten so out of hand...."

Her voice trailed off, as if she realized what she said came out differently than intended. True, his procrastination in enlisting professional help to deal with the ghost allowed the haunting to escalate far beyond what either one had expected.

"Yeah. I'll never forgive myself for that," said David, his mood immediately depressed.

"Honey, I'm so sorry. That's not what I—"

"It's okay," he interrupted, grimacing as he thought of Norm.

"It's not what I meant, and I'm really sorry it came out like that." She moved in close, clasping his gloved hand in hers, and he responded with a faint grin.

"I know you didn't mean it like that." He gently squeezed her fingers. "Besides, it's Christmas. Everything will be fine."

Ruth glanced over her shoulder at them and smiled, perhaps admiring how they seemed so much like true lovebirds, hand in hand and leaning into each other. Once outside the terminal building, they moved to catch up, as everyone walked briskly to the Chrysler.

* * * * *

The minivan pulled up the circular driveway to the Hobbs' home just before six o'clock. The grand Cape Cod stood majestic, decorated in colorful holiday lights Tyler plugged in before they left.

"Now... *that's* a beautiful house. Very fitting for y'all," observed Ruth, once the van stopped and the kids piled out. "It's much roomier than the townhouse y'all lived in the last time I was here. Wasn't it in the foothills someplace?"

"In Lakewood," said David. "With the kids getting older, we wanted a place where they could have room to run around." He turned off the ignition.

"Plus, the schools are a little better, and I'm fortunate to have my practice just a few miles down the road," added Miriam, referring to the pediatric clinic she co-owned with two other doctors. Both she and David arranged their winter vacations to coincide with Ruth's two-week stay in Colorado, with David getting the longest reprieve. He wouldn't return to Johnson, Simms & Perrault, the accounting firm he worked for as an auditor, until after New Years.

"I'll grab Auntie Ruth's bags and join everybody inside," said Tyler, handing his tablet to Christopher and climbing out before anyone else removed their seatbelts.

He ran around to the rear of the Chrysler, and grabbed both of Ruth's suitcases and her coat bag. She continued to keep her carry-on with her, which became increasingly mysterious to Jillian and Christopher.

The scents of cinnamon-apple and pumpkin spice candles greeted them upon entering the house, along with the powerful aroma from the decorated Douglas fir standing in one corner of the darkened living room. Unlike the unearthly chill David expected, the main floor was warm and cozy. The soft drone from the furnace pushing warm air throughout the house gave him a sense of peace and well-being he hoped was genuine.

Jillian and Christopher raced for the privilege of turning on the Christmas tree lights. Meanwhile, David helped Tyler with Ruth's luggage. Together they moved upstairs to the guestroom prepared earlier. She and the younger children settled in the living room, while Miriam fixed everyone a cup of hot cocoa.

Unlike downstairs, the temperature along the upstairs landing seemed much colder than earlier, as if someone had left several windows wide open. Yet, when David and Tyler checked, every window remained shut. Tyler followed his dad into the guestroom. The deep chill pervading everywhere else upstairs gave way to warmth rivaling the living room's coziness. David turned on the light and they stepped inside.

"Well, at least it'll be nice for Auntie Ruth in here, huh, Dad?" said Tyler, setting the suitcase and coat bag he carried at the foot of the bed.

David set the suitcase he carried next to the other luggage. The room was decorated in a mixture of antiques and modern pieces, and a mahogany four-post canopy bed was the centerpiece.

"Yeah… so it seems," David agreed, forcing another smile once he noticed Tyler's uncomfortable expression.

"We'll get the gas folks out here after Christmas to check the lines, since the heater still seems a little out of whack."

He stepped out of the room and over to the hall thermostat in an effort to further sell the notion. Tyler didn't buy it.

"Like that's going to make a frigging difference," he whispered, the sarcastic comment not quite out of his dad's earshot. "Do you want me to catch the light on the way out?"

His voice carried a slight edge as he walked to the doorway where David waited.

"Nah, I'll get it, son."

He motioned for Tyler to head downstairs. David glanced around the room before shutting off the overhead light and closing the door. As he moved to the stairs where his son waited, he thought he heard something coming from inside the guestroom, and paused to listen.

"What is it, Dad?" Tyler looked anxious, as if he wanted to get the hell away from there.

David wondered if, like Christopher, his oldest son had seen any recent apparitions he decided not to tell his parents about. A loud burst of laughter erupted downstairs, startling them both, as Ruth and Miriam shared a mirthful moment in the kitchen.

"It's probably nothing," David assured him, his cheeks sore from an even bigger smile forgery. "Let's go get some cocoa before it's all gone."

"Sounds good." Tyler grinned, seemingly a little more relieved. He nearly ran downstairs, refusing to look anywhere but straight ahead.

David almost did the same thing, but the temptation to take one last look got the better of him. Before he turned off the hallway lights he thought he saw something for just an instant. It could've been extra jumpiness based on the frigidity, and further fed by his previous experiences and what Christopher mentioned earlier.

But he could've sworn that a dark shape hovered outside the guestroom's doorway.

"Dad, are you coming?" Tyler called from the base of the stairs.

"I'll be right there, son."

David glanced again at the guestroom's doorway. Whatever he had seen—or thought was there—had vanished. He moved confidently down the stairs, and didn't look back. Not even when the floorboards creaked on the landing behind him and the small hairs on the back of his neck sprang to life.

Chapter Six

The light scratching and shuffling noises resumed.

Tony Williams, the night security guard assigned to keep watch at Langston Hall, stood from his desk near the storage building's entrance. After releasing an irritated sigh, he moved down the dusty wooden walkway toward the basement stairwell located at the back end of the main floor.

The first two times he heard the noises, he called out to see if anyone was inside the building. Despite the remote possibility he might've overlooked someone hiding in the shadows, a closer look wasn't necessary. Not yet, at least. He completed the first required tour of the evening that consisted of a thorough examination of each door and window lock on all three floors of the former dormitory. Tony followed it up with a quick trip to the bottom of the basement stairwell, where he made sure the thick steel door remained secure. A good hard tug on the handle to ensure the door stayed locked was the easiest part of the assignment. That's what his boss, Vernon Mathis, told him the day before.

"Hello?" he called out, harshly, hoping the annoyance in his voice was enough to get whatever, or whoever, made the noise to take notice. "This building is off-limits per the Dean's office, if anybody's in here!"

After waiting for a response other than the continual scratching emanating from the stairwell, big, bad, Tony "The Tank" Williams was on the way. On the way to deliver an ass-kicking to the MoFo cutting into his study time—be it a small furry critter or a bored prankster from a nearby coed dorm.

For a moment, he thought about the terror he used to deliver to opposing SEC quarterbacks on Saturday afternoons. The kind of thing that got him featured on ESPN's Sportscenter twice in his sophomore year, while playing ball for the University of Tennessee. Life was looking up back then—way up. He considered the possibility of turning pro early, say, right after his junior year. But, he tore his Achilles on the last weekend at Vanderbilt that fall as the Vols' starting weak-side linebacker. And, the rest, as they say, was history for poor Tony. No more fame, no big dollars, and no easy pussy.

"Hello-o-oh!!" He repeated, more forceful as he neared the back of the building.

The annoying noises ceased when he reached the edge of the stairs. He turned on the flashlight and pointed it down the darkened stairwell toward its murky bottom. There was no sign of anyone or anything moving about, with no place to hide. Perplexed, he shook his head and looked around, pointing the flashlight down the hallway toward the main entrance. A fluorescent glow from a long line of grime-covered overhead lamps illuminated the main floor.

He moved to the guard station, which consisted of a small card table and metal folding chair, barely adequate despite the temporary purpose. The chair sat next to the front door and a large window Vernon told him was original to the building when completed in 1918. As with any old building, it got real cold sitting there. Really *damned* cold, and especially late at night.

It sure as hell wasn't the McClung Museum, which was less than a hundred yards from Langston Hall. The McClung was his normal gig every weekend and two nights during the week, eight o'clock to midnight. Right now, Matt Edmonds, the newbie who had just joined the campus police, kept watch at the museum, along with whatever Knoxville police officer was assigned to help out. The two were probably sharing their opinions about the Vols' upcoming bowl game over two cups of steaming coffee at the real guard station, near one of three ten-foot Christmas trees decorating the museum's front lobby. And, damn it if it wasn't warm inside that place, unlike this fucking icebox. This old, drafty building that no longer had an address plate was slated for demolition next summer.

Langston Hall was one of the University of Tennessee's oldest colonial-styled, red brick buildings that once served as a women's dormitory until the mid-1970s. It now housed hundreds of boxes filled with transcripts and other documents, such as outdated student records and even older report cards from years long since past. Now just a storage place for such mundane items, the building hadn't seen a guard staff keeping a twenty-four/seven vigil in more than two decades.

Less than a week after Thanksgiving, Tony got the news from his boss, Vernon—the retired Knoxville police captain who now handled the security staffing for UT's largest campus—that he and five other guards had been reassigned indefinitely to this less-than-desirable post. For the past three weekends, John Campbell had handled the evening shift on his own. But now he spent the eight-hour shift divided between this post and a second hot spot on the other side of campus. Starting last night, John manned the desk from 4 p.m. to 8 p.m.; Tony took over from eight to midnight; and then, Johnnie Mercer—another ex-Vols' football star—relieved Tony at midnight. He could count on Johnnie to run three to four minutes late.

It was supposed to be Tony's only weekend filling in for John, since Vernon promised it would be a brief assignment until Matt was fully up to speed. Since Tony didn't have any classes until January, Vernon took the liberty to schedule him for the same gig right on through Christmas. The new plan was for Matt to be ready to take over by New Years.

He better damn well be ready... and way before that!

It looked like New Years might be Tony's only opportunity for a break from the dreary assignment before January. In the meantime, Tony was already screwed as far as getting meaningful time away from this shit. That is, if he didn't somehow come down with something serious like strep throat or walking pneumonia in time for Christmas Day. He might not be able to avoid working Christmas Eve, but damn straight he wasn't working Christmas Day. Momma was coming down to Knoxville with his Aunt Jolene from Louisville, Kentucky, and he sure as hell wasn't about to freeze his ass in this hell-hole while they were in town.

Tony sat in his chair and pulled out his Poli-Sci preliminary assignment for January from his backpack, and set it in front of him. He glanced at his wristwatch. 9:37 p.m. *Date time, right when things should be heating up!* Tony thought about his roommate's cute steady girl, Gina Banks. Gina was fine... so *very* fine, man. So how come Tyrone was making it with this babe, instead of him? Tony was bigger, better built, had a dazzling smile, and was a hell of a lot more charming than his best friend who migrated south with him from Louisville. Besides, the former 'Tank-man' was packaged large where it counted, and had the stamina to keep a woman like her more than satisfied. Yet, up until now she had easily sidestepped his advances, and threatened more than once to "talk to Tyrone about it" if he kept it up.

He released another sigh, deeper and somewhat sorrowful, and cracked open the textbook. Determined to forget about Gina, Tyrone, or anybody else for now, he planned to lose himself in the book's opening discourse about the fading merits of America's two-party political machine.

The damned scratching and shuffling noises started up again, and just like before, they were coming from the basement stairwell. He tried to ignore them.... Maybe it was just a pack of small rodents, or one big ugly mother rat. Hell, a pesky vermin small enough to escape his detection made sense. After checking twice already, he wasn't in a hurry to get up again. Not without a damned good reason.

But the noises continued and Tony couldn't stop thinking about them. It didn't matter if anything was there or not. It was the simple call of duty to protect what lay hidden behind the locked door downstairs. The whole damned reason he and his other guard buddies were forced to spend their evenings in this condemned, God-forsaken shit-haven that should've been torn down years ago. Something about a few crates filled with skeletons and relics recently uncovered from some 'secret place' up in the Smoky Mountains. Along with one other item brought in this morning, according to Vernon.

He snickered. Who gives a shit about some old bones and the shredded remains of clothing and rusted-out armor worn by some white folks from nearly four hundred years ago? For all he knew, they could've been ancestors to the slavers who kept his family in bondage for the better part of two centuries.

Fuck em' all if that's the case!

The scratching and shuffling noises grew louder... as if something was trying hard to get his attention. *Shit, did the source of the noises just now move closer?* He was definitely unprepared for what happened next, as taut gooseflesh rose upon his arms, neck, and shoulders. The old wooden banister inside the stairwell creaked, and it did so as if someone secured a strong enough grip to pull him or herself upward. But that wasn't the only thing making his skin crawl. Heavy footfalls slowly navigated the stairs.

"Who in the hell's down there?" he demanded, a slight whine creeping into his tough-guy persona, and threatening to erase it.

A little frightened, he followed the urge to have another look inside the darkened stairwell. He stood, pushing the folding chair back noisily as possible against the wooden floor, and using his two-hundred-and-forty-pound frame to make his own approaching footsteps sound as heavy as the footfalls moving up the stairway. To up the ante further, he smacked the steel handle of his flashlight against his palm in a steady, methodical rhythm that was a helluva lot slower than his racing heartbeat.

The tactic seemed to work. The noises in the stairwell ceased. Yet, in the heightened stillness, he heard something else... breathing. Deep and steady, it reminded him of Tyrone when he fell asleep on the couch watching television in the wee hours of the morning in their shared apartment. Only in this instance, he had a pretty good idea that whatever made the breathing sound wasn't sleeping. It merely waited.

Tony whispered a quick prayer and continued down the hallway to the stairs, hoping when he shined his flashlight again into the dimness he'd find a harmless four-legged critter scurrying for cover. Yet, the breathing in the stairwell grew deeper, as if whatever waited there eagerly anticipated the night watchman's approach.

Tony summoned the rest of his courage and flicked his flashlight on, hurrying to the stairwell. The flashlight's beam revealed the same barren cement stairs and worn wooden banister from earlier. The breathing had ceased.

Relieved that the noises must've been an auditory hallucination after all, he prepared to turn around and head back to the desk, smiling sheepishly.

That's when he saw them.

Two shadows didn't disappear when the harsh white glare from his flashlight passed over them. Both were human-like shapes, similar to what one might see under the noontime sun when a person's darker twin can mimic every move. Only the dark pair had their own agenda, swiftly moving up the stairs. The shadows separated from each other, lengthening grotesquely as they moved toward him on either side. Tony noticed dark feathers poking through each figure's flowing dark hair, and that each one carried crimson-streaked coup sticks and knives.

"Ah, *hell*, no!" he shouted.

He swung his flashlight at the phantom figures, connecting with nothing but incredible coldness as it passed through his hand and wrist. In desperate panic, he threw the flashlight at the closest phantom....

Later, all he readily recalled from the ordeal was the flashlight passing through it, along with the sound of the glass lens shattering against the wall and the steel casing tumbling down the stairs. He had made it out of the building, running on wobbly legs and a bum ankle from falling as the phantoms repeatedly dove at him. Tony believed he'd never forget the encroaching blackness that stretched across the walls and ceiling while he stumbled toward the main entrance. Reflected within the door's lead glass window, his eyes looked like two bulging cue balls ready to be launched from his handsome ebony face.

Thankfully, he wouldn't recall much else from that evening until long after New Years. The fragmented images would spawn enough nightmares to force the by-then former watchman to curtail his education at the University of Tennessee. The less painful images in his memory were of him running and screaming through the densely treed lot that separated Langston Hall from the rest of the buildings on Circle Way. The race was futile, and the flitting wraiths continued to dive repeatedly at him while a terrible whistling noise pursued him from the treetops.

The rest of what happened to Tony would come from Johnnie Mercer and Matt Edmonds, who found him three hours later, bloodied and curled-up in a fetal position near the curb of the museum's main parking lot. He was babbling incoherently, while pleading for some unseen menace to leave him the hell alone.

Chapter Seven

The morning sunshine looked promising to Ruth as she gazed out the guestroom's window. The snow-covered landscape under a clear, blue sky didn't look like a hindrance for her Sunday afternoon shopping plans. The view from her room was splendid, and most of the surrounding trees glistened from snow slowly melting. Dripping icicles hung from the branches of a nearby maple, and the kids' swing set in the backyard. To top it off, a small throng of winter-hardy birds called merrily to one another from the higher branches of the surrounding pines and a rather majestic oak at the rear of the property. Their songs lifted her heart.

Nattily attired in tan slacks and a white sweater, she stepped to the mahogany antique dresser against the wall opposite the window to finish the final makeup touches around her eyes. Using the dresser's mirror, she soon was ready to join her nephew's family downstairs. Before she left the room, she took a moment to lift her carry-on bag from beside the bed and set it on the dresser, and carefully removed the jewelry box.

Once relieved of their protective wrappings, the precious diamonds and sapphires seemed to glow brightly in the soft, natural sunlight invading the room through the window. Satisfied, she rewrapped the gems and closed the box, placing it inside the top middle drawer of the dresser since it was empty. She added the trust papers she brought for David to sign, and slid all of the items to the very back of the drawer before closing it.

Ready to join everyone downstairs, she prepared to exit the room. A sudden whisper startled her, enough to where she almost dropped her purse and the eye glasses carried loosely in her hand. Ruth peered warily over her shoulder, but didn't discern anything had changed since her last look around the room.

The murmur was low pitched, and similar to another she thought she heard during the night when she was briefly awakened. She dismissed that one as a gust of wind somehow seeping into her room through a minute crack between the window and its frame. That would also account for how cold it got in the room.

The room had been cozy again when she awoke, nearly an hour ago, but it grew chilly as she stood there. She forced herself to ignore what was happening. Straightening her sweater, she opened the door and stepped out into the hallway, where it was much warmer.

She decided to leave the door open, in hopes the heat from the landing would creep into the guestroom during her absence. Joyful laughter resounded from the dining room below. Christopher and Jillian could scarcely contain their excitement with only one day to go before Christmas Eve.

It's so wonderful to be a part of this!

That's all she would allow into her awareness, paying no attention to the light rustling noises coming from the guestroom as she walked downstairs.

* * * * *

"Hey, Mom, Auntie Ruth is up now!" Jillian announced, as Ruth stepped into the dining room from the foyer. "Good morning, Auntie Ruth!"

Jillian hurried over and threw her arms around her waist. Not to be outdone, Christopher sped toward her from the opposite side of the dining room table. When he abruptly jumped down from his chair, the crystal chandelier that hung above the table swayed enough to draw a stern look from David.

"Oh, my, my!" Ruth bent down to kiss their cheeks as they wrapped their arms around her neck. "You both are such angels of sunshine!"

She straightened, and Christopher latched on to her right arm while Jillian clasped her left hand. Together they walked to the table, laden with an array of breakfast items, and sat down, with Ruth sitting between them. Miriam and Janice Andrews had been busy since daybreak preparing a small feast. David cooked up some biscuits and gravy just for Ruth, who stated she was touched again by the efforts to make her visit truly special.

Janice stepped around the table to meet Ruth where they hugged. The two hadn't seen each other in nearly nine years, and Ruth complimented Janice on her choice to pull her sandy brown hair back in a ponytail, stating she looked even younger than before by revealing her delicate facial bone structure.

"Auntie, the biscuits are light and fluffy and the gravy's seasoned the way you like it, I believe," said David, once the gals were seated again.

"Oh, David, y'all really shouldn't have gone to such trouble on my account!" She dabbed her eyes with the corner of her napkin.

"Honestly, Ruth, it's our pleasure to do so," said Miriam. "And, it's just the beginning. After we go shopping later, David has already booked The Mercantile restaurant in downtown tonight. Best steaks in Denver."

"Well, I'll bet we'll all have big appetites tonight after what I've got planned for everyone this afternoon, at the mall y'all told me about last night," said Ruth. She paused for a moment as the gravy boat and biscuits arrived, courtesy of Tyler sitting next to Christopher. "I'll bet a growing young man like you, Ty, will be ordering a big T-bone or rib-eye tonight."

"Rib-eye," he replied, smugly. Preoccupied with eating, he wolfed down the contents piled on his plate, the sure sign of an adolescent about to hit a growth spurt.

"You think that's going to be enough to satisfy that hole in your leg, sport?" teased David. "Maybe we should order you two rib-eyes tonight."

"I bet I could eat *two* cowboy burgers!" proclaimed Christopher, obviously longing to be seen in the same light as his older brother.

"I bet you can, Chris," Ruth agreed, patting his arm lightly.

Miriam seemed touched by Ruth's sensitivity to her children, smiling while her eyes misted. It made David more remorseful about allowing his impasse with his aunt to last as long as it did. After breakfast, the family prepared to move to the living room, and Janice announced she would join them with coffee, tea, and apple cider once she and Jillian cleared the table. As everyone stood from the table, an immense crash shook the ceiling.

David ran upstairs, with Miriam and Janice following cautiously. The nervous kids and their bewildered auntie gathered in the foyer not far from the foot of the stairs. Sadie scurried underneath the living room sofa.

The disturbance continued until David reached the landing. The air's frigid heaviness had worsened, reminding him of when the house was under siege by Allie Mae's angry spirit. Yet, it also seemed different... there was an element present that seemed even more ominous.

The crash sounded as if it came from a bedroom above the dining room or kitchen. David checked Christopher's bedroom first. Other than the usual assortment of scattered toys on the floor, the room appeared undisturbed. He and Miriam moved to Jillian's room, next, and again nothing seemed out of place. That left the guestroom, where Ruth slept. The door stood slightly ajar.

The air felt uneasy and electric as David approached, his frosted breaths misting toward the ceiling. A cautious peek inside the room confirmed the noises had originated there. Most of the furniture escaped serious damage, except for the dresser and its beveled mirror. The mirror, shattered by one of Ruth's suitcases flung against it, lay in shards covering the dresser top and floor. Ruth's personal clothing and makeup had been strewn about the room. The dresser's top middle drawer lay open and empty, with its back edge barely held within its drawer slot.

"Oh my God!" whispered Janice as she peered around Miriam through the doorway.

Miriam shook her head in disbelief.

"What's going on, Dad?" Tyler called from below the landing. The younger kids and Ruth were huddled nearby.

"We've got it under control, son," said David, though nothing could be further from the truth. "Auntie…you might want to come up here, since it looks like everything took place in the guestroom you're using."

Her face dropped, and she gingerly moved past the children. She gasped upon reaching the guestroom's doorway, looking beyond her nephew to the damage wrought upon her belongings.

"Oh, Lord… O-oh, Lord, *no!*" she stammered, stepping past him and into the room.

David assumed she would be embarrassed and, therefore, concerned about her undergarments tossed about the room. But her focus was on the open drawer. She moved over to it and peered inside, running her fingers through the empty space as if expecting something invisible to still be there. She then bent down to the carpet, running her fingers carelessly through sharp mirror fragments as her frantic search continued.

"Auntie, what are you looking for?" he asked gently, after kneeling beside her. "Let me help you."

She looked at him with tears welling in her eyes. Silently, she gathered the strewn bank papers and accepted his offer to help her stand.

"I was hoping to surprise y'all at Christmas," she murmured, turning to look at Miriam as she held out the papers. Her lips quivered. "This is the trust for the proceeds from the farm that was sold some years back near Pigeon Forge, Tennessee. Do you remember me telling you about it in October?"

David nodded and accepted the papers from her as Miriam joined them.

"That farm sold for *this* much? You've got to be shitting me?"

He couldn't believe it, his eyes growing wider once he saw the trust's current seven figure value. When he showed it to Miriam, she was just as surprised. Ruth nodded sadly to confirm the trust figure's accuracy.

"Auntie... you need this money to get you through your later years—you keep it," he said, handing the papers back.

"Not without your signature, David," she said, waiving him off. "I've got enough money set aside that I don't need this. It'd be put to better use by y'all, especially with the kids getting older and Tyler just a few years away from college and all."

She started to weep, and David moved to comfort her.

"I just don't understand why this happened?" Ruth pointed to the empty dresser drawer. "I brought some jewels that have been in the family for more than eighty years, maybe longer. Now they're *gone!*"

She wept harder, which told David the loss especially upset her. He couldn't picture the jewels in question being more valuable than the trust fund, but he understood the emotional value they might have for her, witnessing similar reactions many times in his CPA work. As his clients grew older, their prized physical assets often became hard to part with—even when the items were valuable enough to eradicate an outstanding debt. Preserving such heirlooms for their descendants became the priority, regardless of any deepening detriment to themselves.

A glowing mist suddenly appeared above the dresser. A pungent sulfuric odor filled the air around them and the mist grew denser. It crackled with energy that grew steadily more intense until a bright flash ripped through the room.

David ushered the women out of the room, nearly toppling the kids who had crept closer and were murmuring about the horrible stench. Then the sound of four glass-like objects hitting a wood top emanated from inside the room. Everyone hushed their voices and listened while the objects rolled from one end of the dresser to the other and back again. David peered inside the room with Miriam clinging to a sleeve. The mist was dissipating, and as it steadily weakened, they could see everything in the room again. Ruth gasped in surprise.

The very diamonds and sapphires she brought to Colorado had reappeared.

David approached the dresser guardedly, with Miriam and Ruth latched onto the back of his shirt as they crept along with him. They watched the jewels vibrate and move to form a line in the dresser's center, upon a crumpled doily protecting the furniture's original dark patina. Janice, meanwhile, tried to comfort the younger kids now crying hysterically. Tyler vacillated between hanging back with his siblings and stealing a peek over his mom's shoulder.

When David, his wife and aunt reached the dresser, the line of jewels shifted into a zigzag shape, with the clear diamond at the top and the shorter gems following from longest to shortest. It startled Miriam and Ruth enough to back away from the dresser to where they almost tripped over Tyler, who had also witnessed the event.

At first glance, it reminded David of what Zorro, the legendary Spanish hero, might leave behind. But something about it frightened him far more than what might lately be considered another typical Hobbs' paranormal experience. He'd seen a similar symbol back in October when he desperately sought to appease Allie Mae's ghost as she sought to kill him. The symbol represented the force that inspired her heightened malice, according to Evelyn Sherman, John Running Deer's granddaughter. He recalled Evelyn's words, that this other entity enjoyed wickedness for its own sake, without cause or provocation.

David believed Allie Mae's spirit was at peace, her axe to grind against the heirs of his lecherous ancestor, Billy Ray Hobson, finally buried in Cades Cove. But the wicked entity that fueled her wrath was a different story entirely. Didn't John's letter from a week ago say something about how he and Evelyn believed the spirit was highly agitated—awakened from its pseudo-rest by some careless desecration of its unearthed tomb within the once-hidden, sacred ravine in Cades Cove?

Despite Ruth's pleas to pick up the jewels before they disappeared again, he pushed everyone back out of the room, urging them to hurry downstairs while he closed the door. The violent disturbance inside the room began anew as they raced downstairs, and both David and Ruth were witness to the door bending out against the hinges before they followed the rest of the family down the staircase. By the time they regrouped in the living room—with their coats gathered from the foyer's hall tree, and ready to flee the house at a moment's notice—Miriam was already on the phone with Sara Palmer, seeking her counsel.

A promising start to the day had just been ruined.

Chapter Eight

"Dinner's ready, everyone!"

Hanna Sherman, John Running Deer's youngest granddaughter stood proudly next to the oak dinner table in John's cabin. The slender, leggy, auburn-haired coed who had just completed the first semester of her junior year at nearby King College in Bristol, Tennessee motioned for John and her older sister, Evelyn, to join her without further delay. She'd spent the past two hours in the kitchen preparing a barbeque rib recipe she picked up from one of her sorority sisters, and could hardly wait for her grandpa and big sis to try it.

"Well, don't make me wait to find out what you think!" she playfully scolded, as they took their places at the table. John and Evelyn were seated at the opposite long ends of the table and Hanna in the middle.

The side of the table across from Hanna's chair sat flush against the rear wall of John's cabin, below a portrait of the girls' late grandmother, Susanne Running Deer. An antique gas lantern, converted to electric long before either granddaughter's birth, cast a soft glow upon the portrait and the table.

"Don't make *you* wait?" teased Evelyn. "What about our stomachs that have been growling since two o'clock this afternoon?"

Her lovely smile matched her sister's. The only significant difference between them, other than Evelyn being two years older and slightly taller than her twenty-one-year-old sibling, was in the color of their shoulder length hair and eyes. Unlike Hanna's hair, Evelyn's flowed raven black, in line with her Cherokee heritage. Hanna's eyes, although shaped the same as Evelyn's, with a delicate slant that also pointed to their mutual Native American heritage, were hazel. Evelyn's eyes were a soft deep brown.

"Just for that, you can help bring the rolls and potatoes over to the table!" Hanna retorted, moving into the kitchen.

She returned with a large serving platter stacked high with enough ribs to feed two or three more mouths than gathered at John's home. Evelyn came right behind her with the potatoes, a loaf of warm bread, and a green bean casserole she somehow managed to balance between the other items without dropping anything. She whistled under her breath once she saw the horde of ribs on the table.

"Unless you're planning on your boyfriend, Guy, and his friends to join us tonight, I believe you've outdone yourself, little sister," chided Evelyn, laughing. "Why on earth did you cook this much food when it's just the three of us?"

"Grandpa will eat what's leftover this week. Right?"

Hanna looked at John, who had taken his seat at the head of the table. He smiled tenderly at her and Evelyn, and then smirked. His granddaughters mistook this reaction as his amusement over their play-fight, when in truth it was on account of how different they were.

Evelyn neared completion of her civil engineering degree with plans of using that knowledge to improve the lot of her Cherokee brethren living on the reservation in North Carolina. Hanna wanted to be a journalist in a big city like New York. Even their style of dress reflected diametrical tastes, with Evelyn wearing comfortable worn-out jeans and a flannel shirt, while Hanna opted for a designer sweater and matching thermal tights. Yet, they rarely fought. Each one was tolerant and nonjudgmental of the other. That aspect made John especially proud.

"The ribs should stay good until the end of the week," he agreed. "At least I'll have something healthy to snack on tomorrow afternoon instead of cake and cookies."

"Are you saying you don't want me to make my traditional German chocolate cake for you tomorrow? You know Grandma wouldn't be happy to hear that." Evelyn feigned hurt feelings with a sorrowful pout.

"I didn't say I wouldn't have *any* cake—just not as much this year," he advised, eyes twinkling impishly. "I can't let this get any bigger, or I won't be able to outrun the momma black bears in spring."

He patted his stomach, which his granddaughters readily agreed had grown a few inches since last Christmas. Much of the weight had been put on since October, after David Hobbs returned to Colorado. Hanna had expressed her worries about him, and he overheard Evelyn tell her it was because he missed the friend with whom he had forged a strong bond.

It surprised him neither noticed he actually lost ten pounds since Thanksgiving. Then again, neither girl knew about the continued assaults he'd endured from the anisgina trying to breach the shaman spells he invoked to fortify his cabin. So far, the angry demon couldn't find a way inside, and was the only reason he agreed to share both Christmas Eve and Christmas Day with the girls at his Smoky Mountain home.

Up until now, during their weekly visits or telephone checkups, neither one had been exposed to the spirit's cacophonous wrath as it bore down on the cabin. It took extra determination to shelter his thoughts from Evelyn, as she would otherwise have figured everything out and intervened by now. He didn't want her involved this time, since it was very dangerous. Even so, it was a near certainty one or both girls would eventually witness the entity's anger. He held out hope it would leave them alone until after Christmas, when his granddaughters returned to Knoxville together.

"All right, Grandpa... just as long as you enjoy yourself tomorrow and on Christmas Day, I can live with that," said Evelyn. "Well, sis, do you want me to say the grace or would you like to handle it tonight?"

"You go ahead. The cook needs her rest after a hard day's work."

Hanna grinned mischievously and winked, and the three shared a good chuckle through the Cherokee blessing Evelyn recited. John's worry about the apparent sacrilege coming back to haunt them was cheerfully disregarded by Hanna. Evelyn offered assurance the Great Spirit should be merciful during a time of such joyous celebration as Christmas.

Excellent ribs, all three indulged themselves, leaving only enough leftovers to cover John through Christmas afternoon. They retired to the living room, where he built a roaring fire in the great stone fireplace dominating the room. Hot chocolate and an apple cobbler Evelyn prepared earlier when she and Hanna first arrived added the perfect finale to Hanna's successful supper.

Outside the cabin, darkness shrouded the entire landscape, with the only light emitted from the porch and security lamps. The kitchen clock's soft chime confirmed the time, 5:30 p.m. A sharp whine accompanied by urgent scratching resounded from the back door.

"Did you want to share any of the leftovers with Shawn?" asked Evelyn, as she rose from her seat next to Hanna on the couch.

Once she opened the backdoor, John's prized husky came barreling into the cabin, scarcely allowing her the opportunity to remove his chain. Grateful to be inside, the dog jumped on her, mauling her blue-gray flannel shirt with muddy paws. She scolded him while cleaning each paw and the imprints he left on her clothes, using a towel John kept near the door for that purpose during winter.

"Come here, Shawn!" John called.

Shawn ignored Evelyn's efforts to finish cleaning his back paws and trotted to his master waiting for him in the living room, wagging his tail broadly and cowering low to the ground. When he reached John's recliner, he rolled over on his back, allowing John to give him a good belly scratch.

"There, there... that's my boy."

Shawn sat up and looked anxiously into his face, as if he had a secret to tell but didn't know how to do it. John frowned, wondering if another visitation would soon come. He looked at Hanna. She seemed lost in the revelry of the evening, sipping from her mug while watching the fire roaring in the fireplace. But, when he looked over at Evelyn, she leaned through the back doorway, peering outside.

A deathlike stillness settled upon the back portion of John's property, while the snow glistened under the near-full moon's illumination. Evelyn frowned and shook her head, ready to step inside the cabin and leave the wintry chill for the fire's inviting warmth. Three small, dark forms fluttered in front of her, landing near the porch's edge.

The black starlings stood in a row. For the moment, they merely looked at her, tilting their heads sideways as if studying the startled woman in the doorway. Evelyn didn't immediately respond to her grandfather's calls to shut the door and get inside the cabin. Instead, she seemed mesmerized watching them. After more than a minute passed, the birds slowly rose into the air, circling one another as they weaved in and out in deliberate movement.

By then she'd already motioned behind her to get John's attention, to come see the strange phenomenon taking place on his back porch. He came over to investigate, but the starlings departed before he arrived, and as mysteriously as they had appeared. Squawking madly, they flew in three different directions—one to the west, another toward the north, and the last to the east. The wind moving through the treetops picked up, and a faint whistling sound echoed across the night sky from the northwest.

Evelyn stepped inside, quickly explaining to him what she had just witnessed. She locked the door and set the deadbolt, but the whistling grew noticeably louder. John's face paled as he anticipated what would come next. Hanna looked at the two of them in the kitchen from where she sat on the couch, a quizzical look on her face as the sound pierced the confines of the cabin.

John urged Evelyn into the living room to rejoin her sister, sighing in relief when he saw the heavy draperies drawn across the large picture window in the upstairs loft.

Are the rest of the curtains closed?

He left the living room to check the main floor's windows, and when he returned he gathered his granddaughters with Shawn near the fire, huddling together while they covered their ears to avoid discomfort from the whistle's painful screech. Hanna looked over at John, worried, while Evelyn put her arm around her.

"Be brave," he whispered, gently caressing the soft spot beneath Shawn's jaw. The husky whined nervously, but John's attention kept him from barking at the unseen menace. "Be brave and brace yourselves… it'll pass soon enough."

His words drew an immediate look of anger from Evelyn, as if she suddenly understood the reason behind his haggard condition.

Wrapping his arms protectively around Hanna, John prepared himself for the next phase of the visitation. The whistling noise abated, giving way to the other sound he'd grown used to. An enormous swarm of hornets approached the cabin's western side. Evelyn surely recognized it. The same sound from October, when she and he unwittingly provoked the anger of the entity whose calling card it was. At the time, they both thought it was worth the risk to aid the innocent David Hobbs in his fight against the ghost who drew her malicious strength from the much older and wickedly powerful spirit.

John recalled how Evelyn never wavered in her compassion for David and her conviction that she did the right thing—the *best* thing for him and the restless spirit of Allie Mae McCormick. Since then, he knew she wasn't so sure. The other spirit that for almost a century shared the darkness with Allie's ghost was seriously enraged—*furious* with both Evelyn and John in October and even more ill-tempered once its ancient resting place in the sacred ravine was desecrated in November by forensic and archaeology teams from the University of Tennessee.

I should've told her the visitations never stopped.

* * * * *

The assault on the cabin continued.

Hanna wept in terror, closing her eyes tightly and invoking the Catholic prayers of her youth, Evelyn tried to make sense of the three starlings and what they might mean. Something about three, instead of four, seemed especially important. Imploring her spirit guides for help, the answer remained just beyond her awareness. Part of the answer to the riddle was missing. Aside from the harsh lecture she planned to give her grandfather for hiding what had obviously been going on for a while now, she berated herself in silence for ignoring her intuitions and instead believing his statements that "everything's just fine". While seething, all at once the message from the birds became clear.

"Grandpa—we need to get in touch with Dr. Kirkland, and David! They're both in grave danger!" she told him, raising her voice above the din.

"I've been trying to *do* just that for the past two weeks!" John replied, perhaps more harshly than he intended. "Dr. Kirkland's out of town, I think, and I can't get a hold of David! The line just crackles... crackles like—"

"It did back in October?" Evelyn interrupted, finishing his sentence. *"Shit!"*

She ran her hands through her hair, seeing in her mind's eye the implications of what this all meant.

"Evelyn—*wait!*" John warned her. "Wait until this passes!"

He couldn't stop her impulsive urge to run and grab his phone, to make the calls he didn't complete. No sooner than she picked up the phone and prepared to dial Peter

Kirkland's number herself, a flash of light flew through the room, knocking the phone from her hand and killing the electricity in the house. Immersed in darkness except for the fire that still burned in the fireplace, she scurried back to where her sister and grandfather huddled by the hearth.

"*Wait!* ...You *must* wait until the anisgina's fury passes over us," he said, his eyes filled with compassion.

This time she heeded his advice, while the sound of angry hornets descended from the roof of the darkened cabin.

Chapter Nine

The doorbell rang just before eight o'clock at the Hobbs residence, announcing the arrival of Sara Palmer. The family had gathered in the living room with Janice, trying to enjoy the strawberry mousse she'd prepared. Still on edge... everyone waited for the slightest hint of another frightful disturbance.

After a later start than planned, an afternoon of Christmas shopping with Ruth proved to be a welcome distraction, and David treated the family as promised to an excellent steak dinner at the Mercantile in downtown Denver. They had just enough time to navigate the Sunday evening Christmas traffic rush to get home in time for Sara's visit, who graciously agreed to come out and meet with them.

"Well, Merry Christmas!" she said, as soon as Miriam opened the front door. Snow flurries swirled around Sara, dancing as a chorus-line of miniature white crystals alighted on her coat and knitted cap when she stepped through the doorway. "Sorry to hear what's been happening lately. I can already feel the presence you told me about earlier today."

Blonde with bright green eyes, Sara Palmer was a stoutly built, though attractive, woman in her early forties. Dressed for the evening's chill, amethyst crystal earrings dangled beneath her navy cap, matching the necklace visible inside her coat. The jewelry was the only thing pointing to her Wiccan affiliation. Her easy smile and soft voice disarmed most anyone offended by her vocation as a professional paranormal investigator and healer. It was enough to win Miriam over when the two met in October, through Janice, and they had become good friends since.

Sara looked warily past Miriam, to the staircase leading upstairs, and glanced to the dining room. Janice emerged from the living room on the right.

"Would you like some dessert?" offered Janice, stepping around Miriam, who closed the front door behind Sara. "I've made a splendid mousse... strawberry."

Janice smiled nervously. Sara returned her smile with a compassionate but wan smile of her own. She carried an additional bag to the blue duffel she brought when working to cure the family of the previous haunting. The brown leather carrier appeared stuffed to capacity. Heavier than the duffel, Sara set it on the floor and offered a warm embrace to Janice and Miriam.

"The mousse sounds delightful, Jan," said Sara, after hanging her coat and cap on the hall tree in the foyer.

She picked up the carrier and Miriam grabbed the duffel. Together they moved into the living room, where everyone else waited. Despite the decorated fir's splendor, the atmosphere was tense and gloomy. The kids huddled on the sofa with their great aunt from Tennessee, while David tended the fire losing its battle with the prevalent chill gripping the room.

"I imagine none of what you're presently doing has made a difference as far as heating your home," Sara observed, before sitting next to Janice on the loveseat. She pulled her duffel up to her lap. Her curly blonde hair fell forward, partially concealing her face. Her green eyes resembled chipped emeralds as she gazed through her hair before brushing it away. A slight smirk remained.

"What's so funny?" asked Janice.

"Perhaps it's nothing," Sara replied. "I was thinking about the last time we were all gathered together in this room, back in October. How I sensed the entity looking at us from afar back then was quite different, as compared to now, when its essence moves freely among us."

She paused, and the smirk faded to a serious look. She also appeared to be listening to something inaudible to everyone else.

"What do you hear?" Miriam's nervous tone drew worried looks from the kids. David noticed Janice seemed just as anxious. Ruth looked lost.

"I'm listening to the spirit's thoughts—not an actual voice, at least not right now," said Sara, her voice solemn. "The spirit is male in orientation. A little envious back in October, he wonders now why he found us so alluring. He can't relate to any of what Christmas is about, and why we're so enamored with such a pretentious holiday. He laughs in contempt, longing for the restoration of a world he once knew and reigned in, whatever that means…."

Her words trailed off as if straining to hear the entity's other thoughts. She shook her head when she could no longer tap into its musings.

Frigid air drifted from the ceiling, as if the air conditioner had been turned on. The flames in the fireplace momentarily retreated. David added two smaller pine logs while prodding with a poker. It wasn't enough to ward off the deepening chill, and everyone looked anxiously for guidance from Sara, whose gaze moved to the ceiling fan and light fixture.

"Chris told us about an old withered man who's been hanging around the living room for the past week."

David's comment drew a scornful look from Miriam and one aghast from his youngest child. Christopher hung his head, perhaps out of fear for what the old man's spirit would do to him for revealing what he'd seen.

"What?" said David, indignantly.

"You *knew* Chris didn't want *anyone* else knowing about that!" Miriam scolded. "Couldn't you wait to tell Sara about that in private?" She moved to where Christopher sat, still holding David in her irritated gaze.

"What the hell am *I* thinking? It should be what the hell are *you* thinking!" David's fury rose quickly and the flames in the fireplace behind him grew strong again, as if responding to his ire. "Some pretty weird shit's going on here, and it's not like we've got all night to wait for an appropriate time to talk to Sara about it! Hell, even she stated the entity is a male—and you didn't blow a gasket over that, did you?"

Miriam had no immediate answer. She stroked Christopher's hair, perhaps the thing she needed for a better perspective. She looked at David with less ire, nodding her agreement with his point. He sullenly returned his attention to the fire.

Meanwhile, Sara's attention remained riveted to the light fixture and the slow-turning fan below it. She rose, and stepped over to it. When she stood directly below the circling fan blades, a strange warbling sound vacillated between high and low pitches. She stared upward in silence, as if spellbound. The warbling increased in speed and shrillness, causing Sadie to launch a series of angry barks while Jillian and Christopher implored their dad to make the noise stop.

Sara fainted, and David caught her before she collapsed. The warbling stopped, but the floor above them creaked. Heavy shuffling footsteps moved across the upstairs landing. David brought Sara to the loveseat, and Janice helped him gently lay her upon it.

"I'll be right back—everyone stay here," he said, quietly.

He moved to the foyer, and the shuffling got louder. The floorboards in the landing groaned as if under an enormous weight.

"Who in the hell's up there?" David shouted.

There was no reply, but the shuffling ceased. Cautiously, he peeked around the corner where the living room met the foyer. The area was completely empty, including the upstairs landing. Meanwhile, Sara stirred on the loveseat, and she weakly called to him. He ignored her pleas to wait for her, and instead crept up the staircase, grimacing when several stairs announced his progress.

When he reached the top of the stairs, he peered guardedly in either direction along the hallway. No sign of anyone, other than the distinct feeling of being observed.

He briefly considered grabbing the jewels from Ruth's room, but decided to wait for Sara's help.

"I feel better now," said Sara, once he returned to the living room. She sat up on the loveseat, and rummaged through her duffel bag. "I brought some new toys with me tonight, including an infrared camera that should help us obtain better evidence to work with. I also have my personal ritual book. But, after what everyone has told me, and what just happened, it seems prudent to wait on any spells for now."

"Can we help you set up your equipment?" offered Janice, glancing around the living room for potential placement spots.

"Perhaps," she said, following Janice's gaze. "However, I'd rather start my investigation upstairs."

"Did you want us to come along?" asked Miriam, reaching for her shoes next to the fireplace.

"Only David... I'd like just him to join me for now," she said. "There's something up there that the spirit is highly interested in... something related to him."

Sara removed the new infrared device from the leather carrier, along with the digital voice recorder David recognized from her previous visit. After removing a small EMF detector he remembered seeing before, she handed him the recorder and motioned for him to follow her upstairs.

Other than the unfriendly chilliness, their ascent to the second floor was uneventful until they reached the landing. A moan that resonated deeply greeted them. Neither one was willing to venture further. The moan was rhythmic, with vibrations strong enough to travel through the landing's wooden railing.

It came from Ruth's room. The door was closed, though it had been wide open when David ventured upstairs a few minutes earlier. Fearing he might lose his nerve if he waited, David led Sara to the doorway. He touched the doorknob, and the moaning sound stopped.

"Are you two all right up there?" whispered Janice, her voice timid, from the stairway's base.

"We're fine, babe—"

"*Sh-h-h-h!*" Sara interrupted, drawing his attention to the air around them. Unnaturally still, except for a slight popping sound that reminded him of the electric cattle fences on his grandfather's Ringgold farm when he was a young boy. A similar current oozed through the air around them now, almost imperceptible and yet enough to send tingling sensations across the exposed skin of his face and hands.

Sara pointed to her EMF detector, where the readout jumped wildly from zero to double digits.

"David? Sara? What's going on up there?"

Miriam called to them from the base of the stairs, and the kids' hushed voices echoed their mom's edgy tone. She started to come upstairs with someone else—likely Janice.

"Don't come up here—*please* stay where you are for now!" said Sara, sternly.

She motioned for David to open the door, and then she stepped into the room, pointing her infrared camera in front of her, as if a shield. Something unseen by David startled her in the dimness, and she quickly turned the overhead light on. The light immediately flickered and died, and then a thick ink-like shadow began to fill the room, quickly obscuring the dresser.

"We come in peace." Sara's normally velvety smooth voice was shaking. She backed into David, who had yet to join her inside the room. "We're here to retrieve some items belonging to the owner of this home's aunt, and we'll be on our way."

David looked at her, frowning, since what he wanted apparently wasn't what she wanted. Yes, he desired the precious stones and trust papers from the room, left in haste earlier. But, he assumed the goal was to find some way to remove the entity—to force the unfriendly pest out of the house, once and for all.

An ominous chuckle emanated from the depths of the room, and the door began to close.

"What do we do now?" David whispered, worriedly. As far as he could tell, their plans to explore the room had just been nixed.

In that moment, it did seem like their thoughts were aligned. She stepped out of the guestroom, capturing as much video as she could from the infrared, with David right behind her. Just before they reached the stairway, the bedroom light came back on and the door slowly swung open.

Does this asshole really think we're going to step back inside the room again?

But that's what they decided to do. This time, David approached the doorway tentatively, with Sara right behind him. When he stepped through the threshold, the door crept open a little more—perhaps from a slight breeze caused by his movement... perhaps not. Maybe the spirit wanted to further intimidate them, as a worse feeling of being watched from all angles hit him full force. Sara's fearful eyes scanned the room while snapping a bevy of photographs using a small standard camera. Grotesque shadowed shapes crept across the walls like bloated giant insects with each flash.

While she seemed to grow increasingly nervous, his fear began to shrink. Rage swelled, fueled by all that had happened as of late. Seething with fury David moved about the room, focusing his heated thoughts toward the coldest and creepiest sections of the room. He pictured the spirit's presence contained in these spots, and he wasn't surprised when the iciness seemed to move out of his way.

"What's wrong, you fucking coward?" he hissed, amazed at the level of contempt beneath his anger.

Sara had also been moving about the room, but now stopped, looking at him in horror.

"That's right, you sick son of a bitch... *Get the HELL out of my house!"* he roared. He stomped around the bed, feeling exhilarated by the surge of energy brought on by his sudden bravado.

From what he knew previously about a malevolent ghost's power and resolve, his brazen actions were a death wish. When his rational mind regained the upper hand on his lower instincts, he worried about the response.

The arctic grip that embraced the room surprisingly receded, and the overhead lights in the room and hallway steadily regained their normal luminance. Sara smiled, still uneasy, but giggling as if she was a young girl.

"I believe the entity just left, David!" she marveled, shaking her head. "I can't believe it! I would've *never* thought this was all it would take, and Lord knows it might still return. But, for now, I feel it's truly *gone!*"

She moved to the dresser where the gemstones were still aligned as the curious snake-like symbol. She carefully scooped them up and placed the gems inside the front left pocket of her jeans. Sara advised David to gather the trust papers from where Miriam left them. Miriam and Janice met them in the hallway.

"Is everything all right?" Miriam moved to David's side, her eyes worried. He met her gaze with a forgiving one. "We heard you shouting from downstairs. Everyone else is waiting in the foyer."

The air around them rapidly warmed, as the heater's efforts were no longer hindered. Nonetheless, she shivered. He pulled her close.

Sara repeated her belief that the entity had taken flight from the Hobbs' beleaguered home. Afterward, they all returned downstairs. David glanced over his shoulder several more times, and once they reached the main floor without incident, he began to relax for the first time in over a week.

* * * * *

"I'd rather y'all just put the damned things in a safety deposit box—at least until you can get 'em insured!" Ruth was visibly irritated at David for insisting the best thing to do in regard to the diamonds and sapphires was let a stranger—this medicine woman named Sara Palmer—take them with her. "It's not like they can easily be replaced if something happens!"

He could tell the deluge of tears dammed up behind her genteel façade might burst through at any moment. Miriam sat beside her on the sofa, arms wrapped around Ruth's shoulders, telling her gently everything would be okay, and Sara was trustworthy. She added how she'd entrust the very lives of her children—the most precious things in her world, along with David—in Sara's hands.

"Auntie, I swear on my very life that I'll never let anything bad happen to our inheritance," said David, soothingly.

He stepped to Ruth's other side, where Janice was seated. For the moment, the kids sat on the loveseat, with Christopher sitting on Tyler's lap.

Sara sat in David's recliner awaiting the outcome of the discussion, stroking Sadie's neck while the dog lay on her lap. She smiled compassionately at Ruth, nodding empathetically to let her know she appreciated her concerns. She didn't join the conversation until Miriam and David convinced his aunt the precious heirlooms would be safe in her possession.

"I promise to not let them out of my sight, and I will only allow my trusted friend, Dr. William Fuller, from the University of Denver see them," she advised. "He's one of the top parapsychologists in the country, and an expert in demonology."

"Demonology?"

David's brow furrowed while he sought to understand what expelling a pesky spirit had to do with devils and such. It brought images of poor makeup and costumes from late night, B-rated horror movies. He chuckled, until he noticed the grave expression on Sara's face.

"Yes, Demonology. Although it appears that the mischievous spirit is no longer here, it's imperative we proceed with utmost caution," she explained. "The jewels seem to have formed a catalyst for the entity's aggression today."

David and Miriam nodded. Sara's somber words affected them all.

"Well, it's getting late, and I still need to finish my Christmas shopping in the morning," said Sara, getting up from the recliner.

She reclaimed her coat and cap from the foyer's hall tree. After saying goodbye to everyone, Janice walked her out to the pickup truck parked in the driveway.

"Don't worry, Auntie," said David, after watching Sara drive away through a window next to the Christmas tree. "Everything's going to be fine. By tomorrow morning, the memory of what happened today will be behind us. It'll be Christmas Eve—the start of a fantastic holiday together!"

He smiled and gave her a warm hug. When he drew away, she gazed into his face. Tears streamed down her cheeks. To most it might appear he'd deeply touched her. David suspected some other reason. Yes, he could tell she was grateful for the newfound bond with him. But, something deeper lurked in her eyes... something plainly obvious once he thought about it later.

The ghost had left their midst, hopefully never to come back. Regardless, it wrought irreversible damage. For the remainder of her holiday stay in Littleton, Ruth Gaurnier would sleep restlessly. In the more comforting light of day, David would catch her frequently looking over her shoulders. Was it the same unfriendly spirit coming back for yet another round with the Hobbs' clan? Or, maybe it was something else... something *worse*, now quickened from her distant, secret past.

Chapter Ten

"See, Grandpa? I told you everything would be okay."

Evelyn held the front door open to John's cabin, wide enough to allow Hanna to move past. Careful to not bump into either one, Hanna's arms were laden with fancily wrapped gifts she and Evelyn purchased from the largest shopping mall in Pigeon Forge.

John stood in the doorway, wearing a slight smile as Evelyn caught up to Hanna in the living room. He paused to watch his granddaughters, giggling near the Christmas tree he'd cut from the edge of his property the previous afternoon with Evelyn's help. The girls did a great job decorating the six-foot spruce the night before, long after the latest assault from the anisgina passed. His only worry had been Evelyn's insistence this morning to finish her Christmas shopping.

He couldn't shake the fear of something worse befalling them. True, as Evelyn confidently stated, the spirit didn't return, and *wouldn't* during daylight. It didn't stop him from pacing between the living room and the kitchen until the girls' safe return. At least their protected well-being meant a more promising start to Christmas Eve than what he had envisioned following the attack.

John stepped outside and stood at the edge of the front porch, sniffing around him. For some reason, the air seemed different. Hell, the entire area felt a lot more like it used to feel before all the excitement of the last few months. Even when the entity was absent, he'd learned to sense its trail. He could literally smell it—the anger, as well as its deep thirst for vengeance. But now he couldn't sense it at all. Maybe it had finally finished its business and left for good. His smile widened at the mere thought of lasting peace after a month of daily assaults.

"It's gone, Grandpa," said Evelyn from behind him. She had removed her goose-down vest, which obscured most of the embroidered University of Tennessee on her sweatshirt, before quietly joining him on the porch. She smiled coyly. "Whether this is truly permanent, we'll have to wait and see."

"Yes… we shall see," he concurred. "I'll be with you in a moment. We'll need a few more logs for the fire tonight." He moved to the corner of the porch, where two stacks of split logs sat.

"Are you sure we'll need more wood?"

She motioned around her. The snow steadily melted in the unseasonable warmth that had embraced the Smoky Mountains since just before dawn.

"The forecast calls for new snow late tonight," he replied, grabbing several logs and joining her in the doorway where she waited. "And the air should cool down again once nightfall arrives."

She laughed while stepping back inside the cabin. "We'll see about that!"

"Yes, we will," he chuckled, closing the door and locking it.

Hanna was busy in the kitchen finishing a cheese ball, and Evelyn returned to her earlier task of setting up the dining table with other goodies. John quietly moved to the table, hoping to begin sampling cookies, veggies, chips n' dip and Hanna's soon-to-arrive cheese ball. The plan today was to snack on the table's spread while a large pot of Evelyn's venison chili simmered on the stove. His favorite dessert, the German chocolate cake, would be the last treat brought to the table.

After a playful reproach from Evelyn, reinforced with a stern look from Hanna, John headed for the recliner with his first loaded plate. He paused to admire the glistening tree standing to the right of the fireplace. Hanna and Evelyn used a mixture of new ornaments, along with the standard collection belonging to their grandmother, which John faithfully displayed each Christmas after her passing six years earlier. A few bubbling-oil lantern lights drew his immediate attention, and he was hit by nostalgia, realizing how much he missed Susanne. Before the feeling of her loss could overwhelm him, he turned on the television and sat down.

The girls joined him in the living room, and after allowing him one college football game, they spent the rest of the afternoon watching holiday classics amid several trips to the dining table. When dusk arrived, John stepped to the back door, lifting one corner of the door window's sheer curtain to peer outside. He turned on the back porch light. The temperature outside was already dropping, and the frost normally covering the porch at night would soon come.

Shawn crawled out of his domed doghouse and approached the back door once he saw John looking through the window, wagging his tail at the prospect of some attention. The husky's demeanor was peaceful, without any hint of skittishness. He didn't paw at the back door. Instead, he sat down in front of it, waiting for John to venture outside.

"Well, are you ready to come join us, my good boy?" John asked, as he stepped out onto the porch.

Shawn jumped up and placed his soiled paws on John's flannel shirt. Unperturbed, John gently removed his paws.

"I'll take that as a yes!" he laughed, unclipping Shawn's steel chain.

Before returning inside, John scanned the perimeter of his property from the back porch while stroking the underside of Shawn's neck. It was impossible to discern as much detail in the deepening shadows as earlier in the afternoon, especially for his older eyes. But the familiar oppressive feeling was still absent. Satisfied nothing evil hovered near his home, he relaxed.

"Grandpa, it's time to open some presents!" Hanna announced from the kitchen, refreshing her tea. "Be sure to wipe Shawn's feet. I'd hate to spend the next hour getting his dirty paw marks out of the new sweater Peter bought me last week!"

She pulled on the bottom of the expensive olive-green sweater to show it off to John, who failed to comment on it. He honestly couldn't tell the difference between it and anything else she'd recently worn in his presence.

"Peter?" he asked while closing the back door, indulging one last look through the door's window before securing the lock. He turned to face his mischievously grinning youngest granddaughter. "I thought Evelyn said you're dating a young man named 'Tommy'."

"I am... well sort of," she said, pausing to cast a wry glance at Evelyn, seated on the couch in the living room. "You always told us to play the field, right? To not get serious until we're out of college, if I remember correctly."

She chuckled when John's initial response was to simply shake his head, wearing a knowing grin.

"Enjoy your youth, that's all," he offered. He turned to the German chocolate cake that hadn't been carved yet. Shawn trotted into the living room and curled himself around Evelyn's feet. John removed a healthy slice, ignoring the girls' amused reactions to the oversized helping. "Because you might not have as much fun again until you're old and gray like your grandpa."

The playful glint in his eyes belied the fact he worried about either one of them settling down before they had a chance to explore career options. It was the mistake their mother, Joanna, had made. Now she was the one acting like a teenager, chasing after a much younger Navy boyfriend while her daughters spent the Christmas holiday with family.

"We can only hope we end up with half your energy by then, Grandpa," said Evelyn, reaching down to pet Shawn's head before rising from the couch and stepping over the dog on the way to the dining table. "Looks like

Hanna and I had better get a piece of cake before you eat it all up!" she teased.

She took a smaller helping from the cake plate, and Hanna followed soon after, taking a slice slightly larger than her sister's. Almost half of the cake had already disappeared. Still teasing their grandfather, they followed him into the living room. As soon as they finished, Hanna took their plates and forks to the kitchen sink while Evelyn retrieved her camera from the guestroom.

Once the girls rejoined John, who sorted the presents beneath the tree, he allowed them to take a quick snapshot of one another posing with him and Shawn in front of the tree. Afterward, he had them sit together on the couch while he handed them presents, saving a couple for each to open the following morning. His eyes grew misty watching them tear into the packages, so much like they'd done as little girls, seated on the very same couch that had twice been reupholstered over the years.

Nearing nine o'clock, Hanna and Evelyn tried on the outfits they bought for each other, and the jewelry John gave to them that one belonged to their grandmother. The charm bracelet especially touched Hanna, having been fascinated with several of the silver charms as a young child. John surprised Evelyn with a diamond pendant that originally graced the neck of his late wife's great-grandmother, the daughter of a prominent nineteenth-century German aristocrat.

Although delighted with their gifts, Evelyn and Hanna voiced worries that their mother, Joanna, might not be pleased by John passing the treasured items to them instead of her, since she was his and Susanne's only child. He assured them the gifts were decided upon long ago, once it became a grim certainty his dear wife would lose her long-fought battle against breast cancer. Joanna would also receive a cherished jewelry piece upon her return from the Bahamas after New Years.

Changing into their original outfits and leaving the gifts in the guestroom, the sisters returned to the living room. John finished cleaning up the strewn wrapping paper, and hung up the fleece-lined jacket they gave him. He began building a warm fire, since the temperature cooled to where the brisk air from outside found its way inside the cabin through the chimney's flue.

"If you don't mind tending to this, I'd like to try to call David, to wish him and Miriam a Merry Christmas before it gets much later." John motioned for Evelyn to come and take the poker. Once she did, he went to the small stone cove housing the telephone.

"Dinner should be done, since it's seven o'clock in Littleton," he said, turning toward the living room. Evelyn brought the fire to hungry flames engulfing the hickory logs. "I'll bet the kids are excited—just like you two used to be." His smile loving, he prepared to dial the Hobbs' home number.

John's smile remained bright as he brought the receiver up to his ear, but then he frowned. He hung up and tried the number again.

"What's wrong, Grandpa?" asked Evelyn, setting the poker back in its tray and moving past Hanna, whose concerned look wasn't near as worried. "Let me hear it."

She joined him as he dialed the number for the fourth time.

"All I get is static—just like what happened when David tried to call his home from here, back in October," said John. He handed the phone to her.

Evelyn placed the receiver next to her ear. She confirmed what John had described. John reminded her that she had insisted David staying with John until the following morning. At that time, Allie Mae's spirit lurked outside, stealthily approaching the cabin from the western woods in her determined efforts to kill David if given the chance. The static was the same... and yet somehow different.

"Did you hear anything else besides the static, Grandpa?"

"No... I didn't." He seemed perplexed by the question. "Let me listen again." He took the phone. The static had been joined by a dial tone. "Do you mean the busy signal?"

He handed the phone to her once more. Meanwhile, Hanna joined them.

"No, it wasn't the busy signal... it was something else," said Evelyn, who exchanged glances with her sister and grandfather. "Maybe I'm mistaken, Grandpa. Maybe I'm overacting to the static."

She hung up and dialed the local time instead. The call went through fine, and she handed the phone to John so he could confirm it.

"Don't worry, Grandpa, I'm sure they're all right," she said. "We'll try again tomorrow, and if we still can't get through, I'll see if I can get in touch with the phone company in Colorado after Christmas."

She smiled warmly, as if selling him confidence in her words. She seemed to forget he could read her thoughts, even as old as he was. The faint, wind-like whistling noise she had heard sounded nothing like a busy signal. And as he absorbed what she had experienced, he realized the noise was there each time the number was dialed, subtle enough for him to miss it.

Regardless, it confirmed his immediate thought and fear. The entity hadn't left after all. It lay hidden someplace close and yet at the same time far away, if such a thing were possible. He knew, as certainly she did, the mischievous anisgina merely waited for the right opportunity to strike. He prayed it didn't happen until after the holidays.

"Maybe you're right. I'll try again tomorrow," he agreed.

He forced a smile for Hanna's benefit, and motioned for everyone to return to the living room. The air had grown quite cozy, the deepening chill from outside banished by the fire's warmth. It made it easier for them to ignore what happened, and they resumed their Christmas Eve celebration.

Evelyn suggested they play a board game, and Hanna retrieved the latest version of Scrabble from John's bedroom closet. Her birthday gift to him the previous August, that night presented the first opportunity to play it together. They played two rounds while sipping whiskey-spiked eggnog and listening to a collection of country

Christmas carols he purchased the week before. Afterward, he retired. Evelyn came next, winning the rights to sleep in the guestroom by virtue of a coin flip.

Hanna and Shawn were alone in the living room. After transforming the couch into her bed for the night, she turned off the remaining lights throughout the main floor, leaving only the outside security lights on and a small nightlight in the kitchen.

It was a few minutes past midnight when she finally laid down on the couch. Shawn curled up on the floor beneath her. Following a busy Christmas Eve and aided by the whiskey in her eggnog, she soon fell asleep. A faint smile was on her face, barely visible in the glow from the cooling embers in the fireplace. The quiet sizzle from the hickory coals obscured the soft rustle approaching the secluded cabin from the west.

Chapter Eleven

While John and his granddaughters lay sleeping near Gatlinburg, David wrapped his arms around Miriam's waist from behind and nibbled gently on the back of her ear. They stood near the kitchen sink, where a load of dishes waited.

"Merry Christmas, darlin'."

He could tell that she hadn't expected the loving advance, even though things were rapidly returning to normal. David was as pleasantly surprised as she that the hostile presence hadn't returned. He even called ahead to make room reservations at the local Residence Inn at the Tech Center, down the road from their Littleton home, just in case. Fortunately, they didn't need the reservations and he canceled them.

"Merry Christmas to you too, my love," she whispered, and turned to face him.

Her smile carried only a hint of worry. David returned her smile with a confident grin, knowing she needed to see it. No one in the household wanted to consider the reality of being forced to flee at a moment's notice if the entity returned.

They embraced tightly and shared a passionate kiss, longer than any they'd shared during the past week and a half. The hectic pace in getting ready for Christmas and

Ruth's visit seemed like a blur, and it left them without opportunities for intimacy.

"Maybe later we can finish what we've started here.... Are you interested?" he said, gently kissing her cheek, chin and down her neck.

"Honey, stop... *David!*" she scolded, her tone playful, but with enough seriousness to remind him the kids and his aunt were in the other room. Janice hadn't left yet, despite the fact ten o'clock fast approached. Christopher and Jillian would be in bed soon.

The promise of a visit from Santa Claus was usually the only thing necessary to get the younger kids in bed on Christmas Eve. This year was different. David openly wondered earlier if it would be the time when they came clean with Christopher about the true identity of Santa. Jillian already knew, as of two years ago, and Tyler had known for the past six years that his parents put the presents under the tree during the wee hours of Christmas Day. Granted, the kids still enjoyed the surprises waiting at dawn, as well as watching their younger brother's excitement over the missing chocolate chip cookies and drained glass of milk set out for ole Saint Nick.

"Okay," whispered David.

He kissed Miriam on the forehead and gave her a sly wink, just as Janice walked into the kitchen. Even though the heated moment passed, she blushed, as if sensing the sexual tension between husband and wife.

"I've cleaned up the last of the dessert plates, and here's what's left of the pecan pie that you love so much, David." Janice moved to the refrigerator, where she deposited the last few pie slices. She set the plates in the sink. "I better get going. I want to try to reach Sara before it gets any later. I must say that this has been the most unusual Christmas we've had together, and at least today has been great. Thanks so much for the excellent dinner and fun evening!"

"Always our pleasure, Jan," said Miriam.

The two shared a warm hug, and all three walked together through the dining room to the foyer where Janice's coat hung upon the hall tree. David felt relieved that the coziness found elsewhere on the main floor had infused the dining room as well.

"What time should I plan to be ready for you all tomorrow, Mir?" Janice bundled in her parka with the scarf pulled up around her face. The temperature had been moderately cold throughout most of the day, but dropped to single digits during the past hour. "Would noon give the kids ample time to open presents from Santa and get everyone ready to come over to my place?"

"Noon at your place will be fine, Jan," said David, after receiving an 'it's up to you' look from Miriam. "We're already looking forward to it!"

"Noon it is, then."

Janice walked briskly to her Subaru sedan parked in the driveway. Once she started the engine, she hurried to Miriam waiting for her at the front door, holding it open to escape the frigid air while the car warmed up. David took this opportunity to check on everyone gathered in the living room.

Tyler sat in his dad's recliner with headphones on, playing a new game while rocking back and forth to one of the CDs he received from Janice for Christmas—a metal album she previously asked permission to give him, since it came with a parental warning sticker. Miriam was at first hesitant, until learning the warning pertained to one song, and consisted of words she, David, and most adults uttered in the most frustrating moments of life. David agreed hypocrisy could only go so far, especially since Tyler had been exposed to worse language from his schoolmates, and almost never repeated any of it in his parents' presence.

Jillian and Christopher remained on the sofa with Ruth, who seemed to relish the attention. She presently read a passage to them from the complete Harry Potter collection she'd purchased for them at the mall. The kids were clearly enthralled, swept up in the allure of Ruth's refined southern accent she employed while reading aloud, as compared to the Tennessee twang she normally spoke.

Ruth looked up briefly from the sofa, as did Sadie, while David passed by, surveying the room for anything unusual. He hid behind a smile that wasn't so much forced as enhanced by the holiday cheer around him. Despite her gracious smirk that met his, there remained a hint of sadness.

Auntie's still affected by what happened yesterday....

He thought about John Running Deer in Tennessee. David tried twice to call him earlier, but couldn't get through. He kept getting the long distance busy signal so common this time of year.

Once Janice drove away and Miriam returned to the living room, David nonchalantly ventured upstairs alone. If the kids went to bed first, he wanted to make sure it remained safe. Since last night, no one had experienced anything unusual or unfriendly. But, he wasn't convinced the hostile presence wouldn't come back—especially after angrily telling the entity to get the hell out of their house.

He moved quietly up the staircase, cursing under his breath when the floorboards squeaked. Once he reached the second floor, he stopped and listened, peering in either direction along the hallway. It seemed deathly quiet, but after focusing his attention for a few minutes, he prepared to head down the stairs.

"What are you looking for, hon?"

Miriam stood at the bottom of the stairs, wearing a knowing smile. Startled, he nearly lost his balance and was a hair's breath from tumbling down toward her. Her frightened squeal matched his surprised gasp. He grabbed the banister's edge and regained his footing atop the staircase.

"You scared the holy shit out of me!" he scolded, rubbing one hand nervously through thick blonde bangs, as he considered how close he came to a hospital visit. "How long were you standing there watching me?"

"You scared the shit out of me, too, Mister!" she retorted. "You could've seriously hurt yourself, David, and possibly me too. But to answer your question, I watched you for the past minute or so, after Chris told me that he saw you sneak out of the living room."

So much for discreet cleverness.

"You're looking to see if it's come back yet, aren't you?"

He nodded sheepishly, shrugging as she released a low sigh. "But I don't think it's coming back... not yet, anyway."

"Hopefully, it won't ever come back." She waited for him at the base of the staircase. "Jillian's sleeping with Ruth tonight, and Ty agreed to let Chris join him. I guess Sadie can stay in whichever room she prefers."

"When did this get decided?" He wrapped an arm around her waist as they walked back toward the living room. "I hope Ty realizes Chris will be up at least an hour before dawn."

"He knows," she confirmed. "He and Jill are just as anxious to see what will be waiting under the tree for them as he is. So, get ready to get your tool belt, Mr. Claus." She winked impishly and gave him a light jab in the ribs with her elbow.

"Hell, I was hoping you'd take care of the main chore this time, Mrs. Claus, and allow me to sit back and watch while I take care of the milk and cookies!" He returned her playfulness with a mischievous grin, spurred by where their jovial mood might lead.

Christopher soon began to nod off, and Tyler retired with him upstairs. Ruth and Jillian followed, leaving David and Miriam alone. They set the presents from Santa around the Christmas tree and shared the treats left on the kitchen table by Christopher. Afterward, they nestled close together on the loveseat. With only the illumination from the Christmas tree and the dying flames in the fireplace, they picked up from where they left off earlier, their passionate kiss in the kitchen being a mere hint of things to come. Soon their foreplay brought them to full arousal, and once David ensured the remaining wood coals were safely under control, Miriam led him upstairs.

Everyone else was fast asleep, and they quietly locked their bedroom door. Forgetting the entity that in David's mind watched from somewhere, perhaps in amused silence, they muffled their orgasms only on account of the close proximity of their children and his aunt at the other end of the hall. Then they fell asleep, Miriam's head resting upon David's chest and limbs entwined in blissful contentment.

Chapter Twelve

"What in the hell's this?" muttered John Campbell, as he ripped the torn piece of notebook paper from Langston Hall's leaded-glass front door and held it to his flashlight's beam. The building was completely dark, and even the security lamps high above on either side of the main entrance were off.

"What the ...?"

That was all he managed after glancing over the hurriedly scribbled note left for him by Johnnie Mercer. Anger turned his gray eyes almost green as he stepped from the entrance and raised his sullen gaze toward the top of the building.

"Goddamned *ungrateful* motherfucker!" he hissed.

Light snow drifted toward the frozen ground, as it had for the past hour. He shook off the tiny white flakes that attached themselves to his bushy red hair, grimacing in disgust as he read the note once more. He positioned the flashlight to clearly see the entire message. The letters were a mixture of cursive and block letters, although John didn't recognize the style of some printed details. But it was definitely Johnnie's script, with his initials at the bottom of the torn page.

'Sorry, man. Can't stay and you shouldn't either. Tell Vernon to find someone else to put up with this shit—I fucking quit! Pay you back later. JM'

"This fucking beats all," whispered John, pausing to shine the flashlight around him.

Definitely no one there. Not even a single visible footprint in the light blanket of fresh snow, other than his waffle-soled shoes. Johnnie must've taken off not long after arriving around eight o'clock., nearly four hours ago. And, to think John agreed to switch shifts so Johnnie could be off at midnight on Christmas Eve, instead of his pre-assigned shift end time of 6:00 a.m., Christmas morning.

John hadn't minded making the shift trade, since it allowed him to pick up two more hours of premium pay. Plus, it made him feel good to help someone whose stated reason for requesting the trade was to spend Christmas with his little boy, who'd just turned three a few weeks back. Still healing from his summer divorce to a promiscuous ex-wife, Tracie, John preferred to work as much as possible during the holidays anyway—at least this year.

He stepped up to the entrance and shined the flashlight through the door, looking for movement inside the building. It was hard to tell, but it looked like the temporary guard station table and chair had been knocked over. Probably by Johnnie on the way out of the former dormitory affectionately known amongst the five guards chartered for this gig as "The Langston Icebox."

He pulled the remaining tape attached to the torn corner of the note from the glass. Part of the taped portion felt greasy, and when he examined it closer under the flashlight's glow, he realized the substance was blood.

John stepped back and looked around again, pointing the flashlight's beam in every direction, a little less angry and a bit nervous. A bevy of images from the late-night horror flicks he so loved filled his mind, feeding his growing apprehension. It wasn't until after he continued to look around that the irrational basis for his unease receded and he regained most of his composure.

Two things were readily apparent. The blood was in such a small amount that it could've come from a pin-prick, or more likely, Johnnie biting his fingernails down to the quick. He'd seen him do that before, usually in monthly briefings with Vernon. The other thing was more intuitive.... *There ain't nobody here but me!* No crazed psychos spying from nearby—only the ones from the film clips in his head.

He smiled, feeling foolish and aware of how silly his lanky, six-foot-four frame might've looked a moment ago, waving his flashlight back and forth warily. *If* someone actually had been watching.

He approached the door more confidently. It was locked.

Well, at least J.M. had the presence of mind to secure the main entrance before he wigged out.

John unlocked the door. The first order of business would be turning the security lights back on, followed by double-checking to make sure no one was hiding somewhere inside the building. He would radio Matt Edmonds and his mentor, Steve Holland, to let them know Johnnie bailed and he would cover the Langston Hall job as a double-shift until Pete Lindsey relieved him in the morning.

The door groaned tiredly as John entered the building, and he lamented out loud about how the assignment would be damned near impossible to manage if anyone else quit. Hell, first Tony Williams ended up hospitalized Saturday night, and now Tony's flakey buddy, Johnnie Mercer, goes AWOL. Who else was left for poor Vernon to rely on next? Probably some stiff from the local job corps was John's best guess.

"Whew!" he whistled under his breath, after turning on the master control for the overhead fluorescent lights lining the main floor. He momentarily forgot about calling Matt and Steve. "What in the hell happened in here?"

In addition to the overturned card table and chair serving as a terrible substitute for the normal campus guard stations, Maxim magazines lay scattered across the floor. John snickered at the sight of Johnnie's preferred distraction to help him get through the many long lonely nights during assignments. Johnnie's customary thermos of hot coffee had been turned over; its contents cold and congealed on the floor underscored the haste in which he vacated his post.

"Anybody home?" John called out merrily, smiling at the image in his mind of Johnnie leaving in haste.

What's the big hurry, tough guy?

The heater kicked on, seemingly in response to his verbal question. He moved to the shadowed section near the building's rear, peering up the stairwell as he shined the flashlight toward the second floor. Detecting nothing unusual, he pointed it down into the basement stairwell. Same old Langston Icebox so far.

Comfortable the building sat empty aside from him, John's next priority was to clean up the mess left by his coworker. Grabbing a roll of paper towels from the only restroom on the main floor, he set out to clean the coffee spill. Once that was taken care of, he picked up the chair and card table. He finished stacking Johnnie's Maxims on one side of the table when he thought he heard shuffling footsteps move across the floor above.

John's pulse quickened. The footsteps continued, and his heart pounded hard until it felt like the organ would push through his throat in an attempt to flee his trembling torso. Embarrassed, he summoned what little courage remained and made his feet walk toward the stairs. His intent was to flick on the switch to the overhead light bulb dangling from a long wire hanging from the three-story ceiling above the stairwell. That would hopefully serve as a warning to whomever was also present in the building. Yet, the footsteps above moved with him, as if the unseen visitor knew his exact location and purposely traced his course to the stairs. John's presence was already fully known by the intruder.

When he arrived at the stairwell, the footsteps stopped. A deep breathing sound resonated above him in the darkness. The air around him quickly grew icy as he reached for the light switch on the wall to his left. He bravely turned on the light anyway, and for a moment the illumination was strong enough to cast a bright glow upon the walls. The light flickered, followed by a loud pop as the naked bulb burst into a shower of tiny glass chips cascading down. This event took place after he saw a large grotesque shadow appear on the wall across from the second-floor entry.

Seeing something like that would scare anyone, John reasoned. No one in their right mind would consider venturing upstairs alone—definitely not without a weapon offering better protection than the can of mace and heavy flashlight he carried. But, the low-pitched groan that suddenly arose from the murky depths of the basement stairwell erased any thought of investigating *anything* at *any* time in this place.

A choking sound accompanied the groan, as if something attempted to clear its throat. It might've seemed somewhat human if not for the slithering sound that soon followed. That wasn't human, nor was the sound of its enormous mass brushing against the darkened sides of the lower stairwell as it climbed the stairs.

Another groan, louder than the first, arose from beneath the floor he stood on.

Was that a smacking sound I just heard? Sounds like that enormous motherfucker's real hungry!

Before he could define the noises further, a high-pitched cackle pierced the air in the stairwell above the first floor. The wooden stairs creaked in rhythm, announcing the owner of the bloodcurdling guffaw was on its way to meet him. The soft red hairs attached to the goose flesh throughout John's entire body sprang to life and his bowels immediately loosened. If the owners of the groan and menacing laughter were out to frighten the night watchman beyond his wits, nothing more was needed. Before either menace reached the main floor, John Campbell fled the building, his terrified cries ripping through the early Christmas morning peacefulness.

He later wrote in his resignation letter that he saw something, although not nearly in as much detail as what he'd eventually tell the Knoxville police detectives investigating three seemingly unrelated homicides. As John turned one last time toward Langston Hall, he could've sworn someone looked out through the open doorway on the first floor. Someone or some *thing*.

Under the fluorescent glow from the row of lights lining the main floor's ceiling, the dim tall figure looked like some old naked man with long groove-like scars on his face and body. His stringy grey hair was matted with clumps of black feathers. The thing that made John think the man wasn't really human was the bright yellow eyes— almost cat like—and the smile. When he smiled at John, he pulled back his lips eerily wide... wide enough to reveal two rows of jagged sharp teeth.

Chapter Thirteen

"Mommy! Daddy! Look what Santa brought me!"

Christopher excitedly held up one of the game controllers for the latest XBox version left under the tree. He reached for the Spiderman skateboard and matching helmet, nearly tripping over the huge pile of wadded gift-wrap paper he'd created in haste to find out what St. Nicholas had brought him.

"Wow! That's *great*, honey!" said Miriam, with as much enthusiasm as three and a half hours of sleep could support. Just as she and David accurately predicted the night before, their youngest child was up as soon as the first hint of dawn crept in through his bedroom window upstairs. "See... didn't we tell you how proud Santa is about your good grades in school, and how you keep up on your chores?"

"I'm sure he remembered all of the projects you helped me with this past summer," added David. "It looks like Santa must've *really* liked the cookies and milk you set out for him."

David pointed to the small table next to the recliner. The empty plate and drained milk glass were all that remained from the Tollhouse cookies Miriam prepared and wrapped in green cellophane for Santa to nibble on while setting up the gifts he brought for Christopher and his older siblings. Tyler seemed very pleased with his new

MacBook, similar to one given to Janice the night before. As for Jillian, she seemed just as happy with the diamond/emerald pendant she received, along with the winter wardrobe collection of new dresses, sweaters, designer jeans, and a genuine pair of jade snakeskin boots she had her eye on for the past few months.

David felt especially proud of his older kids' patience with Christopher's continual badgering about their lists to Santa Claus. They both confirmed several times this morning that they, too, had sent letters to the North Pole detailing their hearts' desires laid bare for Santa and his trusty elves. Even so, David couldn't help chuckling in response to the look on Tyler's face, which clearly announced his suppressed urge to tell his little brother all of the presents under the tree each Christmas morning came from Mom and Dad.

"Well, good morning, y'all!" greeted Ruth, walking gingerly into the living room. Already dressed for the day, with her hair primped and makeup on, she wore a colorful green pantsuit embroidered with sequined reindeer and wreaths.

"Good morning to you, Auntie!" David gave her a gentle hug to start the day.

Everyone else enthusiastically echoed his sentiments. Sadie jumped down from her perch on Jillian's lap to also greet Ruth. Her tail wagged wildly as she pawed Ruth's legs.

"Would you like some coffee or tea to start the day off right?" offered Miriam, tightening the neck on her bathrobe.

"That would be lovely, dear!" Ruth replied. "Don't trouble yourself—I'll be more than happy to take care of it. You just take time to enjoy the kids. Lord knows, moments like these will slip through your fingers like a summer rain."

Before Miriam could protest, Ruth was on her way to the kitchen, pausing to give hugs to her grand nephews and niece. "Would anyone else like for me to fetch them something from the kitchen while I'm in there?" she asked before disappearing from view.

Miriam said she'd take some tea, if Ruth intended to fix a cup for herself. When she confirmed it was indeed what she had in mind, David chimed in that he would also enjoy a cup. Jillian and Tyler soon followed, leaving Christopher the lone dissenter. The youngest Hobbs member wanted a glass of chocolate milk, which David volunteered to get for him. Miriam joined him as he headed for the kitchen, ready to start preparing breakfast.

While the skillets warmed up, Miriam paused to drink her tea, and share light conversation with Ruth in the living room. Seated on the sofa, Christopher and Jillian flanked their great aunt on either side, with Sadie sitting contentedly upon her lap.

"So, did you have any trouble sleeping last night?" Miriam noticed the slight redness around the rims of Ruth's eyes.

"Oh, I slept very well, I believe," she replied. "The question is whether or not I kept y'all up by sawing more logs than a legion of beavers in the Chattahoochee River basin!" She laughed. "David should remember how it was growing up in our house back in Chattanooga, and how everyone snored something awful. Although he didn't snore much as a kid, I'd be surprised if he hasn't kept you up some nights, being a Hobbs and all."

"Usually *she's* the one keeping *me* awake," said David, wryly, earning a prompt nudge from Miriam. "They all snore more than me—including Chris. It can get pretty loud upstairs, Auntie. You have no idea."

"Oh, yeah? We'll straighten this out later, Buster!" chided Miriam, popping him lightly on the back of the head as she stood up to return to the kitchen. David feigned injury, falling out of the loveseat—drawing immediate applause from Tyler and a burst of laughter from Jillian and Christopher.

The mood merry, Jillian nearly skipped into the kitchen to join her mom fixing pancakes and bacon. Christopher seized the opportunity to tell his great aunt all about what Santa had brought him. Her sincere interest in what the youngster had to say impressed David, especially when Christopher told her about the storylines to the three games that came with the new system. That explanation lasted halfway through breakfast.

"Auntie Ruth, would you like to see what I got from Santa?" asked Jillian, jumping up from her chair when finished eating. "One of the sweaters I got looks a lot like the one you were wearing when we picked you up at the airport. And there are *two* dresses, some more sweaters, pants, and blue snakeskin boots. Oh, and see the pendant I got?" She lifted it from where it hung upon her chest as she moved to where Ruth sat.

"Why it's very pretty, dear!" Ruth took a moment to admire the excellent craftsmanship. "You'll definitely want to take good care of it, don't you know!"

David wondered if his aunt thought it was a bit extravagant to splurge on jewelry for such a young girl. Nearly a year shy of the onset of her teenage years, puberty had already arrived.

"Snakeskin boots, huh?" said Ruth, "and such a beautiful color!"

"Yep!" Jillian smiled broadly, and gently tugged on Ruth's arm to coax her into the living room. Christopher ran after them, announcing he wanted to show Ruth the colorful artwork on his skateboard. Meanwhile, Tyler finished his cereal and prepared to head upstairs, announcing the intent to get his shower out of the way.

"Hey, sport... don't you want to show Auntie what Santa brought *you?*" teased David.

"Very funny, Dad," Tyler replied, dryly. "She's great and all, but other than viewing the cool programs on my laptop, I hardly think she'd find any of the RPGs and music I'm into as much fun. Hell, you don't, and you're not even forty yet."

David shot him a look, letting him know he straddled a thin line with his smart mouth.

"Sorry, Dad—I didn't mean any disrespect." Tyler cast his gaze downward, perhaps fearing the upbraiding that often would come in response to a smart remark, at least prior to David's trip to Tennessee in October.

"It's okay son... just watch your tone next time." David's response drew an approving look from Miriam that he mostly missed. The grateful look on Tyler's face was enough.

"I will, Dad. I promise."

He smiled and left the kitchen. David and Miriam were alone in the kitchen, where they snuggled for a moment near the sink. It wasn't the time or place for anything more, but a whispered promise from her to be patient until later sufficed in steering his thoughts onto other things.

He started clearing the table while whistling Jingle Bells. It proved to be an effective distraction. The dishwasher loaded and quietly cleaning its contents, he gently wrapped his arm around Miriam's shoulders to guide her into the living room where they rejoined Ruth and the younger kids.

* * * * *

The trip upstairs was a quick one, as Tyler refused to linger on the staircase. After nearly getting killed by a ghost in October, caution and being fully aware of one's surroundings was how he lived each day since. The approach served him well so far, and even allowed him to catch a glimpse of the 'old tree man' that Chris recently described to his parents, Auntie Jan, Auntie Ruth, and the weird psychic friend of Mom and Jan's named Sara.

Watching the specter move from the dining room to the foyer last week, he felt very grateful it seemed unaware of his observation point on the second-floor landing. But, being woken with the naked sucker glowering at him in the doorway a couple of nights later almost sent him screaming into his parents' bedroom. He would have definitely done so had the apparition not disappeared once he sat up in bed.

The entity scared him worse than Allie Mae's angry spirit. He wasn't sure why, either. It was more a feeling... one that made him certain it wouldn't be good if drawn into a face-to-face physical encounter with it.

"Thank God that's over with," Tyler muttered as he reached the second floor.

It seemed cooler up here than earlier that morning. Or, it could've just been his imagination running a little wild on him after thinking about this shit... hard to say for sure. The milder weather outside usually made it hotter upstairs if the heater ran.

Come on, dude.... Hold it together, Ty baby.

He laughed nervously until he reached his room, where he stripped down to his underwear and set out the wool sweater and a favorite pair of faded Lee's on the bed. Moving to the dresser to grab some socks and a clean pair of briefs, he detected movement out of the corner of his eye. Something crept quietly past his open doorway.

Every nerve and muscle tense, Tyler approached the doorway. He thought about how Allie Mae cornered him in this very bedroom two months ago, as her invisible feet creaked across the landing when she moved toward him. But, aside from the hall's temperature continuing to plummet, he didn't detect anyone else.

He moved to the bathroom. Sunlight poured in through the top portion of the back window above dark blue curtains matching the rest of the bathroom's décor. Even so, he reached in through the doorway to flick on the light. After checking to make sure no one was hiding behind the shower curtain, he quickly closed the door and locked it. Tyler rushed through his routine of brushing his teeth and jumping into the shower with a sense of urgency unseen since his dad took him to a Rockies' game last summer. He put on deodorant and splashed cologne, leaving his hair to dry naturally after combing it back.

With a towel wrapped around his waist, he unlocked the door and stepped into the hall. The air was even colder, and he could see his breath. He turned off the bathroom light and hurried to his bedroom. Just as he prepared to enter his room, a man walked out of the guestroom where Auntie Ruth stayed.

He froze, afraid to take a breath. The man turned to face him, and Tyler relaxed, sighing in relief.

"Dad, you just scared the holy hell out of me!"

Tyler smiled shyly. But a queer feeling washed over him. Yes, the man looked just like David, yet also somewhat different. It wasn't just the tan fedora he wore, or the man's old-fashioned clothes. His hair and beard were a shade darker than his dad's and should've tipped him immediately that it wasn't really David. The biggest giveaway was the way in which the man regarded him, wearing a contemptuous grin to go along with four long reddened scars just below the right side of his jaw. The scars pulsed unnaturally, perhaps in tune with the creepy man's heart.

As if amused by Tyler's horrified expression, the man leaned toward him and said, "Boo!"

Tyler hurried inside his bedroom and slammed the door shut. He listened in terror as footsteps creaked outside the doorway, until they stopped. As he had done when faced with Allie Mae's vengeful ghost, he grabbed the baseball bat above his bed bearing the signatures of his favorite Colorado Rockies' players. Summoning courage, he pulled open the door with the bat wielded as a weapon. The man had left. When he peered down the hall, he watched the figure disappear from the landing on its way downstairs.

His protective instincts kicked in. Clad only in the bath towel, with the bat held ready at his shoulder, he raced after the man that looked so much like his father. There was no sign of the man by the time he reached the stairs, and when he arrived on the main floor the dude wasn't immediately visible either. Peering into the living room, his family seemed at ease, so he knew the man hadn't arrived yet. Tyler backtracked, moving through the dining room and into the kitchen. No sign of the phantom man there as well.

"Son, you'll catch your death of cold dressed like that!" scolded Miriam, who stepped into the kitchen to grab a pot of tea steaming on the stove. "What did you forget?" She looked amused.

"Uh… I'm looking for my brush," he replied, lowering the bat.

David walked in just as he spoke, and eyed him in much the same manner as Miriam.

"So, you need a bat to help you do that?" teased David.

"Uh… I… I um found this in the dining room just now. I guess Chris or somebody left it in there for some reason." He realized how silly he looked, and how inconvenient it would be to try and explain what happened with only a towel protecting his privates. He backed into the dining room, hoping for a head-start upstairs before anyone else wandered into the kitchen. "I'll go back to my room and check again."

He was gone before David and Miriam could respond.

"You do that, sport!" David called after him. "Remember we've still got some more showers to take care of, Ty, so don't mess around in the bathroom!"

By the time he reached the landing, the coldness had already receded, just like it had a few days earlier when the other shit went down in the guestroom. Nonetheless, he kept his bedroom door closed while he got dressed. When he emerged again, the hallway's temperature had warmed considerably.

Once he arrived downstairs, he took another quick tour of the main floor just to be sure the man was gone. Satisfied that the man he'd seen must be yet another ghost, he returned to the living room. For the next hour, he immersed himself in his music and games, secluded from all else by his new surround-sound headset, a gift that came courtesy of Auntie Ruth when they visited the mall the other day.

While his mom and dad made final preparations for their short trip to Janice's place, he noticed the photo album his dad brought back with him from Chattanooga in

October, given to him by Auntie Ruth. It sat near the edge of the coffee table closest to him.

Something to idly flip through while listening to the latest Coldplay CD, he recalled the leather-bound album contained some really old pictures from Tennessee. One picture was of an older man wearing a fedora similar to the one he saw the phantom wearing.

Tyler reached over and grabbed the album, flipping the pages until he found the photograph he sought. He might not have remembered it except for one major detail, since other than the same style of clothing, the image in the album and the apparition he saw earlier didn't share much else in common. They definitely weren't the same age, either. The guy in the picture was in his sixties, and the man Tyler saw upstairs looked several years younger than his dad. But, like the younger man he'd seen, the older man in the photograph had four long scars on his neck. They were quite noticeable despite the faded condition of the black and white snapshot.

"Dad... do you remember showing us a picture here in your photo album, of this old man with four scratches on his face?" asked Tyler, removing the headset when David returned to the living room.

David's arms were laden with a Pyrex dish filled with a sweet potato casserole Miriam prepared.

"Yeah, I do." He paused to look at the photograph and appeared curious as to why Tyler seemed interested in it. "That old guy was your great, great, grandfather, William Hobbs. Remember?"

Tyler nodded. Meanwhile, Ruth stepped out of the kitchen and into the living room, holding a cherry pie she baked the day before. She apparently overheard the mention of her grandfather's name. Her dislike for the man was evident in the deep scowl she wore. Tyler pointed to the picture again, and Ruth told him quietly it wasn't necessary for her to come any closer. She knew the image well enough.

"I think I saw him today," Tyler announced, his voice betraying his struggle in trying to decide if it would be worse to divulge what happened or keep silent and hope it had no significance. "He looked a lot younger."

"Where did you see him?" David asked, after his face fell.

"Upstairs," said Tyler. "I saw him walk out of Auntie Ruth's room and then I tried to keep up with him when he went downstairs. That's what I was really looking for when you saw me holding my bat in the kitchen."

Although his dad went easy on him earlier, he worried about David's reaction now.

"Oh, Lord, *no! ...No!*" Ruth murmured. Her hands began to tremble, the color draining from her face.

"What is it, Auntie?"

She wouldn't answer David. Instead, she nearly dropped the pie before she set it down upon the coffee table and hurried out of the living room. Miriam followed, while David looked for a place to set the casserole dish. He told his kids to hold off going anywhere until he could join them.

Ruth had hurried upstairs with Miriam right behind her. When David and the kids reached the guestroom, Miriam had her arms around Ruth's shoulders as she wept. Tyler noticed the bed cover had been pulled back to reveal her pillow. Something waited for Ruth under the pillow... an item she soon revealed was believed to be gone forever, perhaps lost in the myriad of nooks and crannies of her ancient Chattanooga home.

She held the object out for David to take, her upturned palm unsteady. It was a gemstone roughly the diameter of a quarter and a half inch thick, and the jewel she told the family about two days ago. The completion of a set of five gems intended to be the inheritance of the lone remaining Hobbs clan—the Colorado Hobbs family—descended from the vile and wicked patriarch once known as Billy Ray Hobson. Tyler and everyone else knew the specter he saw was indeed him, and surely the one who left the item under her pillow—his last surviving grandchild.

Based on how it was left for her to find, Ruth declared she considered this particular stone as cursed. A defiled object left for her, like the trinkets the old bastard would leave behind after he violated her as a young girl. It was the reason why she wept, and could barely contain her sorrow and shame.

Watching his dad gently remove the non-faceted jewel from her palm and deposit it in his coat pocket, Tyler could tell he understood her pain. Even as a ghost, the older Hobbs had created senseless suffering, proving he was indeed a "horribly wicked and twisted fuck", as David called him back in November, when he first shared the photo album with Tyler.

David tried to speak, but nothing came out. He hugged his aunt tightly, with Miriam holding on with him. All three wept, while the younger kids looked on anxiously… leaving Tyler to wonder when the next round of unpleasantness would be coming. His gut told him the wait to find out wouldn't be long.

Chapter Fourteen

John Running Deer stood on the back porch, shielding his eyes from the bright afternoon sun. The air felt crisp and cool, but still warmer than it had been earlier. A few clouds dotted the sky, and the forecast called for significant snow by nightfall.

Shawn had almost finished taking care of his business, and would seek to get inside the cabin rather than stick close to his private igloo. Certainly, the temperature was mild enough for the husky to spend the warmer daylight hours outside. John had his granddaughters to thank for his beloved pet's newfound preference to be inside the cabin. He smiled while considering Hanna and Evelyn's copious charms, and how easily they disrupted his routine and turned his watchdog into a demure pup. And, they did it in just a few days' time. He hated the idea of them going back to Knoxville and Johnson City after the Christmas holiday ended.

It made him ache even more for Susanne and the days when his granddaughters were little girls. Before long, they would graduate from college and move on with their lives. Their careers would likely take them even farther from Gatlinburg, Tennessee. He'd already begun preparing himself, and as he had reflected on frequently during the past few days, it was the very thing he coached them to aspire for since completing high school.

Shawn finished and wagged his tail, prepared to meet John on the porch. He stopped, looking out toward the densely wooded area north of John's cabin. His tail ceased to move and pointed downward as he growled protectively, with sharp canines bared toward an unseen menace.

John heard an unusual noise. It sounded as if wooden chimes hung in the branches of the evergreen trees that stood like tall sentinels along the rear border of his property. The objects clanked softly against each other.

Warily, he stepped down the porch's worn wooden stairs and into the backyard, never removing his probing gaze from the trees. He deftly avoided slick patches where melted snow turned the ground into a muddy mess, and removed the chain from Shawn's neck, commanding the dog to stay at his side. Cautiously, John made his way to the area from where the clatter emanated.

The sound of wood on wood grew louder, and Shawn's growls became more urgent, punctuated by agitated whines.

"Steady, boy," John whispered, bending to stroke Shawn's neck. "Stay with Daddy."

He soon discovered the source for the noise. His initial reaction was one of alarm, and he carefully examined the leg and rib bones of a wolf, freshly dead, hung by strips of blood-streaked rawhide and sinew from a stout cedar's longest branch. Beyond the tree lay a pristine forest stretching for miles toward the deepest wilderness of the Smoky Mountains. Wolves were infrequent visitors to his property, and naturally skittish in the presence of mankind.

"What in God's name happened here?" he wondered aloud, motioning for Shawn to wait while he took a moment to examine the immediate area.

The skinned and bloody hide of the animal also hung from the branch, swinging back and forth in a steady breeze. Meanwhile, the wolf's head lay positioned below upon the frozen ground. Its frightened, glassy eyes gazed toward the cabin from the cedar's base. The animal's severed paws were arranged in a ring of four that surrounded its gaping jaw. The entrails and other organs were nowhere to be found.

Feeling increasingly uneasy, John stooped to get a closer look at the wolf's head, noticing trails of dark crimson covered recent snow that escaped the sun's reach beneath the thick evergreen canopy. Moccasin impressions had been left in the snow, along with what looked like an unusually large naked human footprint with odd toe marks.

He followed the trail around the tree, until the footprints abruptly disappeared, roughly thirty feet into the forest. Standing motionless, he listened to the wind for another moment and then returned to Shawn waiting near the cedar. He had assumed his protective buddy would venture closer to the remains out of normal curiosity, but the dog remained where he'd left him, glancing nervously toward the cabin.

"Everything will be okay, boy," John said in a soothing tone, though he knew otherwise.

Gently stroking the husky's neck, he surveyed the scene once more. It had been many years since he'd witnessed anything like this. The last time was when his grandfather, a great shaman who refused to add an English surname or nickname to his Cherokee name of *Tali Awohali Atloyasdi* or Two Eagles Cry, took him as a young teenager to a hidden sacred burial area where Cherokee skeletons from long ago lay exposed in the open air on perched wooden pallets. He recalled how animal bones hung from thatched, wooden pole frames. Weathered deerskin ornamental shields accompanied some of these ancient remains, along with the weapons most favored by each honored warrior.

John's grandfather had told him the sacred mountain gravesite hadn't been used since the mid-nineteenth century. It was carefully camouflaged from Andrew Jackson's armies and others that hunted the Smoky Mountains in search of renegade Cherokees refusing the federal mandate to join their brethren heading west on the *Trail of Tears*. To John's knowledge, no one practiced the protecting or cursing of an area anymore.

Knowing the desecrated wolf was intended for him specifically greatly worried John. It was an even worse portent, in his mind, than the terrible visitations he'd endured for the past month. At least those had a predictable pattern and outcome, where at the day's end he and his family remained safe from harm… at least so far.

"Grandpa? Are you okay?"

Evelyn stood on the back porch, shielding her eyes as she looked in his direction. Fortunately, the wind had died down before she called to him, and the wooden noise of the wolf bones hitting each other was barely audible. His granddaughters being thrown into a panic was the last thing he needed—especially today, Christmas, where they'd already enjoyed a fabulous morning together, sharing presents and merriment around a warm fire in the living room.

"I'm fine—just checking on some deer tracks!" he called to her. "I'll be there in a minute!"

John urged Shawn to head to the cabin. The dog glanced one last time at the woods before trotting to the porch, seemingly relieved to get away from there. He looked back at John a couple of times. But his loving master lingered to try and sense if anyone else was there, hiding within the forest's dense foliage.

If someone was near, he couldn't detect it. John returned to his property, and as he moved toward the cabin he felt less anxious. His home that had seen the births and growth to womanhood of first his daughter and then his granddaughters would protect them all as it had for more than forty years.

"Are you sure it was deer tracks?" Evelyn asked as he stepped onto the porch.

He didn't answer her, and instead looked again toward the woods. Shawn had already coaxed his way inside, where Hanna met the dog in time to clean his paws.

"Hanna said she heard some animal crying in pain early this morning, just before sunrise. But, she didn't see anything when she looked through the back door window. Maybe she and I should take a look later."

"That won't be necessary," John assured Evelyn, forcing a broad smile and praying she couldn't see or sense the plummeting depth of his worry. "It's just deer tracks. Maybe Hanna heard a screeching barn owl. They can sound pretty heartrending sometimes."

The misdirection seemed to work. They shared a laugh at how Hanna often overreacted. John opened the back door, motioning for her to go before him. He followed her into the kitchen, where the scents of cinnamon and nutmeg embraced his nostrils, bringing an additional sense of comfort. The afternoon promised to be as merry as the morning had been.

As he closed the back door, he allowed for one last glance toward the woods. Still no sign of anything, another breeze moved through the trees, awakening once more the now eerie sound of bones tapping against each other. John shuddered and locked the door. Despite several more hours of daylight, he closed the curtain and set the dead bolt. He wasn't taking any chances.

Chapter Fifteen

Just after eight o'clock Christmas evening, Vernon Mathis arrived at Langston Hall. The building looked cold and foreboding as he pointed his flashlight's beam to either side of the cement steps and through the glassed front door as he climbed up to the porch. All the lights were off, both inside and outside the former dormitory, except for a slight glow emanating from the upper stairwell in the rear of the main floor.

It would be consistent with the information he'd been given by Jerry Simmons, the security staff dispatcher who called him at home around six o'clock. John Campbell stated he turned on some internal lights the previous night around midnight, Christmas Eve, and left. That really was all John had to say of importance in his hastily composed resignation letter, which he later delivered to Jerry's desk at the University of Tennessee's main administration office this afternoon, only minutes before his shift started at four o'clock.

Vernon wasn't an unreasonable man, or so he told anyone interested in hearing his perspective on how he ran his crew. Only when a situation severely tested his patience—like tonight, after his entire staff bailed and left him to manage the security functions for both Langston Hall and the McClung Museum alone—would his squared jaw and sharp jowl lines reveal the grizzled, retired police veteran he was. Physically fit with defined, powerful muscles, Vernon wore his hair close-cropped in military fashion, which minimized the ever-increasing loss of his hairline. He liked the fact he looked intimidating, and it usually took a solitary stern glance to coerce obedience in any of his direct reports. When seriously angry, as he was right then, his deep blue eyes flashed as narrow slits two shades lighter. They easily reinforced the venomous power of his words.

"Merry fucking Christmas, you bunch of assholes!" he hissed, and opened the building's front door. He was even more incensed by the fact it was unlocked.

The pussy John Campbell couldn't even get that right. Until last night's fiasco, John had been very dependable. In two and a half years, he'd called out just once, and that was due to a severe flu bug that almost shut down the entire University campus. Vernon couldn't believe he left him high and dry. The fact that the trainee, Matt Edmonds, permanently left his post at the McClung Museum this morning came as only a slight surprise. And Johnnie Mercer, Steve Holland, and Tony Williams were attendance problems just waiting to get fired. He especially couldn't believe the theatrics put on a few nights ago by Tony "The Tank". Some fierce weapon he turned out to be. Fucking crybaby, more like it. Only Pete Lindsey remained loyal. Then again, Pete was just a part-timer filling in one or two shifts per week.

So, now it was all up to Ole Vern.

His buddy, Frank Thomas, agreed to moonlight for him at Langston around ten o'clock. Another surly veteran from Knoxville's finest, unlike Vernon he still had a few years to go before he could collect full retirement benefits. Grateful he could help on such short notice, it allowed Vernon the opportunity to check on another trainee from the other side of campus, Billy Peacock, who agreed to fill in at the museum across the way later that night. Vernon remained hopeful he could rejoin his wife and grandkids at home by midnight—if they hadn't already gone to bed.

He turned on the outside security lamps and also the main floor's long row of fluorescent lights. Surprised to see his breath inside the building, it seemed colder than the subfreezing temperatures outside. His immediate assumption the heater must've died made little sense. Dr. Peter Kirkland told him that it had been fairly expensive to restore, when two of the building's three units were replaced with new ones. Vernon thought the whole extravagance of restoring the building in order for the basement's cold storage area to be utilized was a bit much, until he made a joke about it in the professor's presence. Dr. Kirkland's response was quite curt, and he threatened to find another security chief who would do a better job of protecting the University's interests.

It was one of the few times in recent memory Vernon stooped to kissing ass in order to return to the professor's good graces. Rising medical costs in treating his wife, Maggie, for diabetes made it imperative he not lose the job. The nice salary outweighed the undependable personnel he had to work with. Besides, after appeasing Dr. Kirkland's enormous ego, Vernon became privy to proprietary information about what was stored downstairs.

Nearly two-dozen skeletons unearthed in Cades Cove were kept in the basement's cold storage unit. Some belonged to early English settlers, although many lacked various limbs. All were headless.

Other bones were present as well, and believed to be Native American, with one unusual skeleton much older than the rest. That one was added a few days ago. Afflicted with some gross deformity, it had a lot to do with why the cold storage unit was needed.

Utilizing so much of the security staff to watch over this shit seemed ludicrous to Vernon. But it paid the bills to just go with the flow. The main floor had the same abandoned feel as it did when he first visited the building before Thanksgiving, when Dr. Kirkland wanted to review the security arrangements. The University's maintenance crews did a good job of removing the broken furniture and trash, and relocating scores of boxed records that made it nearly impossible to move from the front of the main floor to the stairwell in the rear.

Vernon saved the University some money by not installing an official guard station, since Langston Hall was slated for a bulldozer next June. Although a century old, the locks on the front door proved adequate, and the security latches for the windows were fully functional. The only change was the thick steel door in the basement, the easiest thing to check for his security staff.

He paused to look around, noticing John left the sticky rags from when he cleaned Johnnie Mercer's spilled coffee on top of the card table. The dried paper towels had since become glued to the table's surface.

"Goddamned slobs," he muttered, scowling. He ran the tips of his fingers across the table top while studying the streaked coffee mess on the floor nearby.

The light from upstairs illuminating the stairwell flickered. Unlike the previous two guards to watch over Langston Hall, Vernon remained calm, cool, and collected. In his mind, everything had a logical explanation. He walked casually toward the stairwell. Once he reached it, the light upstairs dimmed and then grew increasingly bright, as if fueled by a sudden burst of electricity. He remained unfazed, expecting to find a sensible reason for the power surge.

He pointed the flashlight's beam to the bottom of the stairwell. After verifying the door was shut and the lower stairwell empty, he pointed the flashlight upward despite the unnaturally bright glow emanating from the second-floor hallway. The first thing he noticed was the long wire hanging from the ceiling three floors above where he presently stood. Then he saw the hundreds of tiny glass particles on the floor, telling him the light bulb likely exploded. He ventured upstairs.

It took nearly twenty minutes to check every inch of the second and third floors. Returning to the first floor, he snickered about his former staff—the sorry group of little girls pretending to be men. He completely ignored the fluorescent hall light on the second floor flickering after he turned it off, and the suspended double-chain it hung from swinging back and forth behind him.

Must be a breeze caused by me passing by…. Watch out, Superman!

He merrily trotted down the stairs, ignorant of the bulb-less wire swinging wildly above. If he looked up, he might've caught a glimpse of the garish shadows on the stairwell's walls descending toward him.

Once back on the main floor, he set out to clean the mess near the guard station, and whistled a Christmas carol as he stepped into the restroom. He collected a few wetted paper towels and some soap when he heard a scraping metallic noise from the basement stairwell. He paused at the restroom doorway, listening for the noise to repeat. It did. The shrill screech was louder the second time.

Vernon's pulse sped up. He unzipped his guard jacket and reached into the inner left side pocket. Unlike the rules governing everyone else on his staff, he packed some serious heat, courtesy of the license to bear firearms privilege he kept long after his official retirement from the Knoxville P. D.

Vernon pulled out his .44 service revolver. He released the safety from the pistol and stepped out into the hallway. The gun was loaded, which was a standard precaution from his early days on the police force, despite never actually shooting someone since his retirement from being a real cop. The sound of the heavy door downstairs being forced open made him think this might be the occasion where some unlucky fool got to meet Mr. Smith & Wesson.

Glancing cautiously from side to side, he crept to the basement stairwell. He peered over the edge without using the flashlight, holding it in his other hand and ready at a moment's notice to flash it in the face of the perpetrator, or perpetrators.

Difficult to see anything from the middle of the basement stairwell to its murky bottom, the heavy steel door stood open, its shiny edge showing above the deeper shadows obscuring all else. It left him no choice. He had to find out what the hell was going on down there.

He considered using a stern verbal warning, but thought better of it after realizing he didn't know much about the layout of the basement. He knew only where the cold storage unit sat, just inside the doorway and to the right. The last time he actually stood inside the large room, a ton of boxes and more broken furniture pieces were stacked haphazardly to the left of the unit. Everything had been cleaned since then, and unfortunately, a thief or vandal would have an advantage over him. Better safe than sorry.

A shuffling noise moved across the basement floor toward the door, accompanied by heavy breathing. Nervous but unafraid, Vernon moved boldly downstairs. Just before he reached the thickest shadows, he turned on the flashlight and held the gun pointed in front of him.

"All right, you stupid asshole, come out of there with your hands up!" he snarled.

He stepped down to the base of the stairwell when he received no response, other than the cessation of the shuffling noise. The breathing grew heavier. His heart rate had sped up even more on the way downstairs, and now blood pounded noisily in his ears. What made him most uneasy was his awareness that the breathing sound steadily approached the doorway where he now stood, and yet no other sound was audible within the basement. It awakened every inch of gooseflesh along his skin while sending icy chills up and down his spine.

Suddenly, a very tall figure stood before him, partially shrouded in the thick darkness the flashlight couldn't penetrate. Vernon's deepest gut instinct said it was somebody very dangerous, maybe a crazed psychopath. The hardened cop side of his brain reassured him such a notion was pure nonsense—the type of fancied fears sissies pretending to be real men would subscribe to. Listening to his well-honed police instincts, he could almost picture the dim figure sneering. Rather than play coy with this shithead, he motioned with his pistol for whoever was there to step closer to where he could see him.

"I'm going to give you five seconds to get your ass out here," he warned. "You're trespassing, and if you don't want to spend the rest of the holidays behind bars or in a hospital, you better come out...."

He didn't finish. Rather, he couldn't find his voice. The emergence of a tall, grotesque man stepping through the doorway took care of that. Under the flashlight's bright glare, the figure looked especially creepy. The man appeared quite old, and yet the intense malice emanating from the weirdo made Vernon think age wasn't a hindrance. He was sort of like Rob Zombie's Michael in the remake of "Halloween", but more hideous in appearance. The face and body were lined with disgusting groove-like scars. Long gray hair, matted with black feathers, covered much of the dude's form. At the moment, his gaze was directed toward Vernon's feet.

The figure slowly raised his eyes. The contemptuous glare alone almost loosened Vernon's bowels. But, what caused his steady arm and hand to shake noticeably was the color of the eyes. They were yellow, cat-like in appearance, and luminescent with a faint orange fire behind them.

The man—or *thing*, as he now assessed—grinned, seemingly amused by the ex-cop's physical response, and briefly glanced at his crotch as if expecting him to pee his pants. It was enough to arouse Vernon's machismo, and it ignited his anger.

"Party's over, motherfucker!" he seethed, gritting teeth as he spat out the words. His arm steadied, he cocked the pistol to prove he meant business, and ready to put a slug in the ugly mug of whoever hid behind the mask.... It had to be a mask, right? No way in hell would a merciful God make someone look like this guy.

The grin on the ghastly face faded, and it seemed as if the impression Vernon sought to make was successful. He sent a silent fervent prayer heavenward he was right, since he realized the creep giving him the willies was likely also responsible for his staff's disintegration.

The figure raised its hand toward the gun and into the flashlight's glare. Much larger than his own, it bore long fingers unnaturally proportioned compared to a normal hand—or at least the hands of any human he'd ever seen, dead or alive, during the twenty-six years he served as a

Knoxville cop. Long dark fingernails curled tight at the tip of each digit began to twitch.

Fearing the worst, and that the uninvited intruder to Langston Hall was about to make a move to gain the upper hand, he decided to shoot. His intent was to wound the fucker and call 911 for an ambulance, along with a squad car from the Knoxville P.D. It seemed to be the safest alternative with this nutcase, and he feared the dude in the scary old man getup might be carrying a concealed weapon. The image of some insanely huge, sharp machete appeared in his mind. At the same time, the face grinned again, nodding as if to confirm it knew his thoughts.

That was it. Time to put a hole in the motherfucker and see how funny he thought *that* was. Vernon started to pull the trigger.

The fingernails unfurled in the ensuing nanosecond, and before he drew the next breath, his hand was cleanly severed at the wrist. It still held the cocked pistol as it fell to the ground. Blood gushed and he screamed in terror, while the grinning assailant bathed in exquisite ecstasy, letting the crimson spray wash upon its face and torso.

Vernon's shock froze him. He thought about stooping to pick up the gun with the other hand. Yet, the thought remained in its infancy when the monster grabbed his bleeding wrist and shoved it into its unnaturally wide mouth. Gruesome crunching and sucking sounds followed, along with the sound of his heart acting as a slave pump to the thing he realized all too late was in no way human. A stream of images of what he'd lose filled his terrified mind. Would he ever see his grandchildren, Spencer and

Megan, again? Who will take care of Maggie? Someone needed to make sure she gets her insulin shots on time each day, since she's often too weak to administer them to herself.

The last image gave enough strength to yank his arm back, freeing it from the fiend letting out a shriek of cackled laughter. Vernon's arm just below the elbow was missing, and the old man's face looked somewhat different—still hideous but not so old. It grinned maliciously as it chewed on something and spat part of it out. Meanwhile, Vernon felt dizzy and panicked at the thought he might collapse at any moment. But when he realized the spattered pinkish mush lying on the stairwell floor had been the twelve-inch section of his arm inside the thing's mouth, he screamed. It provided a surge of adrenaline to get him up the stairs. The image of his dear wife not surviving long without him gave him strength and urgency to try like hell to get out.

The fiend stealthily pursued him, climbing each stair slowly, as if it had all night. It made Vernon think again of Halloween's Michael, and how that fiend always found a way to catch up to his victims in the horror movies he made famous, plodding zombie-like but somehow able to cut his victims off before they reached a haven. Vernon prayed it wouldn't be like that, but when he glanced behind him, the thing smiled knowingly in the dimness, its jagged sharp teeth stained with blood. Its eyes glowed hotly, and it winked. It was as if it wanted him to know it would catch him. Somehow before he made it to safety, he too was going to bite it just like in a horror movie, and bite it big time.

He found his legs once he neared the guard station. He was less than thirty feet from the front door and his ticket to freedom, and the thing behind him was losing ground. He praised the Lord, especially since the row of fluorescent lights clearly revealed the monster's complete horridness. Unbelievably strange and ugly, but also definitely real... very, *very* fucking real.

Vernon almost made it to the door. The heavy breathing resumed. He was wrong about one thing— actually a lot of things, but this one mistake seemed larger than the rest. The sound didn't belong to the thing pursuing him. It belonged to something else, and it now pursued him in earnest.

Two dark shadows appeared on either side, stretching across the walls. Like the unearthly creature behind him, the shadows had human shapes and other characteristics, such as long hair with the same dark feathers clumped in it. The two phantoms carried knives and coup sticks that appeared quite real, moving ahead just as he reached the door. Desperately pushing on the door latch, he glanced at one of the images and saw a face grimacing in anger. The features were definitely Native American except for the eyes. The eye sockets were empty. Soulless, they opened to a dark void extending far beyond the confines of Langston Hall.

It all seemed like some terrible nightmare, except for the excruciating pain resonating from just below his right elbow, along with the crimson trail the open wound left behind him. That was all *too* real, and he started to feel dizzy. If he could just open the door and tumble outside to safety.

The phantoms didn't stop him, despite reaching the door first. Their essences dissipated as soon as he touched them. The frightful sound of their chilling shrieks hindered him just enough to struggle with the door…. How does one open the damned thing with a pair of fucking Indian ghost faces screaming?

The latch finally opened, and he pushed through the door to the outside, into the crisp night air. He started to smile in relief on the porch—praising God that despite the loss of limb he would indeed see his grandkids and Maggie. He'd call 911 in just a moment, once he made it down the steps from the porch and put some distance between him and Langston Hall. Yet, before he made it down the first step, two boney, powerful hands grabbed him by the ankles.

Without proper security staff on hand—including at the McClung Museum less than a hundred yards away, on a lonely Christmas night with no one around—Vernon's shrill screams went unheard. Pulled inside, the strange looking old man with yellow eyes and sharp jagged teeth dragged him all the way back to the shadows and down into the basement. The thick steel door screeched shut, leaving only the smeared trail of blood.

It was the first clue that told Frank Thomas he and his good buddy wouldn't be sharing a few shots of peppermint Schnapps as previously planned.

Chapter Sixteen

"Huh-h?"

Hanna awoke with a start. The living room in her grandfather's cabin was dark, except for the dying embers in the fireplace and the glow from the back porch light seeping in through a small crease in the backdoor curtains. Evelyn was supposed to sleep on the couch, but Hanna decided to forego her turn to sleep in the guestroom, allowing her big sister to sleep in a bed for the second consecutive night. Shawn preferred to sleep with his master, despite her grandfather's initial reluctance to share his bedroom with the dog. It meant Hanna had the rest of the main floor to herself. She preferred this arrangement, since to her the couch slept more comfortably than either of the beds.

She pulled the thick comforter up to her chin with the expectation of drifting back to sleep. Bundled up, she yawned, feeling the heated air from the fireplace gently caress her face. The clock on the table next to her grandfather's recliner read 1:06 a.m. She watched the blue digital numbers change to 1:07 and closed her eyes... until she heard three light raps upon a glass windowpane.

That woke her up for good. Had she been dreaming? She couldn't say for sure, so she listened. Nothing happened at first, but as the clock clicked over to 1:12, the knocks repeated.

Frightened, she sat up. The knocks sounded like they came from the backdoor's window. She caught a glimpse of someone standing outside and gasped. The shadowed form was visible just to the right of the open crack in the curtains.

She struggled to find her voice, and intended to scream for her grandfather. But then something happened to change her mind completely

"Hanna?" an older woman called.

"Who's there?" she replied.

For a moment, the only response she received was silence.

"It's me… Grandma Susanne," said the old woman. Hanna realized the woman's voice came from the figure standing outside. "I don't have long, sweetheart, so come quickly."

Hanna stood quietly, never removing her eyes from the back door while she put on a housecoat and slippers. Cautiously, she moved to the door while tying the sash around her waist. When she reached it, the shadowed figure stepped out of her direct view, to the right. It made her consider again awakening her grandfather before proceeding further.

"I've got a special Christmas gift for John, dearie," said the woman. Now that Hanna stood closer, it really sounded like her grandma. "It's something I wanted so desperately to give him five years ago, but I crossed over before that could happen. *Please…* let me give it to you to give to him."

The anguish in her voice sounded genuine.

"Grandma… so it's really you?"

Hanna peered through the crease in the curtains, and when she saw an older woman standing there and not some young thug trying to break in, she pulled the curtains back so she could get a good look.

"Oh, Hanna… how I've missed you *so* much!"

The woman stepped in front of the window, removing a tan scarf from in front of her face. She wore a long-hooded wool coat Hanna recalled as her grandmother's favorite choice when dressing for the severe winter weather in the Smoky Mountains. Powdered snow covered her shoulders, and Hanna noticed another inch of snow had fallen since she retired for the evening, just before midnight.

Tears welled in the woman's eyes, and she removed the hood from her head, revealing the long blonde curls that defined Grandma Susanne's look. In fact, she never forfeited her beautiful hair, despite the terrible fight she eventually lost to breast cancer. Her soft green eyes seemed to glow under the porch lights. It reminded Hanna of how she appeared as a little girl, and the delighted welcome she would always get whenever she visited Grandpa and Grandma's mountain cabin.

She didn't understand how it could be possible. All Hanna knew for sure at the moment was the woman knocking on the cabin's back door was definitely her grandmother. Yes, it made no sense at all that a dead person could come back from the grave. But, it must be true, because it was happening right then.

"Grandma!" she said, excitedly, pulling frantically on the locks to open the door. "I've missed you just as much!"

Once the door was open she stepped out onto the porch, throwing her arms around the old woman, her Grandma Susanne. She sobbed, and Grandma Susanne wept as well, although mindful to tell her granddaughter to keep her voice down so as not to awaken Evelyn and John. The two embraced for several minutes until Hanna was ready to let go and hear about the gift Grandma Susanne had for her grandfather.

"Let's take a short walk," said the older woman, pointing toward the northeast corner of John Running Deer's property. "Your grandpa's surprise is something you'll need to bring back with you from the woods. It isn't far from here."

Her smile warm and sweet, Hanna couldn't help being drawn to the radiating benevolence. Clothed in her nightclothes and slippers in the chilled mountain air, she nodded shyly and placed a hand inside her grandmother's palm, ignoring the nagging thought she should first alert her grandfather and sister before venturing into the woods.

Grandma Susanne's hand felt warm, and brought back memories from Hanna's childhood. Strangely, the warmth spread throughout her body, and she scarcely noticed the subfreezing temperature.

Hand in hand, they stepped down from the porch and headed to the woods. The light from the moon illuminated the area. A soft breeze moved through the woods once they moved past Shawn's doghouse, bringing with it the wood on wood sound John heard earlier in the day. Since he didn't tell her or Evelyn about his visit into the woods, she was unaware of the gruesome scene that could be awaiting her. The light from the moon barely penetrated the thick pine foliage above their heads as they walked into the woods. Hanna noticed the bones hanging from the cedar's branch, but assumed they had been there for a while. She didn't see the wolf's coat hidden in the shadows or its head and paws lying at the tree's base.

"Stay close to me, Hanna, and we should reach our destination shortly," Grandma Susanne advised, once they moved deeper into the woods where the trees grew closer together and sure-footing became precarious on sloping, uneven terrain.

The old woman had no trouble navigating the thick dimness whereas Hanna fought to keep up.

After a few hundred feet of dense woodland, they reached a small clearing bathed in the moon's luminance. Hanna's slippers were covered with mud, pine needles and other grit. Even so, she felt privileged. Grandma Susanne pointed to a large boulder in the middle of the clearing and led the way. The top surface of the massive rock was flat and fairly smooth, and she brushed away the snow with her coat's sleeve while motioning for Hanna to sit on it.

"I know it's a little cold, dearie, but we'll only be here for a moment," Grandma Susanne told her, gently patting Hanna's shoulder and stroking her face with the back of her hand.

The warmth from her touch flowed through Hanna's entire being again, rendering her impervious to the frigid environment, despite small misty clouds from each breath.

Once situated comfortably upon the rock, Grandma Susanne took a few steps back, to a cluster of much smaller rocks. She looked over her shoulder at something on the other side of the rocks, unseen by Hanna, who assumed it must be the surprise her grandmother mentioned.

"Now... Hanna, I want you to close your eyes and slowly count to ten, like you used to do when you were a little girl and we played hide and seek in the cabin," Grandma Susanne advised, her loving smile unwavering. "When you're done counting, I'll show you something amazing. A sight that John and even Evelyn would be greatly impressed with, too, I'm sure."

Hanna returned the smile, giggling like the small child she once was. When her grandmother passed away, nearly six years ago, she took it harder than anyone other than her grandfather. Hanna had always longed for a reunion, but she never dreamed it could happen. Eager to participate, she closed her eyes and began counting.

Grandma Susanne continued to smile, with a slight trace of amusement. She stooped and picked up four glistening objects from the snow next to the rock cluster. Gemstones, cylindrical in shape and non-faceted. Two of them were diamonds, along with a pair of sapphires. All four gems were unique enough to be considered priceless, and until very recently, had been in the possession of Sara Palmer in Denver, Colorado, courtesy of David Hobbs.

As soon as Grandma Susanne picked up the stones and stood straight, her warm green eyes melted into hollow sockets. Her warm smile faded into a sardonic grin. She stepped to Hanna, who reached the count of seven. Before she finished, the figure continued to morph into the withered corpse that surely rested under the earth's surface—if Susanne Rae Running Deer were to be exhumed from her final earthly resting place.

The figure could've remained poised to horribly frighten the unsuspecting granddaughter of John Running Deer and his beloved late wife. But, at the last moment, it morphed into its natural state. By the time Hanna opened her eyes to see her grandmother's promised surprise, a repulsive and very tall old man stood above her.

He obscured the moon above, which cast an eerie glow on his long gray hair. The deep reddish grooves in his skin had softened and filled in somewhat after his recent meal at Langston Hall. But his eyes, iridescent and yellow, with pupils that narrowed predatorily as he studied her, were more than enough to elicit a shrill scream from Hanna. She nearly lost her breath once she opened her eyes and found the hideous, naked monster of human deformity standing over her. He didn't even need to flash a full smile featuring his blood-streaked, jagged teeth to get the response, which his shit-eating smirk revealed was the prize he'd hoped for.

The scream may have been all he desired, his bloodlust satisfied earlier. But the fact her scream gave birth to several shriller shrieks seemed to annoy him. He raised a hand holding the four jewels, and unfurled the curled fingernails into bloodstained talons. Hanna's eyes grew wider with fright and her cries more urgent. He hesitated... as if in silent debate about filleting her throat and removing the source of his irritation.

Instead of killing her, he merely blew upon the gemstones, emitting sparks and a puff of black smoke. When the smoke reached her face, she choked, no longer able to breathe, and collapsed on the ground. Confirming she lay unconscious, the monster backed up, raising his hands into the air and clicking his curled fingernails above his head. The wind rustled loudly, and two elongated shadows arose from the higher evergreens lining the southwest portion of the forest.

As they had done within the confines of Langston Hall, the shadows separated from one another and flew to the spot where Hanna lay. As they neared, the shadows shrunk in size and appeared as two dark Native Americans walking on the snow. Their images became lucid once the pair arrived on either side of the naked old man, who was quite taller and more repulsive. Their eyes mirrored the empty sockets of Grandma Susanne's a short while earlier.

The pair's raven-black hair was strewn with crow feathers, and each one was dressed in buckskins, beads, and moccasins. They deferred to the old man's authority, kneeling before him.

"*Agasdi nasgi ageyv!*" The old man's voice rumbled unearthly, as it uttered the command.

The one closest to him moved to Hanna's limp body and gathered her up. The old man smiled in approval, closing his hand around the jewels. He turned toward the northern woods, walking out of the clearing with his companions on either side.

As they reached the edge of the forest, their images blurred and faded into a collective swirling mist rising high into the air. The mist darkened and thickened, spreading like an enormous inkblot elucidated by the moon's brightness. It continued to rise above the tree line until it exploded into thousands of small particles that vibrated and buzzed. Carried by a forceful gust pummeling the virgin woodlands below, the unearthly mass raced north, roaring like an immense swarm of angry hornets.

Chapter Seventeen

"Hello, Auntie."

David spoke quietly into his cell phone. He adjusted the seat cushion of his chair in the waiting area outside the ICU at St. Anthony's Medical Center in Denver, where he and Miriam had spent the last forty minutes. Miriam sat across from him with her arm around Janice, whose eyes were red from the tears she'd cried for much of the past few hours after finding her close friend, Sara Palmer, lying unconscious on the floor of her living room.

"Are the kids giving you any trouble?"

His latest comment drew a curious look from Miriam, until she saw the playful expression on his face. Ruth told him everything was okay, and she asked about Sara.

"Not so good, I'm afraid," he said, the sadness in his voice erasing the wan smile. "The doctors told Miriam and Jan they have no idea when she'll come out of the coma."

He didn't feel it necessary to add one of the attending physicians, Dr. Leonard Puckett, stated he believed Sara might never regain consciousness.

"Yeah, it's really tough on both of them...." David glanced at Miriam with a slight wince. "No, the detectives here earlier are just getting started, so there are no suspects yet.... What's that? Yeah, we believe so...."

He stood to get a better signal, noticing the nurse attendant pointing to the sign next to her station desk that said No Cell Phones.

"Hey, Auntie, let me call you later when we get out of here." He spoke softer while holding the phone close to his mouth. "I will… I promise! Tell the kids we might have to take a rain check on the visit to the mall later. But, we're still on for Shakey's Pizza tonight. We love you, too, Auntie. Bye."

David closed the phone and mouthed a silent apology to the attendant, who merely shook her head before returning to the small stack of paperwork she processed.

"So, how are things at home?" asked Miriam, as she continued to comfort Janice.

"Everyone's fine," he replied. "Jill and Chris are working a puzzle with Ruth, and Ty's occupied for now with Chris' XBox. Apparently, Steve Elliston got one of the same on-line games for Christmas and the two have been going at it for the past hour. He won't break for lunch if Auntie isn't paying attention."

The last comment drew a slight smile from Janice.

David wished he could lighten the load that burdened her heart. According to what she told Miriam over the phone a couple of hours ago, she went to see Sara when she failed to return her calls from Christmas Eve and again on Christmas Day. Janice became especially worried this morning, the day after the holiday, when her second call attempt of the day, around nine o'clock, went to voice mail. She got in her car and rushed to Sara's Cherry Creek townhouse, arriving just after nine-thirty. She found the front door unlocked, and Sara sprawled on her living room floor, unconscious. She was wearing the same outfit she had on Sunday night when she came to their home to investigate the latest haunting.

The police, who arrived with the paramedics, found no evidence of forced entry, and nothing of value was missing from the home. The only things missing were the four precious gemstones David entrusted to her care. He prayed Janice's presumption proved correct—that Sara had deposited them within the heavy-duty vault secured to the floor in her bedroom closet. The police were reluctant to have one of their specialists open the vault, since a clear link between what lay hidden safely inside and the attack on Sara needed to be established first.

She had been left with a deep gash extending from below her left eye all the way down her left arm, ending inside her palm. The injury could've been caused by any of a number of sharp objects, and Janice heard one of the officers speculate the weapon might not ever be recovered. That's the way it often turned out in assault cases.

The immediate issue was how to get Janice to not blame herself for what had befallen Sara. His and Miriam's initial efforts to reassure her were unsuccessful. But, as the afternoon wore on, Janice eventually became more receptive to their comfort, and started to see things in a different light.

Dr. Puckett returned to the waiting room with the latest update on Sara's condition around two o'clock. He advised that although she remained in the coma, her vital signs were good. Her wounds had been thoroughly dressed, and the prognosis for successful healing was positive, although still too early to determine the coma's duration. Curiously, Dr. Puckett also shared that the medical staff remained at a loss as to how Sara fell into unconsciousness. The x-rays, CAT scan, and an MRI had uncovered no physical trauma to her skull. It only added to the mystery of what happened and why.

With nothing more that David and Miriam's presence could accomplish on behalf of Sara, Janice insisted they return home to be with their family. As for joining them tomorrow on a planned trip to Breckenridge, Janice admitted she felt uncomfortable leaving Sara for two days, even though she was under the finest care in the greater metro area. David told her that they would hold off leaving Littleton until late in the afternoon, to give her more time to decide if she'd like to accompany them to the ski resort.

Dying to ask Janice if she knew of any other place Sara might've chosen to hide the jewels, it wasn't the right time. Miriam agreed it would be best to wait until after the initial shock of Sara's attack wore off, perhaps after they returned from Breckenridge. He worried what to tell Ruth, since she never wanted to leave the heirlooms in Sara's possession in the first place.

There was much to consider in light of the attack. Did the sudden cessation of paranormal events in his household have anything to do with what happened to Sara? The fact her coma wasn't due to physical trauma fueled this line of thought. He pictured Christopher's description of the withered tree man, and how the thing later ransacked Auntie's room. Was it too farfetched to think such a malevolent presence would follow an unsuspecting, middle-aged woman home and viciously attack her before she even had the chance to take off her coat?

"Thank you for being here with me this afternoon, David," said Janice, coming to where he stood with Miriam, just inside the exit from the waiting area. They hugged, and he patted her shoulder affectionately as they let go. "I'll call Mir first thing in the morning to let you guys know if I'm coming along or not."

"Take as long as you need, Jan," he told her.

"I'll call you later tonight," said Miriam.

Miriam and David headed for the elevator, waving goodbye before joining another nurse in the elevator, whose shift had just ended. They soon returned home in David's pride and joy, his cherished midnight black BMW Z4. He suggested that she drive, foolishly hoping it might help lift her spirit. When she pulled the car into the exit lane for Littleton from I-25, David's cell phone rang.

"It's John!" He smiled broadly. "I was just thinking about calling him once we got home."

Miriam smiled as well, and motioned for him to take the call.

"Hey, John!" he nearly yelled into the receiver of his cell phone. "It's about time we talked, eh?... Yeah, it was good. Here's wishing you a belated *very* Merry Christmas! How was your holiday? Oh, yeah?... *What?* What do you mean she's gone?"

He turned toward Miriam, whose expression mimicked his own shock. Meanwhile, he continued to listen, offering only short, stunned comments to John Running Deer on the other end. For the next few minutes it continued, while Miriam deftly navigated the snow-packed shortcuts to their neighborhood. David hung up, promising to be there for John if he needed anything—to call him when he knew more information, regardless of the hour.

"What's going on, hon?" Miriam's countenance was clouded with deeper worry than before.

At first, David could only shake his head. "It took John's granddaughter, Hanna, from his cabin late last night," he whispered.

"What took her?"

"The spirit that's been haunting us both."

"What? How's that possible?"

She began to weep. Pulling the Z4 into the long, curved driveway in front of their home, her shoulders heaved as tears flowed. David ignored his own shock and remorse in order to take her into his arms.

Jillian and Christopher dragged Aunt Ruth outside to meet them at the car. Holding Miriam even tighter, David had a clear view through the driver's side window. He greeted their alarmed expressions with a worried smile, silently mouthing "everything's going to be all right."

But, how could it be?

Chapter Eighteen

Evelyn put her arms around John's shoulders after he disconnected the call to David. He turned to her with the receiver in hand, his bottom lip trembling.

"Don't give up hope, Grandpa—we *will* find her."

Her expression was confident, and she fought hard to restrain the wave of dread threatening to overtake her. She had to be strong, if for no other reason than to keep him focused on finding Hanna.

She was the first to notice her younger sister gone at daybreak. Evelyn assumed Hanna might still be sleeping. She carefully took out the skillet, bacon, and eggs to start breakfast, and made as little noise as possible. It wasn't until she glanced in the living room that she saw the empty couch. She didn't panic until a short while later, after searching the entire cabin, and quietly opened John's bedroom door after failing to find her anywhere else.

That's when he awoke. He immediately joined the search, while his worried murmurs grew steadily worse. After seeing Hanna's faint slipper imprints alongside a set of much larger bare footprints on the back porch, they dressed hurriedly. With Shawn's help, they tracked the footprints until they disappeared in a clearing located less than half a mile from the cabin. Thick cloud cover had dispersed, allowing the sun's light to bathe the near-pristine wilderness.

The butchered wolf remains were still covered with ice crystals from the early morning frost. Evelyn paused when she saw the garish sight, casting a suspicious glance toward her grandfather who hurried to track the trail of footprints threatened by the sun. She ran to catch up. Once they reached the clearing, he stood next to the slab-shaped boulder, dropping to his knees while rubbing his hands across the cool surface.

Sobbing, he cried out to his ancestors for help—to return Hanna before the entity could sacrifice her life. He spoke in the native language of his forefathers, and Evelyn was appalled by his plaintive words echoing around them, which he may have forgotten she could translate. She waited for him to finish, and helped him to his feet. They returned to the cabin, keeping watchful eyes out for any sign of Hanna. But, other than her melting footprints, there was nothing.

When John regained enough composure, he told Evelyn about the altar, once part of an ancient chain of shrines in the Smoky Mountains. Apparently, an early North American people created them, and disappeared long before the Cherokee moved into the region. Two Eagles Cry, John's grandfather, showed him a similar altar as a boy, and told him how the people often sacrificed their captive enemies to their bloodthirsty deities. Aware of the altar in the clearing near his cabin, John disregarded its importance, this earlier culture long dead.

Even though Evelyn understood the supernatural nature of what they were dealing with, she suggested they call the police. John, still distraught, told her not yet... at least not until he had a chance to search deeper in the woods. He hastily ate the quick breakfast she prepared and dressed appropriately for a longer stay outside.

Evelyn also dressed warmer. With Shawn, they searched the woods surrounding the clearing for the next several hours. But, to no avail. Discouraged, they came back to the cabin shortly after noon.

John placed a call to the Sevier County Sheriff's Department. Due to the holiday week, the staff had been reduced with everyone expected back by New Years Eve. One of the few deputies available, Jerry Van Heusen, agreed to stop by the next morning once twenty-four hours had passed since Hanna's disappearance. Evelyn watched her grandfather become incensed, but knew he understood as well as she that it would take a hell of a lot more help than the sheriff's department could provide, in order to find and rescue Hanna from the demon.

Perhaps, as John suggested, it had something to do with the long-forgotten spirit people who once ruled this section of North America centuries ago, according to Cherokee lore. The notion seemed ridiculous to Evelyn at first. Yet, how else to explain Hanna's slipper trail that led to the ancient altar, along with the dismembered wolf carcass left at the edge of her grandfather's property? Not to mention the strange toe marks next to Hanna's. John told her the unusual imprints were identical to others he found the day before.

As the sun dipped behind the mountains just before 4:30 p.m., John felt the powerful urge to try to reach David one more time. He called his cell phone, since he could never reach him at the Hobbs' home number in Littleton.

"Grandpa… hang up the phone and I'll prepare my cards for a reading," said Evelyn, gently, taking the receiver from him after he ended the call with David. "Let me at least try to find out what the entity intends to do. Maybe I can also determine the general area where it has taken her."

He almost relented, loosening his grip on the handset. But then he gripped it even tighter.

"I need to make a few more calls, and then we'll see about a reading," he told her quietly. "Why don't you wait in the living room while I call Dr. Kirkland and Dr. Pollack. It shouldn't take long. I must warn them one last time about the bones and relics they took from the ravine…."

He didn't have to finish for her to understand fully what he intended to tell the two esteemed professors from the University of Tennessee. The bones and relics— including the jeweled gold scepter with an extremely sharp ivory edge that Dr. Pollack was especially enamored with from the moment it had been unearthed—must immediately be returned to where they were taken from, and reburied.

That alone wouldn't be enough to appease the spirit's anger. Formal apologies handled the ancient way, with shaman dances and the incantations of the Cherokee, performed in the presence of the two contrite Caucasians while the items were reburied would be the minimum expectation. It would be up to the mighty *anisgas*, the warrior forefathers to come through on John's and her behalf, as they beseeched them to rescue Hanna from her imprisonment in the underworld.

Neither one conceded she might already be dead.

* * * * *

The first call went to Dr. Peter Kirkland, picked up by the professor after the second ring. John was pleased to finally connect with him after weeks of getting the runaround from the Forensic Department at UT, and leaving numerous voice mails. Despite his urge to lash out in anger, John maintained remarkable self-control in discussing what happened. Dr. Kirkland patiently allowed him to tell all that had transpired since Thanksgiving, including Hanna's disappearance. But, when John entreated his help in gathering the items taken from the sacred ravine in Cades Cove, the professor responded with the arrogance that had irritated John since he made the regrettable decision to tell him about the uncovered remains of Allie Mae McCormick.

John lashed out at Dr. Kirkland when he responded as if he heard nothing. The professor's steadfast pragmatism left him shortsighted about the consequences he and Dr. Pollack now faced. The call escalated into a shouting match ending with John demanding he turn the items over or he'd forcibly do it himself.

Evelyn started to move to the kitchen as she watched her grandfather tremble in anger, but he waved her off. Despite Dr. Kirkland hanging up on him, he needed to make one last plea for help. Perhaps Dr. Walter Pollack would listen, being a noted expert in the study of the ancient Native American peoples who once flourished in the southeastern United States.

John dialed Dr. Pollack's home number after failing to reach the professor at his office. Elaine Pollack, the professor's wife answered. His request to speak with her husband summarily denied, she'd already said goodbye and left him with a dial tone before he could say anything else. He called again. This time she responded even more sharply than the previous attempt, telling him to keep his 'Indian affairs' to himself until after the holidays, and to show 'better honor and respect for this time of year like a good Christian.' She tersely hung up, leaving him completely livid.

"Look! Tell your husband that I need to speak to him *now!*" he shouted into the receiver when he spoke to her a third time, his blood pressure raising to the point his chest ached. "If anything happens to my little girl, my granddaughter, because of what he's done, Dr. Pollack will personally pay for it all! You got that, lady? Let me speak to him now—"

Elaine Pollack hung up. All further attempts to contact her husband reached either a busy signal or were directly transferred to voice mail. His shoulders shaking from rage, John slowly returned the handset to the small cove in the kitchen. Evelyn came to him. Tears streamed down his face. She wrapped her arms around him and the two wept bitterly, while the sunset's last vestige waned, giving way to the night's dark wintry chill.

Chapter Nineteen

Shortly after sunset, Dr. Peter Kirkland hurried along the stone pathway leading to the lighted steps of Dr. Walter Pollack's stately Italianate styled mansion. The front door was framed within an immense arch, and he hesitated before ringing the doorbell, casting a third glance over his shoulder toward the eastern woods. The previous two times, right after parking his Jeep in the circular drive of the Pollack estate, revealed nothing definitive to worry about. Yet the unmistakable feeling of being observed and studied by someone hidden nearby, perhaps behind the thick tree line across from the driveway, left him anxious to get inside the house.

The doorbell's polyphonic chimes reverberated through the main floor. Dr. Kirkland raised a gloved hand to shield the porch light's yellow glare while he peered through the small medieval-like window inset on the side of the door. The foyer was dark, and the window reflected a distorted image of a bespectacled middle-aged bearded man, with receding white hair pushed to and fro by the wind.

The foyer suddenly filled with light, illuminated by a large crystal chandelier. A moment later, the heavy wooden door opened, and the delicate face of Elaine Pollack peered out. A railroad heiress whose family was among the oldest money clans in Knoxville, the eighty-acre Pollack estate had been procured a decade earlier by her parents' considerable wealth. Her father's affluence had also been largely responsible for Walter Pollack's rapid rise within the academic ranks, to where he now stood next in line for the Archeology Department's chair position.

Elaine studied Peter Kirkland for a moment, as he stood in the cold, waiting for her to grant him admission inside her privileged abode. Her alluringly soft blue eyes radiated warmth that belied her amused smirk.

"Walter's expecting you upstairs, Peter," she told him smugly, brushing her shoulder length blonde hair away from her face before pulling the door open enough for him to squeeze through.

"I expected Charles to be the one to let me in tonight," said Peter, sliding past her as he stepped into the foyer, the soles of his winter boots echoing on the gray marble floor.

He noticed her dark green housecoat, and wondered if she had taken ill since his last visit, just two days prior to Christmas Eve. He felt a twinge of guilt as he watched her struggle to close the door, but knew she wouldn't appreciate any chivalry.

"He's off tonight," she said, turning to him after locking the door and pausing to peer outside. "Even the family butler deserves a holiday break, I suppose."

"Hmmm," was his only response, followed by awkward silence. He could feel her contempt as she brushed by, and he prayed for something witty to say that wouldn't fall prey to her biting sarcasm.

"Like I said, Walter is expecting you."

She glanced over her shoulder at him just before leaving the foyer, pointing to the adjoining turret and the curved wrought iron stairway that would take him to Dr. Pollack's second floor office.

Dr. Kirkland removed his coat, and added it to the brass hall tree next to the front door. By the time he'd gathered his briefcase and straightened his sweater, Elaine had disappeared. He didn't see her in the living room, as he peered through the railings while climbing the stairs to the second floor. His view was partially obscured by the large flocked Christmas tree standing near the foyer. At least he now had more time to think of something clever to say to her when his visit ended.

He never stopped trying to ingratiate himself on friendly terms after an unfortunate incident involving her philandering husband and a young intern the previous fall. He knew about the affair, but kept it secret—even from his wife, Darlene, one of Elaine's dearest friends. Only Elaine's desire for the esteemed status as a University of Tennessee department chairman's wife kept her marriage to Dr. Pollack intact. Rather than take it out on him, she chose Walter's closest friend and colleague at the university to revile in his place.

Walter's upstairs office sat down the hallway to the right of the stairway. The hall itself reminded Peter of a five-star hotel—the Ritz Carlton would be so lucky to have imported marble columns and an exquisite Mediterranean runner along its length complementing expensive European millwork. The place had even been modeled after a castle in Milan, or so Elaine once told him—back when their speaking terms went beyond mere formality.

"Pete, come on in!"

Walter stood up from behind a massive mahogany desk sitting in front of a large stained-glass window. The window featured a giant falcon as it soared over a mountain stream similar to what lay a few hundred feet from the mansion. Slightly taller than Peter, his curly blonde hair, steel blue eyes and chiseled facial features alluded to a Greek god. Dressed in faded Levis and a pair of house slippers, the outline of his well-toned upper body was clearly visible underneath a red flannel shirt, the sleeves rolled up to his elbows.

"I came as soon as I could," said Peter, as he stepped into the room. He waved off Walter's offer to share a drink with him, sitting in one of the leather chairs in front of the desk. "It's been a long day, and Darlene is expecting me back before seven o'clock. We might have a bit of a problem, Walt." He frowned and set his briefcase on his lap, prepared to open it.

"Not yet," Walter advised, motioning for Peter to wait. "Are you sure you're not interested in helping me finish off the sherry left over from Christmas Eve?"

His eyes twinkled with mirth. The extreme confidence of the man seemed to ooze invisibly from every pore. Peter envied Walter—always had. At thirty-five, nearly twenty years Peter's junior, he seemed impervious to his senior colleague's unease. A lifetime of good fortune kept Walter insensitive to doubt, especially in those around him. Whatever he wanted in life always came easily.

Prestige, wealth, love.... Even when Elaine nearly left him over the tryst last summer with Dorothy Tummins, his lovely young graduate intern assistant, Peter knew firsthand that Walter's belief in everything working out to his liking never wavered.

"No thanks." Peter replied, wearily. He let out a low sigh. "John Running Deer is threatening to file suit against us with the NCAI, once the holidays are over next week."

"So, that's the reason you're so damned glum?"

For a moment, Walter seemed pained for his friend, perhaps real compassion for the man who showed him the political ropes around the university without ever asking for any favors in return. He chuckled as he stepped around the desk and went to the open doorway, peering down both sides of the outside hall before closing the door.

"I promise the situation with Mr. Running Deer will seem unimportant once I share some great news with you, Pete. And, just like that, all of your worries will fade away."

He snapped his fingers to illustrate the point, pausing to add another hickory log to the large fireplace, near where his oversized desk sat. Like the rest of the Pollack castle, no expense was spared in outfitting the office. It was paneled in the highest grade of cherry, along with handcrafted moldings, trim work, and other exquisite treatments throughout the room. Peter often mused on how the room was larger than any of the rooms in his own home—including the spacious den of his three thousand square foot Victorian located a few miles away. A large mahogany bookcase took up the wall on the right side of the fireplace, while a state-of-the-art media center dominated the opposite wall.

Walter returned to his plush, black leather captain's chair on the other side of the desk. He kicked his feet up on the desk's corner and folded his arms behind his head, wearing an amused look.

"Well, don't you want to know what it is?" he asked, after Peter didn't press him for details.

"Sure." Peter sighed again, securing the main latch to his briefcase and setting it down on the floor by his feet. "So, what's the great news you wish to tell me?"

"Rather than tell you, why don't you come over here and have a look."

Walter swiveled his chair toward the immense colorful window behind him. In front of the window sat an older cherry table, with a glass display case upon it. He rose from his chair and walked over to a small, blue velvet bag resting on top of the case.

When Peter reached his side, Walter opened the bag and removed six oblong gemstones, ranging from one to two inches in length. Two of the smooth, non-faceted gems appeared to be emeralds, their brilliant green hue sparkling in his palm. The other stones consisted of three bright orange gems that Walter announced were fire opals, and the last stone was a very rare pink diamond.

Astonished, Peter couldn't utter a sound. Meanwhile, Walter opened the glass case and removed a partially jeweled gold scepter—the prize from November's Cades Cove dig. Peter watched in disbelief as his younger colleague carefully inserted the glistening stones into six grooves along the length of the four-foot scepter. Once inserted, the ornamental staff lacked but five more missing stones—a pair on the shaft, two others from the handle's side, and a much smaller space belonging to a circular gem capping off the base of the scepter's handle.

The scepter's entire length was made from pure gold except the very tip, and bore a network of unusual pictograms and other symbols carved between the jewel slots. Its ten-inch ivory tip had an extremely sharp edge, keen enough to split a baby's hair.

"Where on earth did you acquire the gemstones?" whispered Peter.

He had seen the scepter several times before, proudly displayed within the glass case where Walter kept other artifacts taken from several digs over the past few years in the Smoky Mountain region. Peter readily ignored his closest friend's selfish indulgence, asking only that the human remains recovered from the dig be unchallenged property of the university's forensic department. He hoped to soon procure a more prestigious and permanent home for them other than where the remains were currently stored, in the basement of Langston Hall.

"It took a while to track them down, let alone purchase the jewels far below market value—which otherwise would've placed a severe burden on Elaine's inheritance," advised Walter, chuckling. "They were originally purchased by one of Norfolk, Virginia's wealthiest families many years ago, the McCray's, in exchange for a generous plot of land not far from here, in Pigeon Forge, back in 1916."

"So, perhaps whoever originally sold the jewels to the McCray's might've been involved in the murder of the young girl, whose skeleton fragments were reburied in Cades Cove a month ago," Peter observed. "It might be interesting to follow up on that idea at some future point in time."

Walter shot him a look that clearly said such a notion wouldn't be smart to pursue any time soon. Peter understood. After all, such an investigation could eventually lead to this locale, where the most recent illegal acquisition lay in full view within Walter's office.

"I think you should hear the other news I have to share first, before making a decision on what to pursue next," said Walter, setting the scepter on top of the display case. The staff's gleam briefly cast a golden glow upon the professor's forehead and cheek as he turned to face his colleague. "Do you recall the necklace found near the other skeletons buried en masse, roughly sixty feet from where the murdered girl's remains were discovered?"

"Yes, the one with the initials, 'L. C.' Correct?" Peter's face lit up, intrigued. "So, you were looking into this, I take it, while procuring the jewels that belong to the scepter?"

"I knew this would lift your mood!" Walter enthused, visibly pleased by Peter's interest. "Yes. The same source that led us to the missing jewels also has been working to trace the necklace, along with other items found inside that particular gravesite. Would you believe it turns out the necklace belonged to a young teenager named Lucy Carter, who was Governor John White's niece? And yes,

Pete, we're talking about the same John White who led the second attempt to settle Roanoke Island. Lucy was among the hundred and twenty settlers that came from England with him in 1587."

"No shit?" Peter's voice was a hoarse whisper until he recollected himself. "If what you're saying can be verified, then it'll change the prevailing theory about what happened to those settlers. It'll clear some things up. As you know, it's been a maddening mystery what became of nearly half the group that survived the initial attacks against the settlement at Roanoke."

"Actually, Pete, it only adds to the mystery," countered Walter, his elfin smile refreshed. "How did the dozen unfortunate souls end up in Cades Cove, on the western side of the Appalachians? Did they travel alone as a small band of outcasts from the main group, or perhaps, were they sold to a rogue Cherokee tribe by a hostile chieftain like Powhatan?"

He chuckled again, as if this were a privileged riddle to which he alone knew the answer. Peter started to say something in response, but seemed at a loss for words.

"Peter," said Walter soothingly. He stepped to the bar on the other side of the fireplace and poured himself another drink. When he motioned for Peter to join him, he did this time, requesting a gin and tonic. Walter returned to his desk with drinks in each hand, and continued his point after taking a sip from his sherry. "Why don't you let the matter of what we discovered in Cades Cove rest for now? Give it time to simmer down, and allow enough time for certain things to become… unnoticed."

He grasped Peter's shoulder, and the older man nodded pensively.

"One last thing, and we'll end this discussion about the whole Cades Cove business for tonight," said Walter, his hand still on Peter's shoulder while gently guiding him to the chair. "The relic I have in my possession might not even belong to the Indians—neither the Cherokee and their ancestors, nor even the much older Mississippian Indians. My preliminary study on the symbols carved into the handle indicates it might be from another continent. The closest thing I've been able to find is an ancient pictographic language used in ancient Gaul. Although, the figures represented on the scepter are somewhat more refined than the Gallic examples I've reviewed during the past few weeks."

"I suppose it would be best to wait and see what develops from all of this," Peter observed, sitting down again.

"Exactly!" Walter agreed.

A whistling sound arose from the darkened woodlands to the east of the mansion. The unusual pitch of the noise grabbed their attention, though it was faint at first. As they listened, the whistle grew in volume until uncomfortable. Peter commented on how it resembled some of the Fourth of July bottle rockets he and his pals used to set off during his wild and reckless teenage years. Only in that case, the rocket's scream would quickly fade after it ripped across the sky.

The painful noise continued until it reached the estate, where it ceased with a coinciding thump on the roof.

"Perhaps we should have a look?" Peter rose to his feet, glancing at the ceiling uneasily.

"Perhaps we should," said Walter. Lacking Peter's nervousness, he seemed merely curious as to what could possibly make such a strange commotion. "If we start to smell something burning, my guess would be we were hit by a meteor of some sort. The gas line up here runs through the attic." The twinkle in his eyes quickly returned as he pointed above.

"What else could possibly create a sound like that?" Peter asked, tentatively, while moving to a small French pane window in the corner, between the bookcase and the right edge of the stained-glass window.

He pulled back a ruffled curtain to peer outside, squinting in an effort to see past the flurried snowflakes landing lightly on the glass.

"If it wasn't a witch on a broomstick or Santa making up for lost deliveries, my best supposition remains a small meteorite, similar to one that struck a stable at Pennington Farms last year, just down the road," said Walter. "You remember the furor over that, don't you? But Charles and Olivia Pennington made nearly $400,000.00 from the subsequent sale of the fragments that were still intact— which is a hell of a lot more than was needed to repair the damage. Maybe we'll be that lucky, too, provided it doesn't ignite a fire to burn the place down."

His playful grin never wavered, since the fire prevention system installed in his home was among the finest available. Peter recalled how Walter had told him once how it worked. Not only would an alarm signal immediately be sent to the local fire department, but also an elaborate sprinkler system would quickly contain the fire in its infancy, long before it had a chance to spread. Only some of Elaine's prized artwork and antiques would be at risk, since everything Walter valued was either carefully protected or fully insured.

Peter began to believe it could be a meteorite that made the hellish sound they heard. He closed the curtain and stepped to where Walter stood at the display case, seemingly lost in admiration for his cherished scepter. It frankly surprised Peter that Elaine hadn't ventured upstairs to check on them, since the thud that followed the strange whistling noise seemed forceful enough to resound downstairs. He started to relax when his cell phone rang.

"Well, who could this be?"

Irritated, he brought the iPhone's display closer to his face to see who called.

"Do you need to take your call in private?" asked Walter, returning the scepter to its place inside the display case. "I can check on Elaine while you're on the phone. She contracted food poisoning yesterday, and has been a bit under the weather since."

"It's Jerry Simmons, the security staff dispatcher. He's calling from the main switchboard," advised Peter, wearing a quizzical look since Jerry normally left the admin offices by 4 p.m.—five o'clock at the latest. "It should only take a moment... someone else must've called out tonight. I asked him to call me if we didn't have enough staff to cover Langston Hall. Go ahead and check on Elaine if you would like."

He answered the phone, and covered the receiver while again encouraging Walter to touch base with his wife. Walter headed for the door, but stopped when Peter raised his voice at the dispatcher.

"*What?* When did it happen?"

Walter stood a few feet from the doorway, turning to listen to the excited male voice on the other end of the connection that was clearly audible, even though Peter held the handset close to his ear. Dr. Pollack frowned for the first time since Dr. Kirkland's arrival, perhaps mostly in response to his colleague rising from his chair and pacing angrily while he continued to berate Jerry.

"...Why in the hell didn't you call me earlier—the fucking *minute* you found out there were two dead bodies lying in the basement of Langston Hall!! I'll have your *goddamned job* over this—you hear me, Jerry? Yeah, you had better be there! *I'm on my way!*"

He ended the call, and for a moment gripped the handset tightly; seemingly on the verge of crushing the device. His face turned crimson, and his breaths were shallow. Walter slowly approached and leaned against the front edge of the immense mahogany desk.

"Vernon Mathis is dead," said Peter, gruffly, yet at the same time sounding bewildered. He turned to face Walter, who moved to the nearby bar to set his glass down. "And some Knoxville cop named Frank Thomas is also dead. Pete Lindsey found them tonight after Margaret Mathis called the office, frantically trying to find her husband after Vernon failed to return home this morning."

He didn't mention the fact young Mr. Lindsey was taken to a psychiatric ward, Lakeshore Mental Health Institute in Knoxville, shortly after the police and coroner's team arrived at Langston Hall. Finding the headless and mutilated corpse of his boss, along with the gutted carcass of Detective Thomas left the young man terribly shaken, and barely coherent enough to tell the police where to find the grisly discovery downstairs.

"This is… this is terrible news," said Walter, worriedly. "What was that I heard about them being found in the basement? Have the police been advised yet?"

"Yes, apparently, they've already been snooping around there since three o'clock this afternoon," Peter confirmed.

"God *damn* it!" hissed Walter. He moved around the desk and collapsed into the chair, grimacing in disgust.

"Some of the bones from the dig are gone," continued Peter. He moved over to his briefcase and picked it up. "It's too early to say which ones, but I'm headed there now. I suggest you come, too, since it may take us both to persuade our forensic friends from the police department to not remove anything else!"

He looked over his shoulder to see if Walter followed. He remained seated, his demeanor sullen, as if comprehending the full implications.

"Well, are you coming or not?" asked Peter, once he reached the door and pulled it open. "It will make things a hell of a lot easier if you're there too!"

"No," said Walter, his tone drained of its earlier exuberance. When he looked up at Peter, his expression was blank. "It's better if one of us stays out of the public eye for now. We need a plan... a plan on where to hide this thing so no one is the wiser about its existence." He nodded toward the case.

"You know it's far too late to hide anything at this point, Walt," said Peter, scarcely believing the suggestion. "John Running Deer saw it when your team unearthed it, and anyone close to him surely knows about the scepter by now. Don't you remember the look his granddaughter gave us at the court hearing when the NCAI was awarded their temporary injunction against any further digging in Cades Cove? I'll bet every Indian sympathizer in this region knows about *everything* that was taken from the site—including every skeleton and that *goddamned* scepter!"

His hand shook with rage as he pointed at the glass case behind Walter.

"Hell, even your own staff members were all ga-ga when it was unearthed. The only chance they would forget about it—and it was only an infinitesimal chance— disappeared this evening!"

"Keep your voice down, Pete!" Walter hissed, motioning toward the doorway.

The nearby turret and winding staircase served as an excellent conduit for voices and noises traveling along the hallway and down the stairs. With newfound urgency, Walter rose and made it to where Peter stood before his guest could utter another word.

"Just be cool about it—don't act nervous, man!" he whispered. "This will all blow over as long as we handle things the *right* way. We can't overreact to what has happened."

"Humph! That seems so easy for *you* to say, Walt!" said Peter, though for the moment compliant with Walter's wish to remain discreet. He poked his head into the hallway, quietly surveying both directions.

"I'm sure you can handle this just fine," advised Walter, once Peter pulled his head back into the room and faced him again. "Don't overreact to whatever the cops throw your way, and you'll do great."

Walter's playful grin returned, though slightly shrouded by uncertainty.

"We'll see." Peter shook Walter's hand despite his misgivings, and prepared to head downstairs. "Will you at least secure the necklace, so that if this all turns to shit we'll have it to fall back on?"

"Sure," Walter promised. "In fact, I'll secure it in my safe along with the jewels I showed you earlier, after I remove them from the scepter."

Peter eyed him suspiciously, but then softened his gaze. He had little choice other than to trust his friend to take care of the necklace and jewels. However, he felt certain it was just a matter of time before someone came snooping around the Pollack estate.

"All right, then. I'll call you once I find out more about what has happened at Langston Hall."

"Sounds good, Pete. Take care."

* * * * *

Walter stepped into the hallway and watched as Peter disappeared down the stairs. As soon as he heard his boot heels click against the foyer's marble floor, he returned to his office, closing the door. Leaning against it, he faced the enormous grand window. When he heard the heavy front door downstairs open and close, he moved to the small window Peter had gazed through earlier. Flurried snowflakes found it easier to stick to the glass, as the outside temperature continued to drop into the low teens.

Walter saw Peter's headlights turn on through the iced windowpanes, and felt the urge to wave goodbye. He unlatched the lever and rolled open the window. A gust of chilled snow blew into the room followed by heavy creaks on the rooftop above. He waved to Peter, although unsure if his good friend could see him or not. He waited until Peter began to drive away and rolled the window shut, just as a more powerful gust entered the room, sending flurries that reached his desk.

Dr. Pollack turned from the window, wearing a hopeful smile as he took a step toward his chair. He abruptly stopped before taking another. The display case's top had been removed, and the jeweled golden scepter was missing. He gasped in surprise.

A deep sardonic chuckle erupted from in front of his desk, one that was human and yet at the same time unnatural. Walter's heart began to pound fiercely inside his chest. Before his mind could convince him of a logical reason for what he heard, an immense shadow rose up from the floor, easily obscuring the only exit from the room. In instinctive fear, he stepped back into the corner, toward the French pane window he had just closed. The window's curtain still rustled slightly from when he had shut it only a moment ago.

"Who are you?" he asked, his normally confident voice unsure.

His crisp, lucid mind became muddied as he sought to form an immediate plan for escape. He could only manage a general estimate as to how far the drop would be to the pavement below the second story window. Was it eighteen feet or twenty-two feet? He couldn't remember, but a broken leg or arm would be likely, since the gabled roof below the window was slick from sleeted snow. All he knew for certain was the danger he faced. Danger from the voice, and even worse from the tall, foreboding figure that stepped out from the shadow.

Unsure if what stood before him was human, he did discern the figure as definitely male, naked with a slender but solid, sinewy build. Covered from head to toe with faint scars resembling stretch-mark grooves, its long black hair, streaked with gray, gave an appearance similar to a middle-aged man. The individual might've been dashingly handsome in youth, based on the chiseled facial features. But the grooves and unnatural cat-like eyes, luminous green with bright yellow halos around the rims, gave it a creepy appearance. The monstrous humanoid eyed him knowingly, as if fully aware of the myriad thoughts and observations bombarding Dr. Pollack's analytical mind.

"What the hell do you want from me?" the professor demanded, increasingly nervous as the figure moved around the desk and walked stealthily toward him.

Another chuckle erupted from the throat of whatever this thing was, and the slight grin steadily widened into a full smile. Its mouth looked impossibly large to Walter, but necessary to house the double row of long sharp teeth within. Such observations were his natural habit, and he cowered in the corner. All ideas of escape through the window were gone. There simply wasn't time or opportunity to flee.

It alarmed him to see the scepter wielded so menacingly. For a moment, the strange and grotesque being that held it reminded him of some king or ancient chieftain. The deep ink-like shadow hovering behind the figure acted like an imperial cloak as it closed in on him.

"Look, I'll give you whatever you want! I can *pay* you whatever amount you desire!"

Feeling helpless, he heard how pitiful the entreaty sounded. No doubt he appeared the same way. With nowhere to go, he slid down in the corner, his hands held out pleadingly as the figure raised the scepter with a long boney hand. The other hand was held out as if offering him assistance in standing. That is, until the hand's curled fingernails unfurled, and were ready to strike with five deadly razors.

"No, God, please don't—"

That's all Dr. Walter Pollack could get out of his mouth before his impassioned plea for mercy turned into a blood-curdling scream.

* * * * *

Elaine Pollack watched from a hidden vantage point, next to a Doric column standing between the parlor and living room, as the bastard Peter Kirkland gathered his coat, scarf, and hat. He lingered long enough to scan the area as far as his prescription glasses would allow, seemingly frustrated by the fifteen-foot flocked fir in his way. When he couldn't detect her presence, he opened the heavy wooden door and let himself out. It wasn't until after he closed the door and she heard his footfalls along the chilled concrete outside that she began to feel at peace again. If only it was the last time she would ever see the man.

She smiled at how the last thought lifted her mood, and knew it would have elicited a warm chuckle if she felt better. Even now, her stomach churned.

About to walk into the kitchen to fix something light to snack on, she heard a shriek coming from upstairs. Muffled, it likely came from her husband's office. The much louder sound of breaking glass soon followed.

"Walter!"

She hurried out of the living room, nearly tripping on the foyer's marble tiles. After straightening her slippers, she climbed the staircase in the adjoining turret to the second floor as quickly as her weakened condition would allow. When she reached her husband's office, she hesitated for a moment, surprised by the flurried snowflakes floating through the tiny space between the base of the door and the office's hardwood floor beneath it.

Papa's commissioned window broke—oh, my God!

In a panic, she turned the doorknob and threw open the door, expecting to see a sizeable hole in her favorite of five prized windows in the house.

Ninety thousand bucks down the fucking drain!

Elaine stormed into Walter's office, ready to launch a tirade. She pictured him as he finished off the decanter half-filled with sherry and moving on to the large bottle of Blue Label Jack Daniels he received from a local state senator for Christmas. Knocked-off-his-ass-drunk, he apparently lost his balance and probably pushed that goddamned display case of his into the window—after she'd repeatedly warned him to move it somewhere else.

Set to start her usual lecture, much more harshly this time—with an "I told you so!" preface to launch it—she couldn't muster a word. All she could do was drop to her knees while her mouth repeatedly opened and closed, silently. Like the trophy German brown trout her father caught when she was ten and laid out on the back deck of their stately summer home in New Hampshire, suffocating while it fought desperately for oxygen relief that would never come.

As she feared, her cherished window had been broken, although worse than she envisioned. Only a few shards of glass sticking out from the window frame remained. But that was not the worst, and certainly not what threw her into a state of shock that later proved to be the cornerstone for her nervous breakdown.

Dr. Walter Pollack stared back at his grieving wife upside down from his enormous mahogany desk's spacious top. Torn and gutted, his twisted remains resembled a bloody snake. Contorted in a grotesque 'S' shape, he laid sprawled and positioned meanly upon journals and other reports, with his head barely attached to a narrow strip of the professor's spinal cord.

In an instant, all of the shared memories of love and happiness overrode the recent string of affairs and other transgressions that had broken her heart. When the wave of memories and attendant emotions grew too strong to contain within her heaving bosom, Elaine Pollack finally found her voice. Sadly, no one could hear her grieve or offer comfort. Not even undesirable company like Peter Kirkland, whose car sped along the estate's long icy driveway toward the main roads that would take him back to society.

* * * * *

"What in the *hell* is that?"

Dr. Kirkland adjusted the rearview mirror in his Jeep, glancing out the side mirror to get a better look at the colorful window in Walter's upstairs office. He saw his long-time friend wave through the smaller French pane window moments ago and had responded in kind, although fairly certain Walter had missed his response while rolling the window shut. He assumed all was well, and set his thoughts on what to tell the police gathered at Langston Hall. The creepy feeling of being watched by some unseen voyeur had disappeared, and was long gone. But, when he glanced again at the mansion through the rearview mirror, after the back defroster cleared the remaining ice from his rear window, somehow the immense window in Walter's office had changed.

At first, it seemed like some sort of trick or optical illusion, with hundreds of glass fragments from an explosion suddenly being sucked into the office. His first thought was maybe the object that struck the house had caused a fire after all—perhaps busting the gas line Walter told him about—since such a phenomenon of glass being sucked inward could happen if the fire's oxygen pull and pressure were just right. That thought, however, changed completely when a thick, ink-like shadow poured out through the enormous hole where the window had been. He thought he heard a scream, too, but that could've been the wind.

Goddamn it, Walter!

He almost turned around and went back, since he had a new reason to worry what would become of the prized necklace tied to old Roanoke. The images of being honored in the more important forensic and other scientific journals already less assured, they would become nonexistent if some unforeseen misfortune threatened the necklace's pristine condition. He started to slow down. What changed his mind and convinced him to speed up instead was the shadow had grown much larger, deepening into a thick black cloud. It veered swiftly in his direction, rapidly gaining on his Jeep barreling down the driveway.

At first, all he could do was stare incredulously at the reflection of the eerie object through the Jeep's mirrors. Rising panic reclaimed his attention and he pushed the pedal to the floor, desperate to make it to the main road still a half-mile away. The huge specter continued to close the gap, and as it did, the unmistakable sound of hornets filled the air.

"No way!" he whispered, turning down the heater's blower to listen to the growing noise while unable to remove his eyes from either mirror for long. "No *fucking* way!"

Logic wasn't helping, since no matter how he tried to assure himself the cloudlike thing was just a natural phenomenon that only looked and sounded frightening, his heart remained gripped by terror. The noise was dreadful. What in the hell could sound like an enormous nest of pissed-off hornets in the dead of winter?

He still had a quarter of a mile to navigate before he reached the main road. Meanwhile, he kept a vigilant eye on both the side and rearview mirrors. Without warning, the thing dramatically increased its speed, and the size of the cloud got much, much bigger. The cacophony of hornets became so loud Peter could hardly hear himself think. Frightened beyond all reason, he stomped on the gas pedal, trying to shove his boot into the floor, and nearly spinning off the slick driveway in the process.

Less than a hundred feet from the road, the reflective Ruben Road street sign became visible. But, the ear-splitting clamor and enormous wave of blackness overtook him. Unable to see anything, Peter slammed on the brakes, and the vehicle slid to a stop with one tire leaning over a ditch. Unable to drive further, without first getting help in pushing the Jeep back onto the paved driveway, he prepared for the worst. For the first time in many years, he prayed. He beseeched the Good Lord earnestly to get him out of this situation unharmed by whatever was in pursuit. He pictured making it home to his dearest Darlene, and climbing into their soft warm bed while they snuggled until either she or he fell asleep. *Dear God, please make it so—I'll do whatever You ask of me going forward. I swear I'll be a better man!*

With his eyes closed, the terrifying noise ceased, and when he cautiously peered through his eyelids, the darkness had left. Under the moonlight's glow, he again could clearly see the glistening snow-covered trees and landscape of this portion of the Pollack estate, as well as the yellow lined roadway ahead.

He looked around him, to confirm he was truly alone. He smiled when he didn't see or hear anything strange, other than his labored breaths and the water trickling through the nearby ice-covered moonlit stream running along the border of the property. He gave thanks that his prayer was heard, and vowed to look into rejoining the Methodist church his wife had been after him about for the past several years.

Prepared to get out of the vehicle, to calculate how best to get on the road again, he casually glanced in the rearview mirror.

Peter had time to gasp and that was all. Before he could muster a scream or mount a self-defense, the owner of two glowing green eyes staring at him through the mirror's reflection fell upon him, pulling its thick dark cloak along with it as the monster invaded the Jeep's front seat.

Chapter Twenty

"With everything going on, it might be best to hold off until Thursday for the trip up to Breckenridge," said Ruth, returning to her preferred spot on the sofa. She carried a mug of hot cocoa, and took a moment to blow on it. The heat from her homemade recipe melted the tiny marshmallows to where they disintegrated into bubbling white foam.

Nearing nine o'clock, she had checked on Tyler, Jillian, and Christopher in the kitchen. All three were engaged in a lively game of *Blokus*, Tyler's Christmas gift from Miriam's younger sister, Marlene, living in California. Their laughter erupted, and provided a powerful contrast to the somber mood in the living room.

"Are you sure y'all wouldn't like some Southern cocoa?" she asked.

David waved off the offer. Miriam told her it sounded tempting, and she would help herself to some in a little while. For the moment, they snuggled on the loveseat, although neither smiled. Both had spent the evening with watchful eyes on the telephone sitting nearby, waiting to hear either the latest news on Sara's condition or John's missing granddaughter.

"I've got enough cash on hand to reimburse you for what you'd lose on the first night's reservation," offered

Ruth, resuming her first thought. "I can tell that neither of you have the heart for taking a vacation right now."

"That's awfully sweet of you, Ruth," Miriam told her, smiling weakly. "Your presence alone has made the craziness around here bearable. Our holiday season would be a *very* difficult time—definitely, without the bright spots that you've made happen."

Tears filled Ruth's eyes. She nodded her appreciation, as a worded response would surely bring a deluge of emotion beyond her control. After so many holiday seasons spent with just her beloved companion, Max, the twelve-year old Cocker Spaniel she was forced to put down a few weeks ago, to feel like a valued family member filled her entire being with incredible joy.

"I feel the same way, Auntie," said David, nodding toward Miriam. "And while we appreciate your offer, should we decide to cancel tomorrow's trip, I've got it covered. Besides, the lodge manager is a buddy of mine from college. I'm sure Mark and I can work it out, if we need to postpone or even cancel the ski trip."

"Well… if it turns out that you do need my help to pay for anything, please don't hesitate to let me know," she said, her countenance aglow while she sipped her cocoa.

* * * * *

Relieved that his aunt's disposition had improved, it gave David the opportunity to broach a different subject, where several questions nagged at him. All revolved around the mysterious ruby discovered under her pillow.

He was especially curious as to how the precious stone escaped the entity's notice, and yet drew the attention of his great grandfather's spirit instead.

The most recent urge to bring it up had been inspired by what happened that afternoon, when he held the ruby, admiring its perfect shape and near-flawless clarity. Its only imperfection was a unique cloudiness inside the jewel, most noticeable when exposed to a strong light source.

While waiting for Miriam to join him in the parking lot adjacent to St. Anthony's ER, he remembered the ruby, safely secured inside his wallet. He took it out and held it up to the sun, disregarding the fact some miscreant might accost him and take it. Even now, as he reflected on what happened, his imprudence surprised him. He recalled how a strange calm took over his entire being, and was only interrupted by Miriam's hurried approach and urgings for him to jump inside the BMW so they could get going. That seemed strange, too. It was as if her only worry was to get the heck out of a rough neighborhood. She scarcely noticed the shiny red gemstone he held toward the sky.

The most remarkable thing about the experience, however, came from what he saw inside the ruby. He could've sworn the cloudiness moved, but it stopped when he tried to get a closer look.

"Auntie, I've been meaning to ask you some questions about the ruby," said David. "Would you mind if we talk about it?"

"What sort of questions do you have?" Her smile faded, and she seemed to tense up.

"Just general stuff," he assured her, softening his voice. "Really, it's just a couple of questions. I promise to make this as painless as possible." He smiled tenderly, hoping she would relax.

"I guess it'll be all right." She grimaced as if the mere thought of the jewel induced a surge of arthritic pain. "I sort of wish it'd stayed lost, or that I had the dumb sense to leave it and the others in the bank's safety deposit box for y'all to claim later."

She steadied the cocoa mug on her lap, absently kneading her left arm.

"I can see why you'd think that, Auntie," David agreed, frowning slightly while he watched her massage the sudden soreness. "I certainly don't wish to open old wounds. If what I'm about to ask you doesn't sit well for any reason, I'll respect your right to decline an answer."

"All right."

"The five gemstones have been in the family for nearly one hundred years... correct?"

"Yes."

"Has there been anything strange or unusual concerning them that you've noticed down through the years?" He tried to remain casual while observing her reaction.

"Do you mean like what happened this past weekend and again on Christmas Day?"

He didn't expect her straightforward reply. "Yes," he said, sitting up in the loveseat, hoping for more definitive answers than he originally believed possible.

Ruth nodded, and a wan smile tugged at the corners of her mouth.

"It's been said that ever since Grandpa Will came into possession of the jewels, our family's been cursed." She set the mug on a ceramic coaster on the coffee table before continuing. "Uncle Zach once told my pa and his sisters that they were stolen from a sacred location in the Smoky Mountains. And, truth be told, we've had our share of bad luck down through the years."

"What kind of unlucky things have happened, especially prior to when I came along, if you don't mind my asking, Auntie?" David's curiosity was piqued, as he recalled what he had witnessed in Cades Cove this past October, when forced to relive the night of Allie Mae McCormick's murder. He silently prayed she wouldn't clam up.

"Just a few odd things now and then. The frequency has varied throughout the years, and the events haven't been as bad as they used to be before you were born," she replied, clearing her throat while repositioning herself on the sofa. "But our house in Chattanooga would sometimes be visited by something... something cold and mean— even meaner than Grandpa Will. I often thought he had something to do with it all, like whatever the thing was had come to the house on his account. After he died, I figured we'd be free.... The visitations were just as frightful as they'd been when he was alive.

"Often someone would get hurt. Or, some heirloom, like Grandma Bev's bone china serving plate, would fly across a room and smash against a wall. We learned to stay clear of the cold presence that would move through the darkened halls of our old house late at night, and during the day sometimes."

She paused to take another sip, while David and Miriam waited patiently for her to continue.

"Grandpa used to laugh at us when he was alive, telling Pa, Momma, your daddy, and our older brother, Marvin, that we were a bunch of fools for being frightened by a harmless phantom—especially one that wasn't around on a daily basis." Ruth chuckled sadly.

"So, I take it that Great Grandpa Will could see or hear the spirit's presence. Am I right about that?" David remembered the cold spots and creaking footsteps going up and down the stairs when he was a kid, but he always assumed it was just an old, drafty house. No one in the family slept well, being up and about at odd hours of the night. He figured crashing plates and such were merely byproducts of a dysfunctional family.

"I'm sure he could hear *and* see it," she said. "I recall a number of occasions when Bobby and I caught him talking and hissing at something. Neither of us could discern anything around him, other than the air around us turning quite chilly."

"It sounds like maybe you and Dad had some experiences, too, then," said David, his voice hushed.

Waiting for her to share such an encounter, the phone rang. The ringer sounded more shrill than usual, which startled him and Miriam. He got up from the loveseat to find out who called.

"It's John," he announced, as soon as he recognized John's home number from the Smoky Mountains of Tennessee.

He immediately picked up the receiver and brought it close to his ear. Greeted by a loud crackle, it forced him to pull the phone away. As he did, the noise faded, replaced by the sound of a woman crying.

"John?" he asked, tentatively, once he brought the handset close to his ear again.

"He's in jail, David!" the voice sobbed. "Two deputies arrested him tonight and took him away—he didn't kill anyone!!"

"What? Is that you, Evelyn?"

Miriam got up from the loveseat and ran over to him. He mouthed John had been arrested.

"Oh, my God!" she whispered, moving closer. She tilted her head to where she could hear most of the conversation.

"David, are you *there?*" Evelyn sounded panicked, her voice loud enough for Ruth to hear it clearly. "They say he killed *three* men, including Dr. Pollack from the University. I-I don't know what to do! I'm so *scared!*"

"Evelyn... where did they take him?" he asked, trying to sound calm while fighting growing apprehension. "Was it to a local jail, or did they take him someplace else, like Knoxville?"

"They took him to the jail in Sevierville," she replied, pausing as if distracted by something inside John's cabin. David heard what sounded like a huge windstorm going on somewhere near her. "He Who Cannot Rest, *Teutates*, is back. David, *please* find a way to come here! You're the only real friend Grandpa has—he needs you! Please, *hurry!"*

"I'll see what I can do, Evelyn—I promise I will!" He looked at Miriam, who nodded an affirmation to his words. "I'll need a little time to get everything arranged. I'll call you back in the morning—"

"No—just come, David!" she interrupted, her voice trembling to the point a hysterical outburst was imminent. "I'm *begging* you! Will you *please* find a way to get here right away—*definitely* by tomorrow? *Please!"*

"All right. Yes," he replied, sighing, after looking again at Miriam, whose countenance reflected a curious mixture of worry and suspicion. "I'll call you back as soon as…."

The line went dead.

"As soon as what?" Miriam asked, taking the receiver from him and verifying the steady dial tone. A slight crackle accompanied it.

"As soon as," his voice weak, he wondered why she eyed him so.

"We cancel our arrangements to go up in the mountains tomorrow, I believe." said Ruth, finishing his sentence.

She eyed them thoughtfully, and stood from the sofa. Her expression very worried, David was surprised by the forthright remark.

"I believe y'all have got some important, unfinished business to take care of," she continued. "I guess we'll be heading back to Tennessee a bit earlier than I originally planned. It's not at all the way we wanted things to turn out, but it certainly is what it is. Something's obviously calling you, David, and it's calling you back home."

Chapter Twenty-one

Evelyn shuddered as she pulled a shawl tightly around her shoulders. For the moment, she stood in the middle of the living room of her grandfather's cabin, facing an intense blaze from the fireplace. Despite the heat, she shivered, as if a glacial breeze embraced her.

The mere thought of her grandfather spending the night in the isolated confines of the Sevier County Jail seized her heart. Even worse when she considered Hanna's fate. Missing now for almost two days, Evelyn hoped to resume her search in the morning.

"It's all right, boy… Grandpa's going to be okay," she assured Shawn. Curled up next to her feet, he lifted his chin in an effort to coax her to scratch him in the area that gave him the most pleasure, beneath his jaw and above his chest.

She relented and sat next to him, stroking his sweet spot until he got up and trotted to John's recliner. He picked up the furry chew-toy Hanna bought him for Christmas and carried it over to her in his mouth, nudging her with his nose.

"So, you want to play a little tug-of-war, Shawnnie?" She raised the pitch of her voice to indulge him.

Shawn barked in response and twice more when she pretended to change her mind and not play after all. As if eager for distraction, his tail wagged fiercely when she tried to grab the toy. For much of the next half hour they wrestled on John's black bear rug that lay directly in front of the fireplace. She enjoyed the diversion, too, and they played until the cuckoo clock on the mantle announced midnight had arrived.

Evelyn leaned back on her elbows, casually listening to the clock's chime as it counted the hour. She raised herself up, listening closely to what at first she thought was another sound coming from the clock.

"Sh-h-h!" she told Shawn, after he began to whine again when she wouldn't resume their contest. His ears perked up and he looked toward the large picture window in the loft. A low growl emerged from his throat.

Evelyn's eyes followed his gaze, and her heart galloped until she realized the heavy draperies were drawn shut, from when she and John secured the house the previous evening. A gentle gust of wind caressed the cabin from outside, and the curtains on both floors billowed softly, as if the breeze somehow seeped inside her refuge.

She stood and moved through the main floor at a frenetic pace, making sure every window and door was locked and all the curtains were closed tightly. She raced up the narrow staircase leading to the loft, releasing a relieved sigh once she verified the window and its thick drapes were fully secured. She turned to head back downstairs, and that's when she heard the whisper.

Low at first, she found it difficult to make out the words. Evelyn listened to the voice emanating from the other side of the drapes; she deciphered most of what was said in her native Cherokee.

"Ulisgolvtanv Ayu Hawinaditlv."

The whisper was genderless, breathy, and echoed slightly. The resultant timbre made it hard for her to determine exactly where the voice came from outside the cabin. Perhaps it came from somewhere *inside*—maybe lurking next to the window behind the heavy drapery.

After her initial gasp, she cautiously stepped toward the window. At first tempted to open the draperies and peer outside, she changed her mind. She left her hand poised to pull them back.

"Who's there?"

Silence. Then the voice repeated the phrase, the request to gain access sterner and somewhat menacing. While she tried to decide how best to respond, a deep groan filled the air around her, sending an unsettling shiver through her entire being. The sound echoed across the cabin's tall ceiling, moving from the front to the back of the structure.

"Anagisdi utsatina!" said Evelyn evenly.

Responding in the native tongue of her forefathers, she silently prayed her nervousness didn't hinder her command's effectiveness in getting the presence to "go away!"

A mirthless chuckle resounded from outside the window. Shawn launched into a barking tirade directed at the front door. Evelyn scrambled downstairs, in time to catch a large shadow moving away from the door and out of her direct view. She feared something, or someone, inside the cabin with her, might've caused the shadow. But, then she heard the sound of heavy feet stepping from the front porch as she moved to the front door. She pulled back the curtain to the front window next to the door, and peered outside. A slight indentation in the shoveled snow bank, along the far edge of the porch, indicated someone recently had been there.

She checked the front door's lock and deadbolt to make sure they remained secure, while Shawn turned his attention to the back door. His tail pointed downward as he bared his teeth at some unseen menace, and snarled protectively. Evelyn moved quietly to the door, closing her eyes and chanting a Cherokee incantation to protect her and Shawn.

Everything outside grew very still, as if nature itself heeded her entreaty for peace and protection. The wind ceased to embrace the cabin, and a slight depression of cold air that had steadily descended from the ceiling now dissipated, allowing the warmth from the fire to radiate beyond the living room.

"Come here, boy... come here," she quietly called to Shawn, once she returned to the living room.

She patted her thigh until he turned away from the back door and trotted to her. He glanced several times at the door before sitting next to her.

"It's all right, Shawn. Everything's going to be okay, baby. Whatever was here is gone."

Shawn looked into her face and glanced toward the back door again. After a slight whine, he laid down on the living room floor next to where she stood, his snout resting on her feet. Meanwhile, she warily looked around expecting something else to happen despite her positive reassurances.

For several minutes she waited. All remained peaceful. She moved through the main floor of the cabin, checking to make sure the place remained secure. She paused to straighten her grandfather's largest dream catcher and climbed to the loft. After making sure the drapes were pulled tightly across the large picture window, she returned downstairs.

She sat in her grandfather's recliner, and Shawn leapt up to where his upper body rested in her lap. He brought his face close to hers, breathing rapidly with his tongue out, as if he had an urgent warning he wished to relate quietly. She turned down the TV in order to determine what he worried about. She shared his acute nervousness, and yet, everything remained calm and still inside the cabin... until three light raps resounded upon the back door. The noises came from outside, as if someone lightly tapped their knuckles upon the door's curtained window.

She couldn't be sure, but Evelyn thought she glimpsed the shadowed outline of someone's head, as they tried to peer through a slight crease in the curtain. Enough to get her out of the chair, she uttered another quiet prayer and took a few tentative steps toward the door.

"No need to fear. Everything's all right, dearie," said a woman's voice from the back porch. "It's Grandma Susanne."

The voice sounded warm and comforting, and was filled with assurance. It definitely belonged to an older woman. It sounded uncannily familiar, and in Evelyn's mind, it did closely resemble her dear grandmother's voice—both in timbre and manner. But there was something else about it that seemed as foreign as the other qualities were recognizable. Something that made her hesitate.

She moved two steps closer, lifting her feet to avoid creaks that would normally arise from the pine floor.

"That's it, dearie… come on over and open the door so we can visit," said the owner of the voice, maintaining a cheerful, caring tone.

It sounded so much like Grandma Susanne. Evelyn opened her mouth to speak, but caution again gave her reason to pause. She stopped moving. All of her senses, both physical and spiritual, were fully heightened.

"Ah-h, my dearest Evelyn…. Why do you doubt me?"

The voice sounded amused, which reminded her of the playfulness so characteristic of Grandma Susanne. It was one of the things she sometimes thought about whenever she reminisced about her grandmother—especially in the cabin, where she spent most of her formative years when her mom was busy chasing whatever boyfriend she had at the time. Evelyn's father died in a motorcycle accident when she was five, although her mother hardly grieved. Evelyn and Hanna lived with their grandparents until Joanna, their mother, decided to resume her parenting duties when her kids became teenagers.

"Speak to me, dearie. Our reunion can only last so long, before I must leave again."

"I-I'm coming," said Evelyn, nervously.

She approached the door; close enough to see the silhouette of her grandmother. She could see the outline of her facial features, her curly hair, and even the long charcoal gray coat she favored.

"Do you wish for me to catch my death of cold, Evelyn?" the woman chided her, lightheartedly, again engendering cherished memories from her childhood. "Let me in, dear."

Evelyn reached for the doorknob. Expecting it to be at least as tepid as the last time she touched it, it surprised her the metal knob turned very cold—perhaps as frigid as its partner on the door's other side in the early morning chill. She withdrew her hand and stepped back.

"Grandma Susanne... I loved you as much as I've loved anyone else on this earth. I still do love you," she said to the person standing just a few feet away, separated only by the glass and wood of the back door. "But you're dead. You should return to the holy land near the Three Blood Rivers, and wait for Grandpa to join you and our ancestors. It's what The Great Spirit wants—"

"*Open*, the door, Evelyn!" Grandma Susanne pleaded, interrupting her. "I haven't got much time, dearie, before I must return to the sacred place you speak of. *Don't*—"

"Leave now!" Evelyn demanded. Her tone poised with conviction. "Leave me alone, right *now!*"

"No, I *won't* leave!" the owner of the voice replied, indignantly. "Evelyn, open the door now, before it's too late for mercy.... Or, risk getting the worst whipping of your life!" A slight measure of meanness seeped into the delivery.

"I said go away!"

Evelyn's tone was forceful and louder. Her renewed confidence clearly revealed her growing impatience and disdain for whoever hovered next to the backdoor window. The unnaturalness of the encounter could no longer support the allure of intimate communication with her deceased grandmother.

"Get the hell off my grandfather's property *now,* damn it!"

The silhouette backed away from Evelyn's view, leaving in its place the bright luminance from the moon seeping through the small creases in the curtain, along with the glow from the porch and security lights. A low, sinister chortle rumbled from beyond the back porch, impossibly moving through the log and mortar walls of the cabin. It surrounded her while she instinctively stepped backward into the living room.

"Open the door, you ungrateful bitch!"

A thick, dark shadow moved in front of the door, obscuring all light, while a deeper, menacing voice replaced the much sweeter one from just moments ago.

"I will strip you naked and skin your hide for your dear grandpa to find when he returns home!"

"Anagisdi utsatina!" Evelyn shouted angrily.

She refused to be intimidated further, raising both arms with her palms faced toward the door. She mouthed another prayerful incantation, as she turned her hands inward before thrusting them at the door.

A swooshing noise immediately shook the back wall. The force threw her onto the living room floor. Shawn crawled to the spot where she lay, directing another threatening growl at the back door. But, the dark presence dissipated, leaving only slight wind gusts whistling quietly through the cabin's eves and tiny creases between the doors and windows.

Is it gone?

Evelyn stood and warily looked around. Shawn continued his vigil, with more growls against the menace whose physical presence was temporarily muted. An immense thud shook the entire cabin, confirming the entity's growing displeasure. The varnished, white pine beams lining both slopes of the A-frame's ceiling creaked loudly as if on the verge of a massive collapse.

She grabbed Shawn by the collar and dragged him to the dining table, sliding under it while pulling him along with her. They cowered between two chairs, listening intently. She let out a slight yelp when a chilling voice pierced the air. The voice's terrible cackle reverberated shrilly throughout the living room.

"You stupid fucking bitch—watch now as I pour your sister's warm blood all over your grandfather's cabin-n-n!" the high-pitched voice shrieked with glee. *"Listen as it trickles down the roof—Se-e-e it str-r-r-eam-m-m down the window-w-w-s!"*

"PLEASE leave us alone!" Evelyn cried from beneath the table.

She pulled Shawn closer, the husky no longer resisting her efforts to shield them both. His trembling only fueled her deepening dread.

"Let him in, Evelyn!" cried another voice that she realized in horror belonged to her sister, Hanna. *"He's*

going to kill me, Evelyn—PLEASE open the door before he cuts my—a-a-ar—oh, God, he-l-l-l-p me-e-!"

"*Hanna!*" Evelyn screamed, and moved to crawl out from the table's protective shelter.

She knew the voice could very well be another trick by her invisible tormentor, cleverly mimicking her sister's voice and personality. But she was drawn by the infinitesimal chance the malevolent spirit would spare Hanna. She realized this thing—anisgina or demon—had disguised itself as her deceased grandmother. Perhaps that's how it lured Hanna out of the cabin two nights earlier. She had little choice other than facing the entity head-on.

She came out from underneath the table with Shawn right behind her. Prepared to surrender, she intended to open the door and allow the entity inside before she changed her mind. Another noise pulled her attention toward the apex of the tall ceiling, where a swirling bluish mist hovered. As she stopped to look at it, the glowing haze swirled faster and faster. Its denseness thickened as the color darkened toward purple and then turned deep crimson. Meanwhile, her sister's screams of horror and excruciating pain increased.

"*Don't do it—I beg you, take ME and let her go!*" Evelyn cried, falling to her knees beneath the ever-thickening red mass. It continued to solidify and mutate, gaining a balloon-like shape and bright sheen. Like an overfed tick, it continued to grow until it threatened to burst.

The terrible screams went on, while the strange apparition continued its descending expansion. A flurry of sparks and purple lightning erupted from the image when part of it touched the upper tip of a spirit chaser nailed to the wall below the upstairs picture window. Hanna's cries abruptly ceased, replaced by an inhuman screech followed by a tirade consisting of a strange mixture of Cherokee and other words and phrases that featured harsh cadences—a second language completely unfamiliar to Evelyn. Only a repeated Native American phrase stating "it's too late for mercy" was clearly discernible to her ears, as the inhuman voice shrieked most of its furious tirade in the unfamiliar tongue.

Evelyn's heart sank, knowing she couldn't save her sister. As she sought to plead one last time for mercy, the enormous sac burst. She fainted before the showered foulness reached her, collapsing in a heap while Shawn sought to protect her from a rain of blood and gore.

Chapter Twenty-two

Lying in his cell at the Sevier County Jail, John Running Deer stared at the chipped tiles in the ceiling. All but two other cells on the main floor sat empty. His scheduled arraignment was set for Friday morning, and he remained hopeful it would be moved up to Thursday afternoon, tomorrow.

Someone would surely come to their senses. The charges of first degree murder were completely ludicrous. How in the hell could an old man like him subdue the much younger, athletic professor Walter Pollack, and then butcher and nearly decapitate the man after snapping every bone in the man's back? Much less scale one of the wooden chalices to reach the second floor of the Pollack's exclusive castle estate in Knoxville? And that was in addition to brutally slaughtering a pair of armed Knoxville policemen a day earlier in the basement of a storage building located across from the McClung Museum on UT's campus.

The only substantial link to him for either crime came from the desecrated remains removed from Cades Cove five weeks earlier. That, and the fact he'd lost his temper with Elaine Pollack, the professor's now widowed wife over the phone. Even so, not a single shred of physical evidence connected him to the three deaths. It made him furious about the situation. Meanwhile, precious time had been lost in searching for Hanna. He only allowed himself to think about the unjust charges, not her likely fate. Better to deal with that later, away from here.

Without his old friend, Sheriff Butch Silva, present to vouch for his character and straighten this mess up, all he could do was wait. Helpless. Out of town for Christmas, the sheriff wasn't due back until Friday. It was the very reason the arraignment had been pushed back until then, according to Deputy Jeremy Brown, Sheriff Silva's trusted assistant. Brash, arrogant, and hardheaded, Deputy Brown's worst trait was his open disdain for John's race and heritage. Even if the man hadn't said anything, the hurtful thoughts discerned through John's sentient gifts revealed what the man truly felt toward the Cherokee race and the indigenous peoples who settled America.

Jeremy Brown went home earlier, leaving two other deputies and a dispatcher on duty. The last time anyone came through the jail to check on the occupants happened roughly an hour ago, around midnight. That deputy, a young brunette woman who briefly glanced into John's cell, finished her walk-through and promptly exited the cellblock. The main overhead lights were turned off after her visit, since almost all of the incarcerated tenants were asleep.

John wasn't sure if he could sleep at all, due to rampant thoughts and unanswered questions. He laid down on one of the cell's cots and waited for sleep to come, or more likely the dawn's light.

While starting to drift off, he heard the door at the end of the hall open. Unlike the previous instances, when the jail attendant left the door open until their tour of the cells was finished, whoever shuffled into the hallway closed the door behind them.

He sat up quietly in the bed to listen to the progress of the visitor slowly moving down the hall. He didn't feel frightened, but every nerve stood on edge, quickened by anticipation. Something about the footsteps and presence as it steadily approached the end of the hall to his cell seemed familiar. Unlike the deputies, this particular visitor didn't stop to check on anyone else.

John debated whether or not to get up and approach his cell's barred entrance. Especially once the shuffling figure reached the edge of the cell next to his. The visitor's shadow extended to the cold cement floor in front of him, eerily misshapen in the muted glow of the soft security lights along the hallway. While pulling his legs over the edge of his cot, in preparation to stand and investigate the mysterious person standing less than twenty feet away, a whispered voice addressed him in his native tongue.

"Ayasdi igvyi... golisdi."

He could only make out most of what was said, until the voice repeated the message again.

Seek first to understand.

"Understand what?" John wondered aloud, searching his mind for a possible meaning, and to confirm the owner of the voice, as it seemed *very* familiar.

"Heyatahesdi 'Adatlisvi Awi inage ehi."

No one had addressed John like this since a youngster, using the Cherokee version of his name, which helped him identify who it was standing nearby.

Be careful, Running Deer.

"Ududu?" John cautiously asked, as he whispered his response to the mysterious voice. *Grandfather?*

"...Tali Awohali Atloyasdi."

John smiled for the first time since Christmas Eve, and like a small child about to meet Santa, he jumped off the cot and moved as quickly as he could to the far-right corner of his cell. Still several feet away from where the mysterious visitor stood in the hall, the name delivered to him by the raspy whisperer belonged to the one person who could possibly aid his fight against the anisgina who had taken his beloved Hanna. His grandfather, Two Eagles Cry.

"Ududu!" John cried out, loud enough for one of the other inmates down the hall to stir.

He waited for the man to roll over in his cot before continuing his conversation. Lowering his voice, John addressed him again. The shadowed figure took three steps closer to where he stood with his face pressed against the cold steel bars of his cell.

After John asked a few more questions to confirm the truth of his grandfather's presence, the two quietly conversed together for the next several minutes. John struggled with certain words he had not used or heard since childhood, but his grandfather remained patient with him. Two Eagles Cry advised him how to successfully battle the entity waging war against his family. His last admonishment was for his grandson to call upon all of his ancestors to battle the anisgina and banish it to the dark world beyond the Three Blood Rivers.

John Running Deer tried once more to get a better glimpse of his grandfather's asgina, or spirit, asking for him to move closer. John longed to see him clearly—to be near him again, as he was elk hunting in Kentucky when his grandfather passed away, shortly after John's sixteenth birthday. He declined the request, tenderly telling John that in due time he would see him again, leaving him with one last word of encouragement before shuffling down the hallway.

"Ulanigide!"

It was the last thing John heard him say, and the shuffling sound ceased before it reached the exit. The word and its meaning repeated in his head after he lay on his cot, again wondering if he'd find the restful sleep his body, mind, and soul desperately needed. Or, would he continue to lie awake and watch the dawn's faint light peer through his cell window?

Ulanigide!... Be Strong!... Ulanigide!... Be Strong!...

If only it was that simple.

Chapter Twenty-three

"Are you sure you're okay with doing this?"

David accosted Miriam upstairs in the hallway, Thursday morning. She finished booking an afternoon flight for the entire family to Knoxville, Tennessee. The key factor in making the deal work was the availability of a hotel suite or chalet in nearby Gatlinburg. Neither she nor David believed they would find either available, since Christmas season is a very busy vacation time for the famed Smoky Mountain resort town.

"I can call Evelyn back and tell her that we can't make it."

"We're going, David."

She carried a notepad in hand with the flight and accommodation details, briefly looking at him before moving into their bedroom. Her suitcase and toiletry bags lay open upon the bed and were almost full. Her smile was tense, lacking the normal warmth and allure.

"This must be what we're supposed to do," she said, her tone businesslike. She had her back to him as he stood in the doorway. "Everything has fallen into place for this to happen. The resort in Breckenridge canceled without a fee, and the canceled trip relieved Jan, so she can spend time watching over Sara. Then we got a great deal on the chalet in Gatlinburg, which was a last-minute cancellation by some other family—plus an affordable flight. It all makes sense."

True, David thought. Everything had fallen into place. Even Miriam's partners at Littleton Children's Clinic volunteered to handle the majority of her New Years Eve appointments next week. And the two patients who declined had graciously agreed to reschedule for the following week. He assumed getting out of the Breckenridge deal would be the easy part and everything else would be difficult, if not impossible. It turned out to be just the opposite. In the end, his buddy, Mark Stone, let him cancel without penalizing him. He left it open for David and his family to rebook the reservation at a later time, perhaps in early spring.

Vacationing in Gatlinburg now looked like a potentially fun time for Ruth and the kids, and possibly for Miriam and him—provided they were able to help Evelyn get John out of jail and somehow locate Hanna. It brought to mind two things that made him dread the trip. Number one was Miriam's coolness, which started right after the call from Evelyn last night. He'd already tried unsuccessfully to get her to tell him what was up, but she refused to talk about it. He suggested repeatedly they forego the trip out east, and stick to their original plan of spending the weekend in the Rockies.

He would've greatly preferred telling Evelyn no, despite John's dire situation, rather than deal with Miriam's cold-shoulder. After working very hard the past several months to fix the waning passion in their marriage, he wasn't about to let it disintegrate now. Especially when it appeared the only reason it might happen was because he relented to Evelyn's request to immediately come to John's aid.

David could tell it had something to do with the way in which Evelyn pleaded, and his willingness to come to her rescue. Still, Miriam's immediate cool response after she listened to the conversation surprised him. It wasn't like her to act so insecure. The only time he'd ever seen her show any jealousy in their relationship, was shortly after they first met in college, roughly seventeen years ago. He felt uncomfortable confronting her, just in case it wasn't a jealous impulse after all.

The second thing bothering him was the prospect of facing the entity on its home turf. His thoughts were drawn to the last time, back in October, when he was forced to deal with Allie Mae's angry ghost—a fearsome wraith fueled by the entity's quieter wrath. She almost killed David. How much worse was the situation now, since the more powerful spirit seemed seriously angered at him and John?

Adding to the concern was a dream he had last night, about Norman Sowell. Norm died just before Halloween, and David still grieved over the loss of the best friend he ever had, next to Miriam. Ironically, the previous nocturnal visit he received from Norm came on the eve of his first return trip to Tennessee in October, after David decided he would do whatever it took to make things right with Allie Mae. That visit from Norm was eerily similar to last night's vision. Norm had plenty to say about this trip—much more than the last time they met—and he warned David *not* to go back.

In David's dream, Norman Sowell III looked like he usually did when he was among the living. Dressed in an Armani suit with his jet-black hair combed stylishly, his brilliant blue eyes and gorgeous smile flashed as if they belonged to a movie star. David thanked God, since in the last dream, Norm appeared as a disfigured and grotesque corpse, left in the afterlife to suffer the same agony and humiliation Allie Mae delivered when he died. Grateful for the new vision of Norm, David could finally replace that gruesome picture with a good one.

"I think it's a bad idea, bro," Norm told him in the dream. He stood next to his desk in the posh office that had since been assigned to a new corporate attorney at Johnson, Simms & Perrault, named Stacey Wallace. Blonde, petite, and with great legs.... Surely, she would've been another target for Norm's insatiable lust, if he had known her.

"Yeah, I'm not crazy about the idea either," David agreed. "But, John needs me, man. He was there when I needed him, and I sure as hell can't let him down."

Norm eyed him pensively, while puffing on a cigarette that wouldn't be allowed inside the remodeled grand Victorian mansion where he used to work. He leaned against the front edge of the desk.

"John's a good man," Norm observed. "I can tell you're quite fond of him. He feels the same toward you, too." He exhaled a long stream of smoke rings.

"Well, then, I guess it's best that I go out there and help him," said David. He sat down in one of the plush chairs in front of the desk, the one closest to Norm. "If I don't go, who else is going to help him against this thing?"

A slight smile tugged at the corners of Norm's mouth.

"What?" David asked, indignantly.

He debated whether or not to pick up a cruise ship vacation brochure lying on a small table next to the chair. The ship on the cover appeared to move through the ocean's waves, which made him pause to look closer. The image proved stationary once he brought it up to his eyes, and he later recalled that moment as when he realized the experience was a dream.

"I'm serious, Norm. It's not like *you* can do anything about it, right?"

Norm's smile faded, and he walked to the window next to his desk. David remembered the spectacular view of the downtown skyline Norm enjoyed each day from his office. Only now, the other side of the window was very dark, similar to looking out on a blackout at midnight. The darkness seemed impenetrable.

"No, you're correct. There's nothing I can do for your friend." Norm's voice became a mere whisper as he gazed into the blackness. "She might free me, in order to help you out, David…. But *he* sure as hell won't."

"Who are you talking about?" David sat up straight in his chair.

"*She* and *he*, David," Norm replied, turning to face him. His handsome face was emotionless, like a doll or mannequin's. However, his eyes glowed like sapphire flames. "Allie Mae? Remember? The nice hillbilly lass who impaled me on the fountain in the lobby of this very building?"

"Yeah, like I'd ever forget." David grimaced. "I guess you don't get around much over here, do you, my friend? Because if you did, you might've noticed she was about to send me over to join you just a couple of months ago after I returned to Tennessee!"

"Yes. I suppose it was bad for you as well," Norm replied, the depth of sadness in his voice sharp enough to cut through David's heart, and he cringed. "I had hoped to follow your progress to Gatlinburg, where I heard you faced her. Obviously, since you're still among the living, you succeeded in forcing her spirit from your world. That might explain why I was allowed to leave her prison… to return here and regain some semblance of who I used to be…. "

His voice trailed off and he looked around the room, confused and seemingly unable to recognize the surroundings. He shook his head when he noticed David again, sitting less than ten feet away from where he trembled next to the window.

"*He* is calling," Norm spoke into the air above him, shifting his gaze as if following an invisible presence hovering beneath the ceiling. "Soon he'll be here. It's best that you call this whole thing off before you, Miriam, and your kids get hurt."

"What do you mean?"

Before Norm could answer, his body began to disintegrate, becoming a swirl of tiny glowing particles that were sucked into a swirling stream moving through the window. As it did, it was absorbed by the encroaching darkness. Desperate, David tried to grasp what was left of Norm, but it slipped easily through his fingers.

"Gotta go, bro!" shouted Norm's voice from just beyond the window. "It's too dangerous to stick around. There's no way in hell I'm going back with him—it was bad enough the first time! You need to stay the hell away from him, too, David! Don't go to Tennessee, man—do NOT leave Colorado!"

"Norm, *wait!*"

David tried to wrap his arms around the faint mist, feeling only iciness slice through his arms and hands. The mist quickly dimmed and disappeared, while David called frantically for Norm to come back. Meanwhile, an even deeper chill descended from the ceiling, and before it reached where he stood, he awoke with a start in the warm bed he shared with Miriam. She stirred lightly and turned over, mumbling softly in her sleep. That was around 1:00 a.m., nearly ten hours ago.

"David? David!... Did you even hear *anything* I just said to you?"

He'd been so busy thinking about the dream that he missed most of what Miriam talked about during the past few minutes. Something about what to bring with them for the trip, and something else about what she and Auntie talked about at breakfast. In short, he had no idea what she said and was now headed for a deeper world of shit if unable to repeat what she'd just told him.

"I caught most of it," he began, a weak response, but one he hoped bought him time to think harder. *What the hell did she say?* "I guess I'd better get started on packing, too."

Miriam was halfway done packing her bags. David hoped she would appreciate his focus on grabbing a suitcase and overnight bag out of the closet and immediately getting busy with the same task. For the moment, she regarded him evenly as he brushed by.

"What time again do we need to be on the road to the airport?" He hoped this moved him further from his transgression.

"We need to leave by noon," she replied.

He glanced at the clock on his nightstand, which gave the current time as 11:19 a.m.

"Don't think changing the subject will excuse the fact you didn't hear a damned thing I said just now!"

She retrieved the last items needed for the trip from the vanity in the bathroom, and placed them in her toiletry bag on the bed. She closed it.

"I *was* listening!" he replied, getting angry.

"Oh, yeah? Then what was I talking about?" She smirked knowingly, locking the bag and her suitcase. "I'm waiting, Mr. 'I *was* listening'."

"Well, you were talking about the nice visit with Auntie this morning and what you two have planned for when we get to Gatlinburg. You then talked about the chalet we're renting for the next five days."

Not bad, he decided, despite his growing irritation with her coolness. From her initial look after he finished, he thought he might get lucky.

"It's for six days, which I told you twenty minutes ago. As for the conversation with your aunt? We talked about your family growing up in Chattanooga, since you're so reluctant to share *anything* about *that* with me and the kids!"

She shook her head in disgust, and turned to leave the room.

"Hey, darlin'—I'm sorry. Okay?"

He reached out to stop her from leaving the bedroom without a hug. She eluded him, easily stepping away.

"Just don't dally up here, David," she advised, disappearing into the hallway. "Ruth is making a quick lunch for us all downstairs, which should be ready in a few minutes. Like I said, we need to be on the road by twelve o'clock."

Her tone sounded perturbed. It took all of his resolve not to pursue her and demand she tell him what was up with her shitty attitude. His most recent blunder stopped him, and he regretted not paying better attention to what she said. He would've, if not for that goddamned dream.

"Thanks a lot, Norm," he mumbled.

Without further delay he finished packing. He grabbed the bags and hurried downstairs. David wasn't about to push his luck with his wife's mood.

Chapter Twenty-four

Evelyn sat on the other side of the clear, thick glass supported by a light steel mesh running through it. Not that the window needed it, being bullet proof and all, as part of the latest addition to the recently remodeled wait area at the Sevier County Jail.

"Grandpa, you look *terrible!*" she gasped, as she watched John sit. "You look like you haven't slept for days!"

She started to weep, placing her spread-open palms on the glass. He leaned toward the window and placed his palms against hers. Only the three-inch-thick glass plate separated their connection.

"You shouldn't worry so much about your grandpa—I'll be fine," he assured her, speaking into the intercom. Smiling weakly, he glanced toward the female guard who escorted Evelyn into the visiting area. An attractive blonde, she leaned against the wall next to the room's exit.

"You shouldn't even be here!" Evelyn seethed, casting an angry glance at the guard and a male deputy standing nearby.

"It'll all be taken care of by tomorrow, once Butch gets here," John assured her. He mustered a bigger smile, one she knew was intended to lighten his haggard appearance.

Although John would never admit it, Evelyn picked up his agenda from his thoughts. He wanted to impress two things on her before their twenty-minute visit ended. Number one, she needed to hold onto the hope Sheriff Silva would take care of the misunderstanding, and speak with the homicide detectives from Knoxville who interrogated John for nearly four hours about the triple homicide. Hopefully, Butch could make them see that they not only lacked any tangible evidence connecting John to this terrible crime spree, but also realize the arrest they coerced through the sheriff's department wasn't legal, and set him free.

The second thing he hoped to accomplish was to get her to immediately resume the search for Hanna. With each passing moment, the chances of rescuing her slipped away. Hanna didn't have long.

"You look like you could use some rest, too," he said, scooting his chair in as close as possible to the wooden ledge beneath the window. "Wasn't Shawn good enough company for you last night?" He grinned, wryly.

Evelyn nodded, her eyes sad, and hesitated before saying anything. She feared John might see her thoughts as easily as she had read his. She conceded it might be too late to shelter the anxiety and terror that she fought to keep hidden from his knowledge. Perhaps if he couldn't clearly define the cause for these feelings, she could keep the fact she didn't share his confidence Hanna would be rescued away from his awareness.

Hanna's dead. I was bathed in her blood that took me almost five hours to clean up. Sorry, Grandpa, but your prized black bear rug got the worst of it, and it'll need some special attention to get it cleaned. More than likely,

*you'll want to throw it away or bury it. It's rolled up for
now in the guestroom's closet, wrapped tightly within two
large trash bags that are taped together securely....*

"Shawn did his best to get me to play for most of the
night," she told him, making sure the protective shield she
envisioned for her other, more serious, thoughts remained
intact. She pushed aside all urges to grieve openly for her
beloved sister, and chuckled tiredly to further sell the
humor. "I think it's more of a situation where I'm not
good enough company for him."

"I see." He eyed her, thoughtfully, as if he just now
caught a mental glimpse of her inner war.

"I promise to keep looking for Hanna, Grandpa," she
assured him, moving to block his effort to steal a clearer
look inside her psyche. "I plan to include a deputy or two
from here, now that the required waiting period of twenty-
four hours has passed."

"Uh-huh." John's frown revealed only the depth of
worry weighing heavily upon him, as all of his other
thoughts were suddenly cloaked to her. "Just be sure that
Deputy Jeremy Brown isn't among the deputies that come
along with you."

"The blonde pudgy man with the handlebar moustache
and glasses?" she sought to confirm.

She already recognized the man's disdain for her and
her grandfather when she passed his desk, shortly after her
arrival. Unlike the other employees in the building,
Deputy Brown lacked any sensitivity she could pick up on.
Based on her past experiences, it usually meant an
elemental soul at best.

"Yes," said John, his tone hushed as if expecting her to confirm Deputy Brown as someone she had in mind to help with the search for Hanna.

"Grandpa!" she scolded. "You should know me better than that!"

"Sorry. I just want to make sure you avoid him." He nodded to acknowledge faith in her judgment, despite his protectiveness.

A moment of awkwardness followed.

"You should've allowed me to come here with you last night, after they arrested you," said Evelyn, breaking the silence. "How long did they interrogate you?"

"Deputy Brown kept me in his office for an hour and a half, until the detectives from Knoxville arrived." John frowned. "There were two of them, Detective James Russell and his partner, Thomas Calhoun. Like the warrant stated when I was arrested, they're investigating the University of Tennessee murders. I answered their questions from roughly ten o'clock last night until the detectives finally left to return to Knoxville around two this morning."

"Did they believe what you told them? Surely they realize you couldn't possibly have had anything to do with the murders." Evelyn fought to keep her emotions in check, despite the mere thought of what her grandfather had endured since last night incensed her.

John shifted in his chair, and glanced at the male guard nearby. As if he had something even more important to share, he leaned in closer.

"At first, I'm not sure that they believed my alibi, although one look at me surely told them that climbing up the trellis to the second floor of Dr. Pollack's mansion wasn't likely—for a man at my age, anyway," he chuckled sadly at the irony. "However, by the time the interview ended, I got the feeling they didn't think I killed any of those men—at least not alone."

"So, should I prepare myself for a visit by these detectives, since I guess that makes me your co-conspirator?" She sighed disgustedly.

"I'm not sure… probably all the more reason to get busy looking for Hanna again," he advised. "Stick to the areas about a mile or so around the cabin, unless you feel comfortable with whatever deputy comes along with you. I'm hoping to be out of here early tomorrow morning. My arraignment is at nine o'clock, unless Butch can get me out before then. If he does, then maybe the charges will be dropped, and I won't even have to go to the arraignment."

John nodded, as if he could picture what would actually happen Friday morning.

"I hope you're right, Grandpa," Evelyn said softly, her tone optimistic. "I'll go talk to the cute deputy I spoke to briefly when I first got here. I think I caught his eye, so maybe he'd be willing to help me look for Hanna."

She gave John a playful wink, and he laughed for the first time in her presence since Christmas Eve.

"I love you, Grandpa!" She got up from her seat and motioned to the guard, letting her know she was ready to leave. "Now, get some rest, and I'll see you tomorrow!"

"I love you too!" John called after her, as she walked over to the waiting room's exit. "Be careful!

* * * * *

John waited for Evelyn to disappear before slowly shuffling to the deputy waiting for him. His head low, he hid the streaming tears. The picture in his mind's eye was of his eldest granddaughter weeping as she sought the deputy she described toward the end of their conversation. The tears were in response to what she already knew about Hanna… something terrible had happened.

Chapter Twenty-five

"Well, would you just *look* at this place?" Ruth enthused, after she removed her long overcoat and laid it over a large leather sectional sofa facing an enormous stone fireplace.

She stood in the middle of the living room of the chalet rented by Miriam and David for the next week. The large central room to the chalet was a splendid design of rustic pine logs and smooth river stones from the region, along with the comfort of posh furniture and a theatre entertainment system.

Christopher and Jillian ran into the living room behind her, finishing a game of tag that began shortly after the family's rented Honda Odyssey pulled up to the modern log cabin, perched on top of a high hill on the eastern side of the town of Gatlinburg, Tennessee.

"You're it!" shouted Jillian, as she slapped her younger brother on the back.

Her voice echoed shrilly against the tall, vaulted ceiling. Christopher let out a squeal after getting caught from behind.

"Wow, Mom—this place is so *cool!*" marveled Tyler, as his eyes followed the gaze of his great aunt.

He laid down the bundle of suitcases he carried next to a curved breakfast bar separating the living room from the cabin's large eat-in kitchen. His eyes followed the height of the stone chimney culminating at the apex of the two-story A-frame building. Several tall windows on either side of the fireplace faced a gorgeous view of the Smoky Mountains, which faded quickly as the early evening darkness engulfed the surrounding snow-covered hills. To Tyler's right was a long hall, where three of the cabin's bedrooms sat. To his left was a spiral, wrought iron staircase leading to a loft with another bedroom and the chalet's billiard area.

Miriam soon followed into the living room, and David made his appearance shortly after. He dusted the snow from his boots as he brought in the last of the luggage, and two bags filled with groceries for the next few days.

"This *is* nice!" Miriam allowed a genuine smile of appreciation. She seemed pleased, despite weariness from a trip that had been planned in the morning and carried out in the afternoon.

"Well, it might not be Breckenridge, but I believe we'll be all right," added David, relieved by her new demeanor.

He worried her sullenness would ruin the dwindling holiday spirit. Hope remained that whatever recently caused her to grow distant could be remedied.

"Jill just found a snow saucer lying on the back deck— we can go sledding tomorrow!" Christopher excitedly pointed to Jillian, who stepped through the back door and onto the deck, moving to the purple sled leaning against a tarp-covered hot tub. The hot tub looked large enough to hold six adults at a time. "Is this like the cabin you and Mommy stayed in when you were here in October, Daddy?"

The joyful glow on Christopher's face, before he ran upstairs to join Tyler in checking out the loft and twin billiard tables, resembled the exuberance of Christmas morning. The looks of shock and embarrassment upon David and Miriam's faces were joined by an immediate hurt expression from Ruth. The tiptoed efforts to avoid revealing their fifteenth anniversary trip to Gatlinburg two months earlier had finally failed. She still smiled, although dimly, as she glanced at David. She stepped to the backdoor and peered outside.

"Hey, Auntie... I'm really glad that you're here with us," he told her, gently. He placed an arm around her waist.

For the moment, her attention was focused on the deck and Jillian's investigation of the hot tub. Jillian smiled and waved, and they responded in kind. David knew he only had a moment to try and repair the damage before Jillian came back inside, or Christopher and Tyler returned from the loft.

"I haven't been as good to you as I should've been for a long time, and I truly regret it," he continued, his tone hushed but sincere. "I promise to never disappoint you again in any way. You are *so* important to me, Miriam, and the kids. From the depth of my heart and soul, I'll do whatever it takes to make up for what I've done wrong in the past, Auntie. You'll never be alone again—I *swear* it!"

Ruth gazed up into David's face, studying his expression while her eyes filled with tears. Even though no direct apology had been offered, he hoped she would consider how things had changed for the better. Heck, the two of them hadn't been this close in nearly twenty years. He desperately wanted her trust—to believe in the promise he now made.

Ruth nodded, as if intuitively aware of his thoughts. She wiped her eyes and smiled, readily accepting his embrace when he reached out to hug her. She sobbed quietly in his arms, and he felt the urge to cry. But it wasn't until Miriam joined them, wrapping her arms lovingly around both of them that he gave in to the surge of emotions and let the stress and lingering pain of the past two months flow from him.

It was a healing moment, and all three wept together. Unfortunately, it served to dampen Tyler and Christopher's excitement. Returning to the main floor, they hoped to tell everyone about the four arcade game systems upstairs. Instead, they joined Jillian by the fireplace, after she quietly stepped inside the chalet. Despite their mom's assurances everything was okay, they looked warily at one another, perhaps wondering what unwanted surprise would come next.

* * * * *

"Are they all okay now?"

Tyler posed the question to Jillian as soon as she closed the back door and stepped outside to join him next to the hot tub, where he finished clearing the snow and ice from the tarp's surface. The last vestige of sunlight had slipped away, and the surrounding hills lay shrouded in darkness. If not for the snow clinging to most of the trees, they wouldn't have discerned much of anything beyond the deck's railing, other than the lights from a few neighboring chalets. It reminded him of when he was a cub scout, and David had taken him to a regional jamboree at the Garden of the Gods in Colorado Springs. It was real dark there, too... just not as spooky.

"Yep, everyone's okay," Jillian replied. "Auntie Ruth seems happier than when we were home in Colorado, and Mom and Dad are smiling at each other again—finally!"

She looked relieved, like the recent tense standoff between their parents worried her a great deal.

"Well, let's just hope it stays that way," said Tyler, his smile sly, which drew a giggle.

"Why do you think we really came out here?" she asked, growing serious.

The strange way her question echoed toward the woods was kind of creepy, and she seemed anxious to go inside.

"I take it that you don't believe we came out here because the ski trip in Breckenridge got canceled due to a problem with the lodge, huh?"

His smile turned impish, although he, too, didn't wish to linger outside on the deck—at least not right now. He hoped it would be more fun later tonight, when he and David got the hot tub revved up. He wasn't sure what his dad meant about "possibly waiting until tomorrow", other than he heard his mom say they planned to visit a friend named Evelyn after dinner.

"I've got a hunch it has to do with what happened to us back in October," he continued. "I heard Dad and Mom discussing Dad's friend, John Running Deer. Apparently, he's in jail for some reason, and it sounds like the shit we went through back in October and last week has been happening here too."

Jillian suddenly looked mortified, drawing an immediate sarcastic sigh from her brother.

"Please don't act like you've never heard anyone in this family say 'shit' before!" he chided, mindful to keep his voice low.

"I know that, Buster!" she retorted. "For your information, I'm *not* an idiot! I know all the dirty words and how to use them just as good as you can!"

"Sh-h-h! Keep your voice down, Jill!" he hissed

He looked anxiously toward the window closest to them. Ruth appeared to be reading a story to Christopher, while David and Miriam were busy getting dinner ready.

"Why would we come to a place where things are happening as bad as what's happened at home?" she asked, worriedly. It told him her look from a moment ago wasn't entirely in response to his choice of expressive language. "The Gatlinburg Strip sounds like fun, and there's some skiing here too. I just hope we have fun, and this turns out to be...."

"A good idea?" he finished for her when she hesitated. She affirmed with a nod. Tyler moved to the far corner of the hot tub and brushed the last of the crystallized snow from the tarp, watching it fall into the darkness beneath the deck. "The slopes around here would count as bunny trails back home, but sledding might be fun. At least there are some cool things to do upstairs... like lots of games to play, and a pool table and an electronic dartboard. We can have our own tournaments!"

He smiled to sell it, because he sensed she was more nervous about being here than she let on.

"That does sound like fun, and maybe you're right," she conceded, weakly returning his smile. "I'm going back inside... and you should come with me."

"I'll be there in a moment," he assured her, and turned to gaze out toward the darkness beyond the deck.

Tyler listened as Jillian limped to the back door, wondering if her chronic hip pain was worse in Tennessee than Colorado. With a soft grunt, she opened the back door and stepped inside. For a brief moment, the lively jazz CD David brought and Christopher's laughter poured outside, muted when Jillian closed the door. Without anything distracting him, Tyler quieted his breathing and focused all of his senses toward the darkened forest around him.

A slight breeze moved through the treetops, rustling snow-laden evergreen branches along with those from barren oaks and elms. His heightened senses detected a menace, one that caused him and Jillian to cast nervous glances toward the deck's perimeter earlier. He heard something faint and leaned forward to listen. It was a voice carried by the soft wind caressing his face with unearthly coolness.

"Why-y-y?... Why have you returned-d-d, oh lover-r-r?... My-y Zac-cha-r-r-ri-ah-h-h!"

Familiar with the voice, the memory of it often left him sleepless since he first heard it in October. It belonged to the wraith who haunted his house after following his parents to Colorado from Cades Cove—a location less than fifteen miles from this chalet, tucked away to the east, but in the same Smoky Mountain wilderness.

Allie Mae.

Tyler didn't reply to the voice. Instead, he hurried to the back door, almost tripping on an icy patch. By the time he was inside the sprawling resort cabin, the voice repeated itself, sounding like its owner crouched invisibly on the railing next to the hot tub. The message this time sounded menacing.

Fearing what he might see if he ventured another glance, he refused to look. Whether or not everyone had a good time in Gatlinburg, without a doubt this was a mistake—a terrible, misguided decision to come.

They weren't welcome. Allie Mae's ghost just said so.

Chapter Twenty-six

Evelyn stood on the back porch of her grandfather's cabin. Anxious, despite the bright glow from the porch light and the security lamps located in the rear of his property, last night's visitation remained fresh. Shawn's angry barks directed toward the shadowed edge of the adjoining woodland heightened her unease.

"Come on, boy—come here, *now!*" she urged, forcing herself to ignore the unfriendly presence she sensed glowering at her from the impenetrable darkness beyond the security lamps' reach. The wolf bones clanged noisily against one another on the defiled cedar tree.

Is it just the wind... or another warning?

A deep, inhuman moan emanated from the woods closest to her and Shawn. The dog whined with ears perked high, his aggression replaced by uncertainty.

"Shawn, get your ass over here!"

Evelyn ran and grabbed his collar. She slipped on the snow and her knee landed painfully on the frozen ground, but she managed to remove the leash. Meanwhile, the unseen menace approached, its crunching footsteps in the snow announced its intent.

Shawn nuzzled her, the coolness of his nose brushing across her face. When she stood up, they raced for the back door. Without looking behind, Evelyn opened the door in haste, shoving the dog inside. Only as she slammed the door shut did she see the ink-like shadow, its reach engulfing the area where she'd slipped a moment ago.

She locked the door and set the deadbolt, stealing a peek through the backdoor's curtain. Blackness filled her view, as if a giant void somehow replaced the porch. The glow from the porch light and the twin security lamps disappeared.

She backed away from the door and into the living room. Shawn followed, wrapping himself protectively around her legs. Unlike the night before, a false entreaty hadn't been delivered—the demon didn't attempt to hide its hostility. The last assault from the menace was hardly forgotten, as the faint smell of blood hung in the air, camouflaged by Pine-Sol and Febreze, and a glowing incense stick resting in its holder on the kitchen counter.

The day disappeared quickly after the visit with her grandfather that afternoon. She left him with her chin up and wearing the brightest smile she could muster. He needed it. His despair would deepen soon enough, once he learned the fate of Hanna. She intended never to tell him what happened, when the wicked entity slaughtered her sister—seemingly for its own amusement. She tormented herself with that realization all day, from the wee hours of the morning when she desperately sought to clean up the blood, tissue, and other fluids that surely came from Hanna's violated body.

But as she left the jail, her façade crumbled before the bevy of law enforcement officers crowding the jail's administrative offices. She could no longer prevent the deluge of tears and became visibly angry with herself. Fearing no one among them would take her seriously, a pleasant surprise came when the deputy she'd made eye contact with earlier approached her with a box of Kleenex. Deputy Chris Girard.

Cuter than handsome, with dark brown hair and sky-blue eyes, the deputy guided Evelyn to a secluded section in the building's main lobby. After she calmed down, she presented the proposal she promised her grandfather, and Deputy Girard agreed to accompany her to John's cabin to resume the search for her missing sister. By then, they'd shared a little about themselves. Evelyn's aspirations of becoming a civil engineer dedicated to serving the Cherokee nation impressed Chris, and he told her about his dream of someday joining the CIA.

Evelyn wondered if his intuitions would be strong enough to assure success as a CIA agent—especially after he seemed not to notice the distinct blood scent that hung in the air around the living room when they arrived at the cabin. Prepared to explain what happened the night before, even if it meant possible ridicule, he never broached the source for the acrid smell. Perhaps he acted coy, like a truly gifted detective might behave. Her intuitive insight told her that it wasn't so.

Maybe the fascination with her threw him off. His flirtatious comments became more assertive as the afternoon progressed. It made it easier for her to lead him on a shortened search for Hanna.

She's dead, damn it!

The last thing she needed? A drawn-out tour of a five to ten-mile radius of her grandfather's home with some would-be suitor. A more exhaustive search would come soon enough, with her grandfather, for his peace of mind. Silently, she prayed fervently his release from jail happened first thing tomorrow morning.

Conserving her energy, she limited the search with the deputy to a mere half-mile around the property. Chris Girard readily agreed—especially after finding the decaying wolf-shrine at the edge of John's property. Evelyn sensed how his heart froze once they stumbled upon it, like his soul understood the evil that tortured and killed the overmatched canine predator. Afterward, he led the way to the cabin, eager to trade the grisly sight for some tea and leftover Christmas cookies.

He left around four-thirty, and Evelyn feared he would've stayed longer had she not agreed to give her Knoxville home phone number. A nice guy to go out with sometime, she didn't desire another serious relationship until after graduate school. She waved goodbye to Chris and watched his cruiser drive away, until she could no longer make out the dormant emergency lights.

She watched a steady stream of reality shows on television until sunset, an hour ago. As the last of the day's light disappeared behind the western horizon, she prepared a small meal for herself, planning to share it with Shawn. Having taken care of his personal business outside, his first angry tirade erupted. The shrillness of his barks caught her attention. She ran outside to check on him, and from that moment until now, the prospect of a quiet evening had been lost.

Evelyn recited the prayers taught to her by her grandfather as a little girl. She walked carefully around the living room as she spoke, glancing at the ceiling, and ready for another gruesome event to appear. While speaking the words in Cherokee instead of English, she added two more logs to the fireplace.

So far so good. When the flames and warmth from the fire grew to full strength, she lit a bundle of sage and took it throughout the cabin, along with an evergreen swig she used to sweep out the negative energy from yesterday. She took her time, since she already secured the doors and windows, moving methodically through the main floor and upstairs loft.

When she returned to the living room, Shawn sat facing the back door. His ears were perked up, intently listening to something. He didn't whine or growl, which she took as a good sign. She also listened, more closely.

Faint and almost undetectable at first, a new rhythmic sound surrounded the cabin. It was like chirping crickets, and was accompanied by an eerie scratching noise that made her skin crawl. The strange concoction rose in volume to where Shawn howled and it forced her to cover her ears.

Just before the noise became unbearable, it suddenly ceased. Evelyn's heart beat madly within her chest, hearing only the TV's soft drone and the occasional popping from the hickory logs aglow on the hearth. She stepped over to the coffee table and picked up the television's remote, using it to shut off the TV.

"Tali Wo:-ya Alisaladisgv."

"Huh? Who said that?"

She whirled around, not knowing where the genderless voice originated. It surrounded her. After what happened last night, she realized the dream catchers and spirit chasers covering the walls were of no use against this powerful anisgina. In defiance of her grandfather's magic, the entity seemed capable of moving in and out of the cabin's interior undeterred. The only thing it couldn't do, it seemed, was fully manifest inside the cabin. Last night's attack could've been worse, since other than the horribly mortifying experience of being drenched in Hanna's blood, the spirit remained unable to reveal itself. Something prevented it from happening, and Evelyn could only speculate as to why.

The invisible source for the voice addressed her again, only this time a soft breeze caressed Evelyn's left cheek… the spirit's breath?

'Two Doves Rising'—that's my Cherokee name…. How in the hell did it figure that out?

It made her very uneasy. She'd taken extra precautions to cloak her thoughts since shortly after her arrival for Christmas break, at the first sign of the entity's escalated anger. There was power in a person's sacred name, and she previously worried the spirit might seek her out following the desecration of its tomb. Until recently, the ancient grave lay hidden for centuries beneath sacred soil near John Oliver's cabin in Cades Cove. What chilled her most? The anisgina used the Cherokee pronunciation of her native name rather than the English translation.

Evelyn chastised herself for underestimating the depth of the demon's anger, and its unquenchable thirst for revenge. She also feared for the excavation teams from UT, along with Peter Kirkland. Walter Pollack had already been murdered. She could still hear the professors' disdain, calling her warnings to suspend the project a self-serving crusade. She regretted her unwillingness to fight harder, ignoring the initial dread that had overwhelmed her in November.

"Let-t-t... me-e-e-e ... i-n-n-n-s-s-i-i-i-d-d-d-de!"

The voice turned raspier, reminding her of the great blues singers of the 1940s that her great grandfather, Spotted Wolf, John's father, preferred to listen to when she was a young girl, shortly before he passed to the other side.

"Get the hell away from here!" she sternly responded. She bravely moved through the living room with her eyes closed and arms folded across her chest. Guided by her mind's eye and her gut instincts, she followed an invisible corkscrew trail that widened toward the room's perimeter.

The voice chuckled, as if amused by her determination to stand her ground. In response, she resumed the Native American chant she used earlier, retracing her steps from a moment ago and repeating the entire process anew.

As it had the night before, the entity launched a derisive tirade at Evelyn, shrieking madly with a strange mixture of taunts in several languages simultaneously. She sought to locate the spiritual vortex that allowed the anisgina to sneak in to the cabin undetected. It was *too* damned easy for the demon. If she could push it out and permanently close the doorway, the cabin could be a safe haven once more.

"Anagisdi Utsatina!"

Evelyn uttered the command evenly, careful to focus all of her energy through her mouth and chest as she spoke the words. If she hadn't made it clear to the spirit before, her command to 'Go away!' better be understood now.

A tremor swept through the cabin, and every shiny surface in the cabin shook—whether actual mirrors or mirrored objects. A misty image began to form within the stainless-steel surface of the gas stove, and when she glanced at the large mirror on the wall next to the front window, another similar image emerged. She watched in terror as the image solidified. The garish wraith of a Cherokee warrior gazed menacingly. Its eye sockets were soulless, empty black holes.

"Oh, Shit!"

"Ulisgolvtanv Itsula ayv Hawinaditlv!" *Let us in!*

Evelyn couldn't move, torn between fleeing the cabin and holding her ground long enough to find some way to keep the spirits out. Surprised there were more than one, until then she only sensed the main menace. Her intuitions always provided the upper hand when needed. She didn't know what to do next. What other threat awaited inside the breached fortress?

"Ulisgolvtanv Itsula ayv Hawinaditlv!"

A swirling chorus of voices sounded in unison from inside the cabin. Evelyn's knees grew weak and she thought she would collapse. Her guides touched her, if only long enough to deliver a brief image to her terrified mind.

Cover the mirrors. Do it now!

With Shawn staying close, she ran to the other side of the fireplace and down the hallway to the linen closet. Ignoring the growing din, she grabbed a handful of blankets and towels large enough to cover every mirrored surface in the cabin. Moving to cover each one, she started in the living room since the warrior in the mirror seemed the angriest, and escalated its threats to include graphic details of how it would tear her tongue out and slowly gouge her eyes, clearing her sockets with its bloody knife until they looked like his. The spirit's taunts continued until she veiled the mirror with an afghan her grandmother knitted long ago.

Taking courage from the first conquest, she moved through the kitchen and the rest of the main floor, covering every reflective surface—including all three televisions—before climbing the stairs to the last mirror in the loft. As soon as she covered the mirror's surface, the verbal threats stopped. Nothing more happened until after she returned downstairs.

When she poured herself a glass of wine from the kitchen, she became aware of yet another noise. More familiar, different than anything she recently endured, but also one that occurred the past weekend, during her and Hanna's first night with their grandfather.

It probably started before she even grabbed the bottle of merlot, or the distant whistle may have been too subtle for Evelyn's tired mind. Perhaps her psyche filtered the sound in an instinctive attempt at self-preservation. Regardless, once the noise reached the tree line of the northern forest bordering John Running Deer's property, it grew much louder. The thing that sounded like an immense swarm of angry hornets swiftly descended upon the cabin, slamming into the walls and roof like an ungodly hailstorm, tearing away slats and shingles.

She immediately grabbed Shawn and moved into the hallway. It was the safest place within the cabin, should a tornado ever strike—and this certainly qualified as one in her mind.

"Stay with me, boy," Evelyn told him, as he tried to run into the living room and his preferred spot behind the couch. "It will pass. We'll be safe—I promise!"

Similar to the previous assaults on the cabin's structure, it finally waned in strength. When it did, she led Shawn into the living room, where they sat on the floor next to the fire, anxiously looking around. Every creak in the fifty-year old structure drew a fearful glance.

The sexless voice returned, cackling gleefully just below the ceiling.

"Ah-h-h, poor Evelyn! Po-o-r-r-r Two Doves Ris-s-s-i-in-g-g! You're mi-i-i-ne-e-e! This place can not protect you... leave with me NOW-W-W!"

"NO!" she shouted back at the invisible presence, mustering her courage despite the acute weariness from the spirit's endless antagonism. "Get the hell out of here!"

"Kstaquadu 'ga, Tali Wo;-ya Alisaladisgv!" ~ *Go with me, Two Doves Rising!*

"Adanvsdi Ayv Uwasv!" Evelyn held her ground in telling the entity to leave her alone, despite the hysterics threatening to overtake her at any moment.

"KSTAQUADU 'GA!" The anisgina's anger at being defied was immediate. Its voice much deeper, it thundered like a Vulcan god determined to enforce its will.

"NO-O-O!... Just go away—PLEASE!" she cried, cowering on the floor beside the fireplace. Shawn hovered nearby, snarling. His gaze remained trained on the spirit's otherwise invisible path as it moved through the air above. *"Just GO!... Please, PLEASE, leave me alone!"*

Exhausted physically, spiritually, and most definitely emotionally, she wept upon the cabin's cold wooden floor, no longer listening to the escalated threats from the spirit as it drew near. Nor did she acknowledge its cackled laughter and gleeful digs at her current state once it realized she reached the breaking point.

It seemed like at least an hour was spent like this, although the exact period of time remained a mystery. The entity's taunts eventually faded, becoming infrequent, and dissolved altogether when the doorbell rang. Startled, she sat up and looked toward the door. Shawn, too, sat up, barking loud as he approached the door. Unlike before, his tail wagged. Two shadowed figures stood near the front door. One tried to peer inside the cabin through the front window, while the other, shorter, figure waited for the first one by the door.

Evelyn prepared for another ploy by the entity and its attendant spirits. She quietly stepped into the kitchen and grabbed a long carving knife, wondering what good it would do if the visitors weren't of this world. But it couldn't hurt if it turned out they were.

Armed and ready, she stepped to the door. When she peered through the peephole, she frowned. Shawn's barks became more excited, and Evelyn offered one last prayer for protection. She cautiously opened the door.

Chapter Twenty-seven

"You know... this could wait until tomorrow morning."

David looked at Miriam. Her attention was glued to the dim road before the Odyssey, and she barely acknowledged his words. She squinted in a concerted effort to see through snow flurries and entered the main drive running through the Smoky Mountains National Park. When they watched the Weather Channel back at the chalet, the local report called for six to ten inches of new snowfall by morning.

Even Ruth suggested they should wait until daylight returned before making the trek. But, the strange coolness that had taken over Miriam's persona the night before emerged again, easily pushing aside her warmth and more demure nature. It made David's aunt do a double take, as until that moment, only David and the kids had witnessed the sternness so unlike her.

It gave David the first inkling her reaction and suspicion from the night before, in regard to his response to Evelyn Sherman, was more than a jealous whim. The thought became reinforced less than half an hour ago, when she insisted on driving immediately to John Running Deer's cabin—even after several fresh attempts to call Evelyn failed to get past severe static or an annoying fast-busy signal.

"It's too late to turn back," Miriam tersely advised.

He loathed her attitude, but fought the temptation to linger long on it. After all, in his mind she'd always be the love of his life... he just hoped life with her would be lovable again, and soon. If he could cut out the past twenty-four hours, including the phone call from Evelyn that started the whole uncomfortable business, Nirvana or at least some semblance of peace and normalcy would be back in his life.

Miriam paused to look over at David, her smirk making him think his thoughts were an open book.

"Evelyn sounded like she couldn't wait much longer, remember?"

Miriam's tone right then? It bore a strange mixture of concern, aloofness, and sarcasm. It was likely the end result of a long day, with a hefty dose of stress and a lack of sleep thrown in for good measure. Coupled with the phone conversation she alluded to concerning Evelyn, he recognized the wisdom in keeping his mouth in check. Better to go along with her plan for tonight's visit to John Running Deer's cabin, and go from there.

David reflected on how the evening started. Everyone enjoyed the rib eye steaks he prepared on the chalet's indoor grill. Miriam helped him prepare everything else, and they had even paused to nuzzle and kiss for a moment while setting the dinner table.

The mood began to change after the evening meal, when Christopher wanted to go outside with Tyler. Jillian offered to join them, but Tyler declined. He lashed out at his younger siblings as if the suggestion was instead an invitation to jump into a barrel of burning horseshit.

Ruth seemed aware of the potentially volatile confrontation brewing between the children, as well as Tyler's aversion to going back outside. Despite the frightening incidents that took place in Littleton, it was likely the first time she'd witnessed such a combination of unabashed anger and dire fear in any of the kids.

It made David very uncomfortable leaving the four of them alone in the chalet. Tyler had yet to reveal what unsettled him since that afternoon. Miriam normally would be the first one to take on the protective parental role. This time, however, she merely told their oldest son to remain brave until she and David returned. That alone surprised David, but then she also mentioned they might not get back until the next morning, and had him hurriedly pack an overnight bag while she took a moment to comfort the younger kids.

"Hopefully, Evelyn's actually at the cabin when we get there," said David, casually.

He was unsure how to approach anything that dealt with John's eldest granddaughter. Miriam's response was a positive nod to affirm she hoped the same thing.

"So, you do remember how to get there. Right?"

The road into the park had become icy, and it surprised David it was even open. He noticed the barred gates on either side of the narrow highway, which could be closed at any time. Of course, the road runs all the way through to North Carolina, so closing it would present problems for other travelers relying on the thoroughfare to get them to the other side of the Smokies. Regardless, he preferred traveling along the lonely stretch in the safer light of day. No use arguing about it now.

"The dirt road we'll turn on is coming up ahead… right around this bend, I think," he advised.

He joined her in squinting to see through the windshield, peering into the thick darkness. The headlights provided only faint illumination of the forest on either side of the road.

"What do you mean by 'I think'?" Her response seemed more worried than sarcastic. "You said you remembered how to get there!"

"Yeah, I do remember," he replied, determined to remain calm and not be drawn into a verbal joust he'd surely lose—either factually or emotionally, and frankly either way was just as bad. "But, that was in the full light of day, when I could actually see the landmarks that point to the correct road."

"That's just frigging great!" she whispered, shaking her head while she leaned closer to the windshield.

He did the same, patting her arm once he thought he saw something familiar in the headlight beams' glow.

"There—that's it."

"Are you sure—*what the hell?*"

A sudden gust of wind slammed into the Odyssey, almost pushing them off the road. Surprised, Miriam let out a frightened gasp and briefly lost control on the pavement's slick surface. The vehicle careened from side to side and swerved into a shallow ditch on the right side of the road. They were jerked forward in their seats.

"Are you okay?" Worried for her welfare, he turned on the front dome light.

She looked okay, although a little unnerved. He motioned to take over for the rest of the trip, but she waved him off.

"I'm fine," she said, her tone abrasive. But the glance she shot him was softer, as if she realized her response was severe. "I should be okay… as long as we're getting close to John's cabin."

"It's just ahead… beyond that advisory sign," said David, pointing to the snow-covered signboard detailing the mileage to several park destinations, including Cades Cove. "You'll turn right, and it's just a few miles south of here."

She responded to his confidence, and began to pull out of the ditch and onto the road. The rear right tire was stuck, spinning freely while sending a shower of muddy snow and ice behind the van. Despite trying to maneuver the gears back and forth in drive and reverse, the vehicle stayed put.

"Let me get out and push," he offered. "Just keep an eye out for my signal on when to gun it."

He didn't wait for a reply, knowing there was no other way out of this situation. Hell, it wasn't like they could count on a park ranger or policeman to come to the rescue at this late hour. And, if one showed up, he figured they'd probably get ticketed for being on restricted park property.

He stepped out, zipping his parka when another chilled gust greeted him. The footing tricky, he somehow made it to the rear of the minivan without landing on his ass. The right side of the Odyssey's back end leaned over the ditch, leaving the tire barely visible. David motioned to Miriam, while she watched from her side-view mirror. He began to rock the rear of the vehicle while she hit the gas in rhythm with his efforts.

It took a few minutes to finally make some progress while being careful not to drive the tire any deeper into the rut. Their surroundings were desolate and creepy, and it started getting colder. It was especially noticeable when the wind picked up again.

He became aware of footsteps crunching through the snow, approaching the minivan from the deep shadows on the other side of the road. He saw Miriam's attention drawn to the noise as well, since she had the driver-side window rolled down in order to better communicate with him.

"Why-y-y-y are ya here, Billy-y-y Ra-a-y-y-y?"

The voice sounded hollow and at the same time weirdly sultry... an unsettling combination. But it was also familiar, and one he hoped to never, ever hear again after what happened two months ago.

Allie Mae McCormick.

"Why-y-y-y did ya come back, again-n-n-n?"

The voice sounded less sultry and more menacing, its owner perturbed.

"David—get back in here! *Hurry!*"

Miriam's urgency spurred him on. One good push should do it. One last—.

"Go ba-a-ck-k! Back to yer home, Billy Ray-y-y-y!"

It sounded like the invisible owner of the voice now hovered in the middle of the road. Creaking ice on the road warned of footsteps coming closer to the back of the Odyssey where he pushed with all of his might to get the damned thing back on the road.

"Gun it, Miriam! Floor the van *now!*"

Bravely, he ignored the encroaching frigid presence while Miriam hollered '*I am!*' in response to his gruff command.

"*Le-e-e-av-v-v-ve h-e-r-r-e-e NOW-W-W!*" the spirit shrieked in his ear.

David recoiled, but seeing the tire finally grip a patch of earth below the snow and climb out of the ditch, he gave it one last push before scurrying to the passenger side door, swinging it open and jumping inside. Before he closed the door, he leaned his head out, facing the icy presence that pursued him stealthily from the rear of the vehicle.

"I can't!" he shouted defiantly. "My friend needs me, and there's nothing *you* can do to stop me! 'You hear me, Allie Mae? Leave me the hell *alone!*"

A heavy sigh filled the air.

"That was really *stupid* of you just now, David!" Miriam scolded, after she pulled the van back on the road and gave enough gas to get back up to a safe speed. She had rolled up her window and now glanced nervously around. "Didn't you learn *anything* from the last time we dealt with her?"

She shook her head while he glowered. He locked the passenger door, more as a distraction to keep things civil.

He didn't allow himself to think about what the wraith might attempt next. In the headlights' beam he soon saw the edge of the road heading south to John's place.

"The road's just ahead. Turn here!"

Miriam glanced one more time into the rearview mirror before making the turn. She gasped, almost sliding off the road again. David warily looked over his shoulder in response. A mist-like form pursued them, coming up fast, the bottom of the form bluish with a pair of porcelain-white feet hitting the ice-covered road in patted rhythm. He recalled the blue gown Allie Mae's spirit often appeared in, and when his mind understood that she now ran to catch up, he urged Miriam to floor the accelerator.

"Don't look anymore—just drive!"

Miriam looked at him with pleading eyes, as whatever hardness had seized her since last night finally seemed to be melting away.

"You've got to trust me, darlin'!"

She nodded, while eyeing him worriedly. But without looking back she raced down the road, careful to maneuver the road's curves smartly. He kept his eyes trained on the side-view mirror. When he could no longer make out the ghost's outline of the mist, and they had neared the fork that would take them to John's doorstep, he returned his attention to Miriam. Her knuckles were ghastly white from her tight grip on the steering wheel.

"Okay... we're almost there," he said, making sure his tone and delivery stayed confident and reassuring. "Turn here, and this road will take us right up to John's cabin."

The name of the road was Beaver Falls Trail, though only the 'Beaver' and the first two letters of 'Falls' were visible when the headlights flashed across the road sign. The rest was covered with snow. It was another iced-over dirt road, and Miriam squealed the tires as she pulled the vehicle onto it. She kept the pedal pinned to the floorboard, taking no chances for anything to catch them from behind.

John Running Deer's cabin came into view, illuminated by security lamps. Several lights were on inside the cabin. In all likelihood, Evelyn was there. Miriam parked the Odyssey next to Evelyn's sporty Nissan, and cut the engine. For a moment, they listened to the wind pushing flurried snowflakes against the windows.

"Let's not wait for Allie Mae to show up again," said David, drawing another worried look from Miriam.

Liking her frightened mood so much better than the disdain he'd dealt with lately, he hoped things would get cleared up once and for all when she saw there was absolutely nothing romantic going on between him and Evelyn. Hence, his readiness to go straight to the door.

"Yeah, that's a good idea," she agreed, allowing a deep sigh to escape before glancing one last time into the rearview mirror. "I suppose we should wait to take the bags with us." She opened the driver side door and jumped down.

"That would be my assumption," he agreed, joining her.

He recalled how warm and inviting the cabin had been when fighting for his life two months ago. John's home became David's safe-haven. Something had changed. He was pretty sure Miriam felt it, too, as she hovered close to his side as they climbed onto the front porch. She drew even closer as he rang the doorbell.

Shawn's barks greeted them, followed by an awkward few minutes listening to footsteps close to the door and move away before approaching the door again. Finally, Evelyn opened the door, after twice peering through the window's curtains.

"David?" she asked, as soon as she opened the door, shielding her eyes from the porch light's glare. "What are you doing here?"

"Uh… well, we came as soon as we could," he replied, curious as to why she would ask such a question. *What do you mean 'what are you doing here?' You begged me to come here, and as a result, my wife has been pissed as hell at me—THAT's what I'm doing here.* "Are you okay?"

He looked at Miriam, making sure he had approval before moving forward in the discussion.

"You must be Miriam," said Evelyn, warmly to Mrs. Hobbs. She opened the door, moving an object from her right hand to her left, kept hidden behind her back. She extended her free hand to Miriam, who shook it politely. "Oh, come on in—both of you."

Now that he had a better look at her, he noticed the dark circles around Evelyn's eyes—the tell-tale sign of a recent string of troubled nights. Her smile was almost as lovely as he recalled, but it had since been touched by sadness. He motioned for Miriam to go first and he followed. Shawn brushed against them both, wagging his tail.

"So what brings you to Gatlinburg?" asked Evelyn, closing the door and offering to take their coats.

Miriam looked puzzled as if sorting through some discrepancy between what she expected to find and the actual reality. David knew his look reflected the awkwardness he felt, since he couldn't predict how Miriam would react to him being anything beyond cordial to John's lovely granddaughter.

"You asked me to come here last night," he sought to confirm. She offered only a blank expression. "You were emphatic that I come here right away... so we brought the whole family. The kids and my aunt are holed up in a chalet in Gatlinburg."

Now Evelyn looked confused. "What are you talking about, David?"

"On the phone," he said, after trading perplexed glances with Miriam. "You called us late last night, and said John was in serious trouble and needed me. That's why we came here tonight."

"But, David, how can that be?" she asked, bewildered. She seemingly forgot about the carving knife she held behind her back, casually setting it down on a small table near the door, where John liked to keep his daily mail. "That doesn't make any sense."

"What? How so?" He was even more surprised. Miriam wore a similar expression to Evelyn's after she and David watched her set the knife down.

"Because it's impossible," said Evelyn to David, after glancing briefly at Miriam. "It's impossible because I've never called you—ever."

Chapter Twenty-eight

After the initial shock of being unexpected guests wore off, David and Miriam joined Evelyn in the living room, where they sipped freshly brewed coffee in front of a roaring fire. David recalled fondly, from his previous visit to the cabin, how he and John shared a long talk during the first night of his stay. He relaxed on the couch next to Miriam, watching a friendly rapport develop between her and Evelyn.

Evelyn explained the reason for the towels and blankets covering every reflective surface inside the cabin. Holding up fairly well emotionally, she told them what happened earlier. The entity's wiles and taste for violence far exceeded the frightful attacks brought against them by Allie Mae—which made David worry again about the wisdom of bringing his family. He took the opportunity to begin the description of what recently took place at their home in Littleton, allowing Miriam to share much of the information and filling in anything of importance she left out.

When he mentioned the odd acrid smell in the cabin, still detectable beneath the disinfectants and deodorizers, Evelyn could scarcely explain what caused it the night before, sobbing uncontrollably at the mention of Hanna's name. Grateful for Miriam's nurturing nature, she immediately rushed to Evelyn's side, where the two women cried together. Afterward, Evelyn felt comfortable enough to discuss the shower of Hanna's blood, when the sadistic spirit murdered her younger sister in her presence.

Convinced Hanna was indeed dead, Evelyn refused David's optimism that without a body it wasn't a certainty just yet. He did share her opinion that the spirit terrorizing the Hobbs' household was the very same one tormenting her family and also had murdered at least three other people—including two employees at the University of Tennessee. After speaking to John two days earlier about these crimes, David and Miriam recalled how quickly the news spread to Colorado, as the UT murders made it to the national headlines.

Evelyn advised that the entity went beyond the normal definition of evil, which only added to the mystery of what it sought. While possible it simply wanted to kill everyone associated with the desecration of its tomb in the ravine where he and Miriam had innocently celebrated their fifteenth wedding anniversary, she couldn't shake the feeling the demon was after something specific... something from her, and perhaps from them. Why else would they be duped into coming to Gatlinburg on such short notice?

When Evelyn described the hysterics the spirit would fall into, after she wouldn't give in to its demand to willingly let it inside the cabin, David immediately related it to how Evelyn's voice had sounded when he got the urgent call the night before. Coupled with the fact the entity had successfully impersonated Evelyn's Grandma Susanne, he marveled at its cunningness. He was especially chilled by its ability to pull upon his sense of obligation to John and, although she had yet to admit it, Miriam's jealous streak that had long-since been dormant, only to be awakened by the spirit's passionate impersonation of Evelyn as a desperate, lonely, and sexually vulnerable woman.

But, now… what could they do to defeat it, this fiend whose vileness and power seemed to grow stronger with each new day?

Upon Evelyn's insistence that they stay the night with her and not risk encountering the additional threat of Allie Mae's ghost along the deserted park roads, David retrieved their luggage. He did it before anyone could stop him, mustering his courage and with determination to move quickly, sprinting from the front door to the back of the Odyssey, grabbing the overnight bag and Miriam's toiletry case and locking the hatch in one seamless movement. He raced back to the front porch.

The tiny hairs along the base of his neck sprang to life just before he stepped through the door and into the cabin's warmth. He slammed it shut, securing the lock and deadbolt. But, not before catching a glimpse of something. Was it part of Allie Mae's death attire, the blue gown she favored from the turn of the twentieth century? Or, was it perhaps something else? All he knew for sure was that a purple shadow had crept swiftly toward the door behind him.

"David, what is it?" asked Miriam. "Did you see anything when you were outside?"

She got up from the couch and came to him. He peered through the curtain next to the door, spying at the outside world. The shadow was gone, or at least out of his direct view.

"I may have seen something, but I'm not sure." He wore a smirk he hoped would sell her on the notion he wasn't worried... at least not about that.

Evelyn got up from the recliner and walked to the same window, opening the curtain wide enough to get a good look at the porch and the front of the cabin. Her lack of caution with the window surprised him, in light of the spiritual beliefs she professed the last time. She had yet to reveal the fact she already conceded this aspect of the battle to the entity, and was focused instead on its struggle to materialize inside the cabin.

"What do you see?" he asked, pulling Miriam closer to him.

His wife looked up, and despite her uneasiness, he could see the love in her smile. Whatever had turned her heart against him earlier had finally been vanquished.

"Nothing," Evelyn replied.

She led them back into the living room. Before she sat in the recliner again, she retrieved her laptop from a backpack resting next to the chair. After powering up the device, she accessed the Internet through the cabin's satellite system.

"If we can find out some useful information before the spirit strikes again, it'll enhance our chances of surviving whatever it intends to bring next," she said, motioning for them to sit on the couch. "David, while you were outside,

Miriam mentioned the name it called itself when it pretended to be me last night on the phone. Let me see what I can find out about the name."

"Teutates," Miriam confirmed quietly. "That was the name spoken on the phone last night. You... I mean, your *voice* referred to the entity by that name and also described it as 'He Who Cannot Rest'."

"It's still hard to fully comprehend how clever this thing is, being able to disguise itself as pretty much anyone it chooses," observed David. "It makes you wonder if that's how it tricked Hanna into leaving the safety of this place. It seems the most plausible explanation to me, anyway."

Evelyn looked up sharply.

"What? Did I say something wrong?"

Her reaction worried him.

"No... it's nothing," she said. He could tell her smile was forced. "I just wish I had made that connection right away... maybe in time to have somehow stopped her from leaving in the first place." She wept.

Miriam got up from the couch, prepared to comfort her again. Evelyn waved her off, saying she deeply appreciated her compassion and needed only a moment to regain her composure. But then she asked Miriam if she'd like to join her in searching the Internet for answers.

"It might be easier if we do this together," she sniffed, once Miriam joined her. Miriam gently massaged Evelyn's shoulders while watching her activate the initial search. "Let's Google 'Teutates', and see what comes up."

To everyone's surprise, the page instantly filled with websites that were either devoted to or mentioned the name, with at least nine more pages to follow.

"Well... isn't this interesting?" Evelyn mused softly, clicking on a website near the top of the list, one dealing with deities of ancient Gaul.

As soon as she accessed the site, a list of the gods and goddesses appeared in alphabetic order. Teutates was listed near the bottom. She and Miriam read the god's description and soon learned Teutates' importance placed it among the elite of the Gallic deities. Other names and derivatives were used throughout Gaul and the British Isles, and the Romans placed Teutates on the level of Mars and Mercury.

Visits to other sites showed the same description, along with the fact Teutates, "God of the People", was a blood thirsty deity requiring frequent sacrifices to be appeased. The devotion of the Gallic peoples to their god greatly impressed the Roman poet Lucan, who identified Teutates on the same level as even the highest rulers of the Roman pantheon.

"Well, here's something quite interesting," said Miriam, glancing at David and then back at the laptop's screen. "I remember studying Lucan in my lit course back in college, but I don't recall anything quite like this passage...."

Her voice faded as she silently read the excerpt along with Evelyn.

"What does it say?" asked David.

He sat up straight, perched on the edge of the couch. His interest aroused, it wasn't strong enough yet to get him to join his wife and Evelyn as they absorbed the page's contents.

"It's from Lucan... Pharsalia I, 495-510... whatever that means," said Evelyn, peering briefly over the screen at him. "And those who pacify with blood accursed Savage Teutates, Hesus' horrid shrines."

Miriam shuddered, and looked longingly to where David sat. Evelyn announced she wanted to look at other pages, and navigated away from the website, drawing Miriam's attention back to the screen.

"What about the English name, He Who Cannot Rest— do you see any sites for it?" she asked, while Evelyn scrolled through the earlier search results for Teutates.

"Good idea, let's take a look and see."

She typed in the new name to be researched, which resulted in fewer responses.

Most were from an array of novels and video games, which yielded no further connection to Teutates. Evelyn stumbled on a site belonging to an occult enthusiast named Claude Von Dansving, who also fronted an Austrian heavy metal band called The Death of Dansby. The main page was quite creepy, and it featured hellish Viking skulls alongside buxom vampires with glowing red eyes. Evelyn started to navigate away to the next link on the Google search result page, when Miriam stopped her. A link that read "Teutates: The One Who Never Sleeps" sat near the bottom of Von Dansving's main page. Evelyn clicked on the link, which opened up to a full-screen picture.

"Oh, Shit!"

Evelyn shook her head while Miriam silently mouthed 'Oh, My God!'

That finally got David off his butt to take a look. At first, he couldn't see what held their attention, since the screen on Evelyn's HP wasn't visible until he stood directly in front of it.

The depiction of an enormous, misshapen hornets' nest wrapped within the coiled body of a viper immediately chilled him. A vile mixture of milk-like venom and blood dripped from the image. Surrounding the angry snake and disrupted nest were rows of shrunken human heads, similar to what one might find among cannibalistic tribes of the nineteenth century. Behind the nest stood a very tall figure. Not exactly like the ghoul Christopher told his parents about less than a week ago. But, close enough.

Bearing chiseled features and defined muscles, like a comic book hero, its curled saber-like fingernails dripped with blood. The eyes glared angrily as glowing narrow slits, and were the most definitive characteristic of the figure, aside from the fingernails. They bore feline characteristics with the coldness of the snake before it, and the digital program changed the color of the eyes in a continuous motion from neon blue to deep green, to fiery yellow and finally to a drenched crimson deepening further toward black before the cycle repeated. The surrounding goriness of the image increased as the eyes grew darker, and tapered off when the eyes turned blue, as if the mysterious figure's bloodlust had been somehow satisfied.

Alongside the image sat a volume button, for the moment muted. Evelyn tentatively clicked it after getting encouragement from David. A chilling buzz filled the air around them in stereo, along with a phrase whispered in Gaelic. The words also flashed in neon green script along the bottom of the page.

Evelyn told them the rolled-tongue enunciation of the words reminded her of the strange phrases shrieked at her by the derisive spirit. Evelyn clicked on a small red button next to a Gaelic phrase chanted in gothic rhythm '*Ailgidim conne… ailgidim conne chugad!*' The German translation that first appeared along the page's bottom was no more helpful than the original, so she clicked the button once more. The English translation now appeared.

She shuddered again while joining Miriam in slowly mouthing the words, with David watching silently. Perhaps it was merely a weird coincidence, since what they viewed from the website had been nothing more than a tribute to the ancient Gallic deities and violence that pervaded throughout much of the metal band culture. Yet, the similarities between this and what they'd already experienced couldn't be easily dismissed.

I am coming…

Evelyn set her laptop aside and got up from the recliner, motioning for Miriam and David to follow her throughout the cabin's main floor. They moved quickly, making sure the towels and blankets covered all the mirrors and any other reflective surfaces they came across. Evelyn also advised them to make sure the windows and doors were locked and secured. Whether it was just an empty rock n' roll chant to Von Dansving's loyal following or intended as a threat by the entity in a clever and unusual manner, they couldn't afford to be lax.

...I am coming for you!

* * * * *

"I'll just be a sec, babe," said David, as Miriam stepped inside the doorway to the guestroom.

Other than the living room, it was the most rustic location in the cabin. Furnished in a pioneer motif, the room featured a feather bed piled high in handmade quilts and just enough reminders from John's upbringing among the most powerful Cherokee shaman leaders. Dream catchers and spirit chasers covered all four walls inside the room, while a painting of a warrior sitting proudly on a black mustang amid falling snow in the dead of winter hung above the dresser mirror. The warrior's sullen gaze looked into the room, as if a silent sentinel charged with watching over John's guests.

Already past midnight, and the cabin completely secure from any outside menace, David unpacked their overnight bag. Working quickly, he spread out the contents on the bed until he could figure out where to put everything. Miriam had always been better at it, which often came as a surprise to those who knew them best, since everyone always assumed the CPA would be more adept at organizing things than the pediatrician.

"No need to hurry just yet," she told him, smiling slyly as she closed the door.

She sauntered to the bed and slipped her arms around his waist, nuzzling his neck, just below his beard. At first, it took him aback. Not that he minded her seductive approach, as it was such a welcome change over what she'd been like during the past twenty-four hours. His only lingering concern was her trust, and that she knew beyond a shadow of a doubt he'd never cheat on her.

"I'm *so* sorry, hon," she told him, pausing to gaze up into his face. She pressed against him, her eyes probing deeply into his. "I have no idea why I behaved the way I did," she confessed. "I guess it was something about the voice that just set off feelings I haven't had in years."

His initial response was a forgiving nod, although the mystery as to why the entity wanted him and Miriam to travel to Tennessee puzzled him greatly. What did *it* want? Other than torturing and killing anyone associated with the desecration of its grave, what more could it desire?

She looked away sadly, perhaps picturing what it was like for her so many years ago, and yet how easily she reverted to the behavior following the call last night.

"It's okay, babe. That's all in the past, now," he assured her, pushing aside his own worries.

He brought his hands up the shapely contours of her body, until they reached her face. He gently caressed her cheeks and brushed aside her hair. Her eyes filled with tears.

"I-I... I love you so much, David," she whispered, and buried her face in his chest.

He allowed her to weep for a moment, but not near as long as she allowed Evelyn to pour out her emotions earlier. Not from insensitivity, as he felt incredibly grateful for her change of heart and would've waited hours for her emotional release to run its natural course. Rather, another feeling overrode his appreciation. Something was left unfinished, despite the fact Evelyn assured them nothing else could be done until the entity made its next move.

"I love you very much, too, Miriam," he told her, gently lifting her face to hold her gaze. "Maybe after we get everything unpacked, you and I can snuggle together for awhile before we go to sleep."

He motioned to the bed still covered with clothes and toiletries.

"Maybe," she agreed, eyeing him coyly. "Snuggle, huh? Are you sure you wouldn't prefer to just have your way with me instead?"

She chuckled, and he realized her amusement came from his use of a word she preferred, one that rarely came to mind for him.

"If we had a place like this to ourselves, like the chalet we had back in October, that's exactly what I'd do!" he teased, pulling her closer.

"Maybe we can work something out to where that can happen," she teased, her look seductive. "But, definitely not tonight. Evelyn wants us to come with her when she goes to see John tomorrow. I'm sure you already planned to do that anyway."

"Yeah, I'd like to be there first thing in the morning," he said, turning to the items scattered atop the bedspread. "I suppose we should get ready for bed before temptation gets the better of me. I could use your help in finding a suitable home for this stuff."

"Sure." She grabbed a handful of underwear and socks.

"Evelyn told me about some Cherokee legends that sort of match up with this thing," she said, placing the items inside one of the dresser's top drawers. "Based on her own experiences and after hearing everything you and I told her, she feels the entity may be much, *much* more than just an angry spirit. I think that last website kind of helped her see things differently. She's beginning to believe this thing might actually be one of the more ominous and chief demons among the Cherokee. She called it a raven mocker."

"A raven mocker?"

"Yes," Miriam confirmed. "She said it's been a big part of her people's folklore and occult for hundreds of years. In fact, the Cherokee living on the reservations in both North Carolina and Oklahoma still fear raven mockers."

"So, these things are fairly common, I take it?" A playful smile was spreading across his face. "Do they run in groups, like gnomes and fairies?"

She giggled for a moment, but grew serious.

"Okay, seriously, tell me what she said about them."

His serious tone matched her countenance, although the image of little raven-like sprites bringing invisible attacks to their unsuspecting victims left an amused expression. Miriam refused to reveal anything else until he looked as serious as she did.

"According to Evelyn, a raven mocker is a witch of sorts," she began. "It's more wicked than most, taking on the form of a spectral bird that easily shifts into something human or a shadowy phantom. A raven mocker steals the life of the weak, seriously ill, or dying. They're said to bear the agedness of those they kill, and are covered with wrinkles as a result—like the old tree man the kids saw walking about our house in Littleton."

She paused to make sure he stayed with her, and when he nodded, she continued.

"The legends also state a raven mocker can remove a person's heart without breaking the skin. Evelyn said that as a young girl, her grandfather once told the story of how John faced such a creature not far from here, after it murdered one of his childhood friends who had battled polio, long before there was a vaccine available on his reservation. She'd always assumed the boy died naturally, due to lack of adequate medical attention. She no longer is so sure...."

Her voice trailed off, and she looked at the door. They thought they heard Evelyn call for them from the living room. When they paused to listen, the only sounds they heard were her laughter and Shawn's playful barks.

"I'll go check on her," said Miriam. "Besides, I can take our shampoo and the other bath supplies you packed into the main bathroom, so we won't have to do it in the morning."

"Sounds like a good idea, babe," he agreed, and watched her leave the room.

He removed his keys and wallet from his jeans' front pocket and prepared to set them on the dresser when something slipped out of his hand and landed on the floor.

It was the glistening ruby. Luckily it landed flat and didn't roll away. He picked it up, ready to place it inside his wallet. On a whim, he decided to hold it up to the wagon-wheel light fixture in the middle of the room. Under its brightness, the jewel's smooth contours sparkled in a rich crimson hue, and he had a clear view of the mistiness inside.

The dense mist definitely moved, swiftly as it traveled along the perimeter of the ruby. It crossed the face of the stone until it faced David. To his amazement, an image inside the mist began to solidify, and an eye appeared. It reminded him of the cat's eye marbles he played with as a kid. But the eye blinked coldly, like it belonged to some tiny, mutated reptile. A terrible chill seized his heart when he realized the eye studied him.

What the...?

He nearly dropped the gemstone, passing it from hand to hand as if it might suddenly catch fire and burn him. He looked around the room, desperately seeking someplace safe enough to hide the thing.

The eye squinted, giving the impression it sought to discern his location. Putting the thing back inside his wallet definitely didn't seem like a good enough place, nor did throwing it inside one of the dresser's empty drawers. Strangely, the only appealing idea that popped into his head was how his aunt recently discovered the jewel in Littleton. He shoved the ruby into the crevice between the bedspread and a pillow.

"David... David, what are you doing?"

Miriam paused inside the doorway before heading off to the living room. She eyed him suspiciously, and her eyes squinted like the monstrous little eye a moment ago. But in her case, it was as if she had caught him doing something sneaky... something *dirty*.

"Nothing," he replied, nonchalantly, moving from where he stashed the jewel. His footsteps were stealthily silent, like a midnight-burglar creeping along the wooden floorboards as he rounded the edge of the bed and walked to where she waited. "I was just straightening the bedspread since it was messed up from where I laid the overnight bag."

Why he lied, he had no idea. It was stupid, even pointless... and definitely dangerous if he got caught. Especially after what they'd just gone through. His immediate reason? The rationale of protecting her and Evelyn from whatever lurked inside the ruby—perhaps the implausible home of the old tree man or raven mocker, if that's what the thing actually was. The real truth, however, was he needed time. He needed to come up with a good explanation as to why he brought the damned thing instead of leaving it someplace safe in Colorado.

"Evelyn has done some more research on raven mockers and is waiting to share it with us," Miriam advised. David gently wrapped his arms around her. He led her out of the guestroom and into the hallway.

The pungent scent of hickory emanated from the living room, as Evelyn added three fresh logs to the hearth. The room seemed cozier, and the fire's bright glow provided the only illumination other than the lamp next to the recliner, where she waited for them to come see what she discovered. Shawn lay curled near her feet.

"I shared some of this information with Miriam already."

She paused to take a sip from one of three cups of fresh cocoa she'd prepared.

"Really, the only difference between what your kids have seen and the legend itself is the curved fingernails and the eyes, since raven mockers are supposed to be human… at least at some point in their existence," she said. "I long considered it just a myth among my people that anyone could live off the life force of someone else— like some sort of vampire. But my sister's murder points to such behavior, and I'd be willing to bet the murders linked to Grandpa might be similar in some way."

She gazed at the fire, the burgeoning flames creating enough warmth for them to be slightly uncomfortable this close to the blaze. She protectively pulled the laptop toward her and scooted her body to one side of the recliner to gain some relief from the fire's heat, while David and Miriam stepped to the side of the recliner furthest from the fireplace and looked over her shoulder at the image currently on the screen. It was an etching from a long-forgotten book on Cherokee myths gathered by a pioneer missionary in the region named James Seaton, who lived among the more peaceful tribes in the early eighteenth century. The depiction was of an old witch being chased by a crowd of people throwing rocks and large sticks as the throng pursued her.

"I know what you're thinking—the same as my initial reaction," she said to David, drawing a glance from Miriam that came soon enough to witness his latest smirk. "How on earth could such a frail and unassuming figure wreak enough havoc to where an entire township or tribe would be in an uproar—right?"

He nodded to confirm her accuracy, feeling vulnerable in the presence of the two females on the planet that enjoyed the clearest insight to his thoughts and musings.

Suddenly, loud creaks erupted from the roof, followed by heavy footsteps descending along either side of the A-frame structure. Soon after, subtler shuffling noises resounded from the back porch. All three scanned the living room and kitchen walls and ceiling nervously. Since it fit the description of how the last assault Evelyn suffered started, David assumed they had three ghostly visitors trying to invade the cabin again. Evelyn agreed, and set the laptop next to the recliner as she stood.

"What in the hell is out there?" Miriam whispered worriedly to him, before turning to Evelyn for answers. Neither one could provide an explanation.

"I don't know," Evelyn responded, in a hoarse whisper. All at once her eyes grew wide, and she grabbed them by their arms. "Move with me over by the fire—*now!*"

The cabin's walls shook hard, as if embraced by a violent explosion she sensed coming. Miriam began to whimper, arousing David's protective instincts. He pulled her close with one arm while using the other to help Evelyn steady a large log and throw it on top of the fire.

Flames sprouted up on all sides of the log, as if affected by their urgency.

Shawn growled at the back door, taking a few tentative steps with his tail turned downward.

"No, Shawn—stay with me, boy!"

Evelyn grabbed his collar and dragged him back. He resisted her efforts to turn his head toward her, instead barking angrily toward the hallway. At the same time, an unsettling noise arose from the guestroom. To David, it reminded him of what cellophane sounded like when stretched over a large dish or bowl, to the point of breaking. Rather than wait for what would happen next, he bravely bolted around the corner and down the hallway.

The hallway was incredibly cold, where only minutes earlier it was the beneficiary of the warm blaze. He heard Miriam start to follow, but Evelyn stopped her. Initially relieved by Evelyn's efforts, when he made it down the chilly hall and flipped the wall switch to the guestroom's light he wasn't so sure any of them would remain safe.

A garish human face with green feline eyes greeted him at the doorway from inside the dresser mirror. The mirror's surface stretched beyond anything he would've previously believed possible, hovering several feet beyond the dresser's edge. It reminded him in a way of the big soap bubbles his kids once played with. Only he never imagined those bubbles containing a profile as hideous as the one turned toward him, as if trying to get a better look at him. The sickening cellophane sound announced the mirror's surface was stretching further. The top portion of the mirror's surface shimmered brightly under the overhead wagon-light's glow.

"David, they're coming in here! Oh my God, this can't be real!"

Miriam's frightened cries erupted from the living room, and Evelyn shouted a series of incantations sounding similar to what she used to help free him from Allie Mae's deadly grip. She didn't sound confident. Along with Shawn's hysterical barks, the combined panic distracted him enough to pull his frightened gaze away from the face. He turned to sprint to the living room. But the bone chilling rumble from the voice that belonged to the face in the mirror forced him to hesitate long enough to pause and take another look.

It had moved into the hallway, hovering less than a foot away from his chest, still attached to the thin membrane of the mirror's surface ready to fracture into a myriad of tiny pieces. The cellophane-stretch sound grew more unnerving while the face leered contemptuously at him, bearing a mouth full of curved and pointed sharp teeth reminding him of the Spawn character in the Spiderman comic books he collected years ago in Chattanooga.

"What do you want with us?" David shouted, stumbling as he tried to get away.

Meanwhile, the screams and desperate calls to him from the living room grew more distressed. The only response he received from it was a deep, drawn-in breath. He only had a moment to bolt down the hallway, to rescue Miriam and John's granddaughter and get the hell away from this place.

"I'm coming Miriam—hold on!"

Before he reached the living room, and glimpsed the other shadowed figures stepping from under the cloaked mirror and glassed family portrait, the mirror exploded into a shower of tiny chips raining on his back. The force from the blast sent him flying and he tumbled into the kitchen.

Heavy footfalls pursued him, and yet whatever made them wasn't visible. He glimpsed two shadowy figures grab Evelyn and Miriam, and drag them under the blanketed mirror and picture frame where they disappeared with their captors. Screaming his wife's name, David scrambled over to the mirror where she'd been huddled, crying his name just seconds ago. As soon as he stood up, two incredibly powerful hands grabbed him from behind. Before he drew his next breath, the hands dragged him into the guestroom, where he became airborne and flew through the mirror's shattered frame. The echoes from his terrified screams followed.

Only Shawn remained behind, barking loudly as he chased after David and his invisible assailant. After waiting several minutes for him to reappear in the guestroom, the husky returned to the living room. For much of the next hour, he pawed and whined anxiously beneath the portrait where Evelyn disappeared. He paced restlessly throughout the cabin until the dawn's light arrived, his plaintive barks outlasting the last glowing embers upon the hearth.

Chapter Twenty-nine

John Running Deer hesitated before unlocking the front door to his cabin, listening as Shawn barked incessantly from the door's other side. John couldn't remember a time when he'd heard his prized husky this upset, which pulled on his heart while he forced himself to wait. Something wasn't right... there was some sort of danger nearby. The guides he had long kept secret told him to be especially cautious before stepping inside his beloved home.

"Maybe I should go in first."

Sheriff A. J. "Butch" Silva whispered this suggestion from behind him. In his early-sixties and just a few years away from collecting full retirement benefits from the state of Tennessee, Butch used his tall, lanky frame to steal a peek over John's shoulder. The wind that had recently picked up around them blew his salt and pepper bangs over his polarized lenses, forcing him to slide the sunglasses down his nose while he watched John's hesitation with worried pale gray eyes.

"No... I'm fine," said John, exhausted after two nights of very little sleep.

His voice soft and solemn, he cast a wary glance at the sheriff. A terrible event happened last night... one involving Evelyn. The heaviness in the pit of his gut told him this, and had done so long before his eldest granddaughter failed to show up at the jail as promised by

7:30 a.m. He sat through several criminal reviews at the courthouse while his stomach churned, until finally, the Honorable Benjamin Ashford dismissed John's case. It wasn't the time to rehash the injustice—a visit with an attorney after the holidays would take care of that.

He braced for whatever awaited him and Butch, and unlocked the door. Shawn's barks ceased as John stepped through the doorway. An immediate unpleasant mixture of odors threatened to overpower his and the sheriff's heightened senses. Some came from synthetic cleaning supplies while others, like the lingering hickory and coffee scents, were natural. Underneath them all, however, lurked the faint smell of blood... human blood.

"What in the hell happened here?" Butch wondered aloud, as he surveyed the living room.

He grimaced when his gaze settled on the overturned furniture lying in the middle of the room, and moved on to the mirror, partially covered with a blanket. Most of the blanket hung loosely from the bottom of the mirror's ornate brass frame. Shawn pawed at it, anxiously, causing the frame to click noisily against the wall.

"Evelyn? Evelyn, where are you?"

John's voice shook. There was no response, other than Shawn's ears suddenly pointing upward. She wasn't anywhere inside the cabin, but John couldn't stop himself from calling again. She was gone, just like Hanna. And the owner, or owners, of the minivan parked in the driveway next to Evelyn's sports car were also gone... with Evelyn? He couldn't say for sure. His guides quietly spoke to him, trying to relay some very important information. They talked about a trap and an act of deception.

Notice all of the towels and blankets, Running Deer. Your granddaughter put them there for a reason, but not to hide anything. Think, Running Deer. Yes! Evelyn put them there to keep the uninvited visitors out!

"Visitors?" he whispered to himself, worried as to what this meant and glancing at the mirror where Shawn continued to paw furiously. He called to the dog and the only response he got was a sharp whine before Shawn returned to his obsession.

It's as if I'm not even here. Hell, he didn't even bark at Butch this time.

"Looks like Evelyn might've been working on something before she was interrupted," observed Butch, moving over to the recliner.

Her dormant laptop was open, and a large notepad with the top page filled with scribbled lines lay next to her half-full cocoa mug. Two similar mugs were lying haphazardly upon the floor, where their congealed contents joined to form a sticky, muddy puddle around one side of the overturned coffee table. Butch bent down to examine the notepad, being careful not to touch anything. John's living room had become a crime scene.

"This could be important."

John confirmed Evelyn's handwriting on the notepad. His brow was furrowed while he scanned the page's contents, having to pause at several points where the words and symbols she'd written were too blurred for his aged eyes to decipher. *She's in terrible danger!*

"Evelyn!"

Her name echoed beneath the ceiling's arched apex. The urge to call her name continued to press him. He forcefully shouted her name again. This time, he ran down the hallway where the bedrooms sat with Butch following close behind before the latest echoes died away.

When he reached the guestroom, his eyes fell upon the spray of tiny glass fragments surrounding the doorway. Cautiously, he stepped through the mess and peered inside the room, the exploded particles from the dresser mirror crunching beneath the soles of his shoes. Sunlight streamed through a small gap above the closed curtains to the room's only window, but not enough to see clearly. He turned on the overhead light.

"What in God's name happened here?"

Butch's tone reflected his amazement. He stepped quietly around John. Neither one seemed to notice Shawn had finally shaken his fixation with the living room mirror, panting by John's side. The floor in the guestroom was covered in shiny glass chips, and formed a snow-like dust near the mirror's frame on top of the dresser. All the dream catchers and spirit chasers had fallen to the floor. Even John's prized warrior painting had been knocked from its perch high above the dresser.

The worst damage to the room, though, had been wrought upon the wall behind the mirror's empty frame. The pine logs had been burned away, and a blackened, molten mass of mortar and copper wiring to the electrical outlet was left behind the dresser. Etched in red within the blackness appeared an image.

"Gigv Inadv… *Uktena*?" mumbled John, incredulously, and yet at the same time reverently.

"John… now you know you're going to have to talk straight with me—none of that mumbo-jumbo."

"It means Blood Snake," John told him evenly, after shooting him a disdainful look. "Uktena is the Great Serpent that guards the Land of Darkness beyond the Three Blood Rivers…. It's sort of like the dreaded place between your heaven and hell, the state you call 'purgatory'."

He waited for Butch's nod to acknowledge the Catholic concept taught to him as a boy. Certainly, they agreed the coiled image on the wall resembled a snake or serpent more than any other creature. The hard part was to figure out the connection between it and everything else. Perhaps it was the entity's calling card, or maybe its sign, like the wax seal used in olden times to announce the completion of a transaction. John shuddered.

"Leave it to me, buddy," Butch told him, looking as if he silently called upon the aid from a cherished Catholic saint while patting John on the shoulder. He suggested they return to the living room. "I'll call in some help so we can get to the bottom of what's going on here, *and* find your granddaughters, of course."

Ready to follow his lead out of the guestroom, John noticed something lying on the bed next to the pillows. It was an overnight bag he recognized. He moved to get a closer look at the nametag attached to the bag's handle, and soon shook his head in further disbelief.

"'Someone you know, John?"

Sheriff Silva instinctively reached for his hand radio even before John told him the names written on the tag. David and Miriam Hobbs. It not only added to the mystery, but also confirmed something very bad took place during his absence.

Butch stepped into the hallway and placed a call to the dispatcher, issuing a command for every available deputy to come to the cabin. Grateful, John nodded approvingly when Butch added they needed to bring extra search equipment, but frowned at the sheriff's next request.

"I need you to call Knoxville and get a forensic team out here, Norma," said Butch into his handset, sheltering the receiver while turning away from John. "No bodies, but yeah, the request is warranted. Tell them to get here pronto. From the looks of things, we might have something important... something related to the UT homicides earlier this week."

Chapter Thirty

What the hell?... Where am I??

David anxiously looked around, surprised to find he had been shackled to a cold stone floor. Darkness surrounded him, and the lone light source came from a fiery glow beyond a doorway, roughly two hundred feet away. As his eyes adjusted, dim objects grew easier to define. He could make out the outline of a corridor leading to the doorway. Enormous columns, each five to six feet thick and several stories high, stood on either side of the corridor. Jeweled mosaics featuring serpentine dragons covered each column, and the colorful reptiles appeared to crawl down the columns' length, with the creatures' angry, open mouths, full of sharp teeth, at the base.

As frightful as the images appeared, none of them came close to the hideousness of a face he had recently seen. He couldn't remember exactly when and where that happened. His eyes continued to adjust, and he recognized the motionless forms of Miriam and Evelyn, maybe thirty feet away. Although sitting up, they were chained to a pair of columns on the corridor's other side, clothed in the sweaters and jeans when he last saw them. It was cold enough for their steady breaths to be visible. David shivered in his sweats and T-shirt, since he was about to get ready for bed when all hell broke loose.... Was it in

John's cabin? For some reason, that notion felt right. At the same time, it filled him with terror.

Could this be a dream? It didn't seem likely. Memory brought a flood of images... images of terrifying phantoms with no eyes, and that goddamned repulsive face pursuing him from inside the stretched surface of the dresser mirror. He recalled screaming Miriam's name before two powerful, clammy hands grabbed his ankles and dragged him out of the living room, down the hall, and carried him airborne into the mirror, where his chin banged painfully on the dresser's edge. From there, things got even weirder and far more frightening. He watched helplessly as the wall closed behind him, and he dropped into a deep dark chasm.

Other evidence confirmed the reality of his experience, like the bumps and stinging scrapes on his chest, legs, and face. Not to mention his clothes still carried a raw earth odor.

Regardless, they were here, wherever *here* was. He looked worriedly around, casting another nervous look to Evelyn and Miriam sitting motionless. *Are they still breathing?* It took a moment to discern misty tendrils rising into the air above their heads. What kind of place was this, anyway? Shackles and chains belonged in a prison or dungeon, but the ostentatious place looked like a palace or temple. The massive ornate columns pointed to some grand design.

That looks like real gold inlays along the base of the pillars, and it's probably the same stuff that's glistening inside the cornices high above. Something about the eyes of the dragon face. If I can just get a little closer to the face.

The eyes looked just like the ruby his aunt brought with her from Chattanooga… only much bigger.

"This shit can't be real," he mumbled.

The smooth, cold surface greeted his fingers as he reached up and grazed the ruby eye.

A menacing moan resounded from behind him. The murmur faded, and when he glanced over his shoulder he couldn't see anything. Beyond the reach of the faint illumination in front of him, everything was shrouded in impenetrable darkness.

While debating whether or not he should say anything, to call out to the presence or try to waken Miriam or Evelyn, the moan erupted again. It rumbled through the cold stone floor. His immediate response was to pull desperately on the heavy shackles secured tightly to his wrists and ankles, and he prayed desperately for some way to free himself. Now that he had a better look at the bonds in the dimness, they appeared quite crude with a rudimentary lock. Forged from heavy iron, he wasn't going anywhere without a key.

Something snorted in the darkness. He glimpsed moisture in mammoth, twin mists drifting toward the floor behind him.

If that shit came from the nose or snout of whatever is back there, then it's something very, very big! Gotta get these mothers off somehow. Better do it quickly before I become lunch!

Miriam uttered a soft moan, and Evelyn stirred. The unseen menace lurking in the darkness answered his wife's whimper with a meaner groan, which quickened David's fear for her safety.

"Miriam!" he whispered, harshly, trying to get her attention without creating further agitation for the monstrous creature. "If you can hear me, see if you can slide out of your chains."

"Uh-h-h…," was her initial response. She awoke with a start and found she couldn't move, held fast by the heavy chains. She panicked. "David? *What's going on?*"

"Keep your voice down!" he said, less forcefully. "There's something in here with us and it—"

An angry roar cut through the air, silencing him. He instinctively flinched and pushed himself against the base of the nearest column. An immense black shadow flew swiftly through the air, just beneath the ceiling.

Evelyn was fully awake, and she looked around her in disbelief while Miriam cowered in terror, listening to the leathery flapping of giant wings while the mysterious creature passed over as it moved toward the doorway. Its angry screeches echoed throughout the immense room and drew amazed expressions from all three, transformed into looks of terror when the flying menace sped back toward them, diving much lower on its return trip.

It flew past them again, a reddish blur as it climbed into the air before circling high above. Hovering again in darkness, David hated trying to anticipate what it would do next.

Evelyn joined Miriam in frantically pulling at the chains around their torsos. Scarcely able to move their bonds, Evelyn chanted incantations in a nervous tone matching the whimpering pitch of Miriam's cursed misgivings. Listening, David teetered ever closer to the edge of despair, since Evelyn had seemed so confident, sure of herself and her magic in his previous dealing with her. It definitely wasn't the case now.

Other noises echoed from beyond the lighted doorway in the distance. Unlike the chilling screeches and roars from the menace lurking above, the noises were definitely human in origin. Blood-curdling screams and pleas for mercy from a middle-aged man and a young girl ripped shrilly through the air, drifting down the corridor to them. Another voice was also present, and it resonated deeply in a strange language. The owner of this voice, a male by the sound of it, seemed delighted by the man and girl's cries from obvious suffering.

Both Evelyn and Miriam looked anxiously to David in the dimness, their worried grimaces at first resembled maniacal smiles until they both sobbed fearfully.

"Evelyn, can you somehow slide out of your chains?"

It was David's last hope. Miriam's escalating murmurs told him that she couldn't free herself. Perhaps, and likely, it was the same for Evelyn. He wouldn't allow himself to think all was lost… at least not yet.

"We *can't* do it!" cried Miriam, looking over at Evelyn before turning back to him. "Both of us are *stuck!*"

"*Shit!*" he hissed.

His shackles seemed heavier and colder as his own panic rose. His mind went blank while he desperately sought some other means of escape.

"Hold on, Miriam—I'll think of something!"

"Think of *what?*"

Her exasperation always made it harder for him to concentrate.

"Something!"

"Please, both of you *stop!*" scolded Evelyn, seemingly in control of her emotions again. "Your devotion to one another will serve us so much better than any anger over what has happened to us! We need to put our hearts and heads together and come up with an idea that—*Oh, my, God! Watch out, David!*"

Her courage melted as her eyes were focused on something coming down from the ceiling.

He looked up in time to see an immense, open mouth filled with razor-sharp teeth descending upon him. Similar to the images portrayed on the columns lining the corridor, a pair of glowing red eyes appeared, along with the rest of the enormous serpent's slithering body. The creature's face resembled the Chinese dragons he once saw depicted everywhere in San Francisco's China Town, with huge flared nostrils on its long snout and two rows of immense golden horns on its head above the brow. It veered away long enough to snap its dangerous jaws at Miriam and Evelyn, who screamed and pressed themselves against the columns. It dropped to the floor, its focus solely on David.

The serpent let out a roar that shook the entire room. The enormous columns creaked as if they might crumble.

It slithered toward him. Its mouth opened wider as it approached the helpless, terrified man huddled in a fetal position on the floor. He could only watch and listen, hating the fact he could do nothing about Miriam and Evelyn's frantic cries and shrieks, while the creature's leathery skin brushed against the stone floor as it approached.

Resigned to an imminent death, he called out to his beloved wife, expressing his undying devotion one last time and closed his eyes. The creature's hot breath, laden with the stench of rotten meat filled the air before him. It was the last thing he thought about as it arrived.

Chapter Thirty-one

Sunset came early to the Smoky Mountains Friday night. Or, it felt that way to John. The forensic team finished their examination of his cabin, where sprayed Luminol revealed widespread blood residue upon most of the living room floor and lighter blood spatter on two walls. Despite his and Butch's earlier detection of an acrid scent hinting at bloodshed, his steadfast hope of finding his granddaughters alive overrode the growing mountain of evidence that said otherwise.

"We're all done, I reckon," advised the leader of the team, Sam Roberson.

A tall, slender, steel blue-eyed man in his late forties, with a thick head of salt and pepper hair, he closed the supply case and ushered the rest of his team out of the cabin. Born and raised in nearby Pigeon Forge, John had met Sam once before, during an investigation following a series of break-ins into two of the nearby national park's visitor centers.

"It might take a few weeks to get the final analysis on everything we collected this afternoon. I'm sure that either Butch or the detectives you spoke with recently will be in touch."

"Thanks for your time today, Sam," said John, thinking again about where the collected blood and tissue samples probably came from. *Evelyn? Hanna? Or, both?* "I'll wait to hear the results when you get them in."

He bit his lip while closing the front door. There would be a time to grieve, but not yet. Something inside told him so... a piece was still missing. As long as the puzzle remained incomplete, he refused to accept the loss of those dearest to him. That included David and Miriam Hobbs, who for some inexplicable reason traveled to Gatlinburg yesterday and came to his home. He and Butch gathered the information from the rental agreement found inside the Honda Odyssey, which the Sevier County Sheriff's Dept had since impounded.

"Shawn? ...Where are you, boy?"

John waited for Shawn by his recliner, who ran down the hallway from one of the bedrooms and cowered low as he approached his master. John worried some of the glass chips in the guestroom from the destroyed mirror might get stuck in the husky's paws. Shawn's paws were fine... but something else seemed wrong. Shawn continued to look back toward the hallway, as if expecting someone else to step into the living room.

After pausing to listen with his ears and instincts, John returned to his intended task of carefully clearing away his granddaughter's belongings left on his favorite chair and the table next to it. The laptop was closed and had been set next to the table, after Sam and his staff had finished dusting for prints and collecting possible DNA evidence. Her notepad sat open on the table. It, too, had been checked.

"He Who Can Not Rest?" he mouthed quietly, and then lifted the page to see if other notes followed.

Nearly half of the next page was filled with web page addresses and cross-referenced words and strange symbols. Intending to research the information later, since Butch had hand-copied the web addresses earlier that afternoon, John returned to the first page.

Teutates? Why does that name seem familiar? And, why is this reference about wasps and snakes double-underlined?

"Evelyn was close to finding out something very important," he said quietly.

Did the wasps' reference relate to the anisgina's attacks on the cabin, since a massive swarm of hornets might sound like a giant horde of wasps? The snake reference made him think again about the strange symbol left on the guestroom's wall where the dresser mirror used to be. *Gigv Inadv*. The legendary great snake, Uktena, immediately came to mind, for which scores of Cherokee legends had been created.

While reading the notes about the German occultist's website, he heard a noise. It sounded like a coin or something similar landed on the floor in the guestroom and now rolled around. Shawn's ears perked up, and he growled. John shushed him, motioning with his index finger pressed to his lips to remain quiet while he tiptoed down the hallway.

By the time he reached the guestroom, the noise had stopped. Iciness filled the air. It didn't take his heightened senses to realize a spirit had been here very recently and possibly still lingered. The feeling of being watched from all directions confirmed the notion.

At first glance, not much had changed since his last visit to the room. Something glistened on the floor amid glass chips. Even from where he stood, he could tell the quarter-sized object was a gemstone—a dark fire opal was his initial guess. Cautiously, he stepped into the room while Shawn followed close behind him, and bent to examine the item.

What in the hell is this?

He picked up the gemstone.

My God, it's a ruby!

The stone's size, unusual clarity, and smoothness amazed him. A flurry of images flashed before his mind's eye. Everything from the ornate gold handle to which the gem once belonged to the object's eventual burial deep within the earth was revealed. Recent images briefly appeared... a beautiful girl dressed in a Victorian-style, long blue dress followed by extreme violence to her person. The last thing he saw was an elderly woman carrying the gem in a box with other jewels that once belonged to the splendid scepter.

Surprised by the vision's detailed images, John steadied himself with one hand on the dresser. While unsure if his friend, David Hobbs, had brought the quarter-sized jewel here, he had no doubt it somehow related to Allie Mae McCormick and the ravine she cherished during her lifetime, nearly a century ago.

Allie Mae was definitely the girl he just saw, and he recognized the prized scepter removed from the ravine by

Dr. Pollack. The ruby's smooth surface reminded him of the loose jewels he and Micky Webster, his fellow ranger who helped him find Allie Mae's gravesite, relinquished to the University of Tennessee's Antiquities Department.

While holding the ruby close to the bedroom's overhead light, he glimpsed a shadow pass by the doorway.

"Who's there?" John asked, warily.

Shawn ran out of the room in pursuit of the intruder, but stopped, his tail wagging while he waited for John to join him.

As soon as John joined him in the hallway, he saw a bearded man wearing a tan fedora, dressed in a shirt, trousers, and work boots once the common attire of the mining folk in the region. Standing near the living room, the figure looked down at Shawn, grinning, and raised his eyes to meet John's gaze.

"David?"

John uttered the question tentatively. The man did look like David. Yet, at the same time, he seemed somehow different from the last time he saw him in October. John hoped it wasn't just because the apparition was semi-transparent.

Did the anisgina kill you?

"Nah, I ain't him... just his kin," the man replied.

He pointed to John's hand holding the ruby, and tipped his hat before turning away, moving into the living room where the heavy boots reported his progress. The footsteps headed for the front door and then abruptly stopped.

John ran after him with Shawn barking excitedly at his heels. When they reached the living room, the apparition had disappeared. Its chilled essence hung in the air, despite the warm blaze in the fireplace. John paid little attention to the room's temperature or comfort. He was distracted instead by a tremor within the ruby he held.

Something happened to the gemstone since he first examined it, just moments ago. In the center of the ruby, a mist formed. John grabbed his eyeglasses from the coffee table. He turned on the lamp next to his recliner, and brought the jewel closer to his eyes for a better look.

Holding it up to the light, he was surprised to see a mist moving inside. It also looked like a faint image began to solidify within the tiny haze.

John gasped, covering it with his hand. He anxiously looked around, hoping to find a place to dispose of the thing, as if it had become some sort of venomous spider or other deadly bug poised to bite. A small wooden box sat on the fireplace's mantle, next to a photograph of his daughter, Joanna, taken when she wasn't much older than her daughter, Evelyn, was now. John picked up the box and carefully removed a small silver pinky ring that belonged to his late wife, Susanne. He quickly placed the ring in the breast pocket of his flannel shirt, and deposited the ruby inside the box. He closed the lid hastily, and returned the box to the mantle.

"Hopefully that buys me enough time," he mumbled, worriedly.

John forced a smile for Shawn, who pawed at his pant legs, as if seeking assurance everything was going to be okay. John truly wished he had that hope to give. What he did have was a renewed interest in his granddaughter's research from yesterday. What she had sought gained a lot more urgency now, in light of the most recent events. Confirming the identity of his mysterious visitor would have to wait, although he was almost certain the man was David's ancestor, the infamous Billy Ray Hobson. John's most pressing questions dealt with the ruby itself and what he saw moving inside.

He opened the laptop and waited for it to power up, resting the device on his lap as he sat in the recliner. Luckily, he remembered the guest password Evelyn set up for him, despite his insistence he would never use the damned thing. He viewed the Internet as too much of a hassle to get information that was questionable at best in terms of authenticity. At least that's what he thought before now. Evelyn was on to something with her web search. Perhaps that's where he would find the very key needed to resolve their problem with the angered anisgina, once and for all.

Her notes made sense in light of what squinted at him from within the ruby's glowing center. It was an eye... cold and reptilian like a snake. A chill traveled down his spine as he considered a new possibility. Maybe, the jewel lying within the small box on the mantel belonged to a sacred creature among his people known as The Great Serpent. Until that very moment, John had passed the serpent off as merely an old Cherokee legend, a fairy tale to help his ancestors explain everything from the war between night and day to the inevitable expulsion of his people from the Smoky Mountains. If the mythical creature turned out to be factual, the ruby belonged to the ancient guardian charged with protecting the only path to the underworld—the land of the dead located beyond the Three Blood Rivers.

"The Eye of Uktena," John whispered, his tone reverent as he picked up Evelyn's notepad and began the painstaking course of retracing her steps. If there was still time to undo the wrath of the anisgina, he could think of no better way to rescue his granddaughters, David, and Miriam.

"May the Great Spirit show me how to use this, and to allow me safe passage through the depths of *Tsvsgino* to find them. Allow me to bring them back from hell to the land of the living, safely."

It would be a noble prayer… as long as the owner of the eye didn't come for him first.

Chapter Thirty-two

Tyler woke from a deep sleep. Someone pulled the blankets down to his waist and pushed on his shoulder. That someone now tapped him lightly on the forehead.

"Ty, wake up!" whispered Christopher. "There's somebody moving around in the game area."

At first reluctant to acknowledge his little brother's urgent pleas, grumbling it was likely just the chalet's upper floorboards settling, he rolled over with his back to Christopher. He pulled the bedcovers up to his neck, anticipating a return to the sweet comfort and bliss from a moment ago. Then he heard it.

What in the hell?

"See, I told you!" whined Christopher, his tone more fearful than before.

Tyler's wide-eyed response as he sat up in bed didn't help. Before he could pull on his jeans, one of the balls on the pool table rolled across the slate surface. It bounced against the table's sides before landing inside the corner pocket closest to their bedroom.

Definitely can't explain away that shit!

He stood up and faced the doorway leading out into the loft area. A nightlight near the top of the stairs eerily enhanced the darkened silhouettes of the pool table and several video games. Bravely he stepped forward, with Christopher clinging to the back of his t-shirt. His heart pounded as he listened. Hearing his great aunt's snores downstairs, he waited for some other sound from the billiard area.

"W-who's out there?" he asked, hoping to sound gruff like his dad when pissed off about something, but knowing he couldn't hide his nervousness. Fully awake, he thought about his earlier encounter with Allie Mae's spirit. *God, don't let it be her... please!*

At first nothing, other than the sound of Aunt Ruth sawing logs downstairs. Feeling hopeful, that maybe a logical explanation existed for what they heard, he took a quiet step back toward his bed. A low sigh suddenly filled the darkness in front of him, accompanied by the sound of something brushing softly across the loft's carpet.

Shit!

"Ya shouldn't have come back, Zachariah-h-h!"

They couldn't see her... not yet. Her voice sounded like it came from just outside the bedroom's doorway.

"Quick! Shut the door, Ty!" Christopher urged.

The snores from downstairs ceased.

Frightened as his little brother was, Tyler couldn't move. It was more on account of the voice... it sounded so *hostile*. It was just like when Allie Mae tried to kill him. To his horror, the brushing noise moved through the doorway and into the bedroom. Instinctively, he backed up with Christopher whimpering behind him.

"Someone must die-e-e-e!" The voice was a mixture of sensuality and deepening malice, and it bore a southern twang that only made it worse. So dangerous, and its threat was real. "Yer next! He's comin' for y'all… one by one… until he collects every-y-y-o-n-n-ne!"

"The tree man?"

Christopher's voice barely audible, the question seemed like it slipped out by accident. Tyler turned to shush him before he said anything else, but an amused chuckle floated through the air. Christopher trembled, tightening his grip on his brother's shirt.

She's in here… coming from everywhere! Sweet Jesus, how in the hell do we get out of this?

"Teutates will be here very soon-n-n-n! And when he comes, he won't look so old after yer blood drenches his flesh-h-h!!"

A cold breeze embraced their faces as they stepped back into the dresser.

Shit! Nowhere else to go!

"…Or, maybe he'd be pleased if I got started on ya both first-t-t-!"

If it was just him, Tyler wasn't sure what he would've done. His protective nature took over. The chilled presence invaded his personal space, and the sickening smell of raw meat amid a low wheezing, gurgling noise nearly caused him to hurl. Behind him, Christopher fought to keep from vomiting.

Dad said her face was smashed and her larynx torn away when she died.

Wanting to scream, Tyler couldn't. He was unable to muster so much as a whisper. He managed to break through the fear gluing him to the cool pine floorboards. Ignoring the continued threats and coldness that attacked from all directions, he grabbed Christopher by the arm and ran out of the bedroom. The hairs on his neck standing on end told him Allie Mae followed close behind.

After cracking a knee on one of the arcade games, he led his brother to the stairs. At the same time, the living room light came on.

"What's going on up there?" Ruth called, her tone worried.

As they navigated the staircase's narrow spiral, she appeared. She gave them a slight start, as her face was covered with night cream and her hair set in a protective net.

"You boys all right?"

"No!" shouted Tyler, just before they reached the main floor. "There's someone upstairs—"

"Oh, my Lord!" Ruth interrupted.

Her eyes grew wide, and she took a step back. Jillian joined her, peering up from her side at the thing that captivated Ruth's attention.

The sound of a windstorm emanated from the loft, and as the brothers joined their great aunt and sister in the living room, an immense shadow obscured the overhead lights' glow. Only the illumination from Jillian's bedroom kept the chalet from complete darkness. Her countenance filled with terror, Jillian's mouth formed a silent scream.

By the time Allie Mae's spirit descended on the living room, all four had vacated the chalet's premises. Huddled as a group near a streetlight on the road out front, Ruth dialed 911 from her cell phone. Although their rescue was delayed for an hour, they remained outside in the cold until the Sevier County cruiser showed up. No one dared testing the ghost's resolve to carry out her threats.

Chapter Thirty-three

Painful stiffness brought David back to the living, leaving a strangely comforting dark void. For the moment, he sat with hands bound above him, tied with rawhide straps to a long wooden pole supported by two stone pillars, one on either side. To his right sat Evelyn, her hands not near as severely bound, hanging just below her chin. She was unconscious. He looked to his left. Miriam sat closer to him, her hands dangling low, similar to Evelyn. She, too, appeared asleep.

Quietly he rose to his feet, bringing instant relief to the stretched tendons in his shoulders and wrists. With a better view of his new surroundings, the room was much smaller than the cathedral-like setting from earlier, and circular with roughly a forty-foot diameter. White stone walls decorated in intricate designs and symbols, the same was true for the domed ceiling. Snakes and serpents were the dominant theme, and each reptilian image had been skillfully detailed with small spheres surrounding each one, like angelic halos. The spheres glistened, as if containing small gem chips. Every one of them appeared different from the next, which indicated to David the painstaking effort that created this art.

If that had been all he noticed, his unease might not have escalated so quickly toward panic. The smell of death drew his attention.

What the hell is this place?

Along the lower reaches of the wall lay human remains—some old enough to be mere skeletal parts, while others looked recent. A row of six severed heads sat along the wall closest to a marble altar bearing engravings similar to the walls and ceiling. The heads belonged to three men, two children and a woman. One of the men was African American, and the other two were Caucasian—one older and one just a few years younger than himself. The woman reminded him of Miriam and Evelyn, with dark hair, and the children could be Jillian and Christopher's ages.

Is that what I heard earlier? The terrible screaming of a man and child?

A roaring fire seemed surreal, and almost dreamlike. It burned within a small pit on the other side of the altar, fueled by a pile of bones that remained unscathed by the flames. The skull was most unusual, and was human-like in its ghastly deformity with long sharp teeth. It seemed to be grinning within the blaze that was almost turquoise in color, the flames lapping the edge of the altar table.

David expected to find their captors watching him as he continued to survey this gruesome lair.

They're not here…. But, who in the hell's this?

For some reason, he hadn't noticed two other people in the room, lying on the dusty floor in front of him. The pole they hung from was much lower, and the likely reason for the oversight.

A girl wearing a badly soiled pajama top and panties lay in a fetal position. Shivering from the room's coolness, he could tell she studied him through her disheveled auburn hair obscuring much of her face.

"Who are you?"

The question came from the other person with her, a much older man with thinning gray hair. Similar to her, his upper body was drenched in a mixture of blood and some sort of dark grease. The bifocals he carried on a chain around his neck had been smashed. Unlike the girl, his long overcoat and casual dress clothes protected him from the cold.

"My name's David. David Hobbs."

Miriam stirred.

Shit! I need a moment to figure this out before she wakes up.

"And you are?"

"Dr. Peter Kirkland," said the man. The reply followed an exhausted sigh. He motioned to the girl, still trembling in her fetal pose. "Her name is Hanna. I have no idea what her last name is. She's already been through a lot... probably a traumatic shutdown from the looks of it."

A small rodent scurried across the floor, burrowing itself beneath the chin of the younger man's head along the wall. David grimaced in disgust, while Dr. Kirkland sat up and anxiously looked around. It was as if he might jump out of his own skin from fear, despite his calm and composed disposition just seconds ago. Dr. Kirkland watched the rat's tail disappear inside the head, and shivered almost as badly as the girl named Hanna lying prone next to him.

She no longer studied him, as her sheltered gaze moved to Evelyn. Trauma or not, her countenance reflected recognition. David felt foolish for not realizing right away that it was John's other granddaughter lying on the cold dirt floor a few feet away.

"Where is this place—do you know?" he asked, returning his attention to Dr. Kirkland.

Isn't this the bastard who set all of this bullshit in motion?

David tried not to let his anger seep through, which was difficult to manage.

"Some sort of temple that *he* brought us to," Peter replied, more of an edge in his voice than before, as if loathing the mention of the host. "The girl and I shared the same dungeon until a few hours ago. I don't know what *he* has in mind. Maybe we're supposed to witness some kind of ceremony."

A chill gripped David's heart. Yet, the professor acted as if it was no big deal, like a few guests witnessing an event no more harmful than a passion play. Maybe Dr. Kirkland had also suffered from emotional trauma.

The stench alone should keep him from being so goddamned lackadaisical!

"I take it that you've actually seen our host, huh?" said David.

"Who?" Peter seemed confused, irritating David.

"Teutates."

As soon as David spoke this name, Peter's face turned ashen, while Hanna swung her head up. Her gorgeous hazel eyes opened wide, almost maniacal. Evelyn stirred, too, along with Miriam again. Both women were on the verge of finally awakening from the spell that held them silent. While checking on them, he heard a rustling sound. Softly at first, it emanated from beyond the lone entrance to the room, to his left. Outside the entrance's stone archway, the darkness seemed impenetrable.

The rustling grew louder.

"He's coming! *They're* coming!" the professor whined, gazing fearfully toward the doorway.

The noise was joined by a louder buzz. The professor tried to lower himself to hide behind Hanna, but his bound wrists prevented him from getting close enough to her.

"*Huh?*... What's going on here?" Miriam had awakened. She glanced anxiously around, and gasped in horror when she saw the row of heads resting against the base of the wall, less than a dozen feet away. "Where the hell are we?"

The buzz changed... morphing into something more familiar.

"Sh-h-h-h!" David tried to be calm, but his apprehension overrode concern for her peace of mind.

Hornets. That's what it sounded like. An angry nest of the little monsters. Hell, as the growing dissonance stealthily approached the blackened doorway, it sounded like a massive army of the little fuckers was on the way.

Evelyn sat up straight with a start. Obviously disoriented, she glanced around the room with frightened eyes. Once she locked onto her sister's presence, a few feet to her left, she screamed. She leaned toward Hanna as far as she could manage, while her sister responded in kind. They seemed impervious to the noise causing everyone else to cover their ears. Although they couldn't touch each other, tears flowed, and their reunion would've been almost sweet, if under far different circumstances.

"I call upon the mercy of Teutates—have pity on your humble servant!" Dr. Kirkland rose to his knees, his face reflecting a curious mixture of dread and anticipation. He turned to face the doorway. "Lord of Darkness, I beseech thy favor. *Please* don't take your wrath out on me!"

David shot a worried look to Miriam, but her growing terror preoccupied her attention. Her gaze, like the professor's, faced the doorway. Ditto for the Sherman sisters, once their initial joy subsided.

"Have *mercy! Uha adadolisdi!*"

The use of a Cherokee phrase drew Evelyn's attention. She immediately turned her tear-streaked face toward the professor while he repeated the latter phrase over and over, his tone and emphasis increasing in force against the rising din from beyond the room. The buzzing rustle ceased, and everyone's eyes were fixed upon the doorway. Amid several gasps and the professor's delirious fervor, a very tall figure stepped through the doorway, shrouded by a thick, smoke-like mist as it moved closer to the five captives huddled near the altar.

"*Uha adadolisdi!*" cried Dr. Kirkland.

"Tla adadolisdi!"

The figure's deep response rumbled through the room. The voice resonated unearthly in its force and regality. The irritated tone clearly rebuffed the professor's entreaty. ~ *No mercy!*

Barely visible within the mist, David studied what he could of the tall form. A pair of well-toned human legs, defined like a bodybuilder, but each joined to a disproportionately long foot bearing long curled toenails rolled up at the end of each digit. Almost clownish. Slight vertical grooves marked both legs until shrouded by a gilded tunic.

The mist fell away as the figure reached the altar, its appearance now clear.

What the hell is this thing?

Man-like, yes. But, human? Not necessarily.

A thick, powerful torso, armed with rippling muscles as it moved, supported a massive chest graced by an ivory breastplate of exquisite detail. An agitated golden viper with menacing fangs dominated the breastplate, and the snake's eyes were a sparkling pair of brilliant rubies.

Other human qualities of the nearly eight-foot being were its arms and shoulders, bulging with fierce musculature silhouetted within a long black cloak. Its hands were in no way human, however, and nearly as elongated as its feet. Each long slender finger's nails were rolled up tight at the fingertips.

That wasn't what caused everyone to murmur in fear, while the professor tried harder to hide behind Hanna. The face eyeing them contemptuously accomplished that alone. Framed by a full mane of lustrous black hair hanging loose, chiseled features hinted at potential comeliness, if not for a pair of menacing eyes. Turquoise and cat-like in appearance but with the coldness of a hungry crocodile, they narrowed as their owner surveyed the group.

David lowered himself to the floor, his tendons immediately remembering the discomfort. Still unsure if it was a man of some sort or not, its olive facial skin bore tiny grooves similar to the ones on its legs, arms, and exposed torso. The large head might be a necessity for the immense frame, and the chin sloped to a severe point. It made the mouth much wider than anyone he'd ever laid eyes on.

The figure stepped around the altar, and the strange fire that matched his eyes revealed dark streaks along the altar's sides and a pool of congealing liquid.

Blood!

Evil exuded powerfully from the thing, and David loathed the amused look as it stepped on something unseen on the altar's other side. The snap from breaking bones and a squishing noise brought grimaces to them all, and the figure looked on its horrified audience. Its leering smile revealed a mouthful of long sharp teeth.

"Oh dear God!" whispered Miriam, her wide eyes tearing as she scooted closer to David. He had just discovered a slight looseness in the leather bonds around his wrists.

Evelyn echoed Miriam's response. She quietly chanted her incantations while returning the monster's amused gaze with a sullen one of her own. Hanna trembled, drawing her limbs tighter to her chest, which only frustrated Dr. Kirkland's efforts to seek shelter from the demon he so feared.

Teutates? This has to be him.

A small stream of blood crept toward them from the altar. Much of it was absorbed by the room's earthen floor, but a few tiny tributaries came close enough for the entire group to watch guardedly.

Teutates nodded as if fully understanding Evelyn's pleas for her magic to manifest against him. David could see her growing frustration and the fiend's full amusement. He looked at him, his smirk now mirthful.

He knows what I'm thinking? Shit!

Teutates' gaze moved on to Dr. Kirkland.

"Please... take any of *them!*" he pleaded. "They don't know you, like I do!" The professor's whine grew shriller, and he looked around, thrusting his shoulders toward the others. "The woman behind me, Evelyn Sherman—take her! It's her grandfather's fault this all happened, anyway! Yes, it's true! *Take her!*"

Teutates stepped around the altar and approached the group, his strange toenails scraping against the dirt. Any allure from afar proved grotesque up close. His eyes turned cold, meaner, as he regarded the professor. Bending down, he drew near enough to where the crow feathers in his hair grazed Peter's face.

For a moment, it looked like he might kiss the professor. But in the next instant, his fingernails unfurled and severed the rawhide bonds. He grabbed Peter's arms, dragging him to the altar.

"*Oh, God, no-o-o!*" Dr. Kirkland cried out. "*Take her—not me! Oh, please... PLEASE have MERCY! UHA ADADOLISDI!*"

He fought with all of his might, reminding David of a small toddler struggling against its mother at a grocery store.

"Nihi esga nulisdane ayv!" ~ *You offend me!*

Teutates let out a high-pitched cackle following his condemnation, while Peter continued to cry out "Uha adadolisi!"

For a moment, it looked like his captor might relent, perhaps wearier than irritated by the professor's ceaseless droning. Instead, the fiend roared and slammed him on top of the altar table. The reverberation echoed around them, effectively drowning the professor's cries. Before Dr. Kirkland drew another breath, Teutates pulled out a beautiful jeweled scepter of gold with an ivory tip from inside his cloak. The tip was very sharp, and it easily sliced through his clothes and pierced his sternum. With a sickening rip and tear of the surrounding flesh and ribcage, the professor's heart was fully exposed. Teutates unfurled his fingernails and plucked it out. He held the beating organ in his palm for all to see.

Dr. Kirkland miraculously survived, and while gasping for air, the monster reached into the professor's mouth with the other hand and severed his tongue before he could clinch his teeth. A shrill scream remained stifled in his throat.

"Unworthy of using the ancients' tongue, I've now taken his. And, see? In the end, it did *not* save him!"

The voice was almost mellow. It made the delivery of the words especially chilling. While Teutates casually tossed the severed tongue behind him, where it landed on the wall with a wet splat before sliding to the floor, David worked furiously to loosen his bonds.

Blood seeped from the professor's open chest cavity and mouth, trickling onto the altar before dripping down the sides. The carved snakes and serpents looked even more ghastly. David prayed the man was dead—especially when Teutates began to devour the heart. Only he and Evelyn watched him finish, as Miriam closed her eyes tightly while trying to inch closer to her husband. Seeing Hanna's continued repose in a fetal position, he wondered if she had abandoned her weakened conscious mind, and retreated as far as possible inside herself.

"It's going to be all right, babe," he whispered soothingly to Miriam, who opened her frightened eyes, as if to gauge his confidence. He forced a smile. "I swear I'll figure out something… I swear it on my life!"

A sardonic chuckle erupted from the altar, as Teutates watched the tender moment. His grin reeked of amused arrogance. It looked like he might be finished with Peter Kirkland's lifeless body, and ready to move on. But, first, one more trick for his terrified audience. He lifted the body, tore the head off and turned it upside down above his own head. The corpse's congealing blood flowed down, covering his entire being. The monster writhed in ecstasy, and David watched in amazement as Teutates' body completely absorbed the blood. Even the ivory breastplate became pristine again.

The transformation was incredible. The small vertical grooves in the skin disappeared, and the face and body appeared younger, the muscles bigger. Even the eyes changed, turning a deeper blue. As before, the fire's flame mimicked Teutates' eye color, turning the same sapphire shade. He passed a hand through the top of the cobalt blaze, where the flames licked his flesh but caused no damage.

"Nasgi ageyv soi!" ~ *She's next!*

The voice sounded more powerful, surely energized by Dr. Kirkland's blood. Teutates tossed the drained corpse behind him, and walked to the six heads to add a seventh. He pointed his scepter at Hanna, drawing an immediate protest from Evelyn.

"No!" she defiantly shouted. She pulled at the strap holding her wrists. "Take me instead, and let the others return home—*Please!"*

"Oh-h-h, Two Doves Rising… what an interesting offer you make!" he replied, speaking in English as he moved to the front of the altar. "But, what have you to barter with? You're already mine… mine to do with as I please!"

He chuckled, soulless and without warmth. His grin widened into an impossibly broad smile, exposing all of his blood drenched teeth. Bathed by the strange blue light, they glowed eerily. Evelyn strained against her bonds, desperate to shield her younger sister. Miriam wept, trying to scoot closer to Hanna while David watched, frustrated he could do little. Something worse than Dr. Kirkland's demise was about to befall them—he could feel it, like the air changing just before a spring rain.

Teutates raised his right hand above his head, the one not holding the scepter, and clicked the saber-like fingernails together.

"Galutsv!" ~ *Come!*

Another rustling noise emanated from beyond the doorway, and a large inky shadow moved into the room, separating into two distinct human shapes that approached Teutates. By the time they reached the altar, the specters solidified, taking on the appearance of Native American warriors. Colorless though well defined, the pair kneeled before their master.

"Bring me... that one," he instructed.

But instead of pointing the scepter at Hanna, he chose Miriam.

David's heart sank. He fought in desperation to free his wrists from the bonds, chaffing skin until his wrists bled.

"No... take the one whose family created this mess in the first place!" he cried out. *"It should be me, and me alone, Teutates! Only the slimiest slug would pick on a woman!"*

It almost worked. The blue eyes glowed with heated anger, focused completely on him. The amused grin returned, and the warriors turned to face David and Miriam, wearing menacing scowls beneath empty eye sockets.

"Ayohisdi nasgi ageyv!"

Miriam shrieked in terror as the two phantoms leaped to where she sat, slicing away her bonds and dragging her up to the altar. David screamed to bring her back, pleading to take him instead, while Evelyn shouted a litany of Cherokee curses.

Teutates chuckled, and threw his head back. Shrill cackles echoed all through the room.

Chapter Thirty-four

A pair of tan Chevy Tahoe's pulled up to John's cabin before dawn. He stood waiting by the front door, dressed in a yellow snowsuit, thick gloves, and knee-high thermal boots. Carrying his briefcase and Evelyn's laptop, he approached the lead vehicle from the Sevier County Sheriff's Department.

"Sorry we're running late," said Butch Silva, after he rolled his window down. "We didn't finish marking the site where that family from Oregon disappeared the other night until about thirty minutes ago. Last night's heavy snowfall made it that much worse."

"I understand," said John.

Immediate images of a couple and their two kids briefly flashed across his mind's eye. They had disappeared while hiking near Abrams Falls in Cades Cove. He saw their pictures last night on TV, and they had been missing since Tuesday. *They're dead—murdered by him!*

"Charley and Chris are coming with us," Butch advised, motioning to the deputies in the truck behind him. "We're bringing two snowmobiles along, just in case we need 'em. Snow pack's a bit deep in parts of the cove, so we'll see. Go ahead and get in."

John climbed into the passenger seat, setting the laptop between him and the sheriff. After removing his gloves, he opened the briefcase.

"I brought along some interesting items Evelyn was researching when she disappeared," he explained. "I'll fill you in about everything on the way there."

"Sounds good." Butch gave the ten-four signal to Charley Peacock, and the vehicles headed to the road that would take them deeper into the state park. "You told me on the phone that you want to visit John Oliver's cabin. Correct?"

"Yes," John confirmed. "Our destination is the old ravine not far from there."

"The one we used to take the girls to when we were kids?" Butch looked surprised.

"That's the place," said John, smiling wanly. "Do you remember when the university dug up some remains from the ravine last month?"

"Yeah, vaguely."

"Well, what's been going on lately around here is somehow related to that." John glanced at him, gauging his reaction. Butch didn't give an indication one way or another, although John sensed his willingness to hear more. "Including what became of the family you mentioned earlier."

They had reached the end of Beaver Falls Trail, the road that in reality was just a very long driveway to John's cabin. Butch shot John a surprised look. He looked uneasy. It had something to do with what they found earlier that morning, at the missing family's campsite.

Very bad... lots of blood in the snow.

Butch didn't reply, other than offering a thoughtful nod while turning onto Pine View Road. He didn't say anything until they were back on Cades Cove's main thoroughfare and had almost reached the Oliver property. Meanwhile, John wanted to tell him what he'd learned about the monster, Teutates. Once he realized they would likely arrive at their destination before he could finish, he decided to wait. There was plenty of time to go over this stuff later, as long as they didn't encounter the damned raven mocker.

That's what it is! Something that sucks the life out of the weak and frail.

"John Oliver's place should be just up ahead," Butch advised, clearing his throat. "Now, you said something about the university's forensic team digging up some remains recently. Why would that have anything to do with the missing family I mentioned?"

"It has to do with the ancient knowledge of my people," said John. "Something woke up out there, when Peter Kirkland and Walter Pollack decided to tear up the entire area looking for treasure. They should've kept their excavation to where the murdered girl that I told you about yesterday was buried."

"And you believe this thing that woke up is running around killing folks, huh?"

"Yes. I do."

John eyed him seriously. Butch's immediate response was a snicker, but he stifled it when he saw John's countenance remained stoic.

"Well, good buddy, I'd hate to be the one to face some so-called raven mocker." His efforts to maintain a solemn expression failed when he looked at John again. He chuckled. "Yeah, I read over that stuff I copied from Evelyn's notepad last night. I'm sorry, but that MoJo nonsense doesn't work for me. On the other hand, if we find some trace of where your granddaughters and your friends from Colorado disappeared to, it'll be worth the trip out here this morning."

John nodded, and worried Butch's nonchalant attitude might come back to hurt them. They reached the fork that would take them to the parking area just outside the Oliver site.

"If not, well, it'll mean I'll have to come up with a serious explanation as to why I dragged two of my best deputies out here. That wouldn't be good for you either, because—"

"Stop, Butch, and look!" said John, pointing to the horizon at the edge of the snow-covered meadow in front of John Oliver's homestead. In the distance, beyond the entrance to the old, forgotten path, an orange haze brightened the early morning sky, like a forest fire. It wasn't a fire, John knew. In his mind's eye, he saw what it meant... an amazing transformation had taken place in the ravine.

Butch followed John's gaze, pulling the Tahoe through two feet of snow and to the very spot where two month's earlier David Hobbs had parked his rented Buick. The night he faced Allie Mae's ghost alone. Charley brought the other vehicle alongside his truck, cutting his engine.

"Well, what the hell's going on over there?" Butch whispered. Charley and Chris noticed the glow on the horizon, both cursing under their breath. "I'll call the Fire Department."

"No!" John stopped him from picking up the radio handset. "Not yet. Let's make sure it's a fire before we contact anyone else."

Butch eyed him suspiciously, but relented. John hated using their friendship to seek leverage, but there wasn't enough time to explain why he knew that no natural flames threatened the pristine woodlands a mile or so away.

"I'm ready to get going." John stepped out of the vehicle.

He walked to the short log barrier separating the parking area from the meadow, blanketed in white, after receiving nearly a foot of fresh powder overnight. A trail of faint footprints led from the edge of the parking area to where the trees separated, likely following the obscure path to the ravine.

Someone's already there... probably waiting for us!

"Boys, it looks like we'll need the snowmobiles after all," Butch advised, after he and the two assistants joined him by the meadow's edge. Chris Girard seemed barely old enough to be a policeman, with boyish good looks that made John wonder if he was the deputy Evelyn mentioned when she visited him at the jail.

Good kid... raised well by decent folk.

Tiny, flurried snowflakes clung to Charley Peacock's handlebar moustache. Blonde with gray eyes, and a face destined from birth to become the mug of a grizzled lawman, he nodded to John before walking to his truck to help Butch unhook the snowmobiles in the truck bed. Tinted Raybans shielded his eyes. John knew he thought the trip out here was pointless, but revered the sheriff for whom he'd worked these past eight years.

"I'll ride with Chris, and Charley will take you with him, John," Butch advised once the Kawasakis were unloaded.

Bright red and covered on all sides with orange reflective tape they looked almost brand new. Butch motioned for Charley and John to follow him and Chris. At Charley's insistence, they brought a large bag of flame repellant, despite John's repeated assurances the glowing sky had nothing to do with a fire of any kind. The deputy responded with a snide look.

Once the trucks were locked, Chris and Charley started up the snowmobiles and the group pursued the footprints across the meadow. The Oliver cabin sat off to the right, its snow-buried roof and porch glistening from the morning's first rays of sunlight. They reached the break in the tree line, where deep snowdrifts obscured the path leading to the ravine. The fiery glow seemed more ethereal, its source closer.

The group paused before going further, but not because of that.

"What the hell's going on?"

Butch posed the question while the engines idled softly. The ground rumbled ahead of them, the deep snow shifting amid swaying oaks, elms, and pines. The earth continued to shake until whatever approached from beneath the snow stopped, a few feet away.

A terrible foreboding threatened to suffocate John's psyche. He looked around, searching for whatever studied them... the presence keenly hostile. Even the others seemed to feel it. Butch and Charley's expressions were perplexed, and Chris's countenance was pale, fearful.

John considered going back. But Evelyn and Hanna's lives were worth far more than his own, not to mention David and Miriam. True, they might be dead, but he didn't think so. It felt wrong... still incomplete.

He stepped off the Kawasaki, his feet disappearing in snow past his knees.

"Y'all should go back," he said, and turned to Butch, who urged him to get back on the snowmobile behind Charley. "I must go on, alone. If I find them all and make it back, then I'll see you again soon, my friend. If not, know that I go in peace."

John turned away. The feeling of dire dread from a moment ago lessened, as if defeated by his determination to press forward. He began the solo trek to the ravine, struggling to move through drifted snow.

"Wait!"

When John looked back, he saw Butch confer with his deputies for a moment and Chris joined Charley on his snowmobile, turning the vehicle back toward the parking area. Once the two deputies were halfway across the meadow, Butch brought the other snowmobile to John.

"How long have we known each other?" asked Butch, his smile elfin.

"Going on fifty-two years, I'd say." John returned his smile with a wry grin. "You don't have to do this—"

"The hell you say, buddy!" He revved the engine. "Climb aboard. For better or worse, I'm coming with you. I just pray you know what the hell you're doing, John."

"There's only one way to find out," John told him after a slight pause. "Now I've got six lives to worry about instead of five. Thanks."

"You just worry about finding your little girls and that couple from Colorado, and I'll take care of my own ass!" Butch's smile grew brighter, but his eyes revealed the depth of his unease. "You best get on this thing now, before the ground starts shaking again."

John hopped on, and the two continued. The weird shifting beneath the snow remained quiet, although the air crackled with energy. The feeling of being watched and studied intensified as they moved closer to the ravine, and it became almost debilitating. Meanwhile, the brightness in front of them grew to a near-blinding glare, obscuring most of the trees lining both sides of the dormant streambed.

When they reached the top of the ravine, Butch cut the engine. The dawn's light filled the winter sky, and as it did, the powerful radiance inside the ravine waned. What had been obscured was now clearly revealed. They could only stare.

Tsvsgino.

"What the hell is that thing?"

Butch asked the question, while John considered the irony.

Why, yes, good buddy, that thing you see is an actual part of Hell, Hades or perhaps your Druid ancestors' Realm of Darkness. Tsvsgino is my people's name for the same place... where souls of the damned reside.

The scaffolds and walkways from the University of Tennessee's excavation in November lay scattered across the landscape. The circular, limestone structure jutting out of the ravine's basin appeared responsible, its height rising above the surrounding tree line. At least sixty feet by John's estimation and its width triple that guess.

'Sort of looks like one of Susanne's cornmeal muffins she used to make, with a cylinder base and a big, mushroom-like puff on top. And the grayish upper-half reminds me of some sort of insect haven. A giant wasp or hornet nest?

"Hanna and Evelyn are in there," said John, his tone subdued, unlike the debate raging inside his head. "I'm going in."

"That's a bad idea, John—a *very* bad idea!"

Butch glanced worriedly at him before returning his gaze to the garish structure before them, its hive-like top expanding and contracting, ever so slightly.

"The best thing—the *smart* thing to do is get some back-up in here right away!"

John already made up his mind. He wasn't willing to wait... not while the minute chance of saving his granddaughters was still viable. Hopefully, it was still the case for David and Miriam as well. Getting inside the thing looked like it might be a problem. There wasn't an entrance, at least not obvious to his aging eyes.

It doesn't matter—I'll figure it out.

He stepped off the snowmobile and moved toward the slope nearest to the nest-like structure. A buzzing sound drew his and Butch's attention from behind... someone else was coming.

"Well I'll be damned!" said Butch, cracking a grateful smile. "Charley and Chris are back!"

Fearing the two deputies might stop him, John waded through the snow until he reached the ravine's basin. He moved as quickly as possible, stumbling and almost falling face first while he desperately sought an entrance. Butch shouted for him to come back, while his assistants scrambled down the ravine's embankments to catch him. Their shouts sounded more irritated than their boss's, and it provided motivation to move faster.

Unfamiliar symbols covered the walls, aligned in winding designs and similar to what he discovered in his cabin's guestroom yesterday. A blast of air, warm with an odor of mildew, wafted downward. The puffed-out gray section closest to him expanded, and looked like a giant paper lung with its ventricles open.

Was it breathing?

Quick, Running Deer... step around to the other side, where the images are not so many.

A small tunnel in the snow looked like it went all the way down into the limestone base. Meanwhile, the deputies reached the bottom of the ravine.

Damn it—there's no time left! I need to get inside this thing, NOW!

He dropped to his knees, scooping away snow and ice with his hands. Ignoring Butch's urgent shouts to stop and wait, John paused long enough to cast a glance over his shoulder. As he feared, the two deputies were racing to stop him before he slid inside the tunnel. When they reached him, two wispy phantom warriors appeared, instantly solidifying. Before either Charley or Chris could react, the warriors grabbed their arms and pulled them headfirst into the wall, leaving only the echoes from their shrill screams.

Chapter Thirty-five

If only I'd listened to David!

The thought ripped through Miriam's head. Still conscious, she wouldn't be for much longer. The assault upon her mind and soul was unmatched by anything she'd ever experienced, and when it included her body, death would be assured.

Teutates grinned, as if fully aware of the rampant images feeding her brain. His teeth still dripped with Dr. Kirkland's blood as he drew closer. The stench of blood, raw flesh, and things long dead filled her nostrils. She tried to get away, but the guardians who brought her to the monster held her down, pressed against the marble altar. The table's coldness aroused taut gooseflesh along her backside, from neck to ankles. That was nothing compared to the sheer horror of lying in a pool of congealing human blood, along with small pieces of Teutates' latest victims. Miriam fought to keep the vomit down, her jeans and sweater sopping up enough of the mess to where deep crimson crept toward the front of her garments.

And now this. Please, God, make him get out of my head!

She could hear David scream—begging them to take him instead of her, which she'd never allow. The love of her life, it would be up to him to try and survive... someone needed to be there for the kids.

I'll never see them again, my dearest children!

She turned to her husband. He jerked madly at his bonds, and even with eyes clouded by tears she saw blood run down his arms, as the rawhide strips tore into his flesh. She mouthed *I love you* and would've preferred watching him over what awaited her, but a ghoulish, empty-eyed warrior obscured her view. She gasped, despite already seeing more of the vile creature than she cared to, its breathless hiss enough to get her to turn away.

Teutates remained, amused and patient, the demon Evelyn accurately defined from her web search. Raven mocker. That's what she called it. It was nothing like the pictogram from an old manuscript she showed her. A funny thought occurred to her, which made her wonder if it happens to everyone about to die. While picturing the old hag in the pictogram, running from a tribe of angry Indians after stealing the soul of a sick loved-one, she thought of Little Red Riding Hood.

My, what big teeth you have.

Her musing died before its birth was complete, as a louder, deeper voice sounded in her mind.

The better to eat you with, my dear!

She closed her eyes tight, as the nauseating breath of Teutates drew closer. Near enough to take a huge bite out of her left cheek, she grimaced, helpless and resigned to a terrible demise. His amused chuckle confirmed not only the ownership of the sinister voice within her, but also the monster's delight in her present agony as she wondered what would come next.

Just get it over with. Kill me and let the others go!

More chuckles… joined by dry rasps from the ghouls on either side.

Not yet. More fun first.

New images flowed into her head. A woman and a little girl. The ones whose heads lay a few feet behind her against the wall.

They started with the woman… violated? But how… my God! They touched her! Touched her in a way their boney fingers and sharp fingernails could not, and yet the damage was the same. Raped in her mind … forced to orgasmic explosion beyond anything she ever experienced in life, while her husband watched!

They killed her, gutting the body like a deer and removing her heart and head. The images moved on. Daddy dead, only the little girl remained alive. Sharon was her name.

Dear Jesus, don't make me see this—PLEASE don't make me watch! ANYTHING BUT THIS!

Miriam screamed. She shrieked until she began to pass out. It wasn't enough to keep all of the images out of her awareness, but somehow it lessened the immediate blow to her fraying mind. She heard David's frantic calls, and even Evelyn called her name. Nothing from Hanna yet, although if what she went through in her few days of captivity was anything like this, Miriam understood the reasons for her apparent emotional and mental collapse.

The assault continued… but not to her body.

Her breasts warmed, and her nipples rose against her brassiere. A tingling sensation ran along both sides of her neck to her shoulders, growing more and more intense.

*He's kissing me... soft, moist touches along my neck...
moving down... oh, shit!*

Other tingling sensations began along the balls of her
feet, moving slowly up her legs. To her horror, both
sensations moved between her legs. Pleasure beyond
anything she'd ever known overwhelmed her, and David
was a skilled lover who seldom failed to bring her to
orgasm. Wave upon wave of ecstasy radiated from her
pelvis. She couldn't stifle the moans threatening to
become joyful cries—the complete opposite of what she
felt.

I fucking hate you, you goddamned bastard!

Suddenly, the terrible rapture ceased. Gasping for
breath, Miriam opened her eyes. Teutates and his
assistants stood around her, but she no longer drew their
attention.

"Hanigi Agowadvdi!" ~ *Go see!*

The two warriors' grinning expressions were solemn,
although hard to tell for certain with mainly hollow eye
sockets. In the next instant, they flew out of the room,
moving through the darkened doorway and leaving
shadowed tendrils dissolving in the air.

Teutates grunted. For a moment, his countenance bore
suspicion. He brought his gaze back to her, the hellish
smile soon returning.

Time for a little more fun.

Chapter Thirty-six

Dropped into darkness, John landed hard on his butt. More of a chute than a tunnel, he slid for roughly fifty feet before the drop. Thinking he might need it, he packed a small flashlight within the breast pocket of his snowsuit. After getting to his feet, he dusted himself off and brought it out. Once he turned the flashlight on, the beam revealed a narrow corridor. The ceiling was barely tall enough for him to stand, and appeared to be covered in serpentine drawings that stretched beyond the light's reach.

A wall behind him indicated the only way to go along the passageway was forward. He moved cautiously, on the lookout for the two deputies and the phantoms that abducted them. After traveling roughly one hundred feet through the winding tunnel, he heard the sound of rushing water.

A waterfall? Here in this ravine? Impossible!

It was difficult to picture the water flow's source, as the stream that ran through the ravine dried up decades earlier. Yet, as he moved forward, the soft roar of water moving swiftly grew stronger.

Then he saw it.

A gray marble statue, several stories high, loomed before him. Its carved features were remarkable in their realism. The subject was a mix between man and reptile.

A serpent's body merged with the torso of a man, or something similar to mankind.

He walked up to it, marveling that something like this would be here, inside a weird looking structure inside the Great Smoky Mountains National Park. The details and style of the artisanship seemed much more akin to something he would expect to see in New York or some other big city—or in the standing ancient ruins of Europe and the Middle East.

Definitely the depiction of a deity, the statue's gaze bore anger as it surveyed the opening to the corridor before it. Its arms and elongated hands spread out to embrace, and seemed almost welcoming if not for the sharp talons at the end of each finger. The long predatory teeth were bared menacingly at whoever prepared to leave the safety of the corridor.

Teutates? It had to be.

Behind the statue, a waterfall filled a large basin. As John peered out from the corridor, what awaited further amazed his weary mind. Although his flashlight's beam could only reach so far, the basin fed two streams flowing through an immense gorge. It was an underground chasm unlike any he'd ever seen. Thick marble columns rose high into the air, and another, much larger corridor separated the two streams. The column closest to him bore the image of a glistening serpent in a brilliant array of colors. The craftsmanship's excellence surprised him, as well as the priceless content, assuming precious gemstones were used, as appeared to be the case.

Above the waterfall's din, he heard faint screams floating toward him. Not taking any chances, he ducked down to avoid detection. *Is it a woman or a man screaming?* Where the screams came from was difficult to tell. The only way to explore further meant traveling along a narrow wooden walkway crossing the chasm in front of the statue. It looked sturdy enough to support a young boy or girl, but in no way a man John's size.

"Asdawadvsdi Ayv!" ~ *Follow me!*

Huh?

The voice came as a whisper from behind. John turned to look, but there was no one there. Yet, he recognized the voice. It was the same one that addressed him in the jail cell three nights ago.

"Ududu?"

It felt strange uttering the question, and he prayed it really was his grandfather, Two Eagles Cry, with him now.

"Howaayelvdi Ayv Adatlisvi Awi inage ehi!" ~ *Trust me, Running Deer!*

The urgency in the voice reminded him of how his grandfather sounded when exasperated with him as a kid. Still, one couldn't be too careful with a clever demon lurking about.

The bridge creaked, and when it did, the image of a wolf appeared, its amber eyes aglow under the beam of his flashlight. The wolf whined, pawing the wooden slats of the bridge. It took an invisible push on John's back, strong enough to make him stumble, to get him moving. The wolf wagged its tail and barked, eluding John's attempt to touch it. Ignoring the bridge's incessant creaks and groans, he focused on the wolf, greatly relieved when he finally made it across. Once he stepped off, two of the wooden slats broke, tumbling down to the murky bottom.

Ah, hell, we'll have to find another way out of here.

The wolf whined, drawing his attention to a steep marble staircase that would take him to the corridor. Leading the way, the wolf checked several times to make sure he followed.

John couldn't believe the enormous size of the gorge's main room—in itself many times larger than the structure's outer size indicated. *Is this really the same place, or some other world?* A distant blue light provided enough illumination to discern his surroundings, and the enormous hall he steeped into resembled an immense cathedral or temple. More and more columns came into view, each decorated with the same serpent imagery.

The screams had grown silent, but resumed once he reached the corridor. They were getting louder and more plaintive.

Sounds like a man to me… better hurry!

He soon had a better idea of where the screams originated. Another staircase loomed in the distance, and at the top was an open doorway. The bluish glow acted like a beacon in the cavern, emanating from beyond the doorway and getting brighter as he approached.

That's got to be the right place! I'm coming Evelyn, Hanna! Hold on, everyone!

The wolf trotted faster, and John stepped up his pace. A loud roar suddenly filled the air behind him, followed by powerful wings flapping. He couldn't see the thing clearly, as only its shadow hovered near the top of the columns. It moved very fast, rising toward the doorway where the blue light emanated from, blotting it out... at least for a moment.

It's coming back... for me?

The wolf suddenly whined, cowering low to the corridor's tiled floor before scurrying over to the nearest column's base. John followed, although nowhere near as quickly. He stumbled and fell. The wolf barked worriedly, urging him to scramble to safety. But the opportunity for escape was lost by the time he picked himself up. A colossal dragon descended with its hungry mouth opened wide, poised to devour him.

Chapter Thirty-seven

The pain in his wrists was severe, but David almost freed himself.

Making progress at last!

He kept a worried eye on the altar. Until a few moments ago, he knew for certain the love of his life would perish. At least Miriam hadn't been hurt physically... he was pretty sure, anyway. Yet, with that much blood on her, who knew for sure?

She's breathing... all curled up like Hanna. The other assholes held her, they made her cry. Goddamn them all!

Teutates seemed preoccupied with something other than Miriam. He held his scepter out before him... lost in admiration? The golden handle glistened, covered with jewels similar to the ones his aunt brought last week from Chattanooga. Only one stone was missing, and the barren circular space on the handle looked vaguely familiar.

Quit worrying about shit like that and get these suckers off, man! Don't plan on him staying in that stupor for long!

The observation proved prophetic, as a moment later the two fiends returned, carrying a local sheriff's deputy between them. The man wasn't much older than David, in his late-thirties with similar blonde hair, and he was putting up a desperate fight. He clawed to free himself, screaming between whimpers. It drew a terrified look from

Evelyn, and even Hanna looked up. Miriam remained in her fetal position on the altar's table, trembling.

Teutates smiled and motioned for his assistants to bring the man to him. He pushed Miriam off of the altar, her prone body landing with a thud on the floor. But her life had been spared for now.

David looked up and saw the monster eyeing him, amusedly.

"David Hobbs. Perhaps you will enjoy how we deal with infidels... those who don't believe I am!" he announced, his tone deep and graveled with a touch of mirth.

David looked away. Afraid to look at anyone, and loathe to witness what would happen next, he focused on the floor around his knees. All the while, he worked his wrists.

Hurts like a mother... but the left one is almost through... and the other isn't far behind.

As soon as the phantoms finished dragging their captive to the altar, Teutates brought his scepter to the man's face. For a moment, he studied him while drawing the ultra-sharp ivory tip across his forehead and down each cheek. David peeked in time to see several rivers of blood form, the deputy whimpering louder while his knees buckled.

Teutates brought one of his unfurled fingernails underneath the man's chin, allowing the blood to collect inside it. When full, he brought it to his mouth and drank.

"This is the faint remembrance of you, since very shortly your life force and essence will be gone from this world forever," he told the man. "But as you die, know that you've provided great pleasure and delight this day, and a feast of flesh for my servants."

"Please, I beg you—don't do it! I'll do anything— anything you ask!" the deputy cried out between heartrending sobs, a wet spot in his crotch spreading quickly. *"Don't h-hurt me-e-e! Have mercy, pl-l-e-e-e-a-s- s-s-e!"*

"I understand," said Teutates, his tone soothing. "Perhaps there is a way to work this out... a way that suits you better."

He motioned for the others to release him, and when they complied with Teutates' wish, he pulled him off the alter and close to his bosom, where the pair walked around the altar with the demon's arm placed around the man's shoulders.

Until then, the deputy would've only seen the older, dusty remains along the wall and the fresh blood dripping down the sides of the altar. But the escalated look of horror upon his face confirmed he hadn't seen the row of severed heads until now.

He shrieked and tried to escape, managing one step to freedom before Teutates subdued him. Flinging him like a rag doll over his shoulder, the deputy landed harder than Dr. Kirkland, flat on his back upon the altar, splashing blood from prior victims onto his mortified audience. Teutates held him fast and whispered something undecipherable to the warriors, who had fallen to their knees in deference when he took the deputy from their grasp.

The foul guardians smiled and stood. Savage in their attack, one pulled the man's head back to scalp him while the other ripped open his parka and sweater. David tried to ignore the pitiful cries, glancing at Evelyn who wept near Hanna, and his beloved Miriam, who brought her hands up to shield her ears, and tightly shutting her eyes. But, nothing could prepare them for what came next.

Once the deputy's abdomen and chest lay bare, the warriors tore a hole in his belly. Each grabbed a portion of his intestines and began to slowly devour them. Blood and other tissue flowed freely as the deputy writhed in unspeakable agony, and whose ear-splitting screams poured out hoarsely from his open throat.

There would be no relief, at least not soon enough. Long before he died, Evelyn passed out from the horror, and Miriam came closer to Hanna's comatose state. A feeling of weakness swept through David, his last memory of the event, spurred by revulsion and the sense of kinship with someone whose fate he would soon share. Everything faded to black, where the discordance of Teutates' hearty laughter and the deputy's final cries could no longer reach him.

Chapter Thirty-eight

The flying serpent looked as if it might make yet another pass. It miraculously missed John the first time, its hot, foul breath grazing his snowsuit as he fell backwards. The colorful creature's jaws snapped loudly, closing on empty air.

I must get up! Where did Grandfather's avatar go?

John looked around anxiously, knowing in a matter of seconds the soaring menace would plunge again, correcting its earlier misjudgment. In his mind's eye, the images divided. One showed him escaping certain death, reunited with Two Eagles Cry morphed as a wolf. The other image was an omen of serrated separation, bitten in half with his lower torso and legs falling sideways to the ground, while the upper half provided nourishment to the giant reptile.

In the dimness behind him, near the edge of the corridor, two glowing eyes peered from behind a pillar, twenty feet away. A terrible cramp seized his left thigh, but he ignored it and limped to whatever waited for him, the echo from his boot heels resounding louder than he would've liked. The sound not only revealed his present location, but also his intended destination.

Stay low, Running Deer.... Dive!

The serpent's talons ripped his hood away, tearing it away from the rest of the snowsuit. He rolled away, scurrying around the column's base. The creature's tall shadow hovered nearby, and its claws scraped across the floor's marble squares as it retraced John's prior movements, tracking his scent.

Quietly, he removed his boots, his socked feet chilled by the marble floor. He turned to check on his pursuer's latest location.

"Asdawadvda Ayv Gani!" ~ *Follow my lead!*

It was the voice from earlier, whispered from the shadows roughly thirty feet away. Between two columns, the panting wolf's glowing eyes appeared. Meanwhile, snorts from the serpent distracted him, coming from the other side of the column he presently hid behind.

It's about to find me… I smell its seared breath!

"Edoa Asdudi, Adatlisvi Awi inage ehi!!"

His grandfather's voice called urgently, commanding him to stay close. The glowing eyes vanished. Rather than wait for them to show up in a new locale, John scurried to where he last saw them. The wolf was on the move, and its eyes peered around another column, roughly a dozen feet further away.

John hurried to where the eyes waited. They didn't disappear until he almost reached them, in time to see the faint outline of a furry gray tail move away. He glanced over his shoulder. The dragon landed where he was just thirty seconds earlier. Its mist-filled snorts drifted in the air, hanging as a cloud until the moisture fell to the floor. To his left, the corridor's path approached the base of the other tall marble staircase.

The man's screams were getting worse... he was begging for his life. The screams were definitely louder now from atop the tall staircase.

The doorway where the blue glow is coming from. They're all up there. I can feel their life force... they're not dead yet.

"Galutsv!" ~ *Come!*

Despite the nearness of the menace, the wolf moved back into the corridor. It quietly trotted to the staircase and ascended the stairs. John didn't need further encouragement, stepping light on his feet to avoid detection. The wolf waited, and they hurried up the staircase.

It surprised John that an attack didn't happen sooner, casting several more glances over his shoulder to where he last saw the colorful dragon, amid the tall columns where he left his boots. Suddenly, a loud screech filled the air above where he stood, a few steps below the staircase's pinnacle.

Run!

Flapping wings and an enormous shadow announced its descent. The wolf leapt over the last few stairs, snarling as it turned to face the aggressor fifty times its size. John scrambled up the stairs, wheezing as his heart thudded madly. Strong and virile at his late age, the stress and physical challenge of making it this far caught up with him. Once past the wolf, he started to collapse, even as the hungry dragon bore down.

Just another ten to fifteen feet and I'll be there. I can see the walls to a room on the doorway's other side. Hanna's in there… Evelyn, too!

The dragon landed behind him with a heavy thud, drawing one last weary look from John. Resigned to the likelihood he wouldn't succeed in saving anyone, he collapsed to the ground, cowering from an immense mouthful of sharp pointed teeth.

It could've been where his life ended—*should've* ended. But the wolf he believed to be his grandfather, Two Eagles Cry, wouldn't allow it.

Before the dragon could take the bite to end John's life, the wolf bit the thing on its right leg. It shrieked more in irritation than pain, swinging its wings around, and catching the wolf under its chin. It landed hard on the stairs, yelping as it tumbled down to the corridor. John moved to rescue the wolf, but his grandfather's voice inside his head urged him to keep going… to get through the doorway.

Lacking strength to run, John leaned forward, stumbling the rest of the way. The smell of seared breath followed him, and the angry serpent almost won.

Something else took him. Something with powerful, boney hands yanked him through the doorway. It was the last thing he remembered before passing out.

Chapter Thirty-nine

Searing pain sliced through the sleeves of John's coat. Both of his arms were held fast.

"Ulihelisdi Awiadisi!"

The voice was unnaturally deep, and the resonance caused a slight tremor in the circular room's walls. Not since he was a young boy had anyone used the shorter Cherokee version of his name—one his grandfather shunned.

Welcome Running Deer!

The figure before him was taller than any man he had ever seen. It stood before an ornate altar made of white marble coated in blood. The room was immersed in a bluish glow, created by a roaring cobalt fire fed only by a pile of human bones.

This is where they died... the ones he killed. Sacrificed for amusement. Eight heads in a neat row behind the altar—like the wolf's head and paws left for me at the edge of my property.

The figure smiled, and John knew it read his thoughts. Human in some ways, with handsome features mixed with hideous attributes, the coldness of its cat-like eyes made him the most uneasy. They seemed to bore through him, singeing his sentient awareness as if carelessly sifting through his rampant thoughts.

"Teutates?"

John felt ashamed by his nervousness, since he hoped to exhibit strength in front of Evelyn, who looked terrified. An auburn-haired girl lying next to her trembled in filth…. *Hanna!* Alarmed at her condition and near-nakedness, he lurched forward, instinctive in his urge to rescue them at all costs.

Twin hisses filled his ears. Until now, his captors stayed hidden behind thick veils of darkness, holding him fast with invisible iron-clad grips upon each arm. Their faces materialized on either side. The faint odor of ginger overwhelmed that of death. They grimaced maliciously, made worse by vacant eyes and paper-like flesh peeled away from their foreheads. What surprised him most were black crow feathers in their hair. Although similar feathers adorned Teutates' hair, hanging from ornamental beads in his long raven mane, the simpler manner in which these two wore theirs angered him.

Danuwa analihi! Warriors, both of them… disgraced!

"No more than you, Running Deer," said Teutates, his voice far more mellow as he moved to Evelyn.

Yanked up by her hair with his right hand, in a swift move that escaped John's eyes, the rolled fingernails in his left hand unfurled to slice through her bonds. He brought her close to his chest, pulling her hair back to expose her throat.

"You've deserted the calling of your people, leaving it to a woman. Neither you nor she are worthy of life!"

Evelyn gasped in pain as he wrapped his long fingers through her hair, like rollers, and pulled tighter.

"Don't hurt her! I beg of you, *please!*" John fell to his knees on the dirt floor.

A better view than he would've liked of the row of severed heads, the last one belonged to Deputy Charley Peacock. Wearing an expression of terrible pain and horror when he died, it looked like he'd been scalped first, with enough savage force to tear through the outer rim of his skullcap. Charley must've been the man he heard crying and screaming, offering a plea eerily similar to his own.

Another woman lay trembling next to Deputy Peacock's severed head, which John guessed to be Miriam. He noticed David hanging from a pole.

They're still alive!

Blood poured down David's wrists as he desperately fought the bonds. John looked away, trying not to think about how close David was to freeing himself.

He might be our last hope!

"Why should I listen to you, cowardly man?"

Teutates' voice was gleeful as he addressed John again. He brought his index razor just below Evelyn's chin. John didn't know what to say. If it was possible to save her—or any of them for that matter—he had just one shot. One shot to get it right.

Agatoli Uktena!

His grandfather's voice pierced his mind.

Ududu? Are you in here with us under the guise of a new spirit form? Along with his grandfather's voice came an image of the ruby. *Where is it?* John last remembered seeing it back at the cabin. *It's in the box on the mantle...*

what good would it do anyway? Why are you showing me this, Grandfather?

Teutates paused, and acute interest replaced the smug look.

He still might kill her, but maybe….

The monster withdrew saber-tipped fingers from her throat, reaching within his cloak and producing his gilded scepter. John immediately recognized it.

Something about the way it glistens… spectacular but incomplete.

Teutates smiled, revealing Piscean rows of sharp teeth.

"So, the holiest stone is somewhere near?" asked the monster. Teutates turned the scepter to where John could see the lone empty groove within the ornate handle. Home to the ruby David brought, long ago it had been removed from the ravine by his infamous ancestor, Billy Ray Hobson. "The Eye of Uktena rests in your living room?"

Tla!

The voice of Two Eagles Cry, his grandfather was louder this time. No, the ruby wasn't there.

Did someone already take it? Maybe Teutates or the dishonored ones took it, and he's just toying with us… intent on delivering prolonged agony through our emotions.

"We no longer need you," said Teutates. A very bad development.

No, Running Deer. No one else took it. You have it… you brought it with you when you picked up the flashlight from the mantle. Don't you remember? It's in your coat.

"I was wrong—it's somewhere else!" blurted John. Coyness could either save him or hasten his death. "You'll be wasting your time if you go to my home to look for it. And, if you hurt any of us, you may never find your ruby."

A dangerous gamble and a stupid move if his thoughts gave him away. Teutates gave no indication one way or another, although his expression seemed to soften.

"Uwoyeni nasgi gawohilvdodi.naquu." ~ *Hand it over now.*

Back to my native tongue? He's desperate to make sure he gets it back. Why??

"Nasgi nigesvna nihi tsateli!" ~ *It's not yours!*

"Tla! Nasgi Aquateseli!!" ~ *No! It IS mine!!*

Teutates' voice grew deep again, threatening. He pulled Evelyn closer, bringing the scepter's ivory tip beneath her chin. She screamed and a small river of blood appeared. John cried out for him to stop. His remorse was immediate and profound.

"Don't do it, Grandpa!" Evelyn pleaded bravely. "He'll kill us all if you tell him!"

It was too late. Distressed for her welfare, his thoughts betrayed him. Only for an instant, but he pictured where it lay hidden, tucked inside a small zippered compartment in his snowsuit. Teutates smiled, the scepter's ivory tip bearing Evelyn's blood poised to sever her neck while she sobbed, ostensibly resigned to her death.

"Adanedi nasgi ayv!"

The shadowed wraiths tore open John's snowsuit, eager to comply with their master's command to bring the ruby to him.

"No—get your hands off me!" John shouted.

Undeterred, they rifled through his pockets until one of them located the jewel. As one fiend held it up for his partner to admire, John managed a solid nudge. The ruby slipped from the wraith's boney fingers, landing on the floor. For a moment, it looked like it might roll in a tight circle and fall over. While the pair sought to recover the jewel, it rolled toward Teutates, who reached with one hand while he tightened his grip on Evelyn's hair with the other.

Disquelvdi uyotsuhi!

John gave no indication he heard anything. Two Eagles Cry's latest admonition was shouted with confidence, and John watched as the ruby veered toward the blue fire burning nearby. Before Teutates could grab it, the gemstone rolled into the fire, where it settled in front of the burning skull.

The spell's been broken!

Undeterred, Teutates stuck his long fingers into the flame, intent on retrieving the prized ruby. He quickly drew back his hand, wearing a look of angry surprise. He tried it again with his fingernails fully unfurled. The flame morphed from cobalt to emerald. His fingernails ignited. The green flames raced up his hand, where Teutates' long fingers' flesh split open.

Howling in tremendous pain, he tried to douse the blaze in the pooled blood on the altar's table. When the blaze traveled up his arm, he released Evelyn, tearing out a few clumps of her hair. A slight tremor moved through the walls and across the ceiling, steadily increasing as if determined to seize and destroy the vile place, this temple of death.

The ghostly warriors released John, backing away and worriedly casting their hollowed eyes in every direction. They seemed wary of something unseen and unheard by John and everyone else. A distressed roar from a very unhappy dragon resounded beyond the sacrificial room's doorway.

"Evelyn! Hanna!" cried John, as he ran to his granddaughters.

Evelyn finished removing Hanna's bonds, and his youngest granddaughter looked at him with frightened eyes peering through matted locks. John tearfully embraced them both, while keeping a watchful eye on the monster whose left arm had become a sizzling torch.

Teutates' muscles began to whither and disintegrate, amid flames changing to orange and then yellow. Even the fire supported by the pile of bones changed, burning in natural form and color, as well. The bones themselves turned black before collapsing into a pile of ashes. However, the ruby remained pristine. It glowed radiantly from within the fire's midst.

David finally freed himself. With the demon preoccupied with its survival, he ran to Miriam and gathered her into his arms. Barely conscious, he wrapped her arms around his shoulders.

"We've got to get out of here!" urged John, turning his attention to the doorway.

Teutates' servants remained distracted, their gazes fixed upon the glistening spheres covering the walls and ceiling. Each glowed brightly.

The surge rumbling through the earth grew louder, and the floor shook. The warriors no longer looked to their master for guidance and protection, who was immersed in flames, shrieking in agony as the fire consumed him wholly, without mercy. Meanwhile, the spheres began to vibrate. One by one they detached, floating along the perimeter of the room. Like a small army of crystal bubbles, the croquet-sized orbs drifted in an array of brilliant colors toward the room's only exit, where the warriors cowered. The spheres attacked them, tearing away the fabric of their dark essences. With each hit, a human soul briefly materialized. Colonial pioneers to Native Americans and even Appalachian coal miners appeared, and many more, both male and female.

Joined by similar balls of light crowding outside the doorway, enough souls overwhelmed the pair. They disintegrated, spiraling to the ground as twin piles of black dust, similar to what was left of the pile of human bones, their choked rasps extinguished.

John urged Evelyn to help him carry Hanna, who briefly resisted their efforts. But the spell on her and Miriam lifted. Less disoriented, Hanna seemed to fully recognize her grandfather for the first time. She reached for him to take her, squalling like an infant.

Teutates loomed above them, standing on the blood-soaked altar. Poised to pounce with his arms spread wide, he couldn't follow through with his evil intent. Still immersed in flames, he let out a derisive cackle, followed by a string of threats mostly unintelligible, perhaps from dialects long dead. But instead of leaping on them, he fell backward. From the altar's other side, the fire's sickening pop and sizzle continued to consume him.

A low sigh followed, dispersed into the air, and then came silence. The sorrowful moans from the dragon protecting the temple also subsided. However, for a demon such as this, John doubted the end would be this clean. In his mind's eye, he saw the agony continue... the shrieks of a condemned spirit thrown into impenetrable darkness, forced to feel pain and wretchedness long after the physical form became mere ashes and dust.

"Sorry, my friend, that our reunion is under such dire circumstances," he quietly told David, pausing to gently grasp his arm and careful to not aggravate the wrist wounds. John peered around the altar.

"Well, it certainly wasn't the original plan," David agreed, chuckling sadly, walking gingerly as he peered over the altar's other edge. "At least we now have lots to catch up on."

Teutates, or what was left of his charred and molten body, lay still. Like bacon in a skillet, the skin, eyes, and fatty tissue bubbled and popped, releasing a nauseating sulfuric stench wafting toward them. Small rivers from the melting mass of Teutates' corpse joined to form a large puddle next to a bludgeoned, headless torso of a man lying behind the altar. A light gray mist arose from the demon's disintegrating corpse, drifting down to a small crack in the wall, where it disappeared.

Is that the anisgina's sacred essence? His immortal soul? Or, did he even die? Look—no bones!

John grimaced as he watched the remaining discernible features dissolve into the puddle, steadily shrinking as it fed the growing mist sucked into the crack, pulled along by a powerful draft or vacuum.

John looked at David, whose facial expression told him that they shared a similar conclusion.

This shit's far from over!

"Hurry—follow me!!" John moved to the doorway as Evelyn and Hanna joined him.

David returned to where Miriam waited, helping her stand and guiding her to the room's exit. He paused to grab the gilded scepter lying on the floor. It ignited before he touched it, and he quickly withdrew his hand.

"Don't stop for anything! We've got to get out of here before he comes back!" warned John, just before stepping out of the room.

"Who, Teutates?" asked Evelyn, worriedly, her voice hoarse from her personal ordeal with the demon. "I thought he just died...."

She didn't finish her words, but the expression on her face confirmed her understanding of a different fate.

John watched the images in her mind, including what she picked up from his recent witness of the burning remains of the demon. But unlike his awareness, her spirit followed the anisgina's flight from the room, disappearing into the darkened depths of a hellish world that flourished far below where they presently stood. Gathering strength and malice, Teutates would return... soon. *Very* soon. And when he did, there would be no moment of carelessness. No toying with his prey. Suffering on a level unheard of before… that's what the demon intended to deliver to each of them, individually, next time.

We can't afford to wait—every second counts! I'll lead the way!

But the memory of the broken bridge slats returned to John's awareness. How in the hell would they get to the other side of the bridge? It just wasn't possible. Maybe there would be another way, once they made it past the dragon.

Yes, that's it. Some other way. Let's go!

"Did you hear that?" Evelyn asked, craning her neck toward the blackened chasm, where hundreds of orbs floated, glowing in the distance like colorful fireflies flitting to and fro above the chasm's depth before them.

Hanna raised her eyes, looking in the same direction as her sister. Even Miriam responded, her head cocked to listen intently. Unfortunately, neither male sensed what the females had locked onto… not at first.

The floor rumbled again. Softer, like a seismic aftershock. Fearing the room might collapse, and ready to force everyone out in a mad dash to the bottom of the staircase, John hesitated after his first step from the room's present safety. Not because of the serpent menace from earlier. Uktena remained quiet. Something else gave him pause… something coming.

The multitude of oval lights veered as a group away from the entrance, speeding into the darkened depths to their left until the glow became barely detectible. While the earth's rumble continued to grow louder, yet another hostile surge approached, rising from the darkest depths.

"No frigging way!" David hissed, shaking his head in dismay.

The sound of an immense swarm of hornets, or wasps, filled the chasm. It was an incredible horde of anger roaring as it swerved upward, a swelling black mass barely discernible in the pitch void. The swarm headed for the entrance.

With nowhere to go, Teutates' dying fire provided the room's only illumination. The angry swarm reached the stairs, and moved up fast.

Miriam and Hanna murmured in fear, while Evelyn wept. David was losing his courage, too. All the while, the floor shook harder, making it nearly impossible to stand.

Where are you, Grandfather? Show us a way for escape! Don't desert me now!

The sound of a canine whining rose from a far corner of the room, drawing their collective attention. Nothing was immediately visible that far away, until John remembered his flashlight. He pulled it out of his pocket and turned it on, hurriedly pointing the beam. No sign of the animal, but older remains fell away from the wall across from the altar, near the log pole racks where David and the women had been bound.

Move now, Running Deer! The Great Mother will soon devour this place. Trust and follow me!

"Quick! Everyone over here!" John led the way to where old bones continued to fall from inside the wall.

Once he arrived, a cool draft greeted him. Evelyn and David remarked about it from behind.

A hidden passageway lies beyond the wall?

David and Miriam's faces were aghast, and Hanna resisted Evelyn's initial efforts to get her to stay with the group. A variety of human remains had been piled to block the passageway. Some were old and decayed to the bone. Others were more recent, where the rotting stench announced the presence of putrid flesh long before the flashlight's glow revealed scurrying beetles and maggots feeding on severed limbs and entrails. But this wasn't the time to be squeamish.

"Help me pull the rest of this out of the way!"

John raised his voice above the din now gathered outside the room's entrance. He was the first to reach in and pull out the debris. Entangled with a severed arm turned purple from recent decay, a child's ribcage and shreds of an old-fashioned shirt from more than half a century ago pulled free.

More cold air! If we just don't think about any of what's here we might make it through before it's too late.

"Hurry! We haven't got all damned day!"

John glanced warily behind them, directing the flashlight at the doorway blackened by a deep shadow. The first few specks of whatever made up the swarm crept into the room, twinkling as orange and yellow dots in the light, like sparks from a foundry.

David and the women glimpsed it as well, providing enough incentive to get moving. Amid gasped breaths and dry retches, everyone tore frantically at the human wall, until there was enough of a gap to slide through. As if reminding them to hurry, the wolf barked from within the passageway. Two familiar amber eyes provided encouragement for John to trust and not hesitate.

A thunderous shout from behind announced Teutates' entrance into the room, the swarm swiftly surrounding everyone while the quake seizing the floor traveled up the walls. Miriam and David cried out from stings, slapping at the back of their necks and shoulders.

There really are wasps or hornets with this thing? Shit!

With a persuasive shove, John sent Evelyn and Hanna through the hole dripping with gore. Several prickling stings attacked a small exposed area on John's lower back. He hastened David and Miriam through the hole before either one glimpsed the monstrous giant standing a few feet behind them all.

Relying on instinct, since it was futile to face the angry demon and expect not to become part of the wall of gore, John ducked without looking back. The top half of his snow suit disappeared, and he felt the thick fabric fall away, Teutates' razor talons separating it from him without so much as a snag against the stitching. He might not be so lucky the next time.

John launched himself through the hole, surprised when he landed unharmed on the wall's other side.

* * * * *

The narrow passageway sloped upward at a severe incline, which Evelyn remarked might've been designed to bring supplies quickly into the underground temple. The immediate image that came to John's mind was of sacrificial victims thrown down into the chute. Perhaps the human remains they removed were part of a plug or clog in such a tunnel. He shuddered at the thought—especially with the bloodthirsty fiend responsible for the demand now hovering on the wall's other side.

"Evelyn, take my flashlight and lead the way," he told her, keeping his voice hushed while handing it to her. "David, you and Miriam go next, and I'll follow last."

Evelyn nodded after casting a worried gaze to the area behind John. David and Miriam grimaced from their latest assault, and as the sting grew steadily worse in John's back, he understood their shared plight.

All the more reason to get moving!

He urged everyone to hurry, casting another nervous glance behind him. The flashlight's glow moved away, leaving him in deepening darkness. He sensed something watched from the midst of the gore-filled entrance to the tunnel behind him, and the fluttering mass of stinging insects hovered angrily on the other side of the wall. He could feel the intense malice and frustration from Teutates. For some reason, the demon couldn't follow him and the others...yet. Something else was coming to the demon's aid, to eradicate the problem. Swift vengeance would follow.

Everyone keep moving... Hanna stay close to Evelyn... that's it! Good job everyone... now just a little quicker!

Able to stand at first, he and David scraped their heads on the ceiling. To everyone's dismay, Evelyn reported the passageway's size dramatically shrunk ahead, where it became just big enough to crawl through. There still wasn't a clear indication where this would lead. She grumbled her doubt it led anywhere.

It simply can't be a dead end... and do I always have to ask you, Ududu, to appear and help? Would it be too much to ask you to stay with us? Especially since the buzzing sound is getting louder again. The demon will be on his way in a moment!

"There looks like a sliver of light ahead!" Evelyn announced, after pulling herself into the hole with Hanna clinging to her jean cuffs.

Everyone else waited in darkness until their turn. Miriam went next and David behind her. John heard a muffled cry of excitement from inside the chasm, but couldn't tell if it was good or bad. Meanwhile, the encroaching swarm behind him grew steadily louder.

Teutates has made it through... here he comes!!

"John, get in here—now!" David called. "Evelyn says there's a big opening up ahead, and she hears people out there!"

Spurred by hope, John felt along the walls for the entrance to the narrower section. Just as he pulled himself up into the dark cramped tunnel, the swarm rose fast along the passageway behind him.

They're closing in... fast!

Desperate, he squirmed to keep up, his arms and legs fatigued. David's voice called to him, muffled and moving further away. He could hear excitement ahead. His granddaughters called frantically for him to hurry. Help was coming, and he heard David and Miriam's voices, too.

I can't move... I'm so tired and... and, I'm stuck!

You can still make it out of here, Running Deer! Yes, you can!

A surge of energy accompanied the voice. It was enough to overpower the fear brought by the angry swarm creeping up the tunnel. John could now picture his escape. So simple and clever, yet it was impossible to realize unless he found peace within himself first.

The hornets, wasps, or whatever the little bastards were, managed to squeeze around him. He received multiple stings along his neck and right side of his face. But, the vision remained strong—even when his booted ankles were seized by a mighty grip. John unzipped the front of his snowsuit and wiggled out before the entity could crush the bones in his legs.

Scrambling in a fervent fight for survival, John crawled away from his clothes, while the earthen walls of the tunnel crumbled around him. Clad only in his thermal underwear, he saw daylight. He could even see David and Evelyn, who appeared as stick figures standing at the edge of wherever the passageway led. It widened enough to where he could crouch and move a little faster.

Just a little ways to go. It's good to see Hanna and Evelyn smile again, and David looks relieved. There's Butch, and the kid named Chris is okay. Thank God most of us made it!

Evelyn and Hanna's smiles suddenly disappeared and David's relieved look turned to one of horror. Something painful ripped across John's shoulders and the back of his head, the force sending him tumbling down upon the unstable ground. He landed a few feet from where the limestone entrance to this place gave way to knee-deep snow.

"Everyone get down!"

A multitude of small explosions, and the sound of metal ricocheting off the walls surrounded him. It hastened the structure's final collapse. He heard screams of terror as the earth opened behind him, and a huge maw prepared to devour the unholy temple in its entirety. A monstrous groan followed, while blackness clouded his vision and awareness.

The last thing he remembered was a lone wolf standing between a pair of snowmobiles, where detectives James Russell and Thomas Calhoun and a Tennessee state trooper crouched with high-powered rifles drawn. The wolf panted, smiling contentedly, and then trotted into the nearby woods. No one else noticed.

Only John.

Maybe it's better this way, and things can finally return to the way they once were.

"May the Great Spirit make it so," John whispered, just before he lost consciousness.

Chapter Forty

"Auntie's place is coming up, just beyond those pine trees."

David pointed to the craftsman bungalow built in the early 1930s. The only residence Ruth Gaurnier had ever known, it seemed cold and sullen. He glanced in the rearview mirror, where the looks on his children's faces matched his own. Even Miriam, who remained reticent following the ordeal in Cades Cove that ended yesterday morning, looked concerned. Her brow was furrowed as she peered through the passenger window of the second minivan they rented. The police impounded their previous vehicle, and it wouldn't be returned to the rental car agency in Gatlinburg until Monday morning.

Only Ruth seemed at peace, despite her Chattanooga home's outward hostility. After all it *was* still her home, a place she knew as well as it knew her.

"Wow-w-w!" enthused Jillian, although sounding more like she would if about to mount a scary roller-coaster or visit the commercial haunted houses in Denver during Halloween season. "So, that's your house, huh?"

"Yes it is," said Ruth, her tone relieved.

David wondered if it had more to do with the strange events in Colorado or the harrowing encounter she and the kids had two nights ago in Gatlinburg, or both.

"It's too bad y'all can't stay longer with me," Ruth continued, her sadness slipping through. "But I understand when you can't get the flight home you would've liked. Besides, y'all will need a couple days to recuperate from everything you've gone through, I'm sure."

David understood the last part was intended mainly for him and Miriam, since his wife was due back at work tomorrow, and he would return after New Years Day. Flying back to Denver early tonight left them only a few more hours to spend with Ruth.

It had been a crazy two weeks, and the bizarre events from the past few days were sure to stay with him for a while. Especially the gruesome details of what he'd witnessed in the sacrificial room of Teutates' temple—those would never be erased. His experience with the demon left him broken spiritually. Not to mention his tender wrists and the numerous wasp stings along the back of his neck and shoulders. He felt disconnected, whether that meant from God or his life's purpose here on earth. No matter how he sorted through everything, it would take some time before he felt like himself again.

And I better show up with a smile at the office on Wednesday.

Then there was Miriam. She worried him, and not only because she came very close to being sacrificed. That would've been devastating enough. But something happened to her while pinned to that bloody altar... and something was taken from her. Her innocence? He wasn't sure if that was it or not. Maybe she had lost the part of her that believed in good over evil. Her tender spirit that so loved the simple things in life had been ravished and damaged. Was it beyond repair? Only time would tell.

"Well, come on inside so we can visit for a little while," said Ruth, after David parked the Voyager. "I can fix some orange pekoe tea for anyone interested in having any."

"That sounds nice," said Miriam, pausing to smile at Ruth before gingerly stepping down from the passenger seat.

David sensed her disconnect, although her tone demonstrated a fight to get through it. *That's a good first step.*

"Can we hook up the XBox?" Tyler asked, gathering his backpack containing all of his game gear.

"Son, we won't be here that long… just a few hours," David reminded him.

Everyone stepped out of the van and headed for the porch. The pussy willow's barren wands near the front door brought painful memories from his youth that he quickly pushed from his mind.

"Ah-h-h, Dad!" Christopher whined. "It doesn't take that long to set it up and tear it down. Please!"

Tyler echoed his brother's complaint, which drew a pleading look from Miriam to just go along with the request.

"Really, David, I don't mind if they want to do that," said Ruth. The first one up the steps to her front door, she had her key ready. "I've got an extra TV they can use upstairs."

She unlocked the door and pushed it open. It let out a painful groan, as if the house actually had gotten used to having no one there.

David set her suitcases in the foyer, near the oak staircase leading to her bedroom. Intent on taking them up for her, he paused to take in the essence of the place, which seemed different to him from his late-night visit back in October. It didn't feel the same in daylight.

"Oh, don't worry about those for now, David," Ruth advised, peering around the corner from the kitchen, an empty teakettle in hand. "We can get them later, after we've had a chance to rest."

"Come in here and join us, hon," said Miriam, calling from the living room.

His heart skipped at the sound of her voice. *That sounded almost normal... so soon? Please God, let it be true!*

"All right," he agreed, stepping past Max's favorite pillow, still lying on the floor near the entrance to the living room.

In the final weeks before Ruth had her cocker spaniel euthanized, his arthritis worsened to the point he could no longer climb on her lap. David recalled overhearing her conversation with Miriam about her beloved dog on Christmas Eve.

The kids sat on the long couch, the only early American piece David remembered from childhood. Everything else had been added since then. Jillian listened to her mom and great aunt chat about her extensive bone china teacup and saucer collection, proudly displayed inside a glass cabinet next to the kitchen.

After Ruth carried the full teapot and a tray of holiday cookies into the living room, she set them on the coffee table and settled into her favorite chair next to the television. Miriam sat in a matching overstuffed chair next to her, and David relaxed in an older wooden rocker nearby after adjusting the thick seat cushions to comfort his back's lingering soreness.

For the next half hour they enjoyed the refreshments and light conversation, until the boys grew antsy enough to ask her about the TV upstairs. Ruth rose from her chair to join them, but Tyler assured her that he could figure it out on his own. Once she gave directions on where to find the bedroom with the television set, just off the first landing, he and Christopher grabbed the backpack containing their treasured game system and disappeared upstairs.

Ruth offered to take Jillian on a tour of the old house, but she declined. David assumed it had nothing to do with a lack of curiosity, as more likely either deference to Ruth's arthritic condition or an instinctive aversion to the general spookiness, accentuated by dark oak paneling throughout the house.

"Let me get that for you, Auntie," he offered, when she rose to gather empty the teapot and tray.

At first reluctant to accept his assistance, which he understood was rooted in her strict upbringing as a southern hostess, she allowed him to take the items into the kitchen. When he returned, she was engaged in a lively discussion with Miriam and Jillian. He sat down next to Jillian, content to listen to their girlish banter about the similarities between upbringings, despite a span of three generations in different American regions. It brought a pang of guilt when the time came to gather his wife and kids to resume their trip to Chattanooga's airport.

"Are you sure you don't want me to take these up to your room for you, Auntie?" he asked for the third time, when she declined both his and Tyler's offer to take her suitcases upstairs. He'd even tried to sneak Tyler past her with the heavier suitcase, but she blocked him with the walking cane she used inside the house.

"Yes. Just leave them here in the foyer. I want to go through a few things I brought home from Denver and Gatlinburg first," she explained, motioning to both suitcases. "It'll work out better that way."

David nodded, and the kids each gave her a warm hug.

"I really wish our time together wouldn't have been so... eventful," said Miriam, her eyes tearing up. Ruth nodded in agreement, forcing a warm smile through her own tears. "We will make up for this, and soon."

"Let's not go so long without seeing each other," added Ruth, and reached out for her.

The two women held each other tightly, both seemingly reluctant to be the first to let go.

Ruth motioned for David to come nearer, and when he did, Miriam stepped back, dabbing at her eyes with a coat sleeve.

"Auntie, I'm so glad things are different between us now," he told her, feeling overwhelmed by several emotions, most of them good, although regret for past grudges still hovered nearby. "We'll do this again."

"Yes."

That's all she could muster, her voice choked with emotion. He held her, unable to shake the need to be strong and stoic, while her shoulders shook. Miriam drew close again, her loving arms draped around them both, followed by the kids.

The old saying, parting is such sweet sorrow always made him wonder. *What in the hell does that really mean anyway?* It certainly could never apply to a moment like this.

Just sorrow. There was nothing sweet about it.

The profound notion came with a sense that a potential wrong could be made right... if a different choice, or path, was taken.

After loading the Voyager and pulling out of the driveway, David couldn't shake the feeling that another terrible mistake was happening. *It's not too late... you can still fix this!*

* * * * *

After regaining consciousness in a hospital bed, John accepted David's invitation to come to Denver in the spring, during the kids' school break in early April. The blow to the back of his head and shoulders required nearly thirty stitches to close, but all in all, his doctor told David and Evelyn he would fully recover, and be released in a day or two. She also planned to come along in spring after

Miriam's invitation to her personally, to keep a protective eye on her grandfather. It depended on Hanna's health, since the trauma she suffered while imprisoned by Teutates would linger for a while... possibly years.

The specialists they had talked to at St. Joseph's hospital in Knoxville were cautiously optimistic for a full recovery after Hanna's memory improved last night. Badly dehydrated and malnourished, her vital signs continued to strengthen. The last thing Evelyn heard from the medical staff was they planned to release her sister soon after John, if there were no further setbacks.

As for what happened in Cades Cove, no one talked about it. Other than helping Butch and the Knoxville detectives complete the necessary paperwork, there wasn't a single mention of Teutates and his murdered victims. Better, in this case, to let sleeping dogs lie undisturbed. It was especially true after the five survivors witnessed the demon's physical demise, its burning corpse smoldering near the blood-drenched altar, only to be attacked again by the entity in its preferred form.

David knew in his heart he'd never forget the yellow eyes glaring from within an immense ink-like shadow hovering behind John when the lawmen opened fire. The collapse of the temple immediately followed. John later told him from his hospital bed what the temple originally looked like when he and Butch arrived at the site yesterday morning, which was a far cry from the huge pile of rubble presently sitting in the middle of the ravine. David recalled how the cops lamented about not having a camera handy to capture a photograph after the dust settled, as proof of the immense glistening structure before its destruction.

After David and Butch rescued John and the deputy named Chris assisted Evelyn in helping Hanna and Miriam escape the deep chasm, the detectives and the lone trooper helped carry everyone out of the ravine, using the available snowmobiles and an all-terrain truck that made it to the ravine after Butch called for backup help. In the midst of destroyed scaffolds and walkways set up by the University of Tennessee's archaeology department in November, Teutates' temple that had lain hidden beneath the ravine for untold centuries would again be nothing more than a rumor, if that.

Prior experience told David the demon's fury was likely far from over, its lust for vengeance still unsatisfied—made worse by how its re-emergence ended. Not talking about it wouldn't keep the thing from coming back again someday....

"Hon, you can go now. The light's green."

Miriam's tone as gentle as her touch, she brushed her fingers against the back of his white-knuckled hands gripping the minivan's steering wheel. He hadn't moved for nearly a minute, drawing not only her attention but the kids' concern as well. Less than a quarter mile away from his ancestral home in Chattanooga, he felt the call of the house he grew up in and now belonged solely to Aunt Ruth.

David's eyes blurred and his shoulders heaved, quickly growing more and more volatile until all at once a terrible cry erupted. He sobbed uncontrollably and Miriam threw her arms around him, pausing only to look in the rearview mirror, to make sure other automobiles could maneuver safely around the minivan.

After that, things became a blur for him. Miriam insisted on him exchanging seats with her and drove up the street. The hands of his three children comforted him, massaging his sore shoulders until they were back in his aunt's driveway, where Miriam parked.

He insisted on going up the steps alone. Ruth answered, and for the first time in years he told her that he loved her. Truly, he had loved her all this time. But, it was a love regrettably buried under bitterness and unresolved anger.

David wasn't sure how the words came out, but his aunt understood and accepted. They embraced, holding each other tightly. Tears flowed freely. She hadn't even begun to unpack—her long winter coat still draped over the suitcases. She was ready to go… ready to leave the only home she'd ever known.

Once back inside the minivan, a joyful cry erupted. The kids were pleased, and Miriam was, too. Aunt Ruth would extend her stay in Colorado after all, perhaps permanently. Her nephew and his lovely wife assured her they would take care of any loose ends surrounding a move into the other upstairs' guestroom on LeClair Drive in Littleton, including the sale of one modest craftsman located in southern Tennessee.

One *haunted* modest craftsman, that is.

* * * * *

He watched them leave. All the way down the street. When certain the maroon minivan wouldn't be coming back a third time, he closed the sheers in the upstairs bedroom. His granddaughter's bedroom.

Time to change things, after so many years. It would be his room again, the one he died in. This was his house. He'd fix it up to suit just him and the cocker spaniel he heard rummaging around downstairs.

Billy Ray Hobson smiled. He turned away from the window and moved slowly through the bedroom, adjusting his tan fedora to hide his glowering eyes while his heavy boots caused noticeable creaks in the upstairs floorboards.

It was time to go downstairs and teach that damned little dog a new trick.

Chapter Forty-one

Under a full moon, the *Harvest Moon* since it was the first one in October, a pair of hybrid sport vehicles with the tops down traveled along an old dirt road, overgrown with dying grass and weeds. Several hours after curfew, the Great Smoky National Park sat deserted. The meadow facing the John Oliver Cabin seemed especially eerie under the moon's bright glow. Perhaps coasting with the headlights off, moving past two police patrol cars near Cades Cove's entrance, also had something to do with that.

We're unwelcome?

"I think the old ravine is up ahead!" Jason Pierce called back to the second vehicle.

His deep brown eyes danced mischievously, and his boyish smile further confirmed his impishness.

Who gives a flying fuck if we're welcome or not? At least this should be interesting. Let's see if Polly and Ed freak out once they see the place where all those people died!

"Sh-h-h-h!! Not so loud, y'all!" hissed Stevie O'Guin. He shot him a bird and pointed toward the empty road behind them. "Just in case those bastards decided to follow us, man!"

He dimmed the headlights, though not as much as earlier, when they were on the main road moving through the cove.

"Dude, frigging chill!" Jason responded, laughing. He and Stevie had been roommates for three years, and high school buddies before that, currently attending the University of Tennessee in nearby Knoxville on baseball scholarships. "And, unless you want to fall into a ditch, I suggest you keep the lights on until we've parked."

There were four couples. Jason and Dianne Crowe, his steady girl since sophomore year, sat in the front. Brunette and pretty, Dianne seemed to share his enthusiasm and intrigue in exploring a so-called haunted ravine, her green eyes sparkling in the dash's illumination.

Shikara Khan and T.J. Wallace snuggled in the backseat. Always up for a good time, neither cared one way or another about ghosts, haunted places, or anything else that dealt with the supernatural. A beautiful native of Pakistan, Shikara had abandoned her Muslim tenets as a freshman, while T.J. adhered to just enough of his Southern Baptist roots to stay out of trouble with his parents, living in Jackson, Mississippi. Like Jason and Stevie, T.J. came to UT on an athletic scholarship, in his case football.

Inside the second vehicle, Stevie sat up front with his latest girl, Stefanie Torain, whose warm brown eyes and flawless ebony skin brought comparisons to Tyra Banks, the model from yesteryear. A little on the heavy side, all Stevie cared about was the girl was a total freak—at least that's what he told Jason. Behind them sat the nerdy pair in the group. It took losing a bet on last week's Homecoming game for Ed White to agree to come, and Polly Chambers only agreed to join him since Dianne was her roommate, and wouldn't give her a moment's peace until she said yes. Both blue-eyed blondes repeated the mantra of "it's not good to dabble with the devil". But Jason knew better. They were just two goddamned pussies afraid of their own shadows.

Hell, a good scare might help 'em loosen up a bit, ya know?

A large *Keep Out!* sign soon appeared in the headlights' beams. It was attached to a rusted barbwire fence.

Chris said it'd be like this, man. Dark and desolate, and ain't nobody else around. He told me and Stevie right after the NFL draft that his dad and mom almost died out here a long time ago. Never saw him drunk like that, man, and the dude never talks... but he did that night. Some demon called Teutates wanted to kill his folks and their friends. The motherfucker already killed a cop and some other people—including an entire family.

"We're here!" Jason announced, unfastening his seatbelt while Dianne did the same. Shikara and T.J. already removed theirs once they drove across the meadow. "If you'll grab the beer, T.J., I'll get the wood for the fire."

"Sure, man. Got it!"

Meanwhile, Stevie and Stefanie climbed out of their vehicle, with eyes straining to see into the thick darkness shrouding the area beyond the fence.

"How can it be that dark in there when the moon is so bright?" Stefanie asked her man.

She looked up at the brightened sky above, and back toward the darkness, thick and ink-like. Stevie shrugged his shoulders. The look on his face was one of indifference, like it wasn't a big deal. He wrapped his arms around her waist, pulling her near. It was an effective distraction for the unanswered question. She smiled and looked up into his face. He winked.

That's where the ravine is, man! This ought to be fun... some real fun for a change! And, maybe the girl ghost Chris told you and me about, Stevie, will be here. The one that got her face bashed in by some crazed rapist when this place was just a lover's lane long ago, and who walks around in a bloody blue gown. Do you remember the chick's name, Stevie-boy? Something like Alice or Allison....

Allie Mae.

For some reason, the instant the name appeared in Jason's head, a chill ran up from the bottom of his spine to his neck, and spread across both shoulders. He shivered.

Get a grip, man. You don't want to end up like those weenie-lovers crawling out from the backseat over there, do you? We sure the fuck don't want that to happen!

Once Ed and Polly picked up the cooler and brought it over, Jason pulled out a pair of wire cutters from inside his letter jacket. Directing Stevie to hold up one of the flashlights they brought, he cut through several wires before anyone else could react.

"What the hell did you do that for?" asked Ed, worriedly. The tin warning sign fell to the ground with a loud clang. "We could go to jail for the destruction of public property!"

"And, who the hell is going to know, unless y'all tell 'em?"

Cocky to a fault, Jason waited for another rebuke from the group. When it didn't happen, he picked up the wood waiting at his feet and moved through the fence. Everyone else soon joined him on a rock ledge at the top of the ravine. Now all the girls were murmuring about the surreal darkness before them; a place where the full moon's rays couldn't penetrate for some reason.

"This is really spooky," Dianne whispered to Jason, pulling her coat tighter as if embraced by a deep chill.

Like the other guys with their gals, he paused to comfort her before getting started on a fire.

Everyone was dressed in jeans and sweatshirts, and most wore some kind of jacket. Like Diane, Jason noticed the other girls were pulling their coats tighter. Although hot natured, he noticed the temperature had become cooler once they moved through the fence.

The darkness seemed to lessen a bit, allowing their flashlight beams enough penetration to where they could clearly see what was there.

This is so fucking cool, man... and admittedly a little creepy too!

The rest of the fence formed a corral roughly the size of a football field. It appeared the so-called ravine was long gone: instead, a grass-covered hill with boulders and other debris sticking out of it dominated the center of the cordoned area.

Well here's another thing supporting Chris's tale from that night. He said the temple had been reduced to a hill of rubble.

"Hey, let's get a fire going." Jason picked up several hickory logs and arranged them in the center of the ledge where a quick blaze would be possible. "Once we get it going strong, we can crack open the beer and cook us a little feast."

A slight breeze moved through the treetops along the fence line, drawing everyone's attention. The girls moved closer to their guys, and Dianne nudged him to hurry up. He focused his efforts on building a decent fire, and soon stepped back proudly from a roaring blaze. To make sure it stayed that way, he and T.J. brought more wood— enough to last several hours. Seemingly drawing reassurance from the towering flames, the girls set up blankets around the fire and before long were lounging comfortably. There was plenty of beer to go around, and several packs of hotdogs and bratwurst to roast.

"This is sweet!" enthused T.J., his smile radiant within ebony skin.

"So *fucking* sweet, indeed!" echoed Stevie, leaning toward the fire with a hotdog skewered on a coat hanger.

His rich Irish heritage, including a full head of red hair that framed his freckled face and deep blue eyes, seemed enhanced by the fire's glow.

"Good deal," nodded Jason, glancing around. The gals and even Ed seemed pleased, or at least hungry, each with a hotdog or brat ready to roast. "After we're done eating, it'll be time for some exploring. The place is supposed to be haunted, so why not check it out and see if that's true or not?"

"Haunted? You didn't say anything about this place being haunted. No wonder it's been giving me the creeps!"

At first, Stevie didn't take his girlfriend's anger seriously. But, when Stefanie retreated to the edge of the fence after laying her uncooked hotdog down atop the cooler, he pursued her.

"Baby, come on!" he pleaded. "It's just some story that Chris told me and Jason last spring. Just a story, like anything else. *Boo!*"

He added a nervous laugh.

"Chris? You mean Chris *Hobbs?*" she asked, incredulously. "The football player?"

"Yeah, the quarterback-of-the-future for the Giants," he agreed. "We all got drunk as hell, and he told us a wild tale about this place. That's all it is."

Jason held his breath. If someone asked if big bad Chris ever came out here, he'd have to lie and say he did. Fearless in football games, especially when a critical victory was on the line, Chris refused to even consider the idea of coming out here.

Dude's scared to death of the place, man. He wouldn't even come with me and Stevie to the park in broad daylight.

"I doubt that's all it is," said Polly, pushing her blonde bangs away from her eyes. She gazed into the ravine and at Jason and Stevie. Her eyes looked afraid. *Very* afraid.

"I've heard stuff about this place. Like the ghost of a girl in Cades Cove who sneaks up on lovers who stay in the park after dark. And then those people who mysteriously disappeared twelve years ago. That *did* happen!"

She started to cry, which only made matters worse. Ed immediately wrapped his arms around her.

Ah-h-h Christ! Better get this shit taken care of quick, before everybody wants to leave.

"All right, all right!" Jason moved to block Ed and Polly from stepping down. Everyone else seemed poised to leave, with Stevie losing the battle of keeping Stefanie there. "Let's just enjoy a nice meal, and afterward, if anyone wants to join me in having a look around, then that's cool. Everyone else can enjoy some more beer and roasted marshmallows. How does that sound?"

Hopeful he wouldn't be forced to immediately pack up, everyone but Stefanie agreed. Fearing she would bring a premature end to the night's festivities, a pleasant surprise came when Stevie persisted in his attempts to get her to stay. It worked.

The promise of continued protection and comfort might've taken Stevie away from helping him hold the party together, but at least she wouldn't leave. As for everyone else, once they got some good food in their stomachs and a few more beers, the group became more boisterous, the atmosphere festive.

Dianne and Shikara pointed one of the flashlights out toward the deep darkness, focusing on the trees along either side of the ravine not obscured by the debris hill in the middle. Several trees were covered with names, and

Dianne suggested to her beau they should get a closer look.

Excellent! Better seize the moment before she changes her mind.

"Let's do it!"

He took a beer and pulled her along with an arm around her waist.

They moved into the ravine, Jason balancing her and the beer bottle while she held the flashlight to where they could see. Careful to avoid the sharp edges from what looked like veined white marble sticking out from the hill, they moved through tall grass and wildflower stems until they reached a row of mature oaks along one embankment. By Dianne's count, just over thirty names covered the trees, some encircled by crude hearts. Names like Milton and Bertha made them both giggle, until the flashlight began to flicker and dim.

"Oh, shit, the batteries must be dying," he observed, stating the obvious.

The beam continued to fade, but before it flickered out, he glimpsed something shining near the base of the hill to their left. The small object appeared round when he saw it, glistening red, less than twenty feet ahead of them.

"Did you see that?" he asked.

"See what?"

Apparently not. No matter, before she could stop him, he walked over to it.

The flashlight died. The built-in flashlights in their cell phones wouldn't work either, and when the handsets suddenly died, Diane started to freak out about it.

Especially since only the fire's light behind them offered any illumination, forty to fifty feet away. Jason remained stubborn in his curiosity about the red glowing object, as it looked like some jewel and not a piece of broken glass. Yet, while trying to recall its exact location, he detected movement in the darkness ahead, above the ravine in the thick forest to their right. It was the sound of crunching footsteps—just like their own had been, stepping on dried pine needles, maple and oak leaves. The footsteps were heading toward them.

"Jason, let's get of here—*please!*"

"What's going on down there?" T.J. called. "Y'all okay?"

"We'll be there in a moment!" Jason called back, suddenly seeing the flicker of red again. He scurried over to it and picked up the object.

What's this? Jesus! It looks like a real jewel... red ones are rubies, right? Holy shit—this is fucking amazing!

"You won't believe what I just found out here!!" he yelled excitedly. "It's got to be the coolest damned thing...."

Suddenly he heard it again... closer. There really was someone moving atop the ravine near the edge of the woods. Crunching footsteps and the sound of something swishing, brushing against the leaves rapidly approached.

A dress? Stop it, man! Quit thinking about that goddamned story!

"We're on our way down there, y'all!" Stevie called to him.

He heard excited voices and several people on the way down into the ravine. That brought comfort. Strength in numbers. But, the other noise still approached ahead, moving faster. And, with it came a sigh.

A female's voice? No fucking way!

Dianne screamed. It sounded like she tried to call his name, and then nothing. His legs felt heavy, but at least he could move, where just a moment ago they felt clamped to the ground beneath him.

"Dianne!"

He ran back to where he last saw her. She wasn't there, so he called again. No answer.

"Where the hell are you, babe?"

Still no reply.

"Jason, we're coming, man!" said J.T., sounding anxious. "We're almost there, man. Almost—ah *shit! What in the hell's going on here?"*

Jason whirled around, in time to see the bottom of a blue gown descend into the ravine, maybe ten to twelve feet away. But, was that what J.T. screamed about from the other side of the hill?

Not sure... but you better get moving... Now!

"Dianne? Where are you, baby?"

Moving as fast as possible to the ledge, he could see dancing flames from the fire they'd built. That would be comforting, if not for the footsteps gaining on him.

I can hear her breaths... and gurgling? She's running after me—is this fucking for real?

He slipped on something wet, and when he steadied himself his hand touched warm moistness. He brought it up to where he could faintly see something dark dripping from his fingers onto his palm.

Blood? Oh God, please no!

"Where's J.T.?" Sounding worried, the voice belonged to Shikara. At least, that's who Jason thought it was. Another shriek ripped through the air, but it wasn't hers.

Is that Stevie's chick, Stefanie? Gotta be, 'cause it sounds like Stevie's over there mumbling 'Oh, my God—Oh, my God!'

"What the hell is that thing?" screamed Shikara.

T.J.'s girl sounds closer. Is she looking at the thing that's breathing down my back? So fucking cold... and that gurgling noise. Something just splashed up against my back! Run-n-n-n!

It shamed Jason that he didn't stop and turn to face whatever pursued him. He hated himself for it, and for not searching for his girl. Instead, he sprinted to the ledge.

Shikara let out a shrill shriek, and after he brushed by her, he heard her no more. The same report for Stefanie and Stevie. Like T.J. and Dianne, they were gone.

After Jason climbed up the embankment, he looked behind him. Whatever pursued him had disappeared in the thick shadows. No footsteps, brushing, or the maddening gurgling sound. Gone? Who could say for sure? He looked at his right hand under the glow from the firelight, covered in Dianne's blood. Already congealing, it had dripped down past his wrist.

She's really dead! How can this be? They're all gone! All my friends—the people who matter most to me are all....

What about Polly and Ed?

He saw them. Somehow, they managed to get the keys from Stevie.

Does that mean his body is down there someplace? Did these motherfuckers kill Dianne and everyone else?

They looked at him with blank faces. Ed started Stevie's vehicle and pulled away, his and Polly's emotionless expressions never changing. The car spun around and sped toward the meadow, and the road out of the hellish place. As the engine's hum faded into the night, a noise similar to swarming hornets approached from behind the ravine. At the same time, he felt a vibration against his left hand. The one holding the circular jewel he found. It moved like a roach trying to crawl from his grasp.

Surprised he opened his hand. The vibration stopped, but inside the ruby something moved. In the soft glow from the nearby fire, a clouded haze appeared in the jewel's midst, traveling from the back of the ruby to the front.

Well I'll be goddamned. It looks like some sort of....

Jason gasped in surprise. An eye appeared within the mist, cold and reptilian. It studied him, like a snake or crocodile sizing up its prey.

The eye blinked.

Ah-h-h Shit! It's too late to save anybody but yourself, Jason! Get the hell out of here like Ed and Polly or die. Leave here now or....

He dropped the ruby and ran to the remaining hybrid parked just outside the hole in the fence. Fumbling for his keys, he only slowed down for a moment, but it proved to be enough.

Before he opened the door to climb in, a pair of unseen powerful hands grabbed his ankles. The hands yanked him to the ground and dragged him all the way down into the ravine, his flesh tearing on the sharp rock edges of the ledge and the marble shards jutting out of the hill.

A muffled scream resounded from the ravine, just a mile outside the John Oliver homestead. Then, silence... other than the wind rustling dead leaves across the ravine.

Death for the unwary, another chapter had been added that night to an old legend. The ravine's unholy guardians lie in wait. Always ready for another opportunity to strike.

The End

To be continued in:
Devil Mountain
(Cades Cove Book 3)
Available Now

~~~~~~~~~

About the Author

Aiden James is the bestselling author of *Cades Cove*, *The Judas Chronicles*, and *Nick Caine Adventures* (with J.R. Rain). The author has published over thirty books and resides in Tennessee with his wife, Fiona, and an ornery little dog named Pepper.

To learn more, please visit AidenJamesNovelist.com, or look for him on Facebook (Aiden James, Paranormal Adventure Author) and on Twitter (@AidenJames3).

Made in the USA
Coppell, TX
28 November 2021

66599646R00231